The Road To VEGAS

The Road To VEGAS

L.J. DIVA

★ Royal Star Publishing ★

Chances is an imprint of Royal Star Publishing
www.royalstarpublishing.com.au

Cover design: Royal Star Publishing and Odyssey Books
Cover photo: istock.com/Gerber86
Typesetting in Minion Pro by Royal Star Publishing

Dedications

My gorgeous Michael Weatherly and Carmine Giovinazzo, without the two of you the characters of Diega and Vegas would not exist. The men you are, the men you will be. Go ahead in life and soar.

And to Jackie Collins for writing a particular scene in a book that stuck in my head for over ten years. I knew I wanted to write a book like that. Full of sex!!!!

Prologue

He had followed her.

He was watching her.

Standing outside on the fire escape, peering through the bedroom window of the one room apartment.

He watched her luscious, full breasts rise and fall with every deep breath.

The way her right hand curled under her chin, resting lightly.

The way her legs moved around under the blanket, shifting it aside to reveal their long, soft length.

She was twitching as if having a nightmare.

As if some horrible demon was after her to savage her.

I hope she's having nightmares.

She was promised to me. She was my gift.

My gift to unwrap and have all to myself.

And have her I will.

Chapter 1

She was running, running, running. Blindly, in fear for her life. Running from something, she didn't know what. She just had to get away. Away from the terror. Away from the man in the shadows...

Footsteps pounded behind her on the hard ground, trailing her. It was him. He was following her. Chasing her. Coming for her.

Why? Why is he coming for me? Who is he? What does he want from me?

Suddenly, silence. No sound at all. No sound except for her terrified heartbeat.

Then, a snapping twig, a scuffing of the ground. What was that? Someone's there. I have to get away, I have to hide. Where, where can I hide, where can I go? There, under that old trashcan, he won't find me. He won't see me. I must be so quiet. I must hold my breath so he won't hear me. Oh, why is my heart beating so loudly? He'll hear it, he'll find me. Oh, God, please don't let him find me. Please don't let him get me. Please, God, make him go away...

Tahlia Johnston sat bolt upright, dripping with

sweat, and hitting out at the covers. She thought she was being grabbed, mauled, molested. It took a few moments to realise…there was no one there. No shadows stalking her, no animal waiting to beat her. She was alone.

Again.

"Thank, God," she gasped, struggling for air, her heart racing at a terrified pace. Quickly snapping on the bedside lamp, she took a few deep breaths to stabilise her pulse, looked around, and was very relieved to see no one hiding in the corners. Throwing back the covers, she swung her legs over the side of the bed. Her right foot touched the bare floorboard and recoiled slightly as chills shot through her leg. Gingerly, she stood, the cold now in both feet. Ignoring it, she pushed back her hair and walked around the rat hole of an apartment her mother had lived in.

She wasn't there anymore. She'd died last month.

A sudden pang of anger filled Tahlia's heart, but a tear came to her eye.

"I don't want to be here anymore, at least I don't have her to be responsible for." She rubbed her arms against the chill that now took her, and glanced around at the meagre things her mother had left behind. Not much to show for sixty years. A few knick-knacks, crockery, bits and pieces. Anything that hadn't been smashed and trashed over the last two decades.

She had been here for two days and now wanted to leave. *I can't stay here, I can't,* she thought. *I need to run. I need to go far away an' never come back.*

She couldn't explain *why* she was running. *Why* she

was having nightmares. The last couple of weeks were either a blur of driving and parking behind gas stations for sleep or blocked out of her memory. Just thinking about it gave her chills down her spine and a fear she didn't understand.

I've been scared before, from things I've seen an' what's been done. But not like this.

She took an envelope from her purse and re-read the letter from the New York morgue, trying to piece together what she knew. The letter informed her that her mother had passed away from cancer, and was asking when did she want to collect her for burial.

"How did they find my address?" she murmured. "Unless they went through my mother's things, but even then I don't remember telling her. In fact, when was the last time I saw her…it must have been when I was eighteen or twenty, an' I'm thirty-two now. Seems like so long ago." She wasn't going to reply to the letter, but found herself in the morgue two days ago when she arrived in town.

"Argh," she cried, flinging her hands into the air in desperation, "why can't I remember?" She pictured the steel slab her mother was lying on. Her body all cold and white. She'd walked away without a backward glance.

Tahlia sighed, feeling nothing at the memory of her mother's body. She screwed up the letter in frustration.

Then there was Wayne, her boyfriend. She'd been living with him, and while their life together wasn't rosy, it was all she had. All she was used to. Wayne preferred that she stay home to look after the house, be a good housekeeper, wanted her to stay inside and never go out. Then one day it all seemed to change, and she couldn't remember what happened after that, except for the huge fight they'd had.

Always the same. They'd fight. He'd apologise. She'd stay. It was all she was used to.

But this time, it was their last fight. That much she knew.

The back of his hand had sounded like a gunshot before she fell to the floor. The pain on her cheek was so intense she cried out as blood flew into the air. Her hand found her mouth, covering it, trying to stop the blood from flowing over the carpet. Because Wayne wouldn't like that. He'd make her clean it up, and blood was hard to get out of anything. She knew.

His vengeful eyes had stared coldly down at her as she looked up at him, desperately trying to control her tears. Because Wayne didn't like that either. Her crying. He hated women who cried and called her all sorts of names because of it. Reminded him of his piss weak mother he'd once said in the heat of a fight. *"You bitches are all the same,"* he'd spat, *"can't please a man the way he likes, and when he lets you know, you bawl your eyes out. You're all pathetic. Just like her. And I* hate *her!"*

She shuddered violently at the thought. It still affected her, but then, it was still so fresh. She could feel it. The burning handprint seared onto her face. Into her mind. Her memory. Her soul.

Her hand once again found her cheek.

"God," she said, pacing the room, "is this my life? A

road filled with crap men taking advantage an' getting what they want all 'cause I allow them to. Or is it 'cause I was trained that way?" She ran her hands through her hair and stopped in thought.

Trained?

From the age of eleven, she'd seen each of her mother's new boyfriends raise a hand and strike somewhere on her frail body. There would be furniture crashing and mementoes smashing. A new bruise and a new lie. Although sometimes the old ones were repeated. Her mother had once been so vibrant and full of life, but that was only when her father was alive. Since then, she'd gone downhill in every way. Physically, mentally, emotionally. Her mother was no longer the woman she once knew.

"It ended up like a broken record, my so-called role model. Nothing but a quivering mess of..." Tahlia stopped and glanced around. "Huh," she huffed and muttered angrily into the empty apartment, "I don't even think there's a word to describe it." A tear sprang up and threatened to overflow.

Her mother had been nothing but a doormat. And in the heat of her own fight with Wayne, she'd decided not to be like her. Not to be like her mother. Not to stand there and take it. Again. She decided to fight back. And struggling valiantly to her feet, she swung her right arm with all her might and landed Wayne with a black eye he'd never seen coming. From a woman anyway.

Tahlia smirked sadly and moved around the room. "At least I tried. Unfortunately, he gave me a busted nose for it." She touched her nose gently and gazed into the small, round mirror hanging on the wall. It was still tender and a little sore, but generally okay. Wayne had thrown his own fist into her face making her blood spurt all over the place. Then he'd dragged her into the car and driven her to the hospital to have her nose set, giving the doctors some stupid excuse for why it was broken, mainly because he didn't want her bleeding everywhere. And, of course, he made her clean it up when they got home. It took her hours, as blood was hard to get out of anything. She knew.

"But what has happened since? Ugh!" She racked her brain and stared at herself.

All she saw was the beaten ghost of her mother staring back. Shoulder length lifeless brown hair, long oval face with dark circles and bags, sparkless, empty green eyes, a bruised and slightly crooked nose, cracked pink lips that hadn't smiled in…so long. She looked closely at herself. "Definitely not the girl I used to be. God," her eyes rolled up to the ceiling, "when was I *ever* the girl I used to be?"

There was a scraping sound out on the fire escape.

Her head whipped around toward the window. *It was nothing,* she thought, her heart pounding furiously.

Are you sure?

A huge clap of thunder rumbled ominously above the building. It moved through the apartment, her body. Making both of them tremble with the deep bone-jarring vibrations. Making her even more scared.

The lightning that followed lit up the whole sky as bright as day. Lit up the apartment. Lit up a shadow out on the fire escape. The shadow moved. The light disappeared.

There's nothing out there, she thought determinedly, trying to convince herself out of panic mode. *It was just the storm or something, blowing the trees around an' throwing leaves into the air.* She swiped her hand over her face and found herself sweating. She panicked anyway. Because she *did not* want to find out if she was wrong.

Glancing at the small clock on the bedside table, she saw it was six in the morning. She knew she wouldn't be able to go back to sleep, and didn't want to, so she packed her own meagre belongings into her duffel, and took what she wanted of her mother's. She showered quickly, and left a note for the super, then closed the door to the one bedroom apartment.

A strange feeling swept over her, making her whole body shudder. She stared at the door as her hand lingered on the handle and realised, with an overpowering finality, that this episode of her life was over.

Gone.

Left behind forever. Never to be seen or revisited again. She sighed, relief calming her momentarily, winding its way through her body, relaxing her. There was no longer anything to worry about where her mother was concerned. The critical sarcasms and anger, hostility and hatred. They were all gone.

Another clap of thunder sounded overhead, and she released the doorknob with a start. Remembering the sound and shadow on the fire escape, she tensed again. A part of her was also scared to the bone. Her nightmares saw to that. Terrifying, yet blurry. Memories that wouldn't come to the fore to show her what was happening. Memories she would have to find for herself.

Shifting her duffel onto her shoulder as if it was a heavy burden, Tahlia walked away. Leaving the apartment, and her mother, behind. She tried to quell the rising panic that threatened to stick in her throat. She knew there was something out there. Chasing and hunting. Haunting and frightful. Something lurking in the background. The shadows. The recesses of her memory, her mind, her life.

Always there, felt, but never seen…

Going to her mother's grave, she stood there, the wind whipping her hair all around, the dark clouds hanging low overhead. She waited. Tears didn't flow. Pain didn't come.

She wondered why. *Why* she didn't feel any sympathy. *Why* she didn't feel much of anything. They hadn't seen each other in years, didn't have much communication at all. Her mother had hated her. Never wanted to see her again once she'd left home, never had any contact with her unless she wanted something. And even then, she'd remind Tahlia that she owed her for looking after her until she'd run away from home at eighteen.

That was a joke! She'd left home because it was depressing as hell and she suffered nothing but abuse from her mother and all of her boyfriends. Besides, it was her mother's job to raise her and protect her. And she hadn't. She'd failed miserably.

Anger started to rise, but she stopped it. There was

no need to feel it anymore.

Suddenly, violently, she was enveloped in an ice-cold chill that the lingering storm stirred up. Wrapping her coat tightly around herself to ward it off, she still felt it in her core. That feeling of someone, some*thing*, lurking, there in the background. Turning to run, she desperately looked in every direction, but all she saw were huge concrete headstones in a dark, empty cemetery.

She saw no one.

Nothing.

But someone *was* watching…

Someone *was* following…

*****

Tahlia drove down the east coast, not sure where she was going, where she would stop, or even when. All she knew was, she had to get away from New York. As far away from Maine as possible. And whatever horrific memories still lay there.

Philadelphia was nice, but not far enough. Maryland and North Carolina weren't good either. Driving through Georgia, she continued south to Miami, deciding she wanted the sunshine and heat.

Miami was perfect after the cold winter, and she wanted to stay but didn't have much money and almost no work experience. She made do with staying in the parking lots of all-night gas stations for accommodation, and sleep was fitful.

Day after day, Tahlia looked for work, walking the

streets, asking in every store. Her feet ached and protested in agony every morning when she set out. Her stomach cried out for a nice hot meal. Until finally, late one afternoon, she walked into a small diner. After talking to the manager, she found herself with a job. Since cooking seemed to be her only skill, and she wanted to stay out of the way of the customers, she helped in the kitchen. Her pay covered the cost of a small trailer in the local trailer park, which wasn't much, but enough. And besides, it was far better than parking for the night in a car park.

Organising with her boss to work day shift only, Tahlia made sure she was home before dark because things still didn't feel right. They hadn't since Maine. Nightmares and visions haunted her every moment, asleep or awake. And it scared her. She was still worried about what may be out there.

Watching…

Waiting…

*****

Four weeks later she had settled in, and her job was good. It was definitely hard work. Harder than she'd ever known, but she wasn't going to let it get to her.

The Miami sun was warm on her face, the sea breeze refreshing, even tempting her into the water one day. She hadn't swum much and was a little self-conscious, conscious of the way she looked. Whiter than white skin, old bruises, a figure not so cutting in her swimsuit, but the big baggy t-shirt covered her well enough. She tugged it down so no one would see. So no one *could* see.

She gazed around at all the beautiful bodies on the beach. Topless, well-endowed women with not an inch of fat anywhere on their bodies. Bronzed and sculpted men with huge muscles pointing in every direction.

Oh, dear God, she thought, blushing, and covering her face with her hands in embarrassment as two tightly packaged macho men walked past her with their tiny little swim briefs overflowing with testosterone. *I've never even* seen *men look like that.* She giggled softly and eyed their retreating figures, then blushed even more.

Now feeling very aware of her body, she stayed in the shallows and paddled back and forth, trying to stay away from people so she would be alone.

Feeling herself relax in the warm Miami water, she allowed herself to float along with the current and wondered if it was all over. She had left Wayne…hadn't she? She couldn't actually remember, but knew she must have left because here she was in Miami, a completely different place from what she was used to. And she was by herself, which hadn't happened in a long time. After years of torture, she must have gone out on her own and taken Wayne's car when she did. At least it looked like Wayne's car, but the plates were different, so she wasn't sure.

God, why can't I remember what happened in those two weeks? she thought miserably, walking out of the water and over to her car. Drying herself off, she glanced around, worried that she would be noticed.

Worried that someone was watching…

*****

A few days later, leaving work at five minutes after five, Tahlia walked to her car. A weird sensation slid down her spine as if someone was watching her. She fearfully looked all around, but saw no one. After locking herself in the car she drove off, but kept nervously glancing in the rear-view hoping no one was following. She knew enough to not go straight home, so she drove around for a while hoping to lose whoever it was.

She made it back to her trailer, ran inside, locked the door behind her, and decided there and then to leave in the morning. "I can't do this again," she panicked, "I can't keep doing this. Running 'cause someone might be out there waiting for me, watching me, wanting me. I just can't." She called her boss at the diner and informed him that she wouldn't be returning, then packed her things, changed for bed, and lay down, hoping for sleep.

It didn't come.

Around eleven p.m. she heard a noise outside and shot up into a sitting position, her back dead straight, her ears straining for the slightest sound.

There it was again. She stood slowly, stealthily, one foot on the floor, then the other, then tiptoed the five steps into the living area.

A footstep.

A shadow at the window.

Bang, Bang, Bang.

She jumped. The noise was so loud, and the vibrations so hard, she thought the window was going to break as the person kept banging. They moved on to the next and the next. Banging on the door, rattling the knob, trying to get in.

She stood there, shaking, feeling sick. The sweat poured down her face, her neck, her back, soaking her nightshirt.

No, no, this can't be happening. Why is this happening?

Around and around, every window, every door, the banging didn't stop.

She backed up against a wall, sank down to the floor, pulled her knees up to her chest, and wrapped her arms around herself. "Go away, go away," she whispered, scared absolutely witless. Trying so desperately to shut out the terror that had re-found her.

Finally, it did stop, and with an evil laugh, the person walked away.

Tahlia knew she wouldn't be able to sleep if she went back to bed, so she sat on the floor and pored over her map for almost an hour, using her trusty flashlight so she didn't have to turn the light on in case he was still outside. "Where am I gonna go now?" she whispered, "where am I gonna go?" She tried to think of a place where she would be safe, secure. "What do I do? What do I do? Will I never be safe anywhere?" Shaking her head, she allowed a few tears to fall. "I could close my eyes an' make a stab." So she did. Opening her eyes, she saw her finger had landed on Las Vegas. "Well, at least if he does follow me, he may not find me. It's so crowded an' there's always tourists, so I should be able to lose myself." She dressed quickly, grabbed her bags, and sneaked out to the car. Jumping into the driver's seat, she jabbed the key into the ignition and drove off as quietly as she could.

He watched her as she sneaked out to her car. Laughing a deep throaty laugh, he sat on his bike and lit a cigarette. The flame cast shadows over his face, lighting up deep pools of blue. Blue pools that bored into her, burning with an intensity that surprised him. That scared him. The feeling that engulfed him set him on fire, and he knew he must do something. Do something about the stirring in the pit of his stomach. The stirring in his sizable groin. Do something that would leave a definite impression. Something that would make her forget everything in this world except him.

He watched her start the car and slowly drive away from the trailer. That's all he'd been doing for the last two months. Watching her. Waiting for her.

Followed her to New York where she went to the morgue and stood all alone at the cemetery. He'd felt a strange feeling, watching her there. A feeling that dared to drag up memories. A feeling that started to tease him with the torment of the very bad things that had happened in his own past.

Down the east coast to Miami he went, where he spied on her day after day. She had sensed him here and there, looking around, trying to find him. But she never did.

Tonight, he'd decided to scare her, shake her up. Let her know, yes he was there, yes he was watching. That he'd been there all along and wasn't going away.

Wouldn't leave her alone to have a happy little life all safe and sound from the big bad wolf threatening to engulf her and eat her.

He'd banged on the door and rattled the knob, tried to get into the windows. He hadn't seen her in the trailer, but knew she was there, and that she'd be shitting herself in fear.

He'd gotten a big kick out of it, laughing as he walked away, waiting to see how long it took her to run. It only took an hour. He must have really scared her.

Seeing her tail lights fade into the night, he took one last drag and flicked his cigarette to the ground, blowing out smoke as he gunned his bike into action.

And once again, he followed…

Chapter 2

As she drove across the countryside, Tahlia decided travelling to Las Vegas was the best thing she could do. There was still the uneasiness of whatever it was haunting her. Something she couldn't put her finger on as her memory was still hazy and full of holes.

Alabama seemed really pretty, but she didn't have time to play tourist. There was a need deep inside to get to Vegas. She didn't know why it felt right, as if some cosmic guide was suddenly leading her, pushing her to go. But it was kind of exciting.

Not being able to afford motels, she stayed in parking lots of all-night convenience stores to at least feel some sense of safety. But sleep was ragged, full of nightmares and images she didn't want to think about, didn't want to worry about. But worry she did.

Something lurked deep inside her mind, her memory. Images of blood and a gun, someone there in the background. She hadn't been alone, and try as she might she couldn't make the images clear. Tahlia shook her head to clear her mind of the thoughts she didn't want to think. *I need to get to Vegas, that's all I need to think about.*

*****

Driving down the highway on the third morning of her journey, Tahlia pulled over to check her map. A motorbike roared past, flinging dirt and dust up over the car, its rider not caring. Looking up, she scowled and noticed the bike was an old Harley. "Nice bike… arrogant prick," she muttered. Pushing the map aside, she glanced over her shoulder and accelerated back onto the highway, seeing the man on the bike was already long gone.

Pulling into another small gas station in another small town, Tahlia came to a stop and waited. She glanced in her rear-view and hoped the car that had been following her didn't pull in. "Idiots," she muttered, remembering how they'd tried to run her off the road earlier. All she'd been doing was minding her own business, driving along, and suddenly there were two idiots screaming up behind her in a souped-up truck.

After what seemed like forever, she got out, grabbed the hose herself, thrust it into the gas tank, and drummed her fingers on the roof of the car as she gazed across the barren landscape. The station was actually the last store in a main street that was only three stores long. Population – next to nothing.

Hearing the roar of a truck, Tahlia looked up in worry and disbelief. "Shit!" She held her breath and looked away as they screeched into the station and stopped behind her car. They stepped out of their truck arrogantly and walked around to lean against the front of it.

"Well, well, well, look who we have here," the tall one sneered. "The little pussy we wanted to talk to, but was too much of a bitch to stop and chat." They looked like college punks, with greasy hair and acne, the type who thought their own shit didn't stink, that every female in the world would want them and willingly fall at their feet if they were told to.

Tahlia quickly glanced over them, wondering if she could defend herself if she had to. They were big, and would more than likely overpower her. Violate her in ways she didn't want to think about. She didn't feel safe.

She heard the bell above the door ring and turned to tell the attendant she didn't need help, but stopped before a sound came out of her mouth.

Walking toward her was the most incredible looking man she had ever seen. A man that oozed masculine sexuality from every pore and knew it. Self-assuredness from the tips of his old black biker boots to the ends of his short dark brown hair. A swagger to make a girl blush, and eyes that were deep, smouldering pools of blue to drown in.

He came to a slow stop in front of her, smiling a smile that made her knees so weak she sagged against the car. She grabbed it to keep herself upright.

"Hey, baby…need some help?" His deep sexy voice made her heart thunder.

Tahlia opened her mouth to speak, but not a word came out. The spell of the moment so absolutely brilliant, then so cruelly broken as he turned toward the two college boys.

"I suggest you two get outta here," he said in a low,

threatening tone.

They had been watching the scene with anger, as the woman they had wanted and followed on purpose seemed to be completely taken with the man who was now facing them, threatening them. They didn't like his tone, so they sneered at him, thought he was joking. They stood up to face the man and laughed. They actually believed they could take him on.

"Didn' your mothers teach you to respect women?" the man asked. "I said get outta here," he growled, his voice now louder.

"What are ya gonna do, old man? Teach us a lesson?" They laughed again and turning to each other pretended to throw punches.

The man flexed his muscles, pulled brass knuckles out of his pocket, and slipped them onto his right hand. "Nope, just beat the holy shit outta ya if ya don' go now." His eyes menaced as he took a few steps toward the two punks, flexing his muscles even more, slamming his right hand into his left several times.

Suddenly nervous, and realising they couldn't or wouldn't take him on, they jumped back into their car with a scowl, slammed the doors, and sped off, fading into the landscape.

The gas pump came to a clanking stop. Embarrassed and blushing, Tahlia dragged her green eyes away from the blue pools that were now gazing at her to put the hose back into its socket, aware that he was watching her the whole time.

"Um, thanks, I suppose," she stuttered, somewhat shyly, blushing even more, her insides like jello. "I'd better pay." She hesitantly moved to walk past him.

He stepped over to her and gently pushed her against the car and spoke in a low sexy voice that made her tremble. "I already paid for you."

"Huh?" She was gone. Drowning in deep pools.

"I already paid for you. I saw you pull in an' thought, what a hot woman, how do I get to know her? So, I paid. Decided to come introduce myself, an' deal with those jerks at the same time. What's your name, baby?" he asked, with a smile so white hot it melted everything around him as his voice washed over her like a warm ocean wave. And she surrendered, willingly floating along on the current.

"Tahlia," she gasped gently as he leaned in toward her. He was so close she could hear the pounding of his heart. Smell his hot, masculine scent that was driving her crazy.

He was an inch or two taller than her five foot eight with strong, muscular arms that were on either side of her, keeping her trapped against the car. "Well, baby, you can call me Vegas."

She stood staring into those eyes and suddenly felt bold as a surge of excitement pulsated a driving beat through her. "Give me your number an' I'll call you tonight," she said in a sexy tone that surprised her. She blinked rapidly and blushed deeply.

He grinned his slow, sexy grin that made her hot with anticipation. "Baby, there's no need for that, 'cause you'll be seein' me tonight anyway. I was gonna suggest that we hit the road together. My bike broke down an' I need a lift." His right hand reached up and brushed a strand of her hair aside. "Where ya goin', baby?"

The current that raced through her body was electric. Never before had she felt this way about a man's touch, a man's scent, a man's sexual energy and maturity. His aura was making her want to melt into the embrace of those strong, muscular arms.

"Baby?" he said quietly.

Tahlia realised she had not only closed her eyes, but held her breath too. Letting out a sigh of content, and feeling sexual awareness such as she'd never known, she opened her eyes, finding him even closer than before. Oh, God did he smell good.

"How 'bout it?" He cocked his left eyebrow at the question. "I'll drive."

Feeling even bolder, she made the decision in an instant, not caring if it was wrong or right, good or bad. She just knew she wanted to get to know him. And she did owe him for helping her. Didn't she? She smiled. "Las Vegas. Okay?"

He grinned. "Great. I'll grab my stuff." He walked back into the station, just inside the door, and grabbed his duffel and guitar case which he threw into the back seat.

"Jump on in," he said. She climbed into the front and slid along the bench seat. Getting in, Vegas started the car then looked at her, grinning in excitement. "Vegas, here we come."

They sat in silence for twenty minutes before Tahlia had the courage to look at him. "So, I guess we should get to know each other then," she said shyly.

He looked at her slowly, giving her that damn sexy

grin of his. "Well, baby, as you know, I'm Vegas. I go round workin' where I can get it an' explore the countryside while I'm at it." He looked at the road again.

"Vegas, huh? After the city?" She was *very* curious about the man beside her.

"So I was told."

"Do you have a last name?"

"Nope."

Tahlia glanced out the windshield then slyly back at Vegas. She let her eyes wander over his hard, muscular body. A tanned torso clothed in a tight, white singlet that showed off an inviting nest of brown chest hair, and a chain around his neck with tags and charms. A tattoo on his right upper arm was of a pattern or symbol she had never seen. His muscular arms were straight out, holding onto the steering wheel. He had a kind of rough and ready look about him. Rough around the edges with wild brown hair that stood up all over, and a fine layer of facial hair that would definitely leave burn marks.

He looked ready for anything. Ready for *anyone*.

It was *very* appealing. It was *very* sexy.

Her eyelids were feeling heavy, and she didn't know if it was from being tired and worn out from the last couple of months, or from being sexually aroused. *Don't be silly,* she thought, scolding herself as she looked away. *A man's never made me feel this way, why would I be aroused?*

Wait, her brain screamed to a halt, suddenly stunned. *Did he call me a hot woman before?* Her mind cleared and focussed itself as she thought back to their conversation at the gas station. *"I saw you pull in an' thought, what a hot woman, how do I get to know her?"* Oh, my God, she blushed, *he called me a hot woman, me, me. No! That can't be right? Not with my plain Jane boring old looks. Can it?*

She sneakily glanced down at his skin tight, dark blue ripped jeans and how they hugged him, fitting so perfectly in all the right places. Her gaze landed on his crotch. His wickedly full, bulging crotch. She wondered what he looked like naked.

"Baby?"

She looked up at him and realised he'd been watching her check out his crotch. "Oh, God," she choked and blushed furiously, knowing she had a stupid look on her face. "Um, ah, nice belt buckle," she stuttered and looked out the window.

"Baby…I'm not wearin' a belt."

That grin was back as her head swung around and her eyes searched his. Glancing down again she saw he was right. "Oh, God," she squeaked, grief-stricken and extremely embarrassed. She turned her head back to look out the window and clamped her mouth shut so there wouldn't be any more humiliating comments.

Vegas laughed, low and sexy. "It's okay, baby," he said, lighting a cigarette. "I was checkin' you out too. Besides, you just might get to see what I got in these jeans." He laughed again. The sound sent a shiver up Tahlia's spine. "In fact. I know you will."

Tahlia blushed even more furiously as they drove into the oncoming dusk.

*****

Late that night, they pulled over to a roadside campsite.

"We're in the middle of nowhere," Vegas said, eyeing her. "We'll have to stay here an' get a good night's sleep." He licked his ripe pink lips with his ripe pink tongue.

After seeing them in motion, sleep was the last thing on Tahlia's mind. Especially after that humiliating moment of hers that afternoon. She had been quiet, just thinking about her life and the mysterious man beside her.

For hours Vegas had driven, without stopping or asking her to take over. Occasionally, he turned on the radio and sang along to whatever song was on at the time.

"So, I guess we get to sleep in the car then. You want front or back?" Vegas was watching her intently, his eyes so dark and deep.

"I'll take the back," she said, swallowing hard and glancing away. She didn't have the courage to look at him with his eyes and lips so hungrily wanting.

"Great, I'll get out an' make a fire for some warmth. You got any blankets in this car?"

"A couple of sleeping bags down on the back seat floor," she replied, getting out of the car and stretching her weary body. Another car was just pulling in, the driver looking for a place to park for the night. There were already two other cars there, small campfires burning, people laughing. Vegas got the fire going, then went off to get water from the campsite supply shed.

Tahlia pulled out the box of food she had and

grabbed the sleeping bags to give them a shake. Vegas came back with the bucket of water and asked if she wanted to wash first.

"Sure," she said, carrying the bucket to the other side of the car so she would have privacy to wash and change. Washing, and putting something appropriate for bed on, she walked back around and handed the bucket to Vegas. He'd laid out the sleeping bags and zipped them together.

"I decided we should stretch out for the night after bein' in the car so long…an' keep warm in the meantime." That damn sexy grin was back as he took the bucket.

Blushing furiously, Tahlia sat down on the sleeping bags and slipped her boots off. *We can't sleep in the same sleeping bag,* she thought, *I barely know him. I can't latch onto another man so soon. God, what am I gonna do? Do I ask him to sleep in the car or do I take the car myself? That's it, I'll sleep in the car. But he'll have the fire…an' the sleeping bags. Well, I could unzip them an' quickly get in the car, it shouldn't be too bad, at least it won't be cold hard ground.*

Grabbing some food from the box, she tried to keep her eyes on what she was doing, but her eyes had a mind of their own, looking up to see where Vegas had gone.

She gasped in surprise. He was only a few feet from her at the end of the car knowing full well she could see him.

At her gasp, Vegas slowly lifted that tight singlet up his muscular back and over his head. Tossing it onto the hood of the car he reached in front of him, and

Tahlia heard the rasp of a zip. Slowly kicking off his boots he tantalisingly slid his skin-tight jeans over his curvaceous ass and down his long, lean legs.

Tahlia breathed hard, unable to take her eyes off this sex god in front of her. *Oh, my God what's happening?* she thought. *No man has ever made me feel this way, only beaten an' abused, treated like a lowly dog, or a piece of crap stuck to the bottom of his shoe.*

In fact, she was surprised that any man had ever been attracted to her, wanted to be with her. She was so plain compared to every other woman she saw, and was wondering why *this* man, Vegas, being the hot stud he was, would even look twice, let alone tease her with his sexiness. *And* want to ride to Las Vegas with her.

She felt hot, unstable. Her heart pounded, her blood raced. She was moist between her legs, aching to take him. She glanced at him again and saw he was now completely naked, slowly washing himself with the small towel she had found for them to use.

Vegas dipped the towel into the bucket then held it over his head and squeezed it. The water slowly ran in tiny rivulets down his back and over his hard ass. Tahlia was gasping for breath as he turned to look at her over his shoulder. His gaze burned into hers, his grin spread across his face. Seeing her panting and wanting, Vegas turned around so she could see him. Naked. Raw. Hungry.

"Oh, my God," she gasped.

He was erect, standing to the fullest attention, and now walking toward her. He stood over her, hard, needing. Kneeling down on the sleeping bags in front of her, Vegas took her hand and pulled her to him.

Oh, my God, she panicked, *what's he doing, what's he doing? I can't do this, I can't do this, not after everything I've been through. Not another man. But this man is different. Yes, this man is different. An' I want him!*

As he slowly undressed her, he was gentle. Touching her, caressing her arms, her sides, her breasts. Tahlia gasped and grabbed his arms, and Vegas wrapped them around her as he pulled her against him, their lips meeting in raw passion. His tongue explored the inside of her mouth, tasting her, wanting her. His hands did the same to her body.

She pulled her head back and gasped for air. Her hands grabbed his hair and brought his mouth to her right breast.

He took it, licking and sucking hungrily. His hands ran over her back down to her ass.

Tahlia moved his mouth to her left breast. Wrapping her arms around him, she brought him closer and felt the length of his penis pushing against her crotch.

Wanting. Needing.

His left hand found its way into her hair and pulled her head back. His mouth was now on hers, his tongue thrust in and out, his right hand pushed its way between her legs. His fingers were now inside of her, probing, moving, finding the spot. Tahlia gasped and writhed against him as fireworks exploded in her brain.

Vegas pushed her down onto her back and pinned her hands above her head. His mouth explored her body, setting her on fire. Her neck, where there was a spot behind her ear. The insides of her arms, so soft and tender. Her breasts, heaving in passionate arousal. His hands slid down her arms, her body, following the trail his mouth had left. Each hand found a breast, kneaded gently, making her groan in absolute pleasure. They grabbed her hips and took her wet vagina to his mouth.

"Ahh," escaped from her mouth as his devoured her, thrusting his tongue inside of her.

In and out. In and out. It too found the spot his fingers had. Then suddenly…

Tahlia barely noticed that Vegas had stopped. She opened her eyes groggily and looked at him.

He was kneeling between her open legs, grinning that damn sexy grin of his. Then, with a look in his eyes, he started toward her, like a wild animal on the hunt.

She opened her legs wider to accept him and moved her hands down to his ass. With his mighty thrust, she took him into her.

Wanting. Aching. Accepting.

His hands entwined themselves in her hair. His mouth claimed hers as its own, his tongue thrust in sync with his hard shaft in a wild tribal dance, their hearts beating in thunderous time.

She had never known rawness like this. The passion. The need. She locked her legs around him, holding him closer. His knees were beside her hips so he could thrust harder. His mouth found its way to her left breast and sucked hard. "Aaaahhh," she gasped, feeling both the pleasure and the pain of the motion.

He looked at her, his right hand now massaging her breast, his left still entangled in her hair. "Open your eyes."

She barely heard him, but managed to open her eyes, staring into those dark pools of passion and desire. This was animalistic energy she had never felt. Never known.

Vegas stared into her eyes. His mouth played kisses on hers as his tongue toyed with her. He was fully inside of her. Deeply inside of her. In a place no man had ever been. A place she only wanted *him* to be. A place *only he* would be. His hand now gripped her hip, and with raw force he thrust harder, faster, bringing her to him as the world shook with climactic thrusts. The intense feeling pulsated through her body, racking her with an orgasm she had never experienced as he met her with the wildness of a stallion. Hard... Muscular... Throbbing...

Groggily, Tahlia opened her eyes and wiped her hand over her face. Vegas was lying beside her, watching her. His left arm around her, his right hand under his head. She had been sleeping with her head on his chest, their legs entwined.

"Hey," he said softly.

"Hey," she replied shyly, seeing they were still naked, but wrapped in the sleeping bags. "How long have I been asleep?"

"Awhile."

The sounds from the other campers seeped into her brain and it hit her. "Oh, my God, oh, my God. I hope they didn't hear us." She sat up. "I hope they didn't see us, oh, my God, oh, my God."

"Baby," Vegas drawled. "It's okay. I made sure I parked far enough away an' in a position so no one could see anythin'." He pulled her back down to him and wrapped his arms around her. "It's okay, just relax."

She did, deciding to let the world fall away and just revel in the moment. Snuggling against his muscular chest, she ran her hand through the golden-brown hair she found there.

He kissed her on her forehead and held her tighter.

Her hand found his chain and looked at what was on it. "What are these?"

His right hand covered hers and removed the chain from her grasp. "Personal."

"Why?" she asked.

"They just are." He stared up into the sky as she looked at him.

"Am I going to find out anything about you?" she asked.

"Maybe," he said, grinning as he looked at her. "Get some sleep." Kissing her forehead again, he closed his eyes.

Tahlia lay awake for a while thinking about the man beside her. The man she had taken inside of her and opened herself for. Never before had she done such things with a man. Never before had she felt so alive, so wild, so free. She blushed at the thought of the things she'd done. So blown away that she could do it with such passion and fervour. Blown away by the intensity of it all. After every other man, and every other situation, this was different. *She* was different.

She sighed. For once in her life, she actually *felt* happy with a man. Strange, since she'd only just met him, but still, it was a very overwhelming feeling of happiness. After the years of pain and anguish with all of the men she'd been with, the hell she'd endured, maybe she had finally found a good man.

Good? You know nothing about him, her brain said.

She gazed at Vegas. *Well,* she thought, as she watched him sleep. *I will find out about you an' enjoy every moment.*

*****

Tahlia was being shaken. "What, what," she mumbled grumpily, opening her eyes slightly as the sun hit her face.

Vegas was kneeling over her. "Up an' at 'em baby, time to dress an' go." He stood and threw her clothes at her, then rolled her out of the sleeping bag.

She saw he was ready, and hurriedly washed and dressed as he packed the car, then took the bucket back to the small shed. Walking back to their campsite she saw Vegas sitting in the driver's seat, left foot still on the ground.

"Want me to drive?" she asked, putting one hand on the door frame, the other on her hip.

"No, it's okay," he said, folding the map back up.

"No, seriously. You drove all afternoon an' night. Besides, it's my car."

He looked at her, deciding. "Okay," he said, sliding over to the passenger side for her as she got in and started the car. "We'll stop at the next town for gas," he added.

"Okay, let's go then." Slamming the door shut she

took one last look at their campsite and remembered what they had done. Blushing with pleasure, she floored the accelerator, and as they left, she realised there hadn't been any nightmares. *Wow,* she thought, sighing in relief, *maybe this is finally a new day.*

Soon arriving in a new town, they drove down the main street. "Pretty," Tahlia said.

"Yeah, not bad," Vegas answered, looking for a gas station. "There." He pointed to one, and after she pulled in, he got out to pump the gas.

"I'll go in an' stock up on food," she said, getting out of the car. She managed to find what they needed even though the store was small and didn't have a lot for sale. Vegas walked in at the same time she was done, and they jumped back into the car and drove off, passing the 'Thank you for visiting Fairfield, please come again' sign.

"No, thanks, won' be comin' back," he quipped.

Driving along the road, Tahlia turned on the radio just as one of her favourite country songs came on. "So, is there a guitar in that case of yours?" She glanced at Vegas.

"Yeah, there is," he replied, catching her eye.

"Well, you were singing yesterday, so how about amusing me while I drive an' play me something."

He considered it for a moment. "Okay." Reaching into the backseat, he removed the old, beat-up acoustic guitar from the case, and plucking a few strings and strumming a few chords, Vegas started playing and singing along with the song on the radio.

After three songs Tahlia joined in.

"You sing too?" he asked, staring at her.

"Well, if that's what you call it. I never thought of myself as a singer. I just go along with the song," she replied, looking ahead at the road.

A thought formed in his mind. "Ya know, if we get hard up for money, we could get jobs in bars along the way. Me playin', you singin'." He grinned at her. "After all, it's usually fat, bald, drunk men in bars. I'm sure they'd rather look at a hot woman than a mug like me."

"Who says there aren't fat, bald, drunk women in bars who'd rather look at a sex god like you than a woman like me," she replied with a laugh. "Besides, I'm not hot."

"Well," he said, still grinning, "you could be right. We could take it in turns. If the bar is full of men, you sing. If it's full of women, I sing. An' yeah baby, you are hot."

Tahlia blushed a deep red as she grinned back. "Deal."

*****

Later that evening, they pulled into a new town, tired, hungry and in need of sleep. After finding a small motel, they rented a room and moved in. It was small and plain, enough space for a small table and two chairs, a TV, and a double bed.

Tahlia blushed at the thought of what might come on that bed.

"We have enough to go grab some food," Vegas said, counting his money.

"There was that small diner three stops down,"

Tahlia suggested and locked the door behind them before they set off down the road.

The food was rewarmed and the coffee mediocre, but it was cheap and filling. They sat side by side in a booth sharing a piece of homemade apple pie and snuggling together.

"I've never done this before," she said shyly.

"What?" He scraped up some pie and took a mouthful.

"Shared a piece of apple pie with someone I hardly know," she said with a soft smile.

"Well, baby, you certainly know me now," Vegas replied, a big grin on his face as he pulled her tighter to his side and nuzzled her neck.

The blood rushed to her face as she felt the hardness of his body, remembering the intensity and passion of what they had done the night before, and what would come when they got back to the motel room.

My, God, she thought, *I've never felt this way about any man. Ever. The rawness, the power.* She looked at him, her gaze taking in his features. Gorgeous big eyes that were deep pools of blue. Hot pink lips so right for tasting and kissing. Wide forehead, strong jaw. His brown hair, short in back, longer on top, wildly splayed in every direction which she wanted to run her hands through, hanging on like she had the night before during their wild throes of passion. She blushed at the thought. *My God, he's gorgeous, an' he wants me.* She blushed harder.

Chapter 3

Walking into their motel room, Vegas told Tahlia to shower first.

"You sure?" she asked.

"Sure. In fact, I might join you shortly," he said, looking up from digging around in his bag. That grin was back, and she started to feel a hot, throbbing feeling.

Smiling to herself, she went into the bathroom and undressed. Stepping under the hot, fast spray of water, she let it run over her, washing away all aches and pains. Soaping herself, she relished in it. *God,* she thought, *when was the last time I had a shower an' washed my hair? It's so relaxing an' refreshing.*

Lost in her thoughts, she didn't notice Vegas come into the bathroom. He stepped in behind her, wrapped his arms around her waist, and planted a kiss on her neck. Gasping in surprise, she turned around to face him, finding him already hard and erect. Looking up, she found his gaze burning into her own, and as her eyelids became heavy with arousal, they closed as his mouth covered hers. She dropped the washcloth and wrapped her arms around his neck, pulling him against her, taking his tongue deep into her mouth.

His hands explored her hot, soapy body, sliding from place to place, arousing her even more. Bringing her to the brink, then stopping.

Wanting him, she turned him around, so the spray of water flowed over his body.

Vegas put his hands on the wall in front of him and turned his head to look at her. "Gonna frisk me, baby?" he asked sexily with a grin to match.

"Nope, gonna do a hell of a lot more than that. So shut up an' enjoy." Grabbing the washcloth and soap, Tahlia slowly ran her hands over his muscular arms and down his hard, lean back.

The soap bubbles ran enticingly down into the small hollow of his spine, and over his hard ass, flowing smoothly down the insides of his legs. She ran the washcloth over him, and once he was soapy enough, began to slowly, sexily, rub her breasts, then her body, over his.

Naked flesh sliding over naked flesh in an exotic dance of passion.

Groaning in pleasure, Vegas moved to turn around.

"No," she said, pushing him back. "I'm not done." Gently sliding her hands over him, she moved them around to his front and caressed his manhood.

He pushed her hands away, turned around, and pinned her to the wall. "My turn," he gasped, a wicked look in his eyes.

Tahlia spread her legs so he could stand between them, and took his hard shaft into her hands, stroking, sliding them up and down. Bringing him to the brink then stopping.

Vegas was breathing hard, his hands on the wall either side of her, keeping her there. He gazed deeply into her eyes, and then his manly tongue peeked out from between his captivatingly full lips. Slowly, teasingly, pink and ripe, it licked his lips from left to right.

Tahlia stood mesmerised.

Then it disappeared as his mouth met hers. His hands slid seductively up and down the sides of her body.

Her arms slid around him as his mouth began the exploration. Arching her back against the wall, she groaned as his mouth moved down to her collarbone, drinking from the hollow of her neck.

His hands clenched her ass, pulling her crotch toward him.

She hitched her right leg around his narrow, lean waist.

Teasingly, he pushed against her, then pulled away. He probed a little further, then pulled back.

The third time Tahlia had had enough. Grabbing him, she pulled him to her and inside, groaning an animalistic sound in response. Pushing her head against the wall, she arched her back even more and thrust her breasts towards his waiting mouth.

Vegas pushed her hard against the wall and kept her there.

She grabbed his hair and brought his mouth to hers, not letting go. His tongue, once again, thrusting into her mouth as his shaft thrust into her vagina in a dual invasion.

Ecstasy came in bursts, one after the other, as Tahlia

made small gasping sounds and Vegas grunted with every thrust. Her mouth tasted him, from his earlobe, down his neck, to his collarbone, along his shoulder to his right arm. Seeing the water run over his tattoo, Tahlia traced her tongue over the pattern, slowly, slowly, one line at a time. Biting it gently, she kissed it, then looked at him.

His eyes seemed darker, long lashes framing them, his pupils fully dilated, his face only millimetres from hers. Vegas breathed heavily, his mouth open slightly as Tahlia gently stroked his face, feeling the softness of his facial hair, tracing her fingers along his lips. Her tongue followed suit, her gaze never leaving his. The look on his face raw, animalistic. A hell of a turn on.

With a sudden movement, Vegas shut off the shower and picked her up. She wrapped herself around him as he carried her into the bedroom.

They fell onto the bed, writhing, thrusting, wild, free…

Hours later, Tahlia woke, facing the dark curtained window that had just a hint of the outside light poking around the corners. Vegas was behind her, his left arm around her waist, right arm under her head, their right hands entwined. Feeling hot, thirsty, and dry, she sat up, careful not to wake him as she pulled out of his embrace. Grabbing a bottle of water from their stash, she cracked it open and took a swig, then sat on a chair to watch him sleep.

My God, what a man, she thought, contented as she remembered how they had climaxed in unison, falling into an extremely satisfied jumble of arms and legs. *I can't believe I found a man who does this to me, after all the bastards I've been with. I can't believe he's interested…in me!*

But is he?

Of course he is, otherwise, why is he here with me. Why did he initiate sex last night if he's not? Why pick me? I'm sure he could get any woman he wanted, he's a hell of a looker. All rough an' sexy, knowing how to talk to a woman to sweep her off her feet. He swept me off my feet yesterday. I didn't have to give him a ride…

Oh, you certainly did that last night and tonight…

She blushed. *Yes I did. An' boy, was it one hell of a ride.*

Vegas rolled onto his back, snoring softly. Her gaze slid slowly down his hard, naked body, marvelling at his member, its length and thickness, the things it had done to her in the last twenty-four hours, filling her to a capacity she had never felt. She sensed the blood rising to her face again.

I don't know a thing about him, not sure I care really. Should I, maybe, after all the others I've been with how do I know he's different? In bed he certainly is, having pleasured me in ways I've only ever imagined. But in other ways?

She sighed softly. *After what I've been through, somehow, I just don't care. He is so different, so manly, so much better than all the other men. He is absolute heaven.*

Tahlia gently set the bottle down on the table and thought of trying one of his singlets on. Grinning in delight at the thought of the look on his face, she reached into his duffel and felt soft material. She yanked out the top and pulled it on, still grinning. *Looks good.* Glancing over her shoulder to see if Vegas was still asleep, she decided to look in his bag some more. *Well,* she reasoned, *I should get to know him.*

She dug around and came across something cold, metallic, heavy. Pushing the opening of the bag apart, she saw a gun, and right next to it, a roll of money thicker than her wrist.

Suddenly that wrist was grabbed, and Vegas violently threw her onto the bed. "Don' you *ever* go through my bag again," he yelled, coming over to the bed, pointing at her as she cowered on the corner looking at him in shock and fear. "Don' you *ever... look...in my bag...again.*" His voice was low and threatening, and he glowered at her in anger, then the look changed and softened when he realised she was frightened of him, almost crying, but trying to keep it together, quivering. He kneeled on the bed and moved toward her. "It's okay, baby." His voice now soft, gentle. "I'm not gonna hurt you."

Tahlia moved back even more, almost falling off the bed, and stumbled into the corner of the room. Ready to run, to get away from the horror she had known in her life and was still running from.

"Tahlia, it's okay, baby," he said, stopping, watching her. "I didn' mean to hurt you, just wanted to scare you. I don' like people goin' through my stuff. It's private, ya know." He reached out his hand to her.

She realised she wasn't breathing and gasped for air, shaking and scared. Memories threatened to pour back into her mind. Memories she didn't want anymore.

No, no, she said to them, *go away, I don't want you in my head anymore.*

Her pulse slowed as she took deep breath after deep breath. Seeing the look of concern on his face, a thought occurred to her. There would be no more fear, no more panic and desperation. No more being a victim. *I'm finally going to get tough an' stand up for myself. I can't keep letting this happen to me. I can't keep doing this to me, myself. I just can't. An' maybe he's different, maybe he's not. But so far, he's been okay. No more. I will take, no more.*

Her brain screamed at her. *Don't be stupid! He just threw you across the bed. He's abusive, and there are definitely violent tendencies behind those gorgeous blue eyes of his.*

Maybe there are, but no more, she thought, deciding to give him a chance and take baby steps. She breathed in deeply, exhaled slowly. "I want to see it," she said firmly.

"See what?" Vegas asked, his gaze never leaving her face.

"The gun."

"Why?" He frowned, confused by her changing moods. *God, talk about a bloody complicated woman,* he thought.

"'Cause, if you can have a gun in your bag with a thick wad of money, then I want to see, an' I want you to tell me why you have it."

Vegas looked at her with a mix of emotions, and after a few moments sighed. "Okay," he finally said, getting his duffel. He brought it over and pulled out the gun and money, laying them both on the bed side by side. Lighting a cigarette, he sat next to them, and leaned against the bedhead, looking at her, watching her as she crawled warily onto the bed and picked up the gun.

Tahlia examined it, turning it over and over. The cold metallic weight left an odd impression in her hands. The trigger, so easy to pull if she needed to. *Needed to?* She'd never handled a gun before so where did that thought come from? After a while, she put it down and picked up the money. "How much?" she asked, without looking at him.

"'Bout two thou," he replied, watching her curiously.

"From where?" She still didn't look at him.

"Work, travel money," Vegas said a little uneasily, wondering why she suddenly had a need to know things. His things. *Damn women! Always bein' nosy.*

She pulled the band off and counted. "From where?" she repeated.

"I told you, work," he said, annoyed.

"Have you ever killed someone?" Her voice was low and shaky, and her eyes looked at him with fear and wariness. Her mind was going a million miles an hour with so many thoughts.

"Yeah." Straight and to the point. Just like his gaze.

Her head shot up, and her eyes now widened to the size of saucers. "When?"

"Not long ago." He became stubborn and crossed his arms, not wanting to tell her.

"Self-defence?"

She got no reply.

Vegas stubbed out his cigarette, and picked up the gun and money, placing them back in his bag. Putting it on the floor beside him, he turned to her, and for the first time noticed she was wearing one of his tops. He grinned. "You look good in that, baby."

Her look was questioning.

"Let's get some sleep," he said, lying down. "C'mere baby." He held out his arms, but Tahlia moved away, lying down on the edge of the bed and facing him.

In fear of him.

He looked at her in surprise, then figured that was how things were going to be. Settling in, Vegas stared at the ceiling, thinking about what had just happened. *Yeah man, I've been violent with women in the past, just as dear old Dad had been violent with Mom, an' me. Been sexually active with many women. God the things they taught me. But the woman lyin' beside me now is different. Not sure how, just different. Not a hooker or some crackpot crack head junkie out to score drugs or sex. She's...she's, soft an' ripe an' homely. Like my Mom. Jesus, where'd that come from?* He was surprised that something like that had popped into his head. A picture of his mother came to his mind. *Mom, God, I miss you. I miss you so much an' now, Tahlia reminds me of you. I wonder if you're watchin' down over me, protectin' me. If you can see her, I hope you like her. She's like you.*

He wiped his hand over his face as a few tears escaped. *I'm feelin' emotions an' pleasure like never before.* He gazed at Tahlia sleeping beside him. She twitched. *I've known since the gas station that she was someone special. From the moment I saw her through the glass, then those assholes had come an' started trouble. Well, I took care a them. An' scored me a woman in the process.* He smiled softly. *One hell of a woman!*

Lying beside a man she barely knew, Tahlia tried to sleep. But she was worried, scared. *What am I doing?* she thought furiously. *How could I be so stupid!*

Well, I did tell you, her brain tormented.

Look, she told herself. *Tomorrow is another day, an' I really need to get a grip on my life now. I'm not with Wayne, an' I never want to go back to that sort of life again. But I don't know Vegas. An' that will have to be the first thing I do. Get to know the man he is. If he's different or not. So far, he hasn't laid a hand on me, an' maybe he won't, ever. But I don't know, so it's time to make a few decisions.*

She drifted off to sleep with images floating through her mind. His gun had brought back flashes of images she'd not had since meeting him.

Flashes of images she did not want again…

She was running, running, running. Blindly, in fear of her life. Running from something, she didn't know what, just that she had to get away. Away from the terror, the pain, the man in the shadows…

The gun that was firing. The pain, searing, the screaming, the blood. The blood, flowing from somewhere on her hands. The blood.

It was there, on her hands, making them slick and slippery. She frantically wiped them on her dress, hoping it would stop, not realising it wasn't hers. She kept running. I have to get away, I have to get away, oh, why is he chasing me, why does he want me? Go away, go away, please, go away.

She ran on, her heart pounding as loudly as the footsteps behind her. Where can I hide? Where can I hide, oh, God, please, where can I hide? Wait, there, I can hide there. Quickly now, don't make a sound, he'll hear you, he'll find you. Must be quiet, I must be quiet and not make a sound.

The footsteps stopped…

He was right in front of her…

Tahlia woke with a start and saw it was just becoming light out. The shower was on, the bed empty beside her. She lay still, breathing deeply to regulate her pounding heart, and listening to the comforting sound of the flowing water. She heard him singing. *God, what do I do?* she asked herself, feeling emotionally worn out. He turned the shower off, and she rose and grabbed her bag, digging around for some clothes and toiletries.

Vegas came out with a towel slung low on his manly hips. "Hey, baby," he said, gazing at her with a soft smile.

"Hey," she said, pushing past him into the bathroom and locking the door behind her. Trying to wash her cares away, she stood under the streaming water, letting it run over her. She dressed and walked out, finding that Vegas had already packed the car.

"We okay, baby?" he asked gently, hopefully, standing with his hands in his pockets and a soft look on his face.

She frowned, unsure as she packed her bag. "Maybe."

After eating some breakfast at the diner, they got gas and supplies. Heading off down the highway with Vegas driving, Tahlia was quiet, thinking, trying to make some choices about her life. She was tired of being beaten, used and abused, scared, and until last night thought things had changed.

Finally deciding to become more self-reliant and stand up for herself, she looked at Vegas, wanting to know more about the man beside her. "Have you ever been violent with a woman?"

He looked at her, his expression mixed, not sure whether to answer. After mentally debating with himself he chose to be honest. To a point. "Yeah."

"I want to know."

Sighing, Vegas contemplated lying, but knowing this woman was different to all the others, he needed to be honest and forthright. "I started havin' sex at fifteen, once I was big enough to control a woman, I did to them what my father did to my mother. I guess growin' up in that kinda household, in a ratty New York apartment, it rubbed off on me an' that's all I knew. My parents hadn' been affectionate with each other for…God knows how long. I don' remember seein' any. Haven' had a woman in," he shrugged, "'bout a year. Been travellin' too much." He smiled softly and looked at her. "You're the first one I've had feelin's for, the first one I don' want to hurt."

"Your father abused you an' your mother?" Tahlia asked gently.

He looked back at the road. "Yeah. Actually, thinkin'

'bout it, my father beat my mother all my life. When I was fourteen, she died from a beatin' he gave her one night. He used a frypan 'cause he didn' like the meal she made him. Hit after hit he cracked that fucker over her head till she stopped movin'. I tried to stop him, but he started in on me till I was out of it. Twenty-four hours later, a friend of my mom's stopped by to see her. The door was open a crack, so she came in." Vegas choked on the words.

"Pull over," Tahlia said as he started to cry.

"No, no, I'm okay," he said, wiping away a few tears and regaining his self-control. "I woke up in hospital two weeks later. My father had disappeared, an' my mother was dead. I had nowhere to go, so they put me in foster care. But considerin' what had happened, I changed, became angry, abusive, just like my father. I lashed out at my foster parents one night then ran away. Lived on the streets ever since. Done things you wouldn' be proud of, an' I'm not either. But I had to do them to survive." He looked at her again. "I'm sorry 'bout last night, baby."

"Concentrate on the road," Tahlia said and looked out at the passing landscape, finally knowing a little something about him, wondering if she should tell him her story. "I know what you've gone through," she said eventually. "My mother's boyfriends. She died a few months ago from cancer."

"I'm sorry," he said, his voice soft.

"I'm not." She sighed.

He reached out and grabbed her hand, gently squeezing it in sympathy.

Stopping for lunch and gas, they said nothing, each wallowing in their own self-pity.

Tahlia; for all the years she was abused and used and wondered why her mother did nothing to protect her from all of her so-called boyfriends and their abuse. From *her* abuse. Why her father died and left her alone at such a young age when she needed him so much. Why all the men she kept picking were such lying, cheating bastards, who believed they could abuse her. Emotionally, physically, mentally. Why she never stood up to them and fought back, just standing there to be walked all over like a doormat. Accepting their excuses, their hands beating her face, her body, her soul, and willpower. Why she just stood there, or lay there and said nothing. Did nothing. Why she just accepted it.

Vegas; thinking about his mother's death at such a tender age, and his father's dirty, filthy betrayal. Why for the first fourteen years of his life his father had never loved him, never wanted him. Only ever looked at him with contempt and anger. And why did he go and kill his mother when she was the one woman, the *only* woman in his impressionable young life to show him how to be happy? At least she tried to. At least she loved him and showed it. Unlike his rat bastard of a father. She had fought so hard to protect him. Her son. The little boy she loved so much. His mother had loved him so completely. And he loved her, with all of his fourteen-year-old precocious heart.

*****

Mid-afternoon Vegas turned on the radio just as the news came on the hour.

"The owner of the gas station in Monroe, Mississippi was found shot dead last night. The police say he had been dead at least twenty-four hours and they don't have any suspects. There was no video surveillance, but a Harley was found behind the station—"

He quickly snapped off the radio, but Tahlia grabbed his hand before it left the dial.

"What did you do?" she choked through clenched teeth, looking at him in horror. "What did you do? Did you shoot him? I know that was the gas station where we met, an' no attendant came out, only you, an' you have a gun an' a wad of money. Did you kill him? Did you? Answer me."

He looked extremely guilty.

"Did you? Tell me," she demanded.

"Yeah," he replied quietly. "Yeah," more angrily. "What are ya lookin' at me like that for? Did ya really think I'd never killed someone before? After hearin' 'bout my childhood I'd say the next step for me was killin', so don' be so surprised."

Tahlia was looking at him, thinking, *oh, my God, what have I done. All I did was pull in for gas an' end up leaving with a murderer.* "Why?" she asked incredulously.

"Why?" he repeated angrily. "I don' know. I was desperate for money, my bike was broke down. I shoved somethin' in my pocket an' he saw me, pulled out his old shotgun an' threatened to kill me. So I got in first. That's when you an' those idiots pulled up an' I had to stop you comin' in. You had a car, so I thought, here's my chance to get away." Vegas looked at her, desperately wanting her to believe him.

She shook her head slowly, not knowing what to think. "So, that's all I was, just a getaway plan. You used me." Looking out the window, she felt shocked tears falling.

"*Aw, come on*, like you never killed someone. I know this car's not yours 'cause I heard on the radio that the police are also lookin' for a car matchin' this description. The plates may not match, but I bet this is the car. It belonged to a guy who was shot to death, an' the last person to supposedly see him alive was his girlfriend, *an'* she matched *your* description. So are ya gonna deny it?" He was surprised by her look of absolute horror.

"What the hell do you mean? I didn't steal this car… I…didn't…I think." Her eyes as wide as saucers.

"What do ya mean, *think*?" he demanded, glancing from her to the road and back.

"I don't remember how I got it," she yelled. "I just don't remember." She wrapped her arms around herself.

"Ya don' remember where ya got this car?" Vegas was unbelieving. "Ya have to be freakin' kiddin' me. It was you, wan' it? You killed that guy an' stole his car."

"I don't know, I don't remember. I have a huge gap in my memory, an' I don't remember." Tahlia was now desperate, not believing she could possibly have killed someone and she started sobbing loudly. "I don't remember."

He pulled over, freaked out by her behaviour, and

grabbed her to hold her, but she lashed out, screaming hysterically and she tried to push him away.

"Let me go, let me go." She scratched at his face and arms as he grabbed for her hands, trapping them in his.

"No, I won'," he said, pulling her into his arms.

"No, no," she screamed, then collapsed against him in exhaustion.

He held her tightly, stroking her hair, letting her sob until she was spent. "Tell me what happened."

"No."

"Tahlia." His voice was low, gentle.

"I don't remember, so how can I talk about it, I don't want to." Sitting up, she wiped her face and blew her nose. "I need a drink, what have we got?" Searching through the box, she grabbed a bottle of soda and started drinking. "Well…" she said, glaring at him, "we don't want to sit here all day, let's go."

With a deep sigh and a long look, Vegas stepped on the accelerator, steering them back onto the highway, thinking about her reaction and what the hell he was going to do about it. An hour later he had another idea. "How 'bout when we stop tonight, in whatever small town we come across, we head for the bar an' grab a meal. Some drinks, a dance, a game of pool, some fun. You know, lift our spirits." He glanced at her questioningly.

Looking at him and seeing the eager look in his eyes, she grinned softly and thought about it. *Why not,* she thought. "Okay, sounds good."

*****

He was watching her on her way to Vegas and thought it was such a joke. He laughed. Did she really think she was safe having a man with her? Especially that man? Mind you, she has no inkling of his past or what he'd gotten up to before meeting her. The bad things he'd done. The bad things he'd seen. And here she was all worried about her past and a supposed dead boyfriend she might have killed and left behind. Dear, dear, he thought, smiling to himself. Poor baby…if only she knew about the man she had given herself to, many, many times in the few short days they had been together.

Out in the desert, in the motel room.

"Ah, yesss", he hissed, "the desert."

It had been particularly intense. Tahlia so aroused and high on the giddy sense of passion and desire that she'd orgasmed almost immediately. Poor girl, she was so sex starved. Starved for love, for the slightest ounce of want and need. Craving everything, every touch, every word, every caress as she screamed into the night again and again. That sweet, nubile, pliant body just made for doing those things to. Things she'd never done before. Things she so badly wanted to do again. Over and over.

"Oh, yes, my sweet Tahlia. You will do them again. I promise you that."

Chapter 4

That night, with thick black storm clouds threatening, they pulled into a small town.

"Let's get gas first," Vegas said, driving in.

"Fine, just don't shoot the attendant."

Vegas looked at her, freaked out by her comment.

"Well?" she asked, raising a brow at him as he got out of the car. Grabbing her bag, Tahlia followed him out of the driver's door. "I'm goin' the ladies' to change into something a bit more appropriate for dinner."

She was going to change her attitude because she had a plan.

"Awright. Once I get gas, I'll do the same an' pull the car in over the side." He pointed over to where there were parks outside the restroom.

Glancing at her watch, Tahlia saw it was nearly seven-thirty, and walking into the restroom, she saw there was only one toilet and not much room to change. "Okay," she said, screwing up her nose at the grossness of it, "it'll have to do." She pulled out her outfit and the first aid kit which she'd brought in from the car and slid out the small pair of scissors.

She attacked her clothes with passion, re-creating them to suit her new lifestyle. A lifestyle she was still tentatively creating for herself, and the woman she was going to be. She smiled as she cut the sleeves off her top and made a new neckline, and turned her skirt into half its original size.

Grabbing the hand towel she'd brought in, she turned on the faucet and quickly washed. She pulled on her clothes and stepped into boots, then brushed and fluffed her hair as best she could before applying some make-up. She wasn't all that used to wearing it, having bought herself a few things when she was living in Maine, as Wayne liked her tarted up.

Tahlia pulled a necklace from a small purse. It had been her father's, the only reminder she had of him. She fastened it around her neck and took a few moments to remember him. She threw everything back into her bag and took one final look. Wow, definitely not her. At least, the old her. She was surprised that the small changes she was making were so easy. And she was able to pull them off without too much trouble.

Looking back at the person in the mirror, she hardly recognised herself.

Her mousy looking hair had disappeared and now seemed so full of life. The bags under her eyes were slowly diminishing, the dark circles nearly gone. The colour of her eyes no longer a dull and dreary green, they gleamed with an emerald sparkle and she wondered if it was due to Vegas and what had happened between them. Not him being a killer, which completely freaked her out, but the incredible sexcapades they passionately shared and participated in nightly. She smiled at her reflection and giggled. Definitely the sex! Satisfied with what she saw, she left.

Vegas was smoking a cigarette and leaning against the car. He'd changed into a tight, black tank top and a pair of skin-tight ripped black jeans. He was wearing a belt with a brass knuckle buckle, and a chain hanging from the belt loops.

Tahlia blushed deeply as she remembered her embarrassing mistake that first day.

Vegas had added two more chains with pendants around his neck, and a leather band around his right wrist. His biker boots had been cleaned, and he was indeed one very sexy man.

"God, you look good," she purred, feeling incredibly turned on.

His eyes widened when he saw her. "Wow, you look great yourself," he replied, flicking his cigarette to the ground.

"Well, I thought I would dress up." She looked down at her outfit and smoothed the skirt. "Think it's appropriate for a small town bar?"

He grinned that damn sexy grin and took her into his arms. "Baby," he drawled in a low voice, "it may not be appropriate for a small town bar, but it's definitely appropriate for me."

He ran his hands over her, taking in the white, skin-tight, sleeveless, low-cut top with the rock and roll logo she had on over a black push up bra. The chain around her neck let the guitar pendant nestle gently between her breasts. Skimming down over her very short black denim mini skirt, his hands found their way underneath and stopped.

"That a thong?" he asked excitedly, plucking at it like it was his guitar.

"Yup." She'd topped the outfit with old black cowboy boots.

"Sure ya wanna eat, maybe we could…ya know," Vegas said.

"Sorry, baby, but I'm hungry." She stroked his face.

"So am I." He grinned wickedly.

"*I* mean for food," she replied, playfully pushing his hands away. "Let's go."

As they pulled up to the bar, the rain clouds finally burst, and the rain poured forth. They ran through the door, laughing and shaking themselves off. Walking over to the bar, Tahlia looked around. A pool table to their left, a stage with a band playing beyond that. Tables with people placed around both the stage and a small dance floor. To their right, more tables, booths and a jukebox against the wall. The floor was covered with threadbare old-fashioned carpeting, and the people were staring at them strangely, obviously not liking strangers in their town.

"Hey," Vegas said when they stopped at the bar and sat down on stools. "We get a meal?"

"Sure," the bartender replied, "you want drinks?" He grabbed a pad and took their order.

Picking up their drinks, Vegas rum, Tahlia cola, they went and found a table.

"Well…friendly," she said with a touch of sarcasm. Gazing around through the smoky haze, she saw that the people had gone back to what they had been doing.

After lighting a cigarette, Vegas grabbed her hand and pulled her toward him, nuzzling her, tickling her with his goatee.

"Mmm, you shaved some off," she complained as she gently stroked his face.

"Thought I'd clean up a bit," he replied with a grin before he kissed her.

Their meals arrived, and they dug in, hungrily eating in silence. After checking everyone out, and ordering more drinks, they decided on a few games of pool before leaving.

"I wonder if they have dessert," Tahlia said, craning her neck to see if there was a dessert sign anywhere.

"I'll go check. Why don' you go put some money in that old jukebox? Pick somethin' decent that'll drown out that god-awful band we been listnin' to," Vegas said before walking off.

Tahlia laughed and looked over at the band that was playing on the stage to their left. They were definitely in need of a stylist *and* a serious makeover.

Swinging her hips as she walked over to the jukebox, which was against a wall with framed pictures all over it, she stood reading the song titles. She popped a few dollars in, picked four songs, and went back to the table. Vegas brought back two pieces of pecan pie and two more drinks.

"You trying to make me fat or get me drunk?" She laughed.

"Both," he said, a huge grin plastered on his stubbly face.

The song playing on the jukebox started skipping.

"Oh, no," Tahlia said and looked over at the player.

The sound of the skipping music annoyed Vegas so much he walked over to the jukebox and paused a moment. Picking a spot, he hit it with his fist, setting the song back on track.

She grinned as he sat down. "Who do you think you are, the Fonz?"

Leaning back in his chair Vegas put his thumbs up. "Ayyy," he drawled, making her laugh as his impersonation was spot on.

Once done, they headed for the pool table that had just freed up, and after an amorous round which Tahlia won, Vegas threw down his cue in disgust.

"I'm goin' the little boys' room."

"You're no little boy." Tahlia smirked, watching him stalk off toward the back of the bar where the bathrooms were. She laughed to herself. "Sore loser."

"So, you think you're pretty good huh?" The sarcasm was so obvious it made her turn around. The guy who had spoken slapped down a twenty. "I'm better than you, so let's play."

Eyeing the twenty, and knowing she could easily beat him, Tahlia picked up her cue. Five minutes and seven shots later he threw down his cue in disgust as she shoved the money into her bra. Vegas was sitting off to the side drinking a beer, and grinning like his face would burst. Three men lined up to beat her, but had no idea what they were letting themselves in for.

When they had all skulked off with their tales between their legs, Tahlia walked over to Vegas and took a long swig of his beer.

Wrapping his arms around her, his right hand slid under her skirt, and he growled in her ear. "Baby, I had no idea you were so good at so many things."

She grinned and kissed him passionately, thrusting her tongue into his willing mouth. "Seems I'm good at a shitload of stuff," she said, running her hands over his rugged face. "You'll just have to find out what else." She turned and walked back to the jukebox. Looking over the selection, she picked one of her favourite songs and was swaying in time to the music when Vegas came up behind her. They started gyrating together, and his hands slid under her skirt, feeling her.

"If you two want sex go get a room," a female voice called out. They turned in the direction it had come from. The female bartender was looking at them in disgust.

"We might just do that," Vegas said, his grin back on his face.

A commotion broke out across the room, and they turned to watch. A waitress was being harassed by some pervert who thought he had the right to grab her ass. She promptly slapped his face and poured his beer over his head. His friends at the table laughed in amusement, but he didn't. Swearing at the waitress, he got up to follow her, but at that moment, another man walked over to him and said something in his ear. The man sat down and shut up.

"Good for her," Tahlia murmured.

Vegas grinned again. "A few more rounds of pool, and a couple of drinks, then we'll go."

She lined the balls up, and it didn't take long before she beat him again. He was not amused. Paying for another song on the jukebox, Tahlia turned to see a challenger waiting to play her. "You do know what you're letting yourself in for, don't you?" she asked indulgently of the man when she got back to the table.

There was a cocky grin. "You won't beat me."

"Okay, your loss." Racking up the balls, Tahlia fired the first shot. Her opponent was good and was winning until she hit another ball into the pocket to even the score. As she straightened up, the arrogant jerk who had accosted the waitress slammed down his beer on the pool table.

"Ya, know," he slurred. "We can all see ya want it, 'cause ya not wearin' any panties." He thrust his right hand up under her skirt to her crotch.

Tahlia was incensed that a man could and would do that to her in a public place. Especially one she didn't know from Adam. It made her feel sick to her stomach that one, she was standing there with his hand on her crotch, and two, his mates were having a good old time, laughing and thinking it was funny.

She made a decision. It's time to stand up and do something, not just stand here and take it.

Both of her hands were still wrapped around her cue as it lay on the table and she tightened her grip. Looking at him angrily, she lifted it and rammed the thick end into his groin.

As he doubled over in pain, she brought her right knee up to smash him in the face. He went reeling backward as one of his friends ran at her. She kicked him in the groin and then the face.

Someone grabbed her from behind, so she smashed her head back into his nose, and using the force to lift her legs, she kicked at the man in front of her.

There was an all-out brawl, and everyone in the bar was fighting each other.

The man that she'd kicked had sprawled into tables, and because their beers had been knocked over, those men joined in.

Even Vegas was pounding into a guy who'd jumped him.

Three men came at her.

With a swift front kick, the one before her went flying and swinging her leg back, she kicked the one behind her. Still holding her pool cue, Tahlia swung it around and smashed it into the face of the third guy who fell on the spot. Everyone was fighting. And it was bedlam.

Vegas grabbed her hand and yelled, "Let's go." Running out the door into the blinding rain, they laughed and giggled hysterically as they jumped into their car, gunned the engine, and skidded out of the parking lot.

Still giddy with excitement many miles later, Vegas finally spoke. "Where the hell'd ya learn to fight like that?"

"I don't know. Maybe all the years of abuse, an' meeting you, gave me the guts to finally defend myself an' do something about it, not just sit there an' take it an'…wow, I can't believe I did that." She was in disbelief, having never even thought of doing something like that.

Well, I did hit Wayne, but then he hit me an' that was that, she thought. *Wow! I started a brawl.* She turned on the radio and snuggled happily into Vegas, and he wrapped his right arm around her and planted a kiss on her forehead.

An hour later, Tahlia woke up to hear him swearing and hitting the steering wheel in frustration.

"What's wrong?" she asked around a yawn.

"There's somethin' wrong with the car, damn it. An' there shouldn' be. I check it every time we get gas."

"Just pull over somewhere an' I'll dig the flashlight out an' you can check it."

He looked at her incredulously. "You want me to get out in the pourin' rain an' fiddle under the hood?"

"Well, there's a problem isn't there, an' you obviously know about cars. An' if you do that, then you can fiddle under *my* hood," she said seductively.

Vegas eyed her in anticipation and licked his lips. Pulling onto a flat piece of land just as the car died, he grabbed the flashlight and got out. Lifting the hood, he checked the motor.

After ten minutes, Tahlia was bored and still aroused from the dream she'd been having about Vegas. Getting an idea that turned her on immensely, she dug around in his bag for one of his tops, and taking off her t-shirt and bra, she pulled his singlet over her head. She slipped off her thong and made sure the sleeping bags were easy to grab. Quietly getting out of the car, she shut the door without making a sound. For a few minutes, she stood there, letting the rain soak her, relishing what was to come.

"Fine'ly," Vegas yelled and slammed the hood shut. The light from the flashlight caught Tahlia, and he stopped. "What are ya doin'? Get in." She didn't move, just seductively licked her lips. "Oh, God," he said as he moved toward her and lifted her onto the hood. She locked her legs around him, and he saw she was wearing one of his tops with nothing underneath.

Her breasts heaved in desire as her nipples pushed against the material. Her lips were full and wanting as she gazed back at him, seeing that he too was soaked to the skin. Reaching for his belt, Tahlia unbuckled it, and slowly unzipped his jeans before her hands slid over his ass and pushed them down along with his shorts. She brought her hands to his front, revealing his hard erect manhood, and stroked him gently.

His breath came in short, hard gasps. His mouth merged with hers and tongues mated together.

Pushing the top up and over her breasts, he took both nipples into his mouth, lashing them with his tongue.

She arched her back, giving him full access, groaning in pleasure, grabbing his head, meeting his mouth in a passionate kiss. Tahlia yanked off his top and marvelled at his muscular body.

Taking his hardness into her hand, she slid forward and opened her legs to take him inside of her. Vegas shoved his hands up her skirt to pull down her thong but didn't find it. He looked up at her in surprise before pulling her toward him as she led him into the pleasure garden.

Gasping, groaning, they ground against each other.

His hands on her waist. His mouth all over her wet breasts. He pushed her down against the hood and thrust hard and fast. Her hands ran over his hard, wet body. Her legs pulled him into her. She was racked with spasms and arched her back as Vegas sucked harder on her nipples.

The rain was pouring down in torrents with neither noticing, only relishing in the eroticism of the moment. Screaming in pleasure, throbbing in ecstasy, they came together.

Their mouths mashing. Their tongues tasting. Their teeth biting.

Collapsing against the hood, they gasped for breath, still touching, still aching, laying there for a few moments before Vegas gently lifted Tahlia up and carried her into the car. She had put the seat down earlier, and they lay together, panting in the afterglow, listening to the rain beat against the roof.

But she wasn't done. Still hungry, with her appetite unquenched, she looked at the man before her and pulled him on top of her as their mouths met in more explosive passion.

He hardened again, as his hands tangled in her hair, and his mouth explored her.

She put her boot-clad feet on the dashboard to brace herself, he unbuttoned her denim skirt, and she ripped off the top she was still wearing. Pushing his jeans down his lean legs and yanking them off, Vegas and Tahlia entwined in every way.

His goatee aroused her even more as she felt it on her wet skin. His lips enclosed around her breast, sucking it into a hard bud then it moved down her body. His tongue found the place where his penis had been and was about to be again.

He tasted, tortured, thrusted. In and out. In and out.

Grabbing him, and pulling him back inside of her, that raw, animalistic emotion came back full force.

Hard and thrusting. Aching and throbbing.

The orgasm racked them both.

Chapter 5

As the morning sunlight started up over the horizon and lit up her face, Tahlia opened her eyes to see a brand-new day. Sighing in content, she snuggled further into the sleeping bag against Vegas, his arms tightening around her as he nuzzled her shoulder.

This is the life, she thought. *No responsibilities, no house to take care of. Just cruising along the highway doing what we want. On our way to a new place. A new life.*

What about the old one?

She opened her eyes again. *What about it? I'm not there anymore, I don't remember what happened, so I'm not going to think about it. Get out of my head.*

Knowing they would have to go soon, she reluctantly pulled out of the strong embrace, kneeled on the seat, and rolled down the window. She stuck her head out to see how bogged they were and felt something slide up her leg and play with the hair on her crotch.

She giggled, swatted his hand away, and crawled back under the covers into his waiting arms. He kissed her left shoulder and nuzzled her neck as they lay in the peace and quiet.

Just being together.

"We're not that bogged you know, we should be able to get out okay."

"Mmm, you say somethin'?" He was planting kisses down her spine, and when he came to her lower back that was all it took.

Turning around, Tahlia pulled Vegas back up against the seat and unzipped the bag, so they had room. She straddled him, her body pressed to his, tasting every goddamn hard inch of him and his masculinity. Biting his nipples, making him groan, her hands explored him, followed by her mouth. Sliding over his hard, lean torso, down to his navel where she teased by poking her tongue in.

She followed the trail of hair that travelled from his navel all the way to his pelvis, and gently stroked his lower abdomen, just along the place where it met his groin. He was going to get what he'd been giving her. Grinding and thrusting, she made both of them extremely happy.

Later, Tahlia was still lying on top of Vegas while he stroked her hair. "What a way to wake up an' start the day," he drawled.

She grinned against his chest, her hand lazily sliding up and down his bulging bicep and through the golden-brown hair she was nestled in. "Mmm, we should do that more often," she murmured, running her tongue over his chest.

"Mmm, we should," he replied, catching her tongue with his mouth.

For a few long moments, they just stayed that way.

Being quiet, being together…

Until they finally moved, getting on the road with hours passing by. They didn't speak, just snuggled. Watching the miles of countryside pass them by.

"We should get rid of the car," Vegas finally said.

"What? Why?" Tahlia asked in surprise and sat up to look at him.

He glanced at her. "We're headin' into a big city, an' if you did steal the car an' shoot that guy, then it's best it not be found."

She thought it over, wondering if she was a murderer.

"A friend of mine will meet us 'bout a hundred fifty mile out, we'll burn an' ditch the car. No one will find it." He glanced at her again and tried to gauge her reaction.

She looked at him, still surprised, but a frown covered her face. "When did you make that plan?"

"After our little exchange yesterday, I made a phone call last night. Told him we would be gettin' inta Vegas today, can he help out."

"I don't know." She sighed. "Let me think about it." Moving over to the passenger window and gazing out at the passing landscape, Tahlia contemplated her life again. *Did I kill someone? Did I steal a car? What if I did, is that what the nightmares are about? The nightmares that come an' go. The stranger in the shadows. Running. The gun. The blood.* She hadn't dreamt of a gun or blood until the other night, and now she was scared. *Oh, my God, what if I did? What if I am a murderer? We can't keep the car, if I did it, even though I can't remember, then we just can't keep the car. The cops will find it, then find us…he's right, we have to get rid of it.* "Okay," she said, sighing and turning to Vegas. "Let's ditch the car."

He watched her face intently. "Okay. There's a small town called White Falls 'bout a hundred fifty mile out of Vegas. He'll hitch up with us there. I'll call him when we stop next."

With a dreadful sick feeling in the pit of her stomach, Tahlia agreed.

When they came to the next town and stopped for gas, Vegas called his friend, and they agreed on a plan. They were still two hundred and fifty miles from Las Vegas, so at the next town, he would be waiting. Inconspicuously, he would follow them, and after fifty miles pull over and help destroy the car.

"God, I feel sick," she said as they drove along.

"Baby, ya know we can' keep on in this car. We don' even know if anyone's been followin' us." He noticed the expression on her face.

Tahlia became paranoid. "Oh, my God. What if I've been followed since leaving Maine? That's where we were, I lived with him, although I don't think too many people knew I existed. An' I kept feeling someone staring at me though I didn't see anyone. So I'm surprised the news even mentioned a girlfriend. God, I feel sick."

Vegas hit the brakes and stopped the car just as she opened the door and threw up. Once done, she got back in, and he handed her a bottle of water. "Have a drink an' lay down baby. It's gonna be awright."

Tahlia lay down on the front seat, her head on his leg, and fell into a fitful sleep, only waking when they stopped again.

"We're here," Vegas said, pulling into the gas station and driving around the side.

Tahlia got out and walked toward the restroom in a daze, vaguely remembering she needed to freshen up as Vegas lit a cigarette and walked over to the other car that was there, but she didn't take much notice. Five minutes later when she came out, he told her it was all planned. "What, already?" she asked, a little clearer in her thinking.

"Yep, baby. You ready?"

"No." She shrugged. "But I guess we have to."

Back on the highway, Tahlia noticed Vegas checking the rear-view every few minutes. Turning around, she saw the car that had been at the gas station. It was a navy sedan. Inconspicuous. "That your friend?"

"Yep."

Fifty miles along, the car behind flashed its lights. They pulled onto a dirt track on their right and drove for miles before coming to a stop and getting out.

"Hey, man," Vegas drawled, "This is Tahlia," He introduced them to each other. "An' this compadré, is Manny."

He was Hispanic, neatly groomed, and wearing worn jeans and a grease-stained t-shirt. His jet-black hair as slicked back against his round head, his eyes were as dark as night. He was a tad shorter than her and Vegas, and muscular, yet slim.

"Hi," she said quietly.

He just nodded.

"Awright," Vegas said, and clapped his hands

together, "let's get to work."

After transferring their bags to Manny's sedan, he and Vegas wiped down the insides of the car Tahlia was still not sure she had stolen. A car that had helped make so many memories within such a short time.

"Awright, 'bout ten feet in front of us is an old ravine. We'll push the car inta it an' set it on fire." Vegas turned to Tahlia. "You okay?"

"Guess I have to be," she replied softly, crossing her arms to guard against so many unknown truths and nightmares that would go up in smoke with it.

Vegas and Manny pushed the car into the ravine and dropped burning fuel soaked rags down. Soon there was smoke floating through the air. The smell made her sick again.

"Okay, baby, let's go." Vegas helped her into the back seat of Manny's beat up old car and got into the front. For the next hundred miles, there was either silence or reminiscence, Vegas and Manny remembering old times.

But she wasn't listening. Just sitting there feeling sick.

"Look, baby, we fine'ly made it," Vegas yelled, woohooing in animation. Gazing out the window, Tahlia saw the casinos and hotels as they drove through Las Vegas. It was still afternoon, so the city wasn't alight yet and didn't seem too exciting.

"Manny's puttin' us up till we can get our own place," Vegas said as they pulled into the driveway of a rundown house.

"It's not much," Manny replied. "But it's clean inside, an' you always have a place to stay, man." He slapped Vegas on the shoulder.

Moving their bags inside, Manny showed them to the spare bedroom. "All yours, man," he drawled. "You an' the little lady."

"Hey, man, eyes off, don' even think about it," Vegas threatened.

"It's all right, man." Manny put his hands up in protest. "I have my own little lady."

Tahlia sat on the bed, and running her hands through her hair, she sighed.

Vegas shut the door behind Manny, and sitting next to her, put his arms around her. "It's okay, baby, we can do this," he said, kissing her cheek. "We're in Vegas, now."

She miserably watched him as he put his things away. *When the hell did I decide to shack up with you?* she thought, shaking her head. *An' why has my life taken another downward turn? Burning an' dumping a car, isn't that arson? God, what have I done, what am I getting myself into? We're getting our own place? Did I decide that or Vegas? I don't know, oh, God, what the hell is going on with my life. I feel like it's spinning out of control again an' I've got no say in the matter. This has to change. It just has to.* She buried her head in her hands, feeling the hot tears start. She didn't want to believe it, but she was basically back to where she'd been before.

*****

She was running, running, running. Blindly, in fear of her life. Running from something, she didn't know what. She just had to get away. Away from the terror. Away from the man in the shadows…

Oh, God why is he after me, does he want to hurt me? Does he want to kill me? Why, why would he want to? I don't know him, do I? I need to hide, where can I hide? Where can I go? God, it hurts, the pain, it's searing me, burning me, why does it hurt? What happened to me? Why is there blood on my hands, did I hurt someone, myself?

Where am I, God where am I? Which way do I go? There, I can hide there, under that trashcan, the one at the back of that house. I hope it's empty, I hope I can fit.

The world stopped. All was quiet. No footsteps, hers or his, but her ears were ringing loudly. She took the moment to lift the trashcan and crawl underneath, pulling it over her.

Footsteps stopped…

Her heart stopped…

Her breath stopped…

She closed her eyes tightly, praying that he not find her.

The trashcan moved…

This was it…

Tahlia opened her eyes and saw it was early evening. The sun was setting, sending shadows along the wall, and she realised she was once again in a strange house with a strange man. Sitting up, she looked around. The room was small, plain and painted some shade of blue. The bed was nicely made, and there was simple furnishings. Pushing all horrid memories aside, she opened the door and went in search of the bathroom. Hearing Vegas and Manny in the living room, she continued, coming across the bright yellow kitchen and finding a petite woman making dinner.

"Hello, you must be Tahlia. I'm Maria, Manny's wife." She was small, five feet maybe, long dark hair framing dark chocolate eyes that sparkled. Even white teeth were showed off by a broad smile. She looked Hispanic, like Manny, and radiated a comforting happiness.

"Hi," Tahlia said, gazing at the woman. "Umm, I'm looking for the bathroom."

"Around the corner, second on your right," she said with a friendly grin.

After washing up, Tahlia went back into the kitchen and offered to help.

"We need a salad so you can do that, the bowls are in that cabinet," Maria said, pointing to the one next to the fridge.

When everything was ready, they called the men to the table and sat down to eat. The meal was delicious, but Tahlia wasn't hungry. Listening to Vegas and Manny talking about jobs, she faded out.

Afterwards, as they sat on the porch with an evening drink, Maria engaged her in conversation, which was fine until Manny turned on the radio sitting on the small table between him and Vegas.

"Police are still searching for the killer of the gas station owner in Monroe. There have been no more leads. In other news, the murderer of a forty-year-old man in Maine is also still at large. Police have found no

evidence to suggest suicide, and are continuing to look for his girlfriend, although friends have said he wasn't seeing anyone, neighbours are adamant there was a woman living at the residence who ran from the house after the gunshot. In other news—"

Vegas shut off the radio with a snap. "We don' need to listen to depressin' stuff man." A yawn escaped him. "Well, guess we'd better turn in then." He glanced at Tahlia who was opposite him on a bench seat and saw she was sitting in stunned silence. Their hosts agreed as it was late, and they'd all had a long day.

Getting ready for bed, Vegas looked at her. "You okay, baby?" he asked, seeing her pale face and wondering if she was going to be sick again.

"That's the first time I'd heard anything," she said, sitting on the bed. "I didn't even believe you when you said you'd heard it. God, I don't know what to think." Tahlia looked up at him in disbelief, shaking her head, feeling sick and tired of everything. "What do we do? What do I do? What am I supposed to do…just…keep on running?" She glanced around the room. "I can't keep doing this, I can't keep running." She paced around, not sure what she should do, if anything at all.

"Come to bed, baby, things will look a lot better in the mornin'," Vegas said, taking hold of her arms. He led her to the bed and tucked her in.

They lay on their backs in silence for a while.

"What do I do?" she whispered. "I don't know what to do anymore…it's like my life has been taken over by some, strange…I don't know what, but I don't like it. I've never had to run before. Never had to go it alone like this…" her voice trailed off as sadness overtook her.

"You're not alone, baby. I'm here with you. C'mere," Vegas said softly, rolling Tahlia toward him. She laid her head on his chest, and he wrapped his arms around her. "It'll be okay, baby. I promise."

*****

He glanced her way. So, here they were, at his friend's house until they found their own place. How sweet.

He nearly retched at the thought.

He was still watching. Of course he was. He wasn't going to stop just because they had finally arrived in Las Vegas. Oh, no, he wasn't going to stop at all. Especially after doing it out in the rain last night.

Ah, yes, out in the pouring rain. The memories came flooding back.

Tahlia so delectably wet and aroused as the rain soaked her through to her skin. Her nipples so hard and ripe as they pushed through the singlet that was plastered to her voluptuous breasts. Her garden full of fruit so luscious and overflowing. So ready for eating. So ready for tasting.

I need to taste her, he thought vehemently. I need to taste her and the sweet juices that I will suck from her very core, her very soul as she screams MY name into the night. The torment I will inflict upon her will make her beg for more. My tongue driving her insane as it slides all the way in to taste what is mine and only mine.

His blood boiled in his veins, burning him as it

surged through to his groin. His sizable groin. So ripe itself. So ready to make its way into her wonderful, willing, so wet and willing secret spot.

A spot he would claim as his own. Penetrate with every ounce of strength he had. And he had a lot of it. He was a very strong man. A health and fitness regime saw to that.

He slammed one fist into the other, gripping it tightly as he tried hard to control the pounding feeling inside him. Inside his rock-hard penis.

It didn't work.

Watching Tahlia's soft ripeness, he allowed himself relief. His seeds flowing fast and free from their captivity as his hand did its magic. They were so happy to be let out from their tiny, tortured prison, and he imagined them swimming for their life into Tahlia. His Tahlia. Impregnating her with his life, his blood, his soul. His Tahlia.

"Oh, my dear, you have no idea of what you are about to experience."

He sighed. She had no idea at all…

*****

For the next two weeks, they searched for work. Manny was able to set Vegas up with odd jobs from his friends, but Tahlia had no idea what she wanted to do until Vegas sat her down and told her she couldn't be choosy.

"We wanna get our own place right? Well, baby, we need cash, so that means you need to work too. I been doin' odd jobs an' such to earn some money, an'

Manny's lettin' us stay here for nothin'. Now it's up to you."

"I know," she said, feeling exasperated. She walked over to the window and saw a warm spring day and children playing in the street. "I just don't know what I want. I haven't worked much. The men I was with kept me, didn't want me out there. Just stuck at home. I don't know what I want to do. I don't know what I *can* do except cook." She turned to him and shrugged dejectedly.

Vegas joined her at the window. "Well…you can sing. Maybe we should look around, see if there's any place that wants a singer. Then you could work nights or somethin' an' still have free time."

Thinking about the idea, she felt a little excited and nodded in agreement. "Okay, I'll start looking tomorrow."

"An' I'll ask around," Vegas said, grinning as he hugged her.

*****

For two weeks, Tahlia walked into almost every bar, hotel, and casino, asking if they had a spot open. She was hit on, abused, and yelled at time and time again. She was told, *'no', 'get lost, 'she wasn't what they were looking for', 'she didn't fit their description of a singer'* – in other words she wasn't hot – to 'come back when she'd had some surgery', or a boob job, or dyed her hair blonde. In general, told she just wasn't good enough. Although some did tell her she could go on a list, 'just in case'.

*****

Coming home from work one day, Vegas was grinning from ear to ear, and he spun her around. "Baby, I just might have the answer. *The Montiamo* have some auditions on tomorrow. They're lookin' for singers to backup acts an' stuff, maybe fill in, or do some full shows when there's no act on. I can take you an' give you support, we can rehearse tonight. How 'bout it?"

Tahlia was stunned. "O-o-kay," she stammered. "Oh, my God. What do I sing? What do I wear? I don't have much. What am I going to do?"

"Baby, slow down, it's okay," Vegas said, holding her in his arms. "Wear that tight white top an' that black denim skirt you wore that night at the bar."

"Not exactly appropriate for a big casino," she said, wrapping her arms around him.

"Maybe not. But if you sing a rock song, it'll be perfect."

*****

At one p.m. the next day, Vegas and Tahlia strode into *The Montiamo*. It was a rich, luscious bed of money and power. Ornate artwork hung on each wall, massive crystal chandeliers dangled every few metres and thick, rich red carpeting that made you float as you walked on it. The lobby alone seemed to be filled with millions of dollars, huge fountains with koi fish, and hundreds of people chattering excitedly as they either booked in or prepared for the day's adventure.

A big burly guard quickly walked over to them. "Sir, Ma'am, you are not appropriately dressed for the hotel. I'm going to have to ask you to leave."

"Well, for *your* information," Vegas started, angered by the intrusion, "we're here for the auditions. An' since Tahlia here is singin' a rock song, *she is* appropriately dressed."

The guard backed down. "Sorry, Sir, Ma'am, I didn't realise. The auditions are being held in the concert hall. Walk through the lobby until you reach the atrium, then take the hallway on your left. It leads you to the concert hall. There are signs to help your way."

Tahlia thanked the guard as Vegas glared at him, and they set off to find the concert hall, which was quite large and very up to date with the latest technology.

Walking in, they saw at least a hundred other women waiting. Chairs had been lined up on the dance floor in rows, and there was a pianist on the large stage up front. A table was set up off to the side where auditionees signed in and took a number.

"Oh, my God, I don't have a chance," Tahlia groaned, seeing the women. They were all dressed up, warming their voices, looking like they'd just stepped out of a fashion magazine. They were definitely aiming to win the job. *All* of them.

"Nonsense," Vegas said, grabbing her arm, and pulling her to the table to pick up a number. "You could be just as good, if not better."

Sitting down in one of the back rows, they listened to everyone before her sing. Some were good, getting to sing half a song. Some were bad, being cut off before singing the first full line of the song. Some were fantastic. They were the lucky ones, with the director letting them sing the whole song, and the crowd joining in, clapping and cheering. They got callbacks, while others were told to go home when they begged for another chance. Either way, every woman and girl, depending on their actual age, was dressed to the extreme. Thinking that their short skirts and low-cut tops with big breasts pouring out would get them the job instead of their talent. Tahlia glanced down at her own outfit. *Good grief, why did I wear this, I look just like them.* She sank into her seat.

Three and a half hours later, when she was feeling even more depressed, Tahlia's number was called. She was now in the front row as they had moved up as each row went home. She didn't move, she was frozen in place at the thought of getting up on stage.

"Baby, come on." Vegas nudged her. "It's your turn."

"I can't," she whispered. "I'm scared." Her number was called again.

"Come on, baby, get up there." Vegas dragged her over to the stage and gave her a push up the stairs. The women who had come and signed in after her were giggling and it made her feel insecure. There were at least another hundred women waiting. All looking the same as the first hundred. And she looked just like them. What had she been thinking?

"Well, 102, are you going to sing or not?"

Tahlia stood still, looking out at the faces in front of her.

"Well."

Getting herself together, she told the pianist the name of the song they had chosen and walked to the microphone. Taking it off the stand as the music started, she saw she was shaking. Trying to control the urge to run, she forgot her cue and mumbled an apology.

"Look—" the music director started in an irritated tone, but was cut off by Vegas, as he had purposefully stood next to him.

"Give her a chance," he said and waved at the pianist to start again.

This time Tahlia started to sing. Her voice was quivery, scared, but as she let the music flow over her, her voice became surer. Belting out the song with guts and emotion, she didn't even notice she was one of the few who had gotten to finish a whole song. And when the last note sounded, there was silence, then one by one, starting with Vegas, everyone began clapping.

Vegas was grinning as he came up to the stage to help her off. "Baby, you were amazin'. Even better than I thought."

They stopped before the music director so he could give her a callback form, then Tahlia let Vegas drag her from the room, not even seeing the gorgeous looking man sitting up in the deep dark depths of the balcony at the back of the room.

He had been there for thirty minutes listening to the auditions. He hadn't thought much of most of them and was quite bored until that one woman had been pushed on stage. At first, she just stood there, seemingly petrified, gazing out at the crowd as they tittered. She was another rock chic wannabe in that tight top and short skirt. Great legs, though. She had been nervous, scared even, but once the music flowed over her, she had changed. Become confident. A mix of emotion that allowed her to cry and belt out a note when needed. She was one of the few who had sung a whole song, and he had been so captivated he hadn't wanted her to stop. Exhaling a long disappointed sigh when she did. As she was dragged out of the room by the rough looking guy that had a hold of her arm, he sat back in his seat and said three words to his assistant.

"I want her."

Chapter 6

As Tahlia and Vegas were walking away from the concert hall, he grabbed her and swung her around, planting a kiss on her mouth. "I think ya got it, baby, no wait, I *know* ya got it. Woohoo."

"Let's not be cocky," she said, grinning at him as he put her down. "God, I was so scared, but as the music flowed, so did I, an' it just came naturally." She bubbled over with enthusiasm, having never performed in front of a crowd before.

"Miss, Miss, excuse me, Miss." Someone tapped Tahlia on the shoulder and they turned around. "Miss, I'm Kate Marshall, and I'm here to tell you that you have been chosen for the singing job you just auditioned for."

"What?" Tahlia was stunned.

"Woohoo, what'd I tell ya, baby, I knew it, I knew it." Vegas swung her around again making her dizzy.

"Stop it," she cried. "Put me down." She turned to the woman. "Are you sure? I mean, there were other people after me, an' I just auditioned."

"Miss, I'm sure. The owner was watching, and he saw

many people before you. He knew you were the one. So you're hired, and if you'll follow me, I'll show you to the dressing area where you'll be measured for your stage outfits, and we'll get your details."

In disbelief, they followed her down hallways and through doors to arrive backstage at the costumer's room. While Tahlia was being measured, Kate popped out for a few moments to get the employment forms for her to fill out.

Walking into her boss' extravagant office, she stopped. He was standing at the hugely expansive floor-to-ceiling window that ran the length of the room, and which you could see the whole of Las Vegas through. He looked thoughtful, arms half crossed, right forefinger resting lightly on his chin. He was physically impressive. Imposing. And she'd once had a huge crush. Until she met the man that became her husband. Now it was nothing more than a close friendship. *And* working relationship. She waited.

"Make sure she has the best couture, any and all designer labels. The finest diamonds in the world no matter the cost. Fix the best suite in the hotel for her, and make sure it's brimming with the freshest flowers. She's to have anything and everything she wants, she needs. Get her a car, she can choose, any type she likes. I want her to have everything she desires, anything she asks for. I want her to have it all." His right hand turned into a fist in emphasis.

"Yes, sir," Kate said, quite surprised. Not only by the tone of his voice but by his reaction to the woman downstairs. Excited. Passionate. Alive. She hadn't seen him like this before. No woman had ever had such an effect on him, not that she'd seen anyway. He'd had a few relationships since she'd worked for him, and that was over ten years. He'd never seemed interested in finding someone to settle down with. Or maybe he just hadn't found that 'special someone'. She saw a gleam of something vibrant in her boss' eyes and wondered what he was planning.

She left him to contemplate about the woman he was yet to meet.

The woman he would turn into the star of Vegas.

The woman he would call his own…

Kate walked back into the costumer's room and handed Tahlia employment papers and told her about the job. "You're to live in one of our best suites. You'll have the best couture and jewellery, and tomorrow morning a stylist will be taking you shopping, and you'll pick up a car as well. Right now, I'll take you up to your new suite to let you settle in. Please follow me."

They followed Kate, still in complete shock.

"Oh, my God," Tahlia breathed, "I can't believe this is happening." She shook her head in disbelief. Nothing like this had ever happened to her before, and she'd certainly never thought it *could* happen. She'd had such a sheltered life that she didn't think things like this existed for her, or were even possible.

"We made it, baby, we made it," Vegas whispered excitedly in her ear as they hurried after the woman in front of them.

Stepping into one of the lifts in the now half-deserted lobby, Kate stopped Vegas in his tracks. "I'm sorry, sir, only Miss Tahlia will be staying as *she* is an employee."

Vegas took a step toward Kate. "What do ya mean, I can' stay? She's *my* woman, where *she* goes *I* go." His anger surged, and he fought the urge to punch her.

Tahlia quickly put a restraining hand on his arm and faced Kate. "Look, if Vegas can't stay, then neither do I," she said quietly.

Kate was worried and quickly stepped back out of the lift to call someone on her phone, pacing back and forth during the brief animated conversation. She ended the call and turned to them. "It's okay," she said icily. "You're being *allowed* to stay, even though you're *not* an employee. Follow me, please."

Wondering why she had reacted that way, Tahlia eyed the woman as they soared up in the lift, but upon entering a room on the twenty-third floor, all thoughts flew out of her mind and she gasped. The suite was utterly amazing with a view of Las Vegas from every window.

Tahlia and Vegas stared at each other, eyes as wide as saucers, huge grins across their faces as they ran from room to room.

Gold taps, twin sinks, and a huge frosted glass enclosed shower in the yellow bathroom. King-size bed with animal print spread and pillows in the bedroom, dark fur rug in front of the fake fireplace and a black grand piano in the living room. The dining area had a rich, red wood table with seating for six and was colour co-ordinated with the kitchen that seemed to have everything a master chef would need.

Various artworks, statues, mirrors and vases adorned every wall and table, and crystal chandeliers twinkled brightly as they hung from the ceiling.

Two plush black leather sofas were piled high with red cushions, and exotic looking rugs were placed evenly throughout the rooms on the thick cream carpet. Huge bouquets of fresh roses, the colours of the rainbow, were leaving their heavenly perfume wafting in the air.

It was luxurious indeed, with Tahlia having never seen anything so rich, let alone lived in something so indulgent.

"My God, this is amazing," she gasped, staring wide-eyed and taking in everything she saw, everything she would use and play with. Everything she had never had.

"You'll start in two weeks, five nights a week. Room service is at your disposal," Kate told her before turning toward the door.

"Wait," Tahlia called. "We've been staying with a friend, so we need to get our stuff. Are we able to get a car?"

"Of course. One of the hotel cars will be at your disposal until you get yours. Just ring down to the front desk when you want it." With that, she was gone.

"Oh, my God, baby," Vegas said, grabbing her and swinging her around until they were both dizzy and giggling. "This is amazin', just amazin'." He kissed her then had an idea, and a wicked grin spread across his face. "Ya know…we don' have to go pick up our stuff yet, we could, uhh, christen the suite…maybe…"

"We can't do that," Tahlia said, shocked by his suggestion.

"Why not? It's our suite now, an' besides, we need to celebrate." Still holding her in his arms, he ran for the bedroom and threw her down onto the bed where she squealed in delight. Ripping his singlet off, and grabbing her thong, he had his wicked way with her.

*****

Sputtering in anger and disgust, he picked up his whiskey glass and took a long swig, hoping to wash away the vile taste that was now there threatening to choke him.

Watching that animal touch her made him sick to his stomach. The way he manhandled her. Threw her around. It wasn't the way a woman should be treated, but she seemed to be enjoying the roughness. Squealing and grunting as he thrust himself inside of her.

Over and over.

Tahlia spread her legs wider for him to enter and come inside of her, screaming as she came and kept coming, convulsion after convulsion of orgasmic wave that she rode hard as they rolled all over the bed in a variety of different positions.

God, I need to do that to her!

Take her over and over, thrust inside of her as hard as I can until I can no more.

He knew it would be a new experience for her as well as himself. He would be the kind of lover she'd never had. Never want to let go of.

His penis was stiff with excitement, aching for release as he continued watching.

He vowed there and then to get rid of the man she was with. To make sure he was no longer deserving or worthy of her.
There was only one man who was.
Only one man she would ever need, ever want.
That man would be him.
The glass shattered.

*****

The next day, Tahlia went shopping with the stylist, and since Vegas had quit his job, he went along. Store after store they shopped and bought the best Las Vegas had to offer. Gowns, dresses, $700 jeans and tops. Shoes, bags, hats. Everything she could possibly want or need.

Shopping in a lingerie store to complete the outfits, she modelled style after style for Vegas. He got a big kick out of it, at one point chasing her into the dressing room for some hanky panky, only to be chased out by the middle-aged manageress.

The last thing to do was buy a car, and she knew exactly what she wanted. A blue 1960's Mustang convertible with hot pink leather trim and turquoise detailing.

"Why?" Vegas asked.

"Well, 'cause. I just do," was her reply.

And a blue Mustang convertible was hers.

Falling onto the plush leather couch in their suite in exhaustion, Tahlia watched as several bellboys brought in her packages. "Ahh, what a day," she sighed.

Vegas grinned, and he poured them both drinks.

"Baby, you're gonna be beautiful," he said, sitting beside her on the couch so they could share a few quiet moments now the bellboys were gone. "We should get dressed up an' go out to eat." He put his feet on the dark wood and glass coffee table in front of them.

"No, I'm tired. Let's order room service," she said, putting her feet up next to his. "Besides, I did all the shopping, you don't have anything to get dressed up in." She sat up and gazed into his eyes. "*You* didn't want to buy anything. You're such a cheapskate."

He looked at her in silence for a moment. "Don' change," he said softly.

"What do you mean?" she asked, surprised by his comment.

"I don' wan' you to become this fancy pants person now you have this job. I wan' you to be the same hot woman I been screwin' for the last few weeks." He was worried, afraid of something.

"Are you scared that if I change 'cause of the clothes an' being a star, that I'll leave you?" she asked quietly as she stroked his face.

His anguished look said it all.

"Aw, baby, I won't," she said, kissing him, touching his face, knowing no other man could make her feel the way he did.

Vegas took her into his arms, and they made love with such passion she knew this was exactly where she wanted to be.

*****

Over the next week, Tahlia went through rehearsals and sound checks, costume fittings and set lists, with Vegas keeping an eye on her the whole time. During the breaks, they wandered around the hotel playing some poker in the casino, eating in the fancy restaurants, and having a good time. Tahlia was relaxing, but was also excited and scared at the same time at the thought of having her very own show and becoming a star because of it. Vegas seemed to worry more about it than Tahlia, and she wondered if he had something else on his mind. Though he didn't talk about it, she knew there was something going on that he wasn't letting her in on.

*****

During lunch on Friday, Vegas received a call on his brand-new cell phone that Tahlia had bought him. Manny was asking for a favour, needed Vegas to help him out. And he had to leave that night.

"It's not fair that you have to leave tonight. You know I love the weekends with you 'cause it's when I don't work," Tahlia said, putting her fork down and taking a sip of juice. Her brow furrowed. She was clearly unhappy about the intrusion into their weekend.

"I know, baby," Vegas said, finishing his meal, "but Manny put us up for a month, an' now I owe him. Look, I don' have to leave early, we can get some personal time in 'fore I go," he said cheekily, wiggling his eyebrows. "You know…upstairs." His eyes looked toward the ceiling then back at her.

"I don't know," she sighed, eating the last forkful of

her chicken.

He swallowed the last of his drink and looked at her. "Look, I'll go do some stuff, you go finish up with rehearsals, then I'll see you after," he said, standing.

And with a kiss, he was gone.

Tahlia sighed. "Just not fair," she muttered and slowly wandered back to the concert hall feeling sorry for herself. She caught sight of a man she'd seen in the hotel every day. He was shaking hands with people, patting them on the back like old friends, smiling and joking with them before moving on. Two beefy men in suits and dark glasses followed.

"Mmm, bodyguards maybe?" she mused. "Must be famous or something." Not taking her eyes off him, she bumped into a waitress called Mandy whom she'd met her first day there. They'd liked each other instantly and spoke every day.

"Sorry," they said in unison, laughing.

"You must be staring at Mr Debonaire," Mandy said with a sly smile.

"Who? Him?" Tahlia asked, pointing in the man's direction.

"That's him."

"Who is he?"

"What! You mean you don't know?" Mandy asked incredulously. "*That* gorgeous man is the owner of *The Montiamo*. He walks around every day making sure people are happy. He takes good care of his staff, and if you have a problem, he's the go-to guy. Gives great bonuses too…oops gotta go, duty calls." She ran off to serve a customer.

Tahlia stood for a while, partly hidden by a hotel pillar, watching the man that Mandy had pointed out. He was tall, six foot something, masculine, well built. Dark brown hair that was short in back and swept off his face for a debonaire look. Gorgeous, in a suave, mature, charming way. Finely chiselled lips with a smile that made the women he spoke to drool all over themselves.

Very James Bond-ish.

He looked damn good in that sharp black suit, the matching black shirt unbuttoned and showing off a lightly tanned chest that brought out the gold tints in his soft looking brown chest hair. Chest hair she wanted to run her fingers through…nestle her face in.

"Mmm," she sighed under her breath, completely taken with the man she was staring at. "Bet he could charm the pants off a woman too."

At that moment, as if hearing her, he turned in her direction. And even across the vast people and noise filled room, Tahlia could feel the intensity of his gaze. It lasted only several heart-pounding seconds, but seemed like forever. His dazzling smile broke the moment, then he turned and walked away.

Feeling herself blush furiously at her reaction to him, and such idiotic behaviour on her part, she called herself a fool and rushed off to rehearsals.

*****

Four hours later, Tahlia and Vegas collapsed against each other on their king-size bed and lay panting. The sex had been explosive and raw just like that first night.

"Wow," he laughed, "talk about energy. You certainly had a lot of it."

She blushed furiously, knowing that some of that energy had been because of how she'd reacted to the hotel owner's gaze. "Well, you are going away for the weekend, I need to get my fill," she gasped lightly.

"Well, I can' wait to see how you react to me comin' back," Vegas said, kissing her. He wrapped his arms around her tightly.

"Oh, don't worry, I'll be all revved up awaiting your return," Tahlia joked, wrapping her arms tightly around him. Her mind drifted back to thoughts of the hotel owner and the way he'd smiled at her, as if she was the only one in the room. *Get out of my head,* she thought furiously, *I can't be thinking of you now.*

"Ya, know..." he said after a while, "I don' think we've christened everythin'."

"What do you mean?" Her fingers slid through golden chest hair.

"Well, the sofa, the bed, the shower, the spa. What about the piano?"

"You mean have sex on the piano?" Tahlia asked, looking up at him in surprise.

"Yep."

"Won't it be too hard?"

"Just like me, baby." He grinned that damn sexy grin and carried her to the piano while she squealed like a teenager.

Laying her on the top, Vegas sat at the keyboard, badly plonked out a tune, and sang a song with very explicit lyrics. Playing along, Tahlia writhed and slithered, rubbing her breasts and tweaking her nipples. She ran her hands all over her body and moved into position so that he would see how wet she was when she spread her legs. She looked up to see his face. That raw, animalistic hunger was there.

In one movement, he grabbed her hips, pulled her toward him, and thrust his tongue deep inside of her. Caressing, probing with such skill. Tasting her, finding *that* spot. She moaned in gasps, arching, spreading her legs wider, holding his head with her hands, keeping him there. And just when he brought her to the brink, he stopped. Slowly sliding his tongue out, he let her go, waiting for her to come down from the high.

Stepping onto the piano bench, Vegas crawled onto the piano, hunting his prey.

Her eyes were slightly open, watching him, her legs still spread wide.

And ever so slowly, he entered her. Sliding millimetre by millimetre, his hot, hard flesh, sliding into her hot, wet embrace. Gasping, groaning, she reached for him, he pinned her hands down, and with such powerful control, he slid fully inside of her.

Gasping even harder, Tahlia bucked underneath him, then he was gone.

He had withdrawn, to do it all over again. This time, gently biting her nipples as he entered her.

Again, writhing and bucking, her breath came in hard, fast gasps.

He withdrew and waited.

"What, are, you, waiting, for?" she gasped raggedly.

He looked at her with intensity and rawness. "This."

He penetrated her completely.

In and out. In and out.

Making her scream, locking her arms and legs around him to keep him there.

The intensity was mind-blowing.

*****

Tahlia awoke in bed to find it was early evening, with Vegas coming out of the bathroom already dressed, and room service knocking on the door. "Hey, baby. Sleep well?" He grinned as he buckled his belt. "I ordered room service."

Sighing, she got up and grabbed her robe, knowing it was no use asking him to stay. They had already discussed it, no, Tahlia had discussed it, and Vegas had said there would be no discussion. Period! He was helping Manny out, and that's all there was to it. Manny and Maria had put them up, and now he was paying them back for their generosity. After all, he and Manny went way back, and he'd do anything for him.

"Aren't you having anything?" she asked, sampling the food, which was amazing.

Vegas couldn't stay. "No baby, it's all yours, I gotta go help Manny," he said, kissing her goodbye and grabbing his bag. "I'll see ya in a couple of days." With that he was gone, leaving Tahlia staring opened mouth at the door, brow furrowed, wondering how long it was going to be like this.

After eating the food and watching some TV, she

felt lonely, deciding to have a shower and go to bed. She walked into the yellow and gold tiled bathroom, turned the shower on, and stepped under the hot, fast spray, soaping herself into a rich, thick lather, soon remembering earlier that afternoon.

Blushing all over, she found herself aroused again, nipples hard, wanting, craving her man's touch. Running the washcloth over her breasts, down her body, and between her legs she pleasured herself and arched against the wall, letting the hard, fast spray titillate her. Minutes later, she barely managed to dry herself before stumbling into bed and falling into a deep, satisfied sleep.

*****

He watched her.

Ever since that animal had taken her into the suite and had his way with her.

The sex had been raw, wild. Hell! It had been a turn on, and he'd found himself harden at the way her body moved and slid all over the animal print silk sheets as she flung her legs wide, groping for stability as he took her with such power over and over.

And the piano scene. That man couldn't play, but he certainly knew how to make her writhe and slither with such fantastic finesse that he'd come quickly as he stood there, soiling his expensively made Italian silk pants.

Like he cared about his pants!

Since he was quite an accomplished pianist, he'd imagined it was him on the piano with her, making her scream and groan like a wild woman, and come into his mouth pouring her juices into him as he suckled her innermost self ever so forcefully.

Tasting her. Taking her.

Have to remember that move, he thought, making a mental note.

Then Vegas was gone, and she was all alone. Wonder what is more important than the incredible woman he left behind?

He stood still, naked himself, grasping his hard-on as she'd stepped into the shower, naked, soaping herself into arousal, pleasing herself. It was a definite turn on, and he couldn't wait to be the one to do that to her. He moved his hand up and down slowly, imagining it was her mouth, her pussy, covering him so completely, so hotly. He would soap her naked flesh with his hands, feel every crevice of her soft, pliable body as he fingered her expertly, taking her to places she would only want him to take her.

I will be the one.

That I promise you.

Chapter 7

"Mornin' baby. I won' be back till later tonight. Have a good rehearsal."

Tahlia replaced the beeping phone in its cradle and thought about the call. It was Monday. Vegas had rung to say he wasn't coming back until that night, and it had ticked her off. *Mmm, why does it annoy me so much?* She couldn't figure it out, and after everything they did, she shouldn't be annoyed. Manny and Maria had helped them out, and now Vegas was repaying them. What was so wrong with that? It made her brain hurt just thinking about it. *Ah, screw it! Let's just get to work.*

She went down to the costumer's room to try on several dresses that had been altered, and taking them to her dressing room, she started getting ready for a rehearsal.

Sliding into a fire engine red gown that clung to her body as it skimmed to the floor and trailed behind her, Tahlia stared in awe. It was made of material she had never seen, with large multicoloured gemstones running around the hem of the dress and up either side of the split over her right leg, which came up to mid-thigh, continuing up past the deep vee of the bust, and around the Chinese style collar. Stones were also around the cuffs of the long sleeves.

She slipped into a pair of matching heels and pinned her hair up. *Wow,* she thought, eyeing herself in the mirror. *I've never seen anything this fancy, let alone worn or tried anything on, an' I've certainly never owned a dress like this. I've definitely come a long way, from mousy doormat to…well,* she blushed, *sex siren!* She laughed softly and blushed harder at the thought of herself being a sex siren. *Wait till Vegas gets a load of me in this. He'll wanna rip it right off.*

She studied herself again. Her hair had taken on a golden-brown shine and was no longer mousy. Her skin glowed vibrantly, no more bags or dark circles, and a light tan made her complexion look creamy smooth. Her eyes glowed a fiery emerald green, and her lips were full and ripe. She slid her hands over her hips. Her figure was improving, having lost weight over the previous weeks, and now she was quite attractive. Not Las Vegas showgirl attractive, but quite a looker that drew men's attention wherever she went.

Lost in thought, she didn't see the man in the doorway. "Wow."

She gasped and stumbled back, but quickly regained her balance. "That door was shut," she said, seeing who was standing before her.

"Yes. It was. I'm sorry that I startled you, but I'm not sorry I opened the door. You look…absolutely, incredibly beautiful." He was staring at her with an intense look that told her he wanted her. His gaze hungrily skimmed the rounded curves of her new body.

She blushed again, feeling her blood rush and her nipples harden.

"May I come in?"

She barely managed a nod.

He stepped into the dressing room toward her, still staring, reaching out his right hand. "Allow me to introduce myself. I, am Diega Montiamo. Hotel owner, businessman." Taking her right hand, he kissed it, not taking his eyes from hers. "I see *something* I want, I go after it until it's mine." His gaze seduced her. "Or, *someone*."

Tahlia just stared. She knew it was rude, but she couldn't tear her eyes from his as they were riveted in place gazing into eyes that were so deeply blue. So entrancing. So inviting…

With another kiss on her hand, he backed away and let her go, then, he was gone, closing the door behind him, leaving her panting, shaking, falling onto the couch in panic. "Oh, my God, what a man. Talk about leaving an impression. What the hell is going on? How can I feel this way?" She felt herself start to freak out. He had left her tingling all over, and she shivered, her body full of goose bumps, remembering her hand in his strong manly one.

There was a knock at the door, and she jumped in her seat, thinking it might be Diega again. "Yes," her voice croaked as the music director stuck his head through the door and told her it was time for rehearsal. "I'll be right there," she said, checking herself in the mirror to make sure her reaction wasn't noticeable.

But thanks to that reaction, the rehearsal was rough. Tahlia forgot lines to songs, and cues for the stage because her nerves were shot and she couldn't stop thinking about a certain suave, debonaire man and how he'd made her feel. Basically, it was a shambles, and she got nothing right. Finally stopping her, the music director told everyone they'd pick it up tomorrow when they were in a better frame of mind, and agreeing, she went to her dressing room to change.

Hoping to clear her mind of invading thoughts, she decided to go for a drive. Jumping into her Mustang, she put the top down and cruised the streets of the city, stopping for a bit of shopping. It worked, as for a few hours she forgot about her problems at the hotel until she walked into her suite at five p.m.

Vegas was standing at the window with a drink in his hand. "Oh, my God, you're home," she cried, running over and throwing her arms around him.

"Ow, don'." He flinched and roughly shoved her hands away.

She stepped back, surprised by his attitude.

Seeing the look on her face, his anger disappeared, and his hand stretched out toward her. "I'm sorry, baby."

She saw his black eye. "What happened?" she cried, taking his hand in hers. "Oh, my God, Vegas. What happened to you?" She reached for his face, but he restrained her hands in his, bringing them to his mouth to kiss them instead.

"I'm fine. It's just a black eye an' some," he winced, "sore ribs, but I'm okay."

"No, you're not. I'll call the hotel doctor." She started toward the phone.

"No," he said loudly, "don'. I'm fine. Just got inta a little fight is all. You should see the other guy," he joked.

"Dead is he?" She wished she could take it back. "Sorry," she said, closing her eyes for a moment in remorse before opening them again.

The look on his face wasn't good. "No, he's not." Vegas walked over to the sofa and sat down slowly.

"Well, I guess there'll be no welcome home party for you, then," she said, following him.

Grimacing, he grinned sadly. "Unfortunately, baby."

"Are they broken or bruised?" Tahlia asked, sitting beside him.

"Just bruised I think. I'll be okay," he said softly, squeezing her hand.

"They'd better be," she said, a smile on her face, "or you'll never get your welcome home party. Just think, weeks without sex. Can you *really* go without for that long?" She tried to hide her laughter.

Vegas glared at her in dismay. "Aw, baby, don' tease me. That is *not* funny."

But it was funny, and they both broke out in laughter.

*****

For the next week, dress rehearsals went well, there was no sex with Vegas, and Tahlia constantly saw Diega walking throughout the hotel. He seemed to know when she was there because she always found him watching her. *That* look in his eyes. Like he had a hunger that needed filling, a desire that needed quenching, and only Tahlia could quench his desires and hunger as no other woman could.

The intensity of his gaze freaked her out. It was overwhelming, and at times so full on that she looked away first. It amazed her, that when he looked at her, it seemed to last forever, but was only ever several seconds long. She always kept it from Vegas, of course, she wouldn't *dare* tell him that Diega stared at her that way, it would only make him angry. And she didn't need, *or want,* Vegas angry.

*****

Monday night was opening night, and Tahlia was a little scared, a little excited, as she paced back and forth wringing her hands together.

"It's gonna be great, baby," Vegas said, trying to massage her shoulders.

They were in the dressing room ten minutes before showtime.

Tahlia stared at the floor as she paced. "I know. It's just…I've never done this before an' I'm freaking out."

Vegas grinned that damn sexy grin. "It'll be just fine," he assured her. "An' I'm in the front row supportin' you." He kissed her. A deep passionate kiss. "I'll let you finish up, baby, break a leg." One more kiss and he left.

As she touched up her make-up, there was a knock at the door. "Yeah," she called.

The door opened slowly. Diega was standing there, a huge bunch of blood-red roses in his strong, muscular arms. "These are for you, to wish you luck," he said, not moving.

She stood still, feeling giddy. "Come in," she managed.

He walked in and gently put the flowers on the counter. "Did you notice I knocked and waited for you to say something before opening the door? Then waited again until you asked me to come in." He was smiling a devilish smile and gazing at her *that* way.

She nodded faintly, feeling so weak-kneed.

"I'll let you finish getting ready. Good luck for your first show. I hope that there are many, *many* more." With an intense look, he was gone.

Her heart was racing, and she took a couple of deep breaths to calm herself. "Oh, my God, oh, my God, oh, my God," she gasped.

"Showtime," someone said, knocking on her door and making her jump. She stared at the door for a few seconds trying to get herself together. Straightening her dress, she cast one last look in the floor-to-ceiling mirror that took up half the length of one wall, and smeared on extra lipstick before walking toward the backstage area and waiting until the director counted her down.

She stood in the pre-chosen spot, the music started, the lights slowly came on, and the curtain parted. She sang her heart out, as the songs had been chosen with care. She cried when they were sad, and smiled when they were happy.

Three costume changes later, the show was over, and she received a standing ovation. It had been a full house, and she was completely overwhelmed by the number of people that had come to her first show. The room was filled to capacity, and it was very exciting knowing they had all come to see her. Tahlia saw Vegas in the front row, whistling and cheering, just as he said he would be. *Which he should be,* she thought as she gazed down at him, *considering the ruckus he'd made to have two seats to himself in the front row for every show.* He told the director that because he was Tahlia's boyfriend, he had the right to free seats for every show. The director didn't like it, but had strangely agreed.

Walking off stage, she was on an electric high, an adrenaline rush like she'd never had. Even people she didn't know, or had barely met, were coming into her dressing room congratulating her.

Mandy came rushing in. "Oh, my God, I saw the whole show and it was *so* awesome," she gushed.

"Thanks." Tahlia laughed as Mandy hugged her. "Glad you liked it. It's good that you were able to come, I thought you'd be working."

"I changed my shifts with someone so I could be here for your first night," she said, "after all, we are friends, I wouldn't have missed this for the world."

"I'm glad we're friends," Tahlia said. "I don't know anyone here besides you an' Vegas. I hope we can spend more time together." Five other people came rushing in

"Count on it," Mandy said as Vegas ran in. "I'll let you two lovebirds be alone," she said with a wink and a wave goodbye.

Vegas shooed everyone out of the room, then wrapping his arms around her, swung her around and kissed her. "Ya did it, baby, ya did it, woohoo."

"Put me down," she laughed.

"Get changed an' we'll go upstairs, no wait, don' change, 'cause I wanna get you out of that dress myself," he said, grinning as he pulled her out of the room.

Laughing, they headed for the lift. Stepping inside, they hugged and kissed, and as the doors closed in front of them, Tahlia saw Diega over Vegas' shoulder, standing across the hotel lobby.

Watching her.

In the suite, they slowly undressed each other, touching and kissing. Stepping into the shower, Vegas reached for the washcloth to soap her body.

Tahlia pulled him close, slowly rubbing herself against him and making him groan. "Was that 'cause of me or your ribs?" she whispered.

"Definitely you, baby," he replied softly, taking her left breast into his mouth.

Groaning quietly, she stroked him until he became hard.

He sucked harder, while his left hand massaged her other breast. His right hand found its way down below, his fingers sliding inside, probing the hard sensitive walls into a raging fire.

Spreading her legs and arching her back, her left hand held onto his head while her right gripped him tightly. They brought each other to the brink and stopped.

His fingers slid out of her, and he slid in. Taking her ass in his hands, he plunged inside. Sliding out slowly, he thrust in again. Over and over he thrust and withdrew, slowly then fast, rhythmically in time.

Clinging to him, she clenched the muscles inside of her and he stopped, eyes wide.

"Do that again," he gasped.

With Vegas thrusting, and Tahlia clenching, the hot water flowed down their bodies, making them climax in unison, groaning small guttural gasps.

Stepping out of the shower a few minutes later, Tahlia picked up a towel and rubbed it over his back, gently dabbing at the dark black bruises. "You okay?" she whispered, her lips slowly moving over his hot skin, kissing his shoulder.

"I'm fine," he said softly, grinning and leading her to the bed. They climbed under the covers, wrapped themselves together, and fell into a deep sleep.

*****

He had watched her all night.

The performance was amazing and had brought him emotionally to the brink many times.

You wouldn't know she'd never been on stage before in front of a crowd of people. She was so professional, so good. The way she laughed, the way she cried. As her confidence gained, she had talked to the audience between songs and they definitely loved her.

So did he.

And now, as she fell asleep, he watched her still.

Aching deep inside, he imagined himself in the shower with her. Soaping her skin, slamming her against the wall to take her hard. Sliding in and out of her as she slid up and down. His fingers wreaking havoc in her pleasure spot, making her groan his name in ecstasy.

He slid his robe apart, and his hand worked hard on his manhood, sending him into a frenzy as she climaxed. So did he. Spurting all over himself. "So what," he muttered, "I'll just have another shower."

He leaned back in his chair with relief, knowing that he would soon spurt all over her. "I will make you mine, Tahlia. And I will do, every, thing, I want."

He noticed the bruising on that animal's body and wondered what he'd been up to.

I'll have to keep my eye on him, he thought. Stroking his new hard-on, he continued watching her sleep.

*****

The week went by in a blur. Standing ovations, fantastic shows, Tahlia was on a high. She had never felt this way in her whole life. A great guy, a great job, a great life. Her nerves about her past had calmed down, and she was feeling safer than she had in years. All her problems seemed to have vanished, and it was perfect.

Until Friday afternoon when Vegas got a call. "Manny needs my help again, baby." He picked up his beer and took a swig.

"Again! Is this going to be a regular thing, is it?" She was irritated, and throwing her fork down, glared at him across the hotel restaurant table. "I was going to suggest we go get you some clothes."

"Clothes! What do I need clothes for? I like gettin' around in what I wear," he said, glancing down at what he was wearing. It was the usual. White singlet that showed off his hot tanned body, and ripped blue jeans with black biker boots. The usual.

He smiled secretly to himself. He loved the way all the showgirls stared at him when he passed them in the hallways or backstage. They whistled, and catcalled, and invited him into their dressing rooms for a private show of his own. One, they promised, would last all night. He never took them up on their offer mind you, and he certainly wasn't going to tell Tahlia about it. He had to keep all of that to himself. His little secret.

Just one more in his long list of many.

"I know," Tahlia replied. "But you need some suits for going out to restaurants an' stuff, so we can look good together. Besides, I got my pay today. *It's huge.*"

"Yeah. How huge?" Vegas inquired curiously, taking another swig of beer.

"More money than I've ever had in my life. This is definitely a well-paying job." She grinned. "An' I love it."

Vegas grinned back. "I love it too, baby. I love that you're happy. I love that I get to stay in a swish hotel. But I need to help Manny, an' no," he leaned forward over the table and took her hand in his, "I don' know if it will be a regular thing."

"Do we get the afternoon together, an' will you see the show tonight?" she asked, squeezing his hands and lacing her fingers with his.

"Not the show, baby, but if you're not needed now, we can go upstairs an' do the magical deed." He wiggled his brows and that damn sexy grin was there.

"Unfortunately, I need to rehearse," she said, pulling her hands away, unimpressed by his antics. She saw his expression fall and grinned. "But come watch so I can at least see *you* before you go." Tahlia finished the last of her drink.

"Okay, baby."

Paying for their lunch, they went to the concert hall for the rehearsal, and three hours later Vegas was gone. Off to save Manny from whatever big thing he needed help with this time.

Sighing in frustration, Tahlia sat on the chair in her dressing room, curious about what Vegas and Manny were up to. Drumming her fingers on the counter, she looked at herself in the mirror. "Well, what am I gonna do this weekend?" she asked, glancing around the lavish and very large room.

She had done it up nicely. Comfy blue sofa, lots of big pink cushions, and a multicolour throw rug draped over the back of it. Prints of movie and music stars on the walls, along with funky pictures, pale pink carpet, and a blue metal and glass coffee table. There were vases filled with the roses that Diega kept giving her, and the mirror she was looking into had lights all the way around it, which were turned on as she sat looking at herself. Even the ensuite was pink and blue and very sophisticated.

There was a knock at the door.

"Come in," she called and swivelled around.

The door opened, and there stood Diega. "Hello." His voice flowed like smooth, melted chocolate.

"Hi," she said shyly, blushing and sitting straighter in her chair. She still saw him walking throughout the hotel every day, but they hadn't spoken. Although, he had been leaving a huge bouquet of roses every night for her.

"I noticed that Vegas left with a bag. Does that mean you have to amuse yourself again this weekend?" he asked, stepping into the room.

The dressing room was a moderate size, but his imposing figure filled it to capacity.

A little sadly she replied, "Yeah."

"Well then, let me help you out. Have a late supper with me after the show, and we'll talk about what I can do to make your weekend happy." Deep blue eyes stared intently.

She frowned slightly at such a strange remark. "Make my weekend happy?"

"I'll rephrase. What *I* can do, to make *you* happy." He gave her *that* look, the one he only seemed to have for her. "I'll see you after the show."

He was gone.

Tahlia looked at herself in the mirror. She was beet red, her pupils dilated. "Oh, God," she murmured, gasping for breath. "I thought only Vegas made me feel this way?"

But the way she felt about Diega was different. With Vegas, it was raw and hungry. He was a wild beast and made her feel like a sexy, vivacious woman. No other man had done that, no other man had made love to her the way he did, and she'd never known passion of any kind in the bedroom. Never believed she could feel this way about any man, or that a man could want her like this, ever.

Diega was charming and sophisticated. So manly.

None of her past boyfriends had been that way. Or given her roses, let alone every night. So now, there were two men in her life. "What am I talking about, God, I can't think of Diega. I'm with Vegas an' that's how it is." She sighed, still freaked out, then shook herself and started getting ready for the show.

Two hours later, with the parting of the curtain, the first note of music started. Belting out a rock song, Tahlia stalked around the stage, feeling every ounce of emotion in the song. The audience was quiet until the last note faded, then they exploded with enthusiasm, and the show went on.

Laughing with excitement and adrenaline, Tahlia stumbled into her dressing room. "Oh, my God, that's so exciting," she gasped to Doris, the costumer who had come to help her.

"You certainly got the crowd going, miss," she said, showing her an elegant red silk dress on a hanger. "Here, have a shower and put this on. The boss will be here soon to pick you up."

"What do you mean? Why do I need to dress up?" Tahlia asked, confused.

"I don't know. Something about a late supper and he suggested the dress."

Wondering what Diega was up to, Tahlia jumped into the shower and was out in minutes. Slipping into the ankle-length dress, she fixed the floating sleeves as Doris pulled the zip up on the back. She smoothed the material, and stepped into strappy high-heeled sandals, then checked herself in the mirror. *Wow, this dress is amazing,* she thought, sliding her hands over her womanly hips, and admiring the way it fell in silky, shiny waves. She had just finished her hair and make-up when there was a knock on the door.

Doris opened the door wide for Diega to see Tahlia and excusing herself, disappeared.

"Wow! You look…absolutely amazing." His breath was snatched from his throat at the sight of her, and he couldn't tear his hungry eyes away.

Blushing furiously, Tahlia smoothed the dress again. "Really?" she asked, feeling extremely shy.

"Really." They gazed at each other, eyes locked together. Diega's full of passion, desire, and wanting.

"So…" she swallowed hard, "um…why did I need to get dressed up if we're only having supper?" She could barely breathe and tried to tear her eyes away from his magnetic gaze. She failed.

"I thought we might do a little dancing if you're up to it. I have a private section in the club, and there's an Australian group about to start…" he looked at his very expensive watch, "in ten minutes. How about it?" He clasped his hands together in excitement.

Swallowing her rising passion, she blushed softly. "Okay, sure, lead the way."

Diega offered his left arm for her to take, and shyly, hesitantly, she took it.

Chapter 8

Leading Tahlia through the hotel, Diega walked with the supreme confidence of a man who had everything he wanted. And *everyone* he wanted. That confidence made people turn and stare as they walked past. The men, because they wanted to be like Diega. Have his wealth and gorgeous looks, be the owner of a hotel-casino with all the perks one could want.

And the women, they just glared at Tahlia with insane jealousy, and she could just imagine what they were thinking. *'That bitch, how dare she get her hooks into Diega Montiamo, he's mine.'* And, *'What does she have that I don't? She's nothing special.'*

It was unnerving, in fact, *very* unnerving, and Tahlia felt very unsure of herself having never been in a situation like it before.

Walking into the club, Tahlia saw it was already crowded with people ready to party. The overhead lights were changing colour in time to the music playing, and everyone was in a great mood, ready for the band that would soon be on.

They were led to a private section up a small flight of

stairs and away from the crowd. Diega put his hand on the small of her back as he directed her to their seats, and a shiver of excitement sped up her spine, hardening her already erect nipples.

"Are you cold?" he asked, his voice low and next to her ear.

Tahlia shivered again and gasped. "No." Her breathing was heavy as she sat down on the circular shaped sofa that was in Diega's private section. *Very* private section. It was away from other people with a small dance floor in front, and a clear glass railing so you could see the stage, and so no one fell off the balcony. The lighting was dim, the sofa full of soft cushions, and a small table already had a bottle of wine ready to go. They were at the back of the club and had the perfect view of everything.

"Wow, this is great. We haven't been in here, yet." She tried desperately to cover her emotional state.

"We?"

She faced Diega. "Me an' Vegas. We haven't been here yet 'cause after the shows we always go up to bed." She blushed furiously and realised what she'd just said, and quickly looked down and away.

"To sleep?" Diega inquired seductively, with a dark, sensual look on his face.

Tahlia looked at him and swallowed hard, trying to find her voice. Nothing came out. She was feeling incredibly hot and turned on from his gaze.

The announcer came over the sound system. "Ladies and gentlemen it's time to present the Australian group you're all here to see, Michael, Toby, Phil, and Andrew, give it up for…Human Nature." The club exploded in applause as four guys came bouncing onto the stage in a burst of music.

Glad for the interruption, Tahlia sat back in her seat and tried to concentrate on enjoying the show. But all she could think about was how close Diega was sitting. He looked damn good in that black suit with the matching shirt. *That's all he seems to wear,* she mused. *I've only seen him in black, no other colour. I wonder what brand it is, it looks expensive, probably tailor-made. God, he smells good too.* Her heart pounded as his cologne wafted around her, and she felt drunk on the scent of it. *Definitely James Bond-age.* She gasped. *No wait, I mean James Bond-ish. Oh, God.* She covered her face in total embarrassment and hoped she hadn't said it out loud.

"Tahlia, are you all right?" Diega leant toward her with a concerned look on his perfect asymmetrical face.

She lifted her head to see that face just inches from hers, and was breathless, gasping for air, staring into eyes so blue and so deep she was drowning.

His lushly shaped lips seductively calling to her to let them kiss her.

Oh, God, I want him…

Oh, God, what am I thinking?

She felt like a complete and utter fool at the thought.

At that moment, a waitress came over and put two large plates of food on the small table in front of them. Tahlia, thankful for another interruption, picked up her glass and downed her drink in one swallow. Aware that it was wine. Aware that he was watching her closely. A little *too* closely. She tried to concentrate on the music and wrapped her arms around herself as some form of protection from his seductive gaze. The group on stage were great, singing rock to pop to ballads, and she tried to enjoy it.

"May I?"

Turning her head, she saw Diega standing next to her, holding out his hand to her. "Umm," she breathed, "okay." She gave him her hand, and he led her to their private dance floor.

Taking her into his arms, Diega held her with experience, but not too close. He didn't want to rush her. Although from the way she was reacting to him, he knew it wouldn't be long. He was burning for her, a raging fire out of control setting his loin ablaze. He felt himself harden.

Oh, God, he thought. *I better keep myself in check. I don't want to scare her. Hell, I don't want to scare myself. I can't believe I'm feeling like this. Like a schoolboy with a big crush.* His heart was thundering loudly in his chest like he'd never known with any other woman. He checked himself.

Slow dancing was like floating on a cloud, and Tahlia felt as light as a feather in his arms. As the group onstage swung into an upbeat number, Diega swung her around into a spin. She giggled in delight at the sudden change in tempo, and for a few songs, they tried different dances. For all of her previous embarrassment, she was enjoying herself and was a little sad when the show ended.

Applauding for the group, she turned to Diega. "I

enjoyed this, thank you."

"It's not over," he replied, taking her hand.

"It's not?" she asked in surprise, curious as to what he had up his sleeve.

Diega led her out of the hotel and to a private area near one of the pools. "This spot is reserved for the bigwigs that stay here. But tonight, it's all ours," he said with a smile.

Stepping into a small alcove, Tahlia saw a sofa with cushions and blankets. A spa on one side, an amazing view of the city on the other. She gasped. "Wow, what a view." Sitting down, she sank into the lush cushions of the black leather sofa.

"Isn't it great?" Diega asked, taking off his suit jacket. "Make yourself comfortable, kick off your shoes, wrap yourself in a blanket. We've got more drinks and food. Let's relax." He sat down next to her and offered a glass of champagne as she wrapped a blanket around herself.

"No, thank you. I'd prefer juice or something," she said, feeling a little lightheaded from the wine she'd gulped down before.

"Okay." He poured her a tropical juice and popped a piece of orange on the rim before handing it to her. "There you go," he said and settled back onto the sofa with his own glass.

"Thanks."

Sitting quietly for a few minutes, and taking in the view, they watched the moon shine down. She could hear the city traffic below them, though not too far below as they would only be a few storeys up from the street, but still high enough to have privacy and not be seen.

"God, this view's amazing. We haven't been here either," she said quietly.

"You keep saying *we*," Diega said. "It seems *you* haven't done much here at the hotel."

"Well, *I* haven't," she said. "It's mainly rehearsals an' shows, an' the weekends are spent going out seeing Las Vegas. Although Vegas an' I have eaten in most of the restaurants, an' played a few games in the casino. We do know the place quite well now."

"This is the second weekend since being here that Vegas has left you alone in Vegas. What do you do when he's not here?" Diega asked, annoyed that *any* man could leave her for *any* amount of time, let alone for a weekend every fortnight.

"Whatever I can to amuse myself," she said, putting her glass on the table and wrapping the blanket more tightly.

"That's why I invited you to supper. So that we could make plans to do something exciting over the next two days. Let *me* show *you* Las Vegas," Diega said, smiling excitedly.

"Why? Do you invite all the female staff members out on weekends?" she asked, suddenly concerned that rumours would get around, untruths she didn't need the hassle of denying or defending to Vegas.

"No. Just you." His gaze smouldered.

She shivered and looked away.

"Are you cold?"

"No. I'm fine," she said, pulling the blanket around

her even more tightly. She needed protection from his never-ending gaze. "You're my boss. I shouldn't be seen out with you. It might not look right," she said, shyly glancing at him.

Diega shrugged and was unconcerned. "There's no law that says I can't date a female staff member."

"We're not dating," Tahlia cried in alarm and shifted away from him.

"No, no, we're not," he said, trying to calm her. "I chose the wrong word. I apologise, I didn't mean to imply anything." *God,* he thought, *that was stupid of me.* "Let's get to know each other then," Diega said, hoping that by talking about himself it would calm her. "Let's see," he started, throwing his left arm over the back of the sofa, and moving his body slightly toward Tahlia who was sitting to his left. "My name is Diega Montiamo. I don't look Italian, but the name goes way back in the family, so I was given it at birth. I'm thirty-eight, and if I say so myself, I don't look it. I started working when I was in high school, and by the time I was twenty-five I was the youngest manager ever of a hotel-casino."

"Wow, really?" Tahlia asked in awe, her alarm fading away as she relaxed back into the cushions.

"Yes, I was. After making many investments, and working my way up the ladder, I became a hotel owner by the age of thirty-two. Now, I own several casinos and properties around Las Vegas, and any so-called mobsters don't come near me. They know they won't survive." A slow, wicked grin spread across his gorgeous face.

"What? You, *kill,* them?" Tahlia asked slowly, feeling

a little freaked out. As if she needed *more* violence in her life from *another* man.

The grin disappeared, and a serious look came into his eyes. "No. But they soon learn they can't mess with me."

There was an uncomfortable silence for a few moments as she tried to comprehend what he'd just told her, and she was slightly turned off by his bragging. She shifted in her seat and asked, "Doesn't it seem self-absorbed an' indulgent to name a hotel after yourself?"

Diega poured himself another glass of champagne. "It would be, except I didn't name it after myself," he said, taking a sip. "I named it after my Italian heritage, my parents. Rosalee and Ricardo Montiamo." He looked at her as if challenging her to find a problem with what he'd just said.

Feeling her heart melt for the man beside her, she spoke softly. "That's a wonderful thing to do. Your parents must be proud?"

The comment left Diega uncomfortable. "I know my Dad was. He died one week after the opening." He swallowed hard, fighting back a wave of grief. "And my mother died when I was fifteen. So, if she's looking down on me, I hope she's proud too." He laughed softly as a tear trickled down his cheek.

Tahlia reached out and gently wiped it away. "I know how you feel…what you're going through…"

He was surprised by her touch, and so was she.

Her hand quickly recoiled. "Mmm, we're getting a little too sad here, I think," she said, having a drink.

He offered her a top up, then picked up the plate of

food. "Here," he grabbed a small roll of something and held it out for her, "try these, they're amazing."

"What are they?" She screwed her face up at the smell.

"Caviar rolled in smoked salmon."

"Ew, no thanks." She grimaced and moved her head away.

"Don't you like caviar?"

"No."

"Why not?"

Tahlia shrugged. "Just don't."

"Then how do you know you don't like it?"

She changed the subject. "You don't look thirty-eight." She was looking at him, her eyes exploring his face. He was clean-shaven, with shallow dimples that deepened when he smiled his finely chiselled lips that framed even white teeth. His nose was full and straight, his brow wide and prominent. Eyes that were so deep and blue any woman would drown in them, and his lightly tanned skin looked soft and smooth. He was one of those men who would be considered a good catch indeed. For any woman.

Fantastically gorgeous looks and an even more fantastic billion dollar bank account.

He was leaning on pillows watching her eyes explore him, a sly smile on his face. "Tell me about yourself," he said quietly. He yearned to know more about the beautiful creature before him. Her soft brown hair twisted into a knot, her face lightly made up, gems sparkling in her ears.

He was glad he'd suggested the dress as it showed off

her figure perfectly, the colour bringing a soft blush to her cheeks. Cheeks he wanted to stroke. The silky material slid over her curves provocatively, leaving no room for the imagination, sweeping over her rounded, voluptuous breasts, showing them off to their best advantage, sliding down to cover her womanly hips just right for childbirth.

God, I want her!

"What were your plans for tomorrow?" she asked, not wanting to talk about herself.

Diega, sadly realising this, reluctantly changed tack. "I thought we could do a driving tour of Las Vegas, maybe go out into the desert. Would you like that?" he asked eagerly.

"Yeah, I would," she said softly, blushing. "It's late, I want to head up now, get some sleep. Thank you for tonight." She stood and laid the blanket on the couch.

"Are you sure you won't stay awhile longer?" Diega asked, jumping up.

"No. I'm tired. It's been a long week. A long night." She smiled lightly and averted her gaze.

"Okay. Do you want me to walk you up?" he asked, not wanting to let her go just yet.

She was nervous at the prospect. "No, no, it's okay, thanks anyway. Good night." She headed for her room with Diega gazing intently at her retreating figure.

*****

He watched her as she undressed, putting on a silky, lacy blue nightie, and felt himself harden at her naked body as the material slid over her round, full breasts that he longed to take into his hands.

She was tired from a long week of shows, and he had been at every one. Watching, listening, applauding. Even crying at times at the emotion that poured out of her.

Vegas hadn't been there, that so-called man she slept with. He wasn't there with her now. Curious, what could be more important than this incredible creature wrapping herself in the animal print bedspread as she falls into a deep sleep. I'll show her an animal in bed, he thought, the bedspread making him very eager.

His body ached to be beside her...

His penis ached to release its seed inside of her...

I need to find out what Vegas is up to and use it against him!

*****

Waking up early Saturday morning, Tahlia was alone, remembering Vegas was gone for the weekend. Lying in the quiet for a few moments, she thought about Diega. *Is it right to go out with him?* She was worried about the implications if she did. *All my life men have disappointed, an' from the age of twelve it was hell. Vegas is the first man to make me feel passion, love, desire. Give me the courage an' power to go after what I want. Love? Did I say, love? Do I love him?* She sat up. *Do I love Vegas? Yeah, I think I do.* She blushed, remembering all the times they had been intimate since meeting.

After showering, she considered what to wear. "Jeans an' a top I think," she said to her reflection in the mirror as she picked out her clothes and dressed. About to order room service, there was a knock at the door.

Diega stood there with a room service trolley and a huge grin. "Hello."

"Hi. What's this?"

"Breakfast. May I come in?"

"Sure," she said, opening the door wider for him to enter. "Wow, smells good, looks good too." She breathed in deeply as Diega set up the dining table.

"Eggs Benedict with a side dish of cream, tropical fruit, coffee, juice, toast, and cereal. All you can eat."

Tahlia laughed. "I don't eat all this normally, an' you expect me to now."

"Just eat what you want, but remember, you might need your energy for later," Diega said, grinning suspiciously.

"We're only driving around Vegas aren't we?" Tahlia asked, now suspicious herself.

"Ohhh, we might get out and walk for a while." The grin was still in place.

Sitting down, Tahlia started on the eggs. "Mmm, this is good," she said, tasting a forkful, her face melting with her taste buds as she swallowed.

"It is isn't it." Diega watched the expressions fly over her face as she enjoyed the meal. They ate in silence for a few minutes. "I thought we could maybe drive out to the desert. Or we could just drive around the outer suburbs, get out, look in shops if you prefer," he said, taking a sip of coffee.

"Whatever, it doesn't matter. When buying the clothes for the show we hit every store, an' in my time off Vegas an' I cruise around. So I don't know if there's anywhere left for you to show me," she replied, drinking her juice.

Diega's eyes darkened at the mention of *that* name. "Believe me," he murmured, gazing deeply at her. "There are many things in Vegas that I can show you."

She sat still in her chair and stared into his eyes. The sexual overtone titillated her and ran up and down her spine like shock waves. Tahlia blushed and looked away. "Umm, I'm done. You ready?" she asked, diving out of her seat so she could get away from him.

He smiled slyly at her show of nerves. "Let's go."

The ride downstairs was nerve-racking for Tahlia, standing so close to Diega. She breathed in his cologne as it wafted around her, making her feel heady and weak-kneed. Walking outside, she took great gulps of air to clear her head, and watched as the valet pulled up in front of them in a shiny, new looking black BMW.

"Hop in," Diega said, opening the passenger door.

"Oh, my God. Is this yours?" Tahlia asked, staring in shock.

"Certainly is," he said with a huge grin. "Hop in."

She sat down slowly, not wanting to touch anything in case she broke it.

Shutting the door behind her, Diega strode around to the driver's side and got in. "Look out Vegas," he said, grinning.

The car was amazing, so comfortable, everything you could want. Tahlia had never been in one so flash and expensive, and she settled back in the seat which was soft and luxurious. "This is a great car," she enthused.

"Yes, it is. I figured as a hotel owner I needed the best car I could buy to go with it. It's very me, I think," Diega said, still grinning.

"Certainly is."

The day turned out to be fun. Diega showed Tahlia parts of town she was surprised she hadn't seen yet, and they stopped in stores she hadn't discovered. He bought her a piece of jewellery she oohed and aahed over, but at first had refused, feeling nervous and uncomfortable about accepting it.

"Please, let me buy you something." The look on his face melted her resolve.

"Okay," she sighed, giving in.

But when they were in the sixth store, and he wanted to buy her everything, she put her foot down. "No," she cried. "You need to stop buying me stuff. Just 'cause I gave in on the other things doesn't mean you can now buy me the whole store."

"It's not the whole store…only half the store," he said, grinning mischievously.

"No!" With that she walked out, ignoring Diega's attempts at peace offerings as he ran around after her, trying to buy out every store in the hope of winning her over.

Lunch was at a Mexican restaurant, with sombreros and shawls on the walls, and a charming atmosphere full of fun. Finishing off the afternoon with ice cream sundaes from the local parlour, they drove back to the hotel.

"That was fun," Tahlia said as they walked toward the lift.

"Yes, it was," Diega agreed, carrying her bags. "We should do it again." He was looking at her expectantly.

She wanted to say yes, but kept her mouth closed, and her eyes averted.

The ride upstairs was uncomfortable, and she couldn't wait to get to her suite. Stopping at her door and opening it, she turned to Diega who handed her the bags. "Thanks for today."

"You're welcome. But it's not over yet." He smiled wickedly.

Her heart fluttered. "What do you mean? What are you up to?"

"Why don't you rest up, and then at seven I'll pick you up for some more fun. And wear a swimsuit." He walked away with a wave of his hand.

Walking in and dumping her bags on the couch, Tahlia wondered what he was up to. She grabbed a soda from the fridge, walked into the bedroom, and threw herself onto the bed. *It's four-thirty now,* she thought, setting her alarm clock just in case she overslept, *so I have a few hours to rest and shower.*

She lay back and settled in, closing her eyes and relaxing.

Beep beep beep beep…

Waking up with a start, she found it was dusk already, and turned toward the bedside clock that was noisily chirping away.

6:30 p.m.

Shutting off the clock and diving off the bed, she

managed to be in and out of the shower in record time. Walking into her huge walk-in closet, she reached for the drawer that held her assortment of bikinis.

"I don't want to look sexy," she mused, deciding on a blue two-piece on the conservative side. Putting it on, she threw a plain summer dress over it. Brushing her hair into a ponytail, she decided against make-up. *What would be the point if we're going swimming,* she thought, shrugging at her reflection. She slipped into sandals just as there was a knock at the door.

Running to answer it, she flung it open to see Diega standing there in white summer pants and a matching shirt, his hair loose and carefree, not slicked back. She stopped in surprise. "You're wearing white," she said slowly.

"Yes, I am," Diega answered back just as slowly, a grin on his face.

"Well, it's just that you're always in black," she said, blushing.

"You notice what I wear?" He raised his left eyebrow in amusement.

"A bit hard not to when that's all we see you in." She blushed again. "Um, so are we going swimming?" she recovered.

"Yes, we are. Let's go." Diega offered his arm for Tahlia to take as she shut her door behind them.

Instead of getting into the normal hotel lift, they continued down the thickly carpeted hall and around the corner.

"Where are we going?" she asked in surprise.

"You'll see."

Reaching the end of the second hallway, they stopped in front of a lift Tahlia hadn't seen before. Diega put a key card into a slot, pressed four buttons on a pad, and the doors opened to reveal a rich red interior, just like the lobby, from the carpeting to the wallpaper, to the gold trim and a small crystal chandelier. They slid quietly up four floors.

When the doors opened, and they stepped out, Tahlia gasped in surprise and delight.

Chapter 9

Before her lay a tropical paradise, and walking through a flower drenched arbour into the living area, she saw they were on top of the hotel.

"Oh, my God, this is amazing. You've created paradise on the roof of the hotel." She ran to the railing and looked over the city as the sun set, realising for the first time that she was scared of heights. "Okay, shouldn't have done that," she quavered dizzily and almost fell backward.

"Are you all right?" Diega took hold of her. "Here, come and sit down." He walked her to the couch which was circular, large, and very soft and cosy with lots of pillows.

Looking around, Tahlia saw a well-stocked kitchenette with grill, a dining area, a pool table, and a grand piano. "You have a grand piano an' pool table up here?" She was even more surprised as her wide eyes took everything in.

"Yes. I use this as my retreat at the end of a long day. I come up here, relax, play, read. Watch the sunset. The couch is large and circular because it turns into a bed, so sometimes I sleep up here in the summer and wake with the sun. It's amazing, all right."

He watched her face as excitement and wonderment crossed it, thankful he had made the right choice for their night together. "There's a TV, DVD, cd player if I want to watch a movie or listen to music," he said, pointing to the medium-sized cabinet in front of them, "and the swimming pool is over there behind that lattice." He pointed to somewhere behind her. "I wanted to keep it separate from the living area."

"It's like an apartment or one of the suites," Tahlia said and looked up. "What about when it rains?"

"There's an automatic roof that can be moved over to keep the rain off. Being up here when it's raining is just as amazing. With all the latticework the place is kept very cosy and warm." He searched her face with a meaningful gaze as he lowered his voice to add, "and very private."

She looked at him, seeing the way he was gazing at her, getting his meaning. "So…we were going…swimming… were…we?" She averted her eyes and grabbed a cushion, holding it to her chest as her face burned.

"A bit later," he said, seeing she was uncomfortable, "in the meantime, let's eat and talk." Pressing a button on a remote, Diega motioned to the waiters who walked through the door with trays full of heavenly looking food.

They sat at the dining table, and a meal of lemon and chive Barramundi, garden fresh salad, fruit and chocolate cake followed. Diega offered champagne, but Tahlia politely refused, preferring juice.

After finishing the last mouthful of cake, she leaned back in her chair. "That was delicious," she murmured, licking her lips in appreciation.

"One of my favourites," Diega replied, picking up his wine glass. The waiter cleared the table, and they were alone again.

Looking up into the starlit sky, Tahlia sighed. "God, it looks so close. Like you can reach up an' touch them."

"Maybe you can," Diega said, pulling a piece of paper from his shirt pocket. "This is for you." He presented it to her.

"What is it?" she asked, taking it.

"Read it."

It turned out to be a certificate, stating that a star had been named in her honour.

"You named a star after me," she gasped in surprise and looked at him.

He beamed back at her. "Yes, I did, and it has been registered, so it's all legal."

She looked up into the starlit sky again. "Which one is it?" she asked, her excitement growing.

"Come, I'll show you." Diega held out his hand, and she took it. Walking over to the side of the roof, she saw a powerful telescope sitting on a platform. Looking into it, Diega adjusted the angle and stepped aside. "Take a look."

Tahlia looked into it. "Which one?"

"The bright one, shining over all the others."

She gazed at the star for a few moments and then at Diega. She didn't know what to say. Shaking her head sadly, feeling so overwhelmed and joyous at the same time, she looked at the ground. Closing her eyes, her brow furrowed as a single lone tear trickled down her cheek. She wiped it away, feeling so bewildered at having a star named after her. "I…don't know what to say. This feels a little strange. I've only been here a few weeks, no one's ever done something like this…this feels strange," she said, finally looking at him.

"Why?" Diega asked softly, feeling his concern grow as he gazed at her intently. His hand reached out to touch her arm, then seeing her discomfort, his hand retreated, and he decided to change the subject. "Okay, let's listen to some music for a while, and we can talk about other things. What you like about Las Vegas, favourite movies, music, TV shows." He walked to the living area and turned his expensive music system on. Choosing a cd, he slid it into the player and adjusted the volume as music wafted over the rooftop. Tahlia was grateful for the few moments to collect herself.

For the next hour they danced and talked about their favourite movies, Tahlia's – Gone With the Wind, Diega's – The Godfather. Favourite TV show, bands, music. She was having a good time, feeling relaxed. Secure.

"Now, how about that swim," Diega said. Taking her hand, he led her past the vine-covered lattice and over to the pool. Letting her go, he walked over to a small electrical box on the wall, pulled a few switches, and turned around to watch her face as the underwater lights came on. They changed colour sporadically, flicking on and off in different synchronizations. As he undressed, he was glad he had suggested a swim as her excitement pleased him.

Immensely.

"Wow, this makes it look good," she enthused, taking off her dress. Turning, she saw his muscular, lean body. His tan reflected the gold in his brown chest hair that slowly, teasingly, snaked down into the snug navy swim trunks that clung to his taut ass perfectly, and framed his long, lean legs. He definitely looked after himself.

Blushing, and feeling incredibly hot, Tahlia hadn't even realised she was staring at him. Seeing him staring back at her with an extremely satisfied look on his face, she flushed in embarrassment, fairly running for the pool stairs and sliding into the water, swimming to the other end. *Oh, God, I can't keep doing this,* she thought. Turning, she saw Diega swimming toward her. Her heart pounded as he glided up with just his face out of the water.

"Wanna race?" He headed back.

Glad the moment was over, she swam after him.

Four laps later they stopped, laughing and out of breath.

"Not fair," she cried, "you're better than me. I haven't swum in…" she frowned, "ages." She tried to remember as she thought about it.

"Ages?" He floated beside her.

Her mood descended rapidly, sadly. "Yeah, ages, let's change the subject." She slowly swam back before being dunked under the water. "What'd you do that for?" she sputtered when she came up.

"You wanted to change the subject," Diega said,

grinning wickedly as he splashed her.

"War!" she declared, splashing back.

For the next fifteen minutes, they splashed and dunked, trying to outdo each other until Tahlia finally cried enough and swam for the side. As she reached for the ladder to pull herself out, Diega's hands grabbed the ladder before her. Startled, she gasped and spun around.

He was barely inches from her, still hanging onto the ladder.

She was trapped, her brain not functioning.

His eyes were dark pools, gazing at her with passion and desire, his wet lashes framing them, dark against his skin. His body so close she could hear the beating of his heart.

She felt electricity run through her veins, her nipples harden, her womanhood ache for him. Gasping for breath, she barely had room to tread water, and with nothing to hang onto, she didn't want to grab Diega. His full lips parted, and he leaned in toward her, his eyes still gazing into hers.

Just before their lips met, she jerked her head away. "What are you doing?" she cried, putting her hands on his chest in the vain hope of pushing him away. She stopped and looked at him. Her hands trembled. His chest hair felt soft beneath them, and she felt his heart pounding harder from her touch.

His eyes smouldered and burned into hers. He said nothing, just breathed rapidly. Diega was desperately trying to control his desires, but it was so incredibly hard to calm his racing heart, not to mention the hardening in his groin. His manly erection became more prominent, and he wanted Tahlia to notice what her hands were doing to him, wanted them around him, stroking him, touching him.

But her hands were nestled in his chest hair, and he liked the way they felt against his muscles. He wanted her with such fierceness and power that his own hands were clamped to the ladder like it was a lifeline. He stared at her, seeing the confusing war of emotions rage through her as she tried to get them under control.

"No, no," Tahlia cried, snapping out of it. She pushed him away, climbed up the ladder, and grabbing her dress, she fled to her suite.

Diega watched her run as he stepped out of the pool. She was like a scared deer, and he swore at himself for pushing her. It had only been their third time together, and he'd decided not to push but couldn't help himself and made a move. Now, she had run off in fear. *I'll have to back off,* he thought, sighing and heading for his own suite.

*****

She was running, running, running. Blindly, in fear of her life. Running from something, she didn't know what. She just had to get away. Away from the terror. Away from the man in the shadows...

She would have to hide, hide where, where, there, under that trashcan. Why is it so slippery? Her hands grabbed for the can, but it slid through her fingers. She quickly rubbed them on her dress, the smear making two dark stains. What is that, oh, my God is it blood,

blood, why is there blood on my hands? Why?

Wait, what was that, it's him, he's coming for me, I must hide, quickly. She pulled the can over her head and curled up, quiet as a mouse. At least she hoped it was quiet. Her heart was thundering in her chest like a galloping stallion, her breath rushing from her mouth.

What was that? A footstep, silence. It's him, oh, God it's him. He's found me, dear God he's found me. She heard gasping, scared for a moment that it was hers. It wasn't. The man stopped in front of the can. There was a bang on the top. *He had found her.*

The can moved.

She was caught.

No, no he can't find me, he can't find me.

A heavy weight lay on top of the can, and she heard deep breathing. *It was him. What was he doing? Sitting on top of the can? Don't let him find me,* she prayed, *dear God, please don't let him find me.* The weight moved. *This is it,* she thought, *I'm dead.*

The footsteps retreated.

Her breath came rushing out of her mouth in a tidal wave.

She was safe.

For now…

*****

Sunday morning, Tahlia woke late, groggy, and still in her bikini. Crawling out of bed, she showered and ordered room service. Deciding to stay in for the day instead of facing Diega, she rang down to the front desk to give him a message. "Tell him I'm not feeling well an' am staying in," she said and hung up.

Curling up on the couch, she ached for Vegas. At least when he was here, she didn't think of Diega. Didn't want him. Didn't yearn for his touch.

Liar! Of course, you think about him and want him and yearn for his touch. You are such a liar! Liar, liar, pants on fire!

I am not! God, I have to stop thinking about Diega. I can't have him. I shouldn't want him. God, what am I gonna do?

She rang Mandy. She needed to talk, and Mandy was her only friend.

"Mandy," a voice slurred.

"You still in bed?" Tahlia asked. "It's past twelve."

"Well, I partied hard last night," Mandy said, now sounding a little more awake. "And since this is my day off, I get to sleep in. What's wrong?"

"I need to talk to someone, can you come up?"

"There in ten," Mandy said, before the click of a dial tone.

Thirty minutes later, she arrived.

"You said ten," Tahlia laughingly accused her as she staggered in wearing big black sunglasses, a summer dress, and sandals.

She was all of five foot five and a redhead. Her curls bouncing wild and free now, but always tied back for work. She loved to party on Saturday nights since she had Sundays free, and always made a beeline for the cute guys at a party. And they lapped up her attention, loving her white skin and freckles, bubbly personality, and *very* curvaceous body. Mandy was lucky enough to live in the apartment building at the back of *The Montiamo*. It was owned by the hotel and was for staff who didn't have anywhere else to live.

"Well," Mandy replied, "I tried my best. There's only so much I can do on a Sunday after partying so hard." She sprawled over one of the sofas and accepted the soda Tahlia offered. "God, I so need this." She cracked it open and drank half of it in one big gulp, then burped loudly. Lying down, Mandy glanced at her friend. "So, what's this all about?"

"Diega."

Mandy looked at her curiously. "What do you mean… *Diega*?"

"He invited me out yesterday an' I went. We had a nice time, some lunch, some shopping. Then last night he took me up to the roof for dinner."

"What!" Mandy shot up from the sofa. "He invited you up to the roof? He never invites anyone up to the roof. In fact, most of us don't even think it exists 'cause no one's ever seen it." She was gaping at Tahlia incredulously. "He invited you up to the roof?" she repeated. "He never invites anyone up there." Her voice drifted off as she dreamt about it. "Tell me, tell me everything." She came back from dreamland. "What does it look like, what can you see? *What did he do?*" Her brows shot up teasingly. "He must have done *something*. Spill the details girl. Now!"

Tahlia blushed a deep red.

"Ha," Mandy cried, "I knew something happened. Tell me. Tell me now."

Tahlia swallowed. *How much should I tell her,* she thought. *I've never had a girlfriend before, I don't know how to handle situations like this.* She looked down. "Um, not much," she said, blushing even more deeply.

"Liar," Mandy cried, "you're blushing too much for *not much.* Spill it all."

"Well, he took me driving around Las Vegas an' bought me some things."

"Like what?" Mandy demanded.

"Ah, some jewellery, an' a nice Mexican shawl that I saw in the restaurant we ate in."

"Okay, what else. Up on the roof baby, tell me 'bout the roof." Mandy was leaning forward in her seat excitedly. She'd never dated Diega Montiamo, hotel-casino owner, billionaire businessman, and didn't know anyone on the staff who had. Until now. *And thank God Tahlia's now a good friend,* she thought. Glad that she'd found someone she could get all girly with and have shopping trips and get-togethers with. She was a bit of a loner, just like Tahlia, having moved to Las Vegas a year ago on her own. Her family was on the other side of the country, and she felt lonely. A lot. But now she was happy that she'd finally found someone she could call a good friend. A best friend. A girlfriend. "Well," she demanded.

"Well," Tahlia started, not sure she should say anything, or if she did it might end up making the whole situation worse. "It's very nice, an' you get a great view of the city. An' we had a nice dinner, an' he presented me with a certificate that said he'd registered a star in my name—"

"Wait, what?" Mandy interrupted. "What do you mean he registered a star in your name?"

"Well, apparently you can have a star named after someone," Tahlia said. "An' it's all legal an' stuff."

Mandy stared at her dreamily. "He paid to have a star named after you. That's *so* romantic. Oh, my, God. He named a star after you." She stared off dreamily again before coming back to earth. "So, what else?"

"Well, um, after dinner we went for a swim an' played around an' stuff, an' then he tried to kiss me, but I ran 'cause it was wrong an' I didn't know what to do or what to say an' oh, my God what do I do?" The words came out in a rush and seeing Mandy's shocked face, Tahlia wished she'd kept her mouth shut.

"Oh, my, holy, freakin', mother, of, God," she said. "He kissed you," she screamed. "Oh, my God, he kissed you." She moved over to Tahlia and hugged her. "You have to tell me everything and tell me now."

"Wait," Tahlia cried, trying to disentangle herself, "he didn't kiss me. I said he tried an' I ran." She felt tears overflow and roll down her cheeks. "An' now I don't know what to do," she sobbed.

Mandy held her tightly. "What do you mean you don't know what to do? He kissed you. *Diega Montiamo kissed you.* As far as I know, he's never kissed any of the staff, but now he's kissed *you.* Oh, my God, he kissed you. What's so wrong with that?"

"Vegas," Tahlia sniffled, looking at Mandy.

"Ah," she said, suddenly realising the seriousness of the situation, "you *do* have a problem don't you."

*****

Monday morning was sunny and bright when Vegas rang. "I'll be home round three, baby," he drawled. "See ya then."

Rehearsals ran from one to three p.m., so she was just finishing up when he walked into the concert hall. She ran into his arms, and he swung her around and kissed her. "Let's go upstairs," she said, dragging him to the lift.

When no one else got in with them, she wrapped her arms around his neck and thrust her tongue into his mouth. He reciprocated, and they didn't stop until their floor.

Stumbling through their door, they ripped each other's clothes off, not even making it to the bedroom. Falling onto the couch, they hungrily ran their hands over each other. Their tongues tasting and exploring after their time apart.

"Oh, God, I missed you," Tahlia gasped as his tongue slid inside of her. He grabbed her breasts roughly, squeezed, kneaded. He bit her nipples hard.

"Ow, that hurts, don't," she cried and shoved his head away. His look was different, not the Vegas she knew.

"Ya know ya wan' it that way," he growled, low and throaty, thrusting into her hard.

It hurt.

"Vegas stop it," she cried louder, pushing at him. "You're hurting me." She was close to tears.

Vegas looked at her, and his expression softened. "Oh, God, baby, I'm sorry. I'm so sorry." He stroked her face. "I'm so sorry. I didn' realise. We play rough a lot, an' I…I didn' realise I was rougher than usual. I'm so sorry." The look on his face was now one of sorrow and concern.

Forgiving him in an instant, she locked her arms around him and pulled him closer. "It's okay, let's just…let's just lie here a bit an' take it easy."

Their faces were beside each other, their eyes gazing into the others.

"I'm sorry."

"It's okay," she said, kissing him.

Gently, slowly, they continued until they were done.

"What happened?" she asked.

"When?"

"This weekend. You haven't been like that with me. Then you go away an' you come back different. What happened?"

Sitting up, Vegas avoided her gaze. "I don' wanna talk about it, baby," he said, and headed for the shower without a backward glance.

*****

He watched them, knowing that animal was back in town after his weekend away. They'd started making out in the lift, stumbling into their suite. What he had done to her next was disgusting.

Rape even.

And she had forgiven him in an instant, still allowing him to make love to her, be inside of her. How could she do that, how could she let him touch her after being so rough?

A real man didn't do that.

A real man didn't hurt the woman he was with.

A real man didn't bite and force himself onto or into a woman.

But then Vegas wasn't a real man.

He was a vile, filthy animal that needed to be shown what would happen to him after mistreating a woman.

His woman.

His Tahlia.

He sneered in contempt at the man he hated. Looking down at the papers in his hand, he noted the company Vegas had kept over the weekend.

Very interesting.

The beginning of his downfall.

*****

Vegas was very loving that week. At every rehearsal, every show. He desperately wanted to make it up to Tahlia to show her how sorry he was.

"Baby, listen," he said to her on Friday night after the show. "I'm so very, very sorry for the way I treated you on Monday, an' I wan' to make it up to you by lettin' you…" He waved his hands in the air in front of him as he tried to find the right phrase.

"What?" she asked, watching his face.

"Well, let's just say, I been a very bad, bad, bad boy an' I need to be punished, baby."

Walking into their bedroom, Tahlia saw rope on the headboard and a whip on the bed. "Oh, my God," she cried, bad memories starting to niggle at her mind.

"What the hell are you up to?" She looked at him as if he were insane.

"I need to be punished baby, an' you're gonna punish me." That damn sexy grin was back, and she melted. Jumping onto the bed, Vegas lay on his back, spread-eagled every which way. "Tie me up, baby."

Standing still a moment, Tahlia decided if she wanted to participate. After all the times she'd *not* been in control, now, it was finally her moment to take charge. *So, why the hell not?* she thought.

She jumped on top of him to tie him up. Ripping off his top, she grabbed his right hand, tying it first, then his left. Stopping, she thought for a moment, then ran into her closet.

"Baby, where'd you go?" Vegas called, eagerly looking for her.

"To get something," she said, coming back with a dark silk scarf.

"What's that for?" Vegas queried, unsure.

"For blindfolding you," she said, grinning wickedly as she wrapped it around his head.

"Blindfold huh, woohoo let's get kinky." His grin was ear to ear.

Once she had tied it securely, she got off the bed. Standing there looking at him, she wondered what to do, then got another thought.

"Baby, where'd you go?"

She said nothing as she undressed and crawled onto the bed from the end. Slowly moving up toward him, she kissed his navel and poked her tongue in.

He gasped. "Oooh, baby," he murmured.

"Shhh." She planted kisses up his torso and ran her tongue through his chest hair. He moaned lightly. She stroked his arms and ran her fingers down his sides while she kissed his body. After minutes of teasing, Tahlia took her revenge. Roughly grabbing his belt, she unbuckled it, and pulling down his jeans, yanked them off.

"Oh, God, baby," he gasped. His shorts followed his jeans, and when he was naked, she strapped his ankles to the end of the bed with the rope he had left there.

Turning back to him, she saw he was hard and erect. To tease him more, she massaged his legs roughly. Moving her hands up and down his thighs to make him harder.

He was gasping and grunting as she stroked his testicles, making him buck and thrash around.

She stopped and watched him, waiting until he calmed down. Slowly rubbing her naked breasts against his manhood, she ran her hands over him, making him groan even more.

Moving up to his face, she played kisses on his body, his neck, his jaw, finally thrusting her tongue into his mouth, then pulling it out.

"Oooh, baby," Vegas moaned as she sat on him, one leg either side of him.

She took him roughly, biting, grabbing, thrusting her tongue in and out of his mouth. The kisses passionate. She writhed against him, feeling his hardness rub against her. Aching for him, she kneeled above him and teased the tip of his penis with her vagina.

"Oh, God, baby, oh, God," Vegas cried.

Tahlia slowly slid down over his hard erect shaft.

Down, down, down.

Engineering the penetration herself, she felt him inside of her, then quickly rose so he was out.

Gasping hard, Vegas pulled against his bonds.

Again, slowly, slowly, she slid down, down, down. Down, down, down.

Her inner muscles adjusted to his hot, hard fullness.

"God, baby now, God," he cried louder.

Moving around in slow easy circles, she didn't touch him, just let her pleasure garden tease him. Revelling in the sense of taking him, owning him, making him hers, all on her own terms.

Finally reaching the brink, he thrust upwards, and she grabbed his sides as they ground together. The fire erupted and flared through them as the sexual energy roared around, catapulting them into another dimension, making them climax in screaming ecstasy.

Tahlia collapsed against him and ripped off the blindfold. She was still wrapped around him, feeling him still so hard inside of her.

"Baby," Vegas gasped raggedly, "undo me."

Reaching up, she pulled on one end of the rope allowing his left hand to be free.

Yanking off the rope around his right hand, Vegas caged her in his arms and kissed her passionately. "God, baby, what you do to me."

She grinned wickedly and laid her head on his chest, nestling in the hair there, hearing his heart pound wildly. "Well," she said, breathing hard, "you are my stallion. I decided it was time to take you for a ride."

Chapter 10

Waking up hours later, Tahlia tried to move her right arm, but couldn't. *Oh, Gawd, waz wrong,* she thought sleepily, *I probly slep on it.* Shaking her head to clear her foggy mind, she looked toward her right arm and found her hand had been tied to the headboard. Gasping, she reached over to untie it, only to find her left hand too was tied.

"Oh, no, no, this can't be happening." Moving her legs, she found Vegas had bound her feet as well. This was not good. "No, no, Vegas," she yelled, not seeing him.

He walked out of the bathroom, still naked, holding the whip in one hand, and slapping the end against the palm of the other. Stopping at the end of the bed, he looked at her with an expression she had never wanted to see again. All the old memories of pain and torture came flooding back, and tears flowed down her cheeks.

"No, no, please no, I'll be good, I promise, just please don't. Let me go, let me go," she begged, pulling at the ropes. But they wouldn't give.

Vegas crawled onto the bed, thinking she was playing along. He slid the whip slowly up her leg to her pelvis, and pushing it against her, found the entrance he was looking for.

She became hysterical, screaming, "No. No. Don't, let me go, let me go, oh, God, don't do this, let me go. *No.*" The scream was so loud Vegas fell back in surprise. She was flailing, pulling at the ropes, trying to get free. "Get away from me. Get away from me. Let me go, let me go." She was thrashing around, and he saw that something was seriously wrong.

"Baby, baby, it's okay. I'll undo the ropes." Feeling out of it, Vegas pulled at the ropes on her hands then her feet.

When they were free, she dived off the bed and pulled the sheet with her.

"Baby."

"No. Get away from me," she screamed, running into the closet and slamming the door shut behind her.

Vegas stood there in utter confusion. She had never reacted like this before, so he had never seen her this way. She was completely freaked out. Scared to absolute death.

He didn't know what to do, and he stood in the middle of the room trying to think. Hearing her sob loudly, he decided to leave her alone and sat on the bed to wait.

He tried to get his heartbeat in check as it pounded wildly. He was now completely freaked out himself, having never experienced this with a woman before. He ran his hands through his hair and over his face, hoping to wipe away what had just happened.

God, what the hell was that? What the hell happened

to her for her to go nuts that way? I know I haven' done anythin' bad to her…that's it, it must be some other boyfriend that did somethin' to her. It must have been pretty bad for her to react like this, just 'cause I tied her up an' used a whip.

He ran his hands over his face again. He was sweating, hot, completely confused as to what had unfolded before him not minutes ago. He looked around the bedroom, but his gaze reverted back to the closet where he could still hear her sobs coming through the louvered doors.

"God, what do I do?" he asked. Receiving no reply, he grabbed a can of soda from the kitchen and sat back on the bed to wait out the mess before him.

When thirty minutes had passed, he went to the closet door and knocked gently. "Tahlia," he called softly. Her sobs had slowed to a muffle, and he could hear ragged breathing. "Baby." Knocking again, he opened the door.

She looked at him in terror, clutching her knees to her chest, rocking back and forth.

The sight of her tore at his heart. Ripped at his core. "Tahlia. Baby. What's wrong?" His voice was soft as he took a step toward her.

"No, don't come near me," she cried, backing into the corner.

"Baby…it's me…Vegas. I'm not gonna hurt you, baby. It's okay. It's just me." He was beside her, sitting on the floor and wrapping his arms around her while she sobbed again, letting out years of anguish and fear. Stroking her hair, he murmured softly, "It's okay, baby, everythin's awright." He waited for her to stop.

Finally, feeling empty, Tahlia sat up and wiped her face. Looking at the man beside her, she wondered if he would ever hurt her like those in her past.

"You okay, baby?" Vegas asked quietly as he stroked her face.

She nodded uncertainly. "I'm okay."

"Tell me. What happened to you?"

Tahlia gazed at him as she thought about it. Deciding she wanted to unburden, she nodded again. "Hold me," she whispered and started her story.

"My Dad died when I was ten. Up till then, I had a normal childhood. I was born in Australia, my parents moved here when I was six. We lived in California for a few years, then moved to New York. After he died, Mom fell apart. She lost her job an' ended up with casual jobs an' deadbeat boyfriends." Tahlia cried softly. "My twelfth birthday was the worst of my life. My mother didn't bother all that much, just got a horrible stale cake from the supermarket. I didn't…"

She wiped away her tears. "The only present I got was Mom falling into a drunken stupor after sex with her boyfriend. When he was done with her, he came into my room." She sobbed harder. "He got into my bed, an' when I tried to scream, he put his hand over my mouth. He told me if I struggled he'd kill me. An' I didn't want to die, but I didn't want him to do the things he did either." She broke down. "I was no longer a little girl."

Vegas held her tightly, crying with her, feeling her pain. His heart ached for her like it had never ached for any woman before. He wanted to make it go away, wanted to make it better. Wanted to kill the son of a bitch that did it to her.

"Mom didn't believe me when I told her. A week later I was really sick, an' she didn't want to take me to the hospital, but one morning she couldn't wake me, so she took me. The bastard had given me a disease, an' all my mother could do was yell at me for seducing her boyfriend. She blamed me. She blamed *me.* For *everything.* For her boyfriend leaving, for getting a disease. She even said I deserved it for trying to take him away from her. She blamed me for my Dad's death. She said it was all my fault he was dead 'cause he had gone out to buy me some books. An' if he hadn't been out, he wouldn't have been killed."

"Oh, baby, I'm so sorry," Vegas said softly.

"The doctor an' the police told her to get rid of the boyfriend or have me taken away. She didn't care if I was, but it didn't matter 'cause the boyfriend had left the night before."

Tahlia took long deep breaths, trying to calm herself down. "I retreated into myself for years. We moved around a lot, more jobs, more boyfriends. She threw out everything I ever had, so she didn't have to pay to move it. I had nothing, except some clothes. At eighteen boys were interested, an' in the hope of finding love, I slept with them, trying to fill a void." She laughed lifelessly. "Didn't work. I ended up just like my mother. In abusive, loveless relationships." She sniffed. "Until Wayne…"

"Wayne?" Vegas asked.

"The man that's dead. Wayne Brady," she replied, looking at him. "I'm still having nightmares, but only when you're not here. There's still only bits an' pieces but, I just can't tell," she said, putting her head in her hands, feeling absolutely exhausted.

"Tell me what you see, baby."

She looked at Vegas and shrugged half-heartedly. "I'm running, there's shadows, there's someone, a gun, blood, him on the floor. It's always the same. A gunshot, blood on my hands. I don't know if I did it, an' it scares me Vegas. It *really* scares me." She was shaking as she sat there, even though his arms were around her.

"It's okay, baby. No one's after you. I'll protect you," he said, once again stroking her hair. "How 'bout we go get some sleep."

"I don't know if I *can* sleep but, okay," she murmured, suddenly feeling emotionally, physically, and mentally worn out.

Vegas led her to the bed and tucked her in, then removed the ropes and whip so she wouldn't see them. "I'll get us some drinks. You wan' a soda?"

"Yeah," she mumbled, gazing listlessly through glassy, tired eyes.

Vegas walked to the fridge, thinking about what he'd just heard. *God, that's rough,* he thought, *an' I had to go make it worse. I wonder what else has happened to her, if she'll be able to put it behind her?* Bringing back sodas, he climbed into bed beside her. Taking her into his arms, he kissed her forehead. "Everythin'll be okay, baby. I promise."

*****

He watched them.

His bottom lip quivered as he held back tears. Had seen her tie him up and do what she wanted. He wanted her to do that to him. It had been a real turn on imagining himself underneath her, Tahlia slowly covering his manhood, moving in circles. He felt his hard-on explode almost instantly, and was glad that he was only wearing his robe. He was getting a bit sick of soiling his silk pants, but knew he couldn't help himself when it came to Tahlia. And besides, he could afford new ones. He leaned back in his chair. Relieved. Satisfied.

God, he wanted her, desperately, like no other woman he'd known.

When she was asleep, that animal had tied her up, and when she woke, she completely freaked out, screaming and crying, and he'd been as confused as Vegas when Tahlia ran into the closet and slammed the door. Watching her sob was gut-wrenching, and caused him such agony.

Tears rolled down his cheeks as he gazed at the woman he loved. His heart aching and breaking at the pain she was in, wondering what he could do to help her.

When Vegas had gone into the closet, he'd gotten her to open up. Feeling every ounce of her pain and misery, he'd sobbed as he listened to her story. He wanted to take her into his arms and comfort her, love her, tell her he would make it all right, make all the pain go away.

He wiped away some tears, and decided to find out about this Wayne person, and show her she was not a murderer.

She *was the woman he loved.*

*****

Saturday morning they woke late, but it didn't matter, especially after last night.

"Mornin', baby," Vegas murmured into her hair. It was soft and silky and seemed to float all around her like a golden-brown halo. He loved the way it felt when it was sliding over his body, and how he could tangle his hands in it when they made love. But now wasn't the time to think about that.

"Morning." She smiled sadly.

"You okay this mornin', baby?" he asked, concerned as he stroked the soft, warm skin of her cheek while her head lay on his chest.

"Tired, but okay. It was good to get it all out. I've never told anyone before."

"Really? Why, baby? I feel honoured that you told me." Vegas lay there feeling quite proud that she had opened up to him, and *only* him.

Feeling hungry, she sat up. "You order room service an' I'll jump in the shower."

"Wan' me to join you, baby?" he asked, leaning up on his elbow to face her.

"No, it's okay," she said, kissing him. She wanted to be alone for a few minutes to go over what had happened last night.

Stepping under the hot spray, Tahlia thought about every moment of the ordeal. The sex had been wild and crazy, but afterwards...it was awful. Not Vegas, he hadn't known what she had gone through, but being tied up had brought back so many bad memories. Her life had been horrid. Absolutely horrid. She had never opened up to a man, but Vegas was different. Wonderful, incredible, a man she had never thought she would find. Never be with. Sighing, she mused out loud. "I never thought there would ever be a man to make me feel like this. I can't blame him for last night. He didn't know about my past."

"Baby, lunch is here," Vegas called through the door.

"Coming." Turning off the shower, she grabbed a towel and dried herself, dressing before joining him at the table.

"I can't believe we slept so late," she said, sipping her juice.

"It was a long night, baby," Vegas said. He finished his first cup of coffee and picked up a forkful of eggs. "Do you wan' to stay in or go out?"

Looking out at the view, she considered the idea. "We should go out. The air will do us good, an' besides, you still have to get some decent suits, my treat. An' a Harley. Did you say your bike bombed? I'll buy you a new one."

Vegas grinned. "Baby, you are not gonna buy me a bike. I can afford one myself, an' there just happens to be one I have my eye on. As for the suits..." He shrugged. "I don' need any."

"Yes, you do. I want to see what you look like in a suit," she looked at him sexily, "you might look absolutely gorgeous." She wiggled her brows at him.

"Don' I already, baby?" he drawled, that damn sexy

grin on his face.

"Yes, you do, but you'll look even more gorgeous an' sexy in a suit. So, no arguing. We're going shopping," she said and collected her things.

Vegas protested again and was still protesting fifteen minutes later when they jumped into the Mustang and set off. Tahlia had inquired at the front desk as to where the best men's wear shops were, and arriving at the first one, she parked the car.

Looking around, Vegas tried on five suits before getting bored. "Baby, I really don' need a suit," he grumbled, standing in front of her with his hands on his hips like a defiant child about to throw a tantrum.

"You do, an' we'll not stop till you get one," Tahlia said, pulling him out of the store.

Two stores later, they found it. Not just one, but several. Pure black was definitely his colour in different styles and cuts. They matched shirts perfectly. Blue brought out his gorgeous eyes and red the hints of colour in his hair.

In a black suit and blue shirt Vegas had to agree. "I do look more gorgeous an' sexy don' I, baby?" He paraded around like a male peacock on the hunt for a female.

"Yes, baby, you certainly do."

Once they paid and packed the car, they drove to the Harley Davidson dealership Vegas directed her to. The bike he wanted was jet-black and chrome, with turquoise and royal blue detailing.

"It's gorgeous," Tahlia breathed. "An' the blue matches my 'Stang."

"It also matches my eyes, baby. Ya really like it?" He

grinned like a child in the world's biggest toy store.

"Hell, yes!" Tahlia exclaimed as she jumped up and down, clapping her hands together in excitement.

"Great, let's buy her."

Half an hour later, with the papers signed, Vegas rode out of the lot with Tahlia following him back to the hotel. Telling the valet to take her car and send their parcels up to their room, she jumped on behind Vegas, donned the turquoise blue helmet he'd bought just for her, and they roared off into the setting sun.

Just the two of them, riding wild and free.

They got back to the hotel late, but it didn't matter. Especially after last night.

Tahlia was still exhausted. She'd never unburdened her secrets with anybody before and was very surprised that she'd told Vegas about what happened to her as a child. Life had been hell after that, and she didn't like talking about it, but had Vegas not started the game of tying her up, then she wouldn't have gone through so many emotions and now been so tired. On the way upstairs, she hugged him tightly, feeling his energy seep into her body and renew her spirits.

"God, I loved it," she cried, kissing him, "we have to go for another ride soon." He carried her out of the lift and to their door. Kissing and giggling, they stumbled inside.

"I love it too, baby. The wind in your hair, your woman on the back ridin' wild an' free." He spun around, Tahlia still in his arms, making her squeal and laugh.

She slid down his body slowly, gazing into his eyes, her passion rising inside of her, her pelvis on fire for his manhood. "An' I just *looove* the feeling of something hard an' throbbing between my legs," she breathed seductively.

Vegas made an o shape with his mouth, his eyes widened, and his brows shot up in anticipation. He licked his lips as Tahlia slid out of her jacket and kicked her boots off, before grabbing his singlet and pulling it over his head.

Taking his hand, she slowly led him to the bedroom. Falling onto the bed and pulling him on top of her, they kissed, and after quenching their desires spent a quiet night lying in each other's arms.

*****

Sunday morning, Tahlia rang down to the front desk and made a reservation, then they hopped on the bike to enjoy the day.

Arriving back at the hotel around six, Vegas wanted to go to bed.

"No. I've made plans. So have a shower an' get yourself into one of your new suits. We're going to dinner." With a raised eyebrow, Vegas stalked off to the bathroom, and she got one of his suits ready. When he was finished, she jumped into the shower after him, and he was dressed when she got out.

"Yum," she purred. "So good I could eat you."

He grinned. "Well, then, how 'bout we stay here, an' you can eat me all night, baby."

"Down boy." She laughed, and playfully slapped his hand away.

The meal at one of the hotel's fancier restaurants was amazing, and afterwards, she led him outside to the reserved section by the pool that Diega had taken her to. They kicked off their shoes and snuggled together under a blanket on the sofa.

"What a view," Vegas said, enjoying a glass of the hotel's finest champagne.

"Amazing isn't it," she agreed.

Their gaze wandered over the city lights and up to the stars above.

"Definitely the best way to end a day," he said, grinning as he kissed her. "We should do this every night, baby."

"The night's not over yet," she said in a low, sexy tone that made his eyes widen in desire. Seeing it was totally dark, and the area completely deserted, Tahlia pulled Vegas to his feet.

"What are you doin'?"

Sliding his suit jacket off, she laid it on a chair and started to unbutton his shirt.

"Whoa, baby, not here," he said, looking around.

"Don't worry. The place is completely private. I reserved it this morning. Besides, we did it out in the middle of nowhere, *several times.* So what's wrong with this?" she asked in mock anger.

"Nothin' at all, baby." His grin was back, and he relaxed.

He slid his hands up her mini dress to pull it over her head.

She pulled his shirt off then grabbed his belt, undoing it, sliding her hands into his pants, pushing both them and his shorts down. Their hands sped over each other as their mouths kissed hungrily.

He unhooked her bra and massaged her breasts with the palms of his hands, circling over her nipples, making them full of desire. God, he loved the way they felt, her skin starting so soft and velvety, becoming so hard and hot.

Groaning in pleasure, she pushed his hands into her panties, making him feel her. Then they were both naked, kissing, touching.

Vegas began to lift her onto him.

"No, not yet." she gasped and led him to the spa. Stepping into the hot bubbling water, they joined and became one. She wrapped her legs around his waist, and her arms around his neck as they kissed passionately. Vegas held onto her waist, lifting her, making her slide slowly down his hard shaft of sexual lust.

Groaning in unison, they let the water arouse them. Sliding up and down, Tahlia gasped raggedly in pleasure. Vegas sucked on her nipples, moulding her breasts. She clung to him as she climaxed, with Vegas holding back until she was done. When she collapsed against him, he slid his right hand between her legs and touched her clitoris. She cried out and arched into a spasm.

"What are you doing?" she gasped as he continued toying with it. Her body rocked back and forth trying to ride the pulsating wave. There was a painful tinge to it that only made it more powerful. When she was on the brink, he held her tight and plunged home.

Afterward, lazily treading water on her back, letting the bubbles play over her breasts as they gently floated on the surface, Tahlia grinned. "Bet we're not the first couple to do that in here." Her fingers slowly swept back and forth over her right breast.

"Probly not, baby," Vegas drawled, lighting a cigarette. He hungrily eyed her bouncing bosoms as the bubbles seductively slid over them. *God, I wan' to drink the water that's running over them, then do bad things to those breasts. God, I love those breasts! God, they're great breasts!*

"How long have you smoked?" Seeing the hungry look in his eyes, she spread her legs wide.

"Seems like forever," he replied, after thinking. He grabbed her and brought those bouncing bosoms to his mouth, unable to resist them any longer as she drunkenly giggled at the tickling she received.

Picking her up, he carried her to the couch and laid her down, then lay on top of her. She grabbed the blanket that was over the back of the sofa and pulled it over them.

Listening to the bustling city below them, they lay quietly together. Feeling his facial hair tickle her face, she giggled and stroked it. Gazing into each other's eyes they slowly moved together, kissing softly, touching gently. Having Vegas inside of her was the most incredible feeling. He was hard, sure, wanting, and taking him into her was all she wanted. The sexiest man she had ever seen, with muscles bulging in every direction. He was strong, and it thrilled her when he threw her on the bed. She found herself always aching for him deep inside, like at that moment.

He climaxed inside of her, and she felt his seed flow through her.

Sighing in contentment, they lay together.

*****

He had seen them.

From the only place you can see the poolside lounge and spa.

He had watched them.

In the spa first, her delectable breasts bouncing on top of the bubbly water. Breasts he wanted to take into his mouth and suck and chew on until they were red and raw, savouring their taste, their smell, their feel.

Then Vegas carried her to the couch where they made love under a blanket.

He was worried. After the scene two nights ago, he was surprised she wanted him to touch her. He'd treated her so cheaply, like some hooker he'd picked up on the street. Using a whip on such a lovely young lady was not the way to treat her.

"Vegas," he hissed, "I will whip you senseless for what you did to her."

She'd let him be inside of her. Obviously, Vegas was not like other men. The men she had previously been with. The bastards that used and abused her like she was a rag doll they could throw around and treat like garbage.

He's still an animal! *he thought viciously.*

He lowered his binoculars as they walked into the hotel.

He had seen them.

He had watched them.

Chapter 11

Monday morning dawned bright and warm, and Tahlia had an idea, so over breakfast she talked to Vegas. "How about one night this week you come on stage with me an' we sing a few songs together?" she asked excitedly.

He looked at her as he reached for his cup of coffee. "I don' know baby, you're the star. Why would you wan' me on stage with you?"

"'Cause I do!" she exclaimed, picking up a bagel and splitting it in half before smearing cream cheese all over it. "I want you on stage singing with me. You can play your guitar, I can sing backup you sing lead. I sing lead, you backup. How 'bout it? Please say you'll do it. Pleeease," she begged and giggled.

Vegas watched her excited face with a smile. "Make it later this week baby, but not Friday, an' I'll do it."

"Ooooh, thank you, thank you, thank you." She jumped up and hugged him, smothering him in kisses.

"Okay, baby, okay," he said, laughing and disentangling himself from her grasp before she sat down and attacked her cream cheese bagel and scrambled eggs.

*****

That afternoon at rehearsal, Tahlia mentioned the idea to the music director, and after listening to them sing a duet, he agreed. "How about Thursday night?" he asked. "It can be one of the sets, four or five songs."

"Sounds fantastic," she said and walked onstage for the rehearsal.

Vegas flicked through the song catalogue the director had and came across some songs he'd loved from years ago when he was a kid. "How 'bout these, baby?" he drawled when she came to him afterwards.

"Oooh, I like that one, oh, an' that one. I was thinking about these." She pointed to three songs she loved. "An' if the set goes well, maybe we can make it a weekly thing?" She tickled his earlobe with her tongue. "Pleeease."

"We'll see, baby, let's get through this week first," he said, grinning as he tried to catch her tongue with his teeth.

*****

Thursday night before the show, Tahlia and Vegas were in her dressing room getting ready for their set together.

"Now remember, it's the third set, an' don't forget your guitar," she reminded him for the hundredth time.

"Relax, baby," Vegas drawled, strumming his guitar. "I'll be here waitin' when you come off for a wardrobe change. It's okay, relax."

"I'm just nervous. I mean I'm nervous before every show, but especially nervous now. Why aren't you nervous, you should be nervous, why aren't you nervous, I am," she babbled and looked in the mirror one last time.

"It's okay, baby, I'm not nervous," he said, looking at her, "an' it's time for set one, so go." He pushed her out the door.

Tahlia breezed through the first set, then the second, before rushing off stage for a change. She ran into the dressing room. "Quick," she cried, yanking off her dress and pulling on skin tight jeans and a black leather vest. They both ran for the stage not a moment too soon.

Walking back out, Tahlia spoke to the audience. "I thought for a change, that tonight I might do something a little different. Tonight, I have invited someone to share the stage with me. He's someone extremely special to me, an' he's insanely gorgeous. An' I've known him for months. Please put your hands together, for my partner, Vegas." Holding her arm out to welcome him, she smiled lovingly as he swaggered out. God how she remembered that swagger.

Standing at the microphone that had been put there for him, Vegas nodded to the audience when they applauded. He was wearing his guitar, and as the lights changed, he started to strum. There was a look of concentration on his face while his fingers played with the strings. There seemed to be no nervousness as he closed his eyes and let his hands feel their way over the guitar. His left hand was holding down the strings as his right plucked them in just the right spots.

Vegas sang lead with Tahlia on backup. A heartfelt ballad filled with pain. Their voices playing in perfect tune and harmony together, floating along on the same wavelength, the same melody.

There was silence as they finished and launched into another song as the people started cheering. Two duets later, they both walked off stage to a thunderous applause.

Tahlia quickly changed for the last set. "They love you," she cried out excitedly.

Vegas grinned. "Yeah, they do, baby, but I'd rather watch you. Off you go." He pushed her out the door again.

Going upstairs later, they laughed, excited by the show. "We have got to do that every week," Tahlia insisted. "We just have to!"

"I'll think about it, baby," Vegas drawled, and they headed for the shower.

*****

The next day Vegas left, still on a high from the night before. Tahlia was getting sick of him leaving every second weekend, but Vegas said it just wasn't up for discussion.

"Discussion my foot," she mumbled, sitting in her dressing room before the show. Another bouquet of roses from Diega sat on the counter, the perfume drenching the room in a sweet heavenly scent. He was still leaving one every night. Vegas thought it very inappropriate and that he should teach Diega to leave her alone. She had calmed him down by reminding him that Diega was letting him live there even though *he* wasn't an employee.

She hadn't spoken to Diega for two weeks. Not since he tried to kiss her in his pool and she'd run away, freaking out. Seeing him in the hotel every day, a tremor of lust would race up her spine, making her skin sizzle. She wanted to run to him every time but held herself back. She knew that if she did run to him, it would be inappropriate, and she didn't need problems with Vegas.

When Diega noticed her across the room, his smile lit up his face, but would then fade away into a look of sadness. Like someone had died, or a part of him had died instead.

Tahlia knew she was attracted to him, and if Vegas weren't in the picture, Diega would be the one. But if it weren't for Vegas, she may not be where she was, and that meant *NO* Diega. She sighed in frustration. *God. How can I have feelings for two men at the same time?*

*****

Saturday morning, Tahlia decided to stay in. Going to the hotel spa, she was worked on from head to toe. A massaging facial, body wrap, mud mask. She was waxed and scrubbed, filed and buffed, and after three hours she felt completely rejuvenated. She ate a lunch of Cajun chicken salad, and then it was time to spend a few hours by the pool. Lying in an open, but private cabana, sipping icy fruit juice, she was reading when

Diega sat down on the pool lounge beside her.

"Hello."

She looked up in surprise, not sure what to say after the last time they parted. "Hi," she finally managed.

"I see that you're alone again."

"Yeah. It seems to be a regular thing now." She felt nervous with Diega so close, remembering his tanned, muscular body, and the way his swim trunks had skimmed his hardness. Now, he was in his usual black suit and matching shirt.

And damn he looked good.

"I also know that you spent the morning in the spa getting the works. You look very…refreshed," Diega murmured, eyeing her appreciatively.

"I thought once a month would be a good thing," she croaked, her mouth dry. "Since I work five nights I have to look my best." She flushed as his gaze roamed her body. She had chosen a sea green bikini, which wasn't skimpy, but a little revealing.

"Well, you definitely look your best. Do you have sunscreen on? You don't want to burn." He reached for the bottle.

"I have it on, it's okay," she said quickly, fighting the feelings creeping up inside of her. Her nipples hard, wanting his touch, so she crossed her arms in front of her to hide them. Rushing on nervously, she said, "I have to stay out of the sun, after all, you can see my spots, I need to be careful." She was rambling now, unable to stop, trying not to let her feelings show. "I hate my spots. There's so many I wish I didn't have them. I call myself the world's largest dot-to-dot puzzle," she joked.

Diega grinned. "Well." His velvety voice was low and seductive as he leaned toward her. "I love puzzles… can I play?" His eyes were dark passion filled pools calling to her to come swim in them.

Tahlia was breathless, mesmerised, unable to look away. She didn't know what to say or do, her heart was thundering, her blood sizzling through her veins. She didn't notice her book fall from her grasp until it landed with a thud on the ground between them.

The moment broken, Diega looked down and picked it up. "Nancy Drew, Girl Detective." Handing it back to her, he grinned and leaned back in his seat. "I was a Hardy Boys guy myself."

Tahlia nodded, gazing at him. "I can see you as Frank Hardy."

"Really? Not Joe?" He was surprised.

"Definitely Frank. Tall, dark, handsome. Straight head on your shoulders, not a hot head like Joe."

"Yes, I see it now." He nodded in agreement. "I had a whole set of Hardy Boys with the blue spines when I was a kid. In fact, I still have them somewhere. They came in handy when…when my mother died. I read them about five times each." His face fell at the drenching up of old memories. "How about you, how long have you read Nancy Drew?"

Not sure how much she wanted to reveal, she started slowly. "Since I was a kid. My Dad would buy me a book every time one came out. But as I got older things, circumstances, changed." She didn't want to go on.

"What happened?" Diega asked quietly.

She sighed and looked away. "My Dad died when I

was ten, so I stopped getting books, an' Mom couldn't afford them when we moved 'cause we had no money. She got rid of all of them an' I had nothing." She wiped a few tears away, feeling sad. "Every time we moved to a new town I would raid the local library, getting my hands on what I could. It's just been since getting this job that I've had the money to restart my collection. This is one of the newer series. An' I've discovered online auction sites, so I've been able to get a lot of what I used to have an' then some."

Diega's heart melted at her story. Knowing the pain of losing a parent, he wanted to make her pain go away, resolving there and then that he would. "Do you have them displayed in your suite?" he asked.

"Kinda. Some are stacked on the small bookcase in the living room, but most of them are packed up in boxes."

"Well, we'll have to do something about that, won't we. Will you join me for dinner?" He looked hopeful.

"I don't know if that's a good idea," Tahlia said slowly, remembering the heat they had generated in his pool that night.

"I understand completely. You're unsure, following my actions two weeks ago, and I apologise for making you uncomfortable. I should not have pushed myself on you. I'm very sorry." Diega looked at her apologetically, waiting.

She smiled slowly and was impressed. No man had said sorry before, besides Vegas when he'd hurt her that time. But despite the warning siren going off in her head, the flashes of his lips closing in on hers, the softness of his chest hair, and the heat of his skin, she so desperately wanted to be with him. Was that wrong? *Of course it was, but hell who cares an' besides, what harm would it do,* she thought. "Okay, but only if it's in one of the hotel restaurants."

"Okay. Be ready at seven. I'll see you then." Walking off, he chatted and joked with swimmers as Tahlia gazed at his retreating figure.

*****

At six, there was a knock on the door, and Tahlia ran to open it. "You're early," she cried, thinking it to be Diega. Before her stood Doris, her costumer, and Nicky, who was the hair and make-up stylist for her shows.

"We were told to come and help you, miss," Doris said, carrying a dress bag which she put on the couch. "We're to get you ready for dinner."

"Really? Did Diega do this?" She was very surprised.

"Yes, miss, now let's get you ready."

There was a flurry of excitement as the two women worked their magic. At five minutes to seven, they were done, and Tahlia looked in the full-length mirror in her closet.

The dress was stunning. An array of blue hues in a silky, shiny fabric that shimmered as she turned, bringing out a hint of blue in her sparkling green eyes. The bodice was low-cut and cinched at the waist, the skirt flowing to her knees. The sleeves were quite wide and floated around her elbows. She stepped into matching heels and spun around, the gorgeous gems sparkling in her ears were way beyond dazzling.

Diega had not only bought her the dress, but matching jewellery. Earrings, necklace, bracelet. All shades of blue. No man had given her jewellery before, ever.

Her shoulder length brown hair was swept up into a French twist, and her make-up was perfect. She felt very glamorous and elegant, having never owned anything like what she was wearing. This was still new to her as she was only now becoming used to wearing glamorous clothes for her stage shows. But that was for work, and this was personal. A man had bought her a gorgeous dress and matching jewels.

The knock on the door sent Doris and Nicky scurrying, and they left as Diega walked into the suite, ready for seeing his Tahlia.

"Are you read…eee?" He stopped in his tracks, his eyes widening in surprise. *My God, she's beautiful. I have to have her,* he thought. "God you look amazing, beautiful, incredible, stunning," he breathed, unable to control his thoughts as they spilled out. Her curves were killing him, making him hard in an instant, hoping she didn't notice, hoping she did. The soft curving of her voluptuous breasts into the dip of the neckline, the way the dress skimmed down seductively over her womanly hips.

Smiling, Tahlia spun around slowly, taking in his appearance. Crisp black tuxedo and white shirt which was undone a few buttons revealing his soft chest hair. His hair was slicked back neatly, and he was cleanly shaven. The scent of his aftershave wafted throughout the room. Damn, he looked good.

"My God, you look amazing," he repeated.

Walking up to him, she shyly kissed him on the cheek. "Thank you for the dress, an' the jewellery is beautiful," she said, touching the necklace. "No man's ever given me such incredible gifts before, I don't know what else to say," she shrugged, "except, thank you."

"Diamonds," Diega answered, eyeing her hungrily. "Beautiful, incredible diamonds."

"Oh, my God, Diega, no, diamonds. They must be so expensive. I can't accept them." She was distraught. Her head shook no, yet her eyes were saying yes as she reached for the back of the necklace. Her hands were trembling, so she tried to grab at an earring to remove it. "I can't accept them, I can't," she cried.

Diega caught her hands in his and kissed them. "My darling, my beautiful sweetheart, diamonds belong around your neck. You deserve them. You deserve the very best of everything. And I can give you everything you want. Anything your heart desires. Anything you crave," his voice dropped to a whisper as he leant toward her and kissed her.

Electricity raced through her as his lips met hers in a slow sensual dance. It was only a moment, but the power scared her, left her gasping for breath.

Diega wanted to rip the dress from her body, to ravish her there and then. To touch her soft ivory flesh, feed on her sweet plump lips, satisfy the incurable passion and desire he had for her. His feelings must have been noticeable, because Tahlia pulled away, shaking.

"Don't, please," she begged in a whisper and wrapped

her arms around herself trying to calm her blazing nerves.

Seeing her intense discomfort, Diega backed off, gathered his thoughts, and cleared his throat. Running his hand over his mouth, he looked around and laughed nervously. "Again, I must apologise. I seem to act before I think and I'm very sorry. I can't seem to control myself around you very well. I understand if you don't wish to have dinner with me." He saw the war of emotions on her face. "I'll leave." He turned and walked toward the door.

"No! Wait," she cried out, trying to sort her own feelings out.

Her brain was screaming. *NO. What did I tell you this afternoon? There will be trouble, trouble I tell ya. TROUBLE.*

Her heart was pleading. *YES. You want to be with him, you know you do. To feel his fingers skim your body, his arms around you as you slow dance. His soft luscious lips on yours 'cause God they make you sizzle.*

She went with her heart.

There will be TROUBLE, her mind screamed again, but she ignored it, feeling dizzy and lightheaded with lust.

Diega had been having his own mental conflict. *You FOOL, how could you keep pushing her. Every time a little more and she runs. God look at her face, her emotions so bare, so real. Please God, let her say yes. I so desperately want to be with her, have her, make her mine. Please let her say yes.*

"I…I still want to have dinner with you." Her fingers

touched her forehead as she got a hold of herself. "Otherwise, this stuff will go to waste," she joked and tried to cover her emotions by twirling the skirt of her dress.

Diega grinned softly. *YES!* he thought, *she said YES.* He held out his left arm for her to take. "Shall we?" he asked softly and escorted her downstairs.

They dined at the best restaurant in the hotel. Diega had a private area that was just for him, ready at all times, and Tahlia was enjoying herself despite the inner war from before.

They drank fine wine and ate delicious seafood. Dessert was the best tasting raspberries and rich Belgian chocolates. Dancing to the music playing overhead, she felt alive in Diega's arms. She felt special. Wanted. She tried to keep her feelings in check not wanting to lead him on. Wanting *him* to lead *her* on.

"Tahlia."

"Mmm?" She hadn't realised her mind had wandered.

"Are you enjoying yourself?" Diega asked, spinning them around.

The touch of his hand on her back sent her tingling. *God, he dances so well that I don't want to stop.* "Yeah. Yeah, I am." The scent of his aftershave drifted around her as they danced cheek to cheek, and before she knew it, she sighed. "Mmm, God you smell good."

He pulled back, gazing at her as she blushed. "I taste good too," he said lightly.

Her heart pounded furiously as she stared into his eyes. Unable to move. Unable to breathe. Rooted to the spot as time stood still.

He watched her as she watched him, the blush rising from her neck to her cheeks as she tried not to fall apart. His heart was pounding just as furiously as hers, and he knew because he could hear it. He could see the soft flesh of her left breast twitch softly, beating in time with the pounding muscle beneath.

Diega stood still, holding her, the one woman he wanted more than any other in the world. The one woman he would make his. And only his. He breathed in her perfume, light, fruity. It combined with her own womanly scent and held him captivated, in a place where all things, all time, just fell away. He was completely taken. Taken to a place he never knew existed. Never believed he could go to. A place he never wanted to leave.

Time, unfortunately, came back to the present, and he found himself once again standing in the middle of the restaurant dance floor.

"Would you like more wine?" he asked lightly as he caught his breath.

"Um, no. I'm…ah…feeling a little lightheaded," she muttered, feeling foolish.

"I don't think that's from the wine," Diega said, gazing intently at her.

She breathed heavily, unable to tear her gaze from his. "I should go," she gasped in a rush of words as a headiness came over her.

"Do you have to?" he asked, his voice low and seductive.

"No," she whispered, her voice barely audible as everyone around them disappeared.

Taking her hand, Diega led her through the hotel,

thinking a tour might give them time to catch their breath. They stopped in one of the clubs to see the band playing, and after a few minutes they moved on to the casino where she played a few slots. Passing a blackjack table, Tahlia asked Diega if he played.

"I do play several games, but not here. Once a month I get together with some friends, and we play a few rounds. Relax. Have a drink."

He led her to the lobby where a pianist was playing for the public. Nodding to him, Diega sat down when the player got up. Moving his hands expertly over the keys, he began to sing a song she had never heard. It was a romantic ballad full of love and passion, and the way he gazed at her while he sang made her feel hot and *very* aroused.

God, she thought, *just when I was calming down from before an' feeling normal again.* She was embarrassed by the attention since the crowd had stopped to listen, and politely applauded when the song was over, knowing it was her he had been singing to.

"Thank you, thank you." Diega bowed to his audience and stepped over to Tahlia. Holding out his arm, he led her outside to the maze of gardens.

Walking around the rose garden, she gave her praise. "How long have you played, you do it so well. An' I've never heard that song before it was beautiful. Where's it from?"

Diega's laugh was light. "Whoa, one at a time, ah, well, let's see. How long have I played, all my life just about. I was one of those children who sang and danced around the house wanting to be a rock or pop star. We had a piano, so I was always tinkling the ivories, and along with my books, music helped after my mother died," his voice softened.

Tahlia knew the pain.

"I picked up every instrument I could get my hands on that summer and learned how to play it. And even though I moved into business, running then owning hotels, I continued my passion for music. I haven't written a song for years, but lately, I've had amazing inspiration." He turned to face her, his hands on her arms, holding her. "I've felt such incredible desire to write again, to put all my thoughts into song. To tell of my love and passion for a woman I've met. The same passion I see in you, *saw* in you at the audition. I'd been watching for about half an hour, and while others were good, there was something about you. Something different." His gaze was dark and seductive, and turning her on immensely.

Feeling incredibly nervous, she glanced around at the gardens. "Wow, the, ah, gardens look beautiful at night, the lights show it off perfectly. They really do," she mumbled, barely breathing, not wanting to look at him in case she gave in to her heart that was pleading to taste his luscious full lips.

"Tahlia." His voice flowed gently, like warm honey, and it made her look up. Gazing deeply into her eyes, he leaned toward her while pulling her against his chest.

YES, YES, her heart screamed as their lips met and sizzled. She clung to him, the electricity setting her on fire as he softly moved his lips over hers. She reacted, delving her tongue into his mouth, tasting him, his tongue, and the manliness inside.

Pulling back, she looked at him in shock.

He was shocked too that she had reacted. Before he could say or do anything a scared and guilty look came over her face.

"I, I can't, I'm sorry," she cried, fleeing for the safety of her suite.

Diega watched her run, feeling shocked and surprised, aroused and encouraged. She had reacted to him by kissing him back. She'd never done that before, always pulled away and ran, scared by her feelings. But this time, she had returned the kiss, and now he knew that she wanted him too, but was scared and worried about letting her feelings take her over. He would capture her heart and make her love him as he knew only she could. Only she would. But she had fears buried deep inside, and he was very determined to rid her of all of them. Determined to make her his.

Chapter 12

Sunday morning, Tahlia was going through her books when there was a knock at the door. When she opened it, she saw Diega and several other men were standing there.

"May we come in?" Diega asked with a smile.

"Um, okay," she replied, unsure of who the men were and why they were coming into her hotel suite with tool boxes in their hands.

She was also feeling very uneasy after last night. However, Diega didn't seem affected at all, like their kiss had never happened. Like her reacting to him had never happened. *How dare he forget what happened last night,* she thought, furiously.

What are you angry for, it's not like you're dating or a couple or anything, you have Vegas. So what are you angry at Diega for? her brain asked.

Oh, God, you're right. What was I thinking?

Obviously, you weren't!

Deciding to play it cool like Diega, she watched as he looked around the room.

"Right here, I think," he said, pointing to the space to the right of the door. "Then you can use the L shape of the two walls and have the bookcases together with a desk in front. And maybe a small shelf system or cupboard to separate the space from the entrance."

"What's going on?" she asked, confused.

"Remember yesterday by the pool, when we talked about your Nancy Drew books?" Diega asked, facing her. "You said there wasn't enough shelving. Well, these men are going to measure the space, and put in bookcases so you can house your books."

Tahlia was shocked. "You don't need to do that," she said, shaking her head.

"I want to. The bookcases won't take long, and I'll even help you put your books out." He smiled at her as the men finished up.

"We'll be back soon," he said, and they all left.

She stood there for a moment and shook her head in disbelief, then walked over to the small shelving unit that was already there. A quarter of her books were on it, so she carried them to the dining table before moving the boxes that held the rest, only stopping long enough to order lunch.

Thirty minutes later, Diega arrived with room service, having rung the kitchen to order extra for himself. While they sat on the couch eating, the workmen drilled holes in the wall so they could bolt the bookcases in place.

"I can't believe you're doing this," she said between mouthfuls of smoked chicken wrap. She felt her heart pound at the intensity of what he was doing for her.

Diega looked at her, wishing he could tell her how he felt. *She must already know after what happened last night. She kissed me back.* He remembered the softness of her lips as if they were there now, lying under his, imprinting themselves on his memory, his soul. He loved her, and he wanted her. *I'll tell her soon, just not yet. I must get her away from Vegas by showing her what an animal he is. Then, she'll come to me with open arms. And an open heart.*

"Well," he said softly, "I know how important the things that you love are. From our conversation yesterday, I saw how important Nancy Drew was to your childhood. Just like the Hardys were to me. Since you've started your collection again, you need somewhere decent to display them, and so, I'm supplying glass door bookcases."

Looking at him with tears in her eyes, she barely managed a thank you, laughing softly as she wiped her face.

"You're very welcome," Diega replied, wanting to wipe those tears away himself.

"We're done, sir," one of the workmen said, and they left after Diega thanked them.

"So," he said excitedly. "Let's unpack."

Deciding which shelves to keep for which books took a while. They had a good time though, moving sets from shelf to shelf until Tahlia found the right places for everything.

"God, I didn't know there were so many," Diega said, handing her some books.

"Well, there are ten different series," she replied, laughing. "I only have a few, but I'm definitely gaining on them all."

"Ten! The girl gets around," he said, laughing with her. "What have you got so far?"

"The Series, the Files, Be a Detective, although there's only six books in that set. Super Mysteries, Notebooks, On Campus, a spin-off called River Heights, Girl Detective, Girl Detective graphic novels, an' Clue Crew. Not to mention pc games, toys, board games, collectables, movies an' TV series, books on Nancy, or Nancy an' the Hardys, reference books, you name it, it's out there, an' after all, the girl *is* in her eighties." Tahlia gasped for breath.

"If all that's out there," he said incredulously, unable to comprehend it all, "then there's a lot more to come. Isn't there?"

"Yep." She turned from Diega to look at her collection. "I love the internet. I've managed to get the whole set of 124 Files in one go. I've got all the new series, plus been able to track down the 36 Super Mysteries, 69 Notebooks an' 6 Be a Detectives. I've nearly completed the River Heights an' On Campus series, plus the pc games. I've got some reference books too, here have a look," she said, handing a book to Diega. He flicked through it and she continued.

"The original series is the biggest at 175 books. Problem is, there are many printings. White spine djs, picture spine djs, yellow spine picture covers, the equivalent to your Hardy blue spine books." She glanced at him. "There are three different sets of paperbacks, plus hardcovers, an' special editions. Not to mention all the foreign editions. My God, there's so many," she said, flopping down onto the couch beside Diega who had sat down when she handed him the reference book.

"So, that's why you wanted a blue Mustang convertible. Nancy Drew drives one," he said, looking at her with dancing eyes.

"Yeah," she said, blushing, "it is. But by the time they gave her one, it was the mid-eighties so she would have had one from then. Whereas every time I think of her car, I see a sixties 'Stang, so I got one of those." She grinned at Diega who grinned back.

"I can see they mean a lot to you, reminds you of the happier times of your childhood," he said quietly and looked at her. His heart ached for her, knowing what it was like to have a childhood ripped apart by the tragic loss of a parent. It was unfair. It wasn't right. He vowed to change her life.

"Yeah, they do," she said softly.

"Well," he said, looking back at the book in his hands. "I think I'll have to do my own research on Nancy Drew and scour your collection, so I know what to get you that you don't already have." *I'll do a lot more than that,* he thought, *I'll buy her everything she doesn't have. And then, she will love me.*

"You don't have to get me anything. You have given me this amazing suite. Believe me, I've never lived anywhere so fancy. You supply all my clothes an' accessories not only for the stage, but you pay for a personal credit card. Yes, I do know that you pay for it." She looked at him as he gazed at her in surprise. "Apparently I'm the only one with a "staff credit card"," she made quotation signs with her fingers, "no one else has one. So, everything I buy, you pay for. An' now," she motioned in the direction of the bookcases, "this."

Diega turned his body toward her and took her hands in his, suddenly very serious. "Tahlia, I want to make you the star of Las Vegas, and if that means buying you everything you need or want then so be it. Besides, this suite is reserved for stars, and *you,* are definitely a star." He gazed at her deeply. "I want you to have everything," he said, his voice low. "*Everything* your heart desires."

Tahlia felt the world spinning. Never had any man offered her whatever she wanted, and she already felt extremely lucky to have her job and the suite. And here was Diega wanting to give her anything and everything she would and could ever want. She didn't know what to do. Should she take him up on his offer, or tell him it was inappropriate for him to be saying such things. She shifted nervously on the sofa and glanced away.

Seeing her discomfort, he let go of her hands and walked over to the shelves to stand in front of them. "Do you like the desk in this position? Maybe you need a big comfy chair so you can sit and read."

Glad the moment was over, she moved over to him and put the reference book on its shelf. "I don't need a chair. I can sit on the couch, an' the desk is fine."

"Are you sure?" he asked, turning to her.

"I'm sure," she reassured him with a smile.

"Well, then, I will leave you to your collection." He walked toward the door.

Surprised he was leaving so suddenly, she called out, "Diega." It stopped him, and he turned to her expectantly. "Thank you, so much, for everything." She felt the heat rising to her cheeks. "Really, you've given me so much already, an' it's more than I've ever had in my whole life. An'" she paused, "it's more than I could ever hope for. Thank you." She tentatively walked over to him and reached up to kiss him on the cheek.

His arms automatically slid around her waist.

Pulling back, she was still so close to him, and both of them were breathless.

He kissed her.

Tahlia kissed him back, and her arms slithered around him. Their mouths moved together in a syncopated rhythm, their tongues delving, probing, tasting.

Tahlia reluctantly pulled back out of his embrace. "You should go," she breathed, her head spinning out of control as she toppled into a hazy passion filled abyss. She cleared her throat and crossed her arms in front of her, hiding her burgeoning nipples poking through her thin top.

"Have dinner with me?" he asked gently, gazing into her eyes.

She gazed back, breathing hard, but thinking about it. "I don't know…"

"Please." His gaze seduced her, wanted her. He stood still, letting the effect of their kiss bring her to the answer he knew he would get.

She sighed and closed her eyes for a moment trying to decide. She felt herself swaying, not sure if she actually was, or if it was her mind playing tricks. Deciding it was all too hard and she didn't have the energy to fight, she finally gave in. Opening her eyes, she saw his now eager look. "Okay, but nothing formal," she said.

"I'll pick you up at seven," he said as his luscious lips spread into a smile.

"Okay," she breathed, still lightheaded, and watched him leave.

Sighing, she sat down on the couch feeling aroused. Her blood sizzled. She dropped her head into her hands. *Oh, God, am I missing Vegas or do I want Diega?* She knew her body reacted to him and God he was so amazing. Diega made her feel like no other man had. Vegas certainly didn't make her feel this way.

Vegas? Vegas who? her brain demanded. *What are you doing?*

I'm falling in love, that's what I'm doing.

Oh, please, with who?

With Diega. No wait, I can't be. She panicked, and her eyes widened in fright.

Why can't you be? It's not like Vegas is here anymore. He leaves you alone and expects you to what, just sit here and wait for him and never look at another man. Ever?

Oh, God, what am I gonna do? I can't have both of them.

You have to make up your mind little girl, you can't go on this way.

Yes, that's it, I have to make up my mind. But it's already made. I'm here with Vegas an' that's all there is to it.

Is that all there is?

Yes! That's all there is, she thought determinedly.

*****

At seven that night, Diega knocked on the door.

When she opened it, he was leaning casually against the door frame dressed in black jeans and a tight, short-sleeved black shirt that showed off the tanned, muscular arms crossed over his chest, making his muscles bulge even more.

"Still in black I see," she purred, her heart thundering as she took in the sight of his muscular arms and body and God what they could do to her. "You really don't dress in any other colour."

"Occasionally, but pretty much black." He grinned, seeing the look of lust on her face as she eyed him, and it stirred him. "You look great," he said, taking in her red floral silk mini dress. It clung to every sexy curve of her body, and he wanted to slide over those curves to taste the soft, sweet, sensual flesh down between her…

"So, where are we going?" she asked, bringing him back from dreamland. She saw his hair was parted on the left with a carefree lock over his forehead.

"Up on the roof. I thought I'd grill."

Tahlia was unsure, remembering what had happened in his pool. "I can't, after last time, we shouldn't…" she muttered, her voice drifting off. Her gaze slid down the bridge of his nose to the chiselled line of his jaw and the way his lips curled up at the ends.

"We're not going swimming," he promised.

Melting at his smile, she grinned. "Okay, let's go grill," she said and followed him around to his lift. When they walked out onto the roof, she saw everything was ready.

"Okay, here we go," Diega said, throwing some burgers

on. "We'll have burgers with salad, fruit and cake for dessert. How does that sound?"

"Sounds great, my stomach can't wait," she said, pouring them both drinks.

Fifteen minutes later they were eating burgers.

"Mmm, this is good," Tahlia mumbled around mouthfuls. She wiped sauce from her chin. *Wow, he's gorgeous, an' he cooks.*

"It is good, even if I do say so myself," Diega agreed, wanting to lick the sauce off as it dribbled down her delectable chin.

Dessert was just as good.

"God I love this chocolate cake. I have it all the time. It's so light and fluffy."

"If you eat it all the time how do you stay in shape?" Diega eyed her figure hungrily.

"Lots of sex," she said, then choked on the piece she'd put in her mouth before making the comment. Closing her mouth, she flushed the same colour as her dress, and swallowing awkwardly, played with the rest of her cake.

"Lots of sex suits you," Diega flirted seductively, his voice low and throaty. He gazed at her hungrily, feeling like he hadn't eaten in days, if not weeks. He wanted to eat her, eat every tasty morsel that she was.

Unable to look at him, Tahlia rushed over to the railing and gripped it for dear life as she gazed out over the city. *God what just happened,* she thought, feeling her blood boil through her veins. *I can't do this, I can't do this, deep breaths, count to ten slowly.*

Diega came up behind her and grabbed her arms,

turning her around to face him. "I want you," he breathed and pulled her toward him. "I've wanted you from the first moment I saw you at your audition." He kissed her passionately, the way a real man kisses a woman. With power and desire. Lust and hunger. It was running so deeply through his veins that the fierceness of it penetrated through to his very core. Scared him to the marrow of his bones, and exhilarated his living, gasping soul. His tongue plundered her mouth with a desperate need to taste her and the chocolatey sweetness inside.

It was pure tongue sex!

She feebly tried to push him away, but couldn't hold on any longer. *I...can't...do this...* The thought vaguely floated through her mind for a second before she gave in, kissing him back with a force she'd never felt before.

Their hands raced over each other's body. Their mouths crashed together.

Tahlia's hands slid down his body and underneath his shirt to feel him. Finding the snap buttons on his shirt, she ripped it open, yanked it down his shoulders, and threw it onto the ground. Her hands and mouth explored his hard, muscular torso, her tongue ran over him as his hands slid over her.

Pulling her mouth back to his, Diega picked her up and carried her over to the couch. They fell onto it, their mouths still kissing hungrily. Their bodies were on fire, a raging fire that was out of control, blazing across their inhibitions unable to be quenched.

Tahlia groaned in pleasure as his hands seared down

over her body and under her dress, sliding it up to reveal a red bra and panties.

He pulled down her bra, wanting to feel, wanting to see, wanting to taste. "Oh, my God," Diega gasped, tasting her body – it was like fine wine – moulding her breasts into the shape of his hands, bringing louder groans from her.

Tahlia cried out as his chest hair came into contact with her naked flesh, setting her bare breasts alight with such intensity she thought she was going to burn up and explode. His lips were doing so much damage as they moved over her skin, tasting her sweetness, drinking her like she was the only thing that could quench his thirst.

His right hand slid down over her body and thrust into her panties, so ready to feel her wet womanhood and what he'd done to it.

"No...wait...don't." The breath tore out of her throat, and she grabbed his hand. "No, wait, I can't do this," she gasped raggedly and pushed him away. Rolling off the couch, she swayed to her feet, fixed her bra, and pulled down her dress.

"Why can't you do this?" Diega demanded, getting up and grabbing her. "Why can't you do this?" he repeated, pulling her to him.

"No," she cried, trying to push him back. "I can't do this. I can't, it's not right. I'm with Vegas. I love him, we're a couple. I won't cheat on him." She looked at him desperately, wanting him to understand the predicament he'd put her in. The one she wanted to get out of. After all, she was with Vegas. And that's all there was to it. But she had feelings for the man before her.

That was undeniable, and she wouldn't deny it if she were asked anyway.

"Vegas," Diega spat the name with contempt. "You mean *that animal* that leaves you alone every fortnight to go off and do *God knows what with God knows who*. The animal that doesn't treat you the way you deserve to be treated. I love you, I want you, I *want* to make you happy. I *want* to give you everything your heart has ever desired." He pulled her to him, seeing her cry at his words. He was on the verge himself, just dying inside at not making her his. "Let me love you. Let me love you. Let me make you happy," he whispered and kissed her again.

"No," she cried, pushing him away with new found strength. "I won't cheat on him." She ran for the stairwell that would take her down to her suite.

Diega was desperate.

He was angry.

So angry he picked up a glass from the coffee table and threw it at the doorway Tahlia had just fled through. "Damn that man, that animal," he violently waved his arms around in emphasis, "he doesn't treat her right, but here she is, she doesn't want to cheat on him. Ha! If only she knew."

Breathing hard he sat down on the couch, put his head in his hands, and cried out in frustration over the woman he loved.

*****

He breathed hard, aching for her, watching her cry for

a while before falling into a fitful sleep.

He'd watched her perform that week. Every week. And was very disturbed to see Vegas join her onstage during Thursday night's show. The audience had thought it was great, the women swooning over that filthy animal. Then Friday, he was gone again.

Seems he prefers the occasional company of ill-gotten people instead of being with her. I don't think he's ever told her he loves her, he mused. He had heard her say it several times, but all Vegas had said was, 'me too, baby'.

Alone for another weekend, she'd gone to the spa then laid by the pool in that fetching bikini that showed off a light tan. Dinner was in one of the hotel restaurants.

She thought her life was so easy, with her job and a suite to call her own. Yet her life was becoming so complicated, with so many men wanting her. Loving her. Needing to make her theirs while hiding their secrets in the past. Hoping they stayed there. Taken care of. Well hidden. For no one to ever find out about.

Little does she know, he thought, taking a sip of wine, that her life is about to be so much more devastating. So painful, yet, so joyous at the same time.

He smiled wickedly. She really has no idea.

He loved her. He wanted her. He would have her.

Looking at the photo of Vegas in his hand, he knew it wouldn't be long.

Chapter 13

Monday afternoon, Tahlia was sitting on the sofa in her suite when Vegas barged in, slamming the door behind him. Knowing that action well from years gone by, she said nothing, her eyes wide, her heart pounding. She watched him as he stalked into the bedroom and threw his bag down on the floor, leaving it where it landed.

He showered, and walking out with a towel around his hips, dug into his bag for a cigarette. Lighting it, he took a long drag and held it, then blew it out in an exhausted sigh. He came into the living room and noticed her for the first time. "What are you doin' here, don' ya have rehearsal or somethin'?" He sounded angry to find her.

Puzzled, Tahlia just looked at him, not sure what to say. She knew angry men and infuriating them was not a good thing. But then Vegas was different. Wasn't he?

"Well?" he demanded and then noticed the bookcases and desk. "What the…where'd they come from," he said, waving his arm toward them. "Diega, that's it in' it. *He* did that."

Becoming angry herself, she snapped. "Rehearsal is

over, I'm sitting here reading a book, an' *yes,* Diega put the bookcases in for me. *Not* that it's any of *your* business."

The look Vegas gave her showed several emotions. It went from dark and angry that she spoke to him that way, to shocked and surprised that she had stood up to him. Finally, it softened when he realised he had spoken badly. "I'm sorry, baby."

"Whatever," she sighed, going back to her book.

"What do ya mean whateva?" Vegas yelled a moment later. "What's gotten inta ya? I go 'way for a weekend, I get back an' ya give me lip." He strode over to the sofa, so ready for a confrontation, *especially* after the weekend he'd had. But Tahlia stood up to face him before he got there.

"Oh, please, what's gotten inta *me. You're* the one who keeps leaving every fortnight an' this is your third time. Every time you come home you're a little different. Just a little bit, but it's definitely noticeable. You talk a little different, you act a little different, a bit more angry, a bit more rough. Now I know that you may have been this way before I met you, considering what I know, but you had never been that way with me till your weekends with Manny. Whatever you're doing I want it to stop, or I don't know if I can continue putting up with it. I'd had enough of abuse before I met you, I won't put up with it again. *Not* from *you.*" She was breathing hard and on the verge of tears.

Vegas looked at her as if weighing up what to say. "I told you last time, baby," his voice low and menacing, "my weekends with Manny aren' up for discussion."

His tone lightened. "But I'm sorry if my actions weren' appropriate. I don' wan' you to leave, baby." His hand reached for her.

She pulled away, not sure if she wanted him touching her. "That's what it may come down to."

Vegas angered again. "Yeah, right, *you're* gonna leave *me*. What are ya gonna do without me? I made you, I brought you here, an' if ya hadn' noticed, *I'm* not the only one in this room with problems, baby, *so are you*. Secrets that you don' wan' anyone knowin'. Wanna keep 'em locked away hopin' no one will find out. Well, I may have shot the attendant, baby, but you killed ya boyfriend. So don' stand there with that shocked look on ya face 'cause you heard it months ago on the radio just like I did. An' in fact, I heard it again this mornin'. The cops are still lookin' for the killer. A woman, a brunette woman. Oh, wait, that's you," Vegas yelled, pointing his finger at her angrily.

"You heard it again…this morning?" she asked in a small voice, suddenly worried. She had been feeling safe, like it was finally, hopefully, over.

"Yeah, baby, I heard it this mornin'." He looked at her, now worried himself. *If the cops catch up with her an' arrest her, then we may be kicked out of the hotel. An' while my dealin's with Manny brings in money, it may not be enough to help her. Doesn' matter,* he thought, *the owner, that Diega guy that's always watchin' her will pay for everythin', an' I won' have to worry. I just can' let 'em find out what I been up to.*

Tahlia was pacing back and forth across the living room with an extremely worried look on her face. "I'm not a killer. I didn't kill him." She felt like she was on the verge of a breakdown. All these months she had hoped and prayed that it was over. The police hadn't come to arrest her, no crazy stalker had tried to hurt her. Wasn't it over?

"Doesn' matter if you did, baby, he abused you, you can say it was self-defence." Vegas stopped her and held her close. "It's okay, baby, I'll protect you. I won' let anythin' happen to you." He pulled back, took her face in his hands, and kissed her. "I'll make everythin' better, baby, I promise. I won' come home all grouchy an' mean, an' I won' hurt you ever." Staring deeply into her eyes, he went on. "I love you, baby. I love you an' I don' wan' to lose you. I love you." He kissed her passionately, his tongue sliding inside her mouth, stroking hers.

All thoughts of her past melted away as she kissed him back, totally elated that he had finally told her he loved her. She had said it many times herself, but he'd never returned it. Now, they ran their hands over each other, feeling the burning desires.

"You don' have to go yet do you, baby?" Vegas gasped.

"No," she mumbled against his mouth as he unhooked her bra and pushed her panties down. He'd already ripped her clothes off, so she yanked his towel down and wrapped her legs around his waist when he picked her up.

Not for a moment did they let go, falling onto the bed in a tangle of arms and legs, mouths and tongues. Vegas kissing and sucking every inch of her, his passion undeniable. Tahlia writhing and bucking as his fingers slid inside of her, holding him there, not letting go.

"Aaaahhh," she moaned, her voice tilting up at the end. Vegas thrust his tongue back into her mouth in synchronized movements with his fingers. Reaching the brink and going over the edge in seconds, she cried out in pleasure.

"More, more."

His fingers didn't let up, moving in circles inside of her, hard then soft. Circling the sensitive inner walls of her inner world, blowing her mind, making her quiver like an arrow that had just hit its target. Continually hitting the spot, her spot, making her convulse as shock wave after shock wave pounded through her.

She rode them.

High and low. Fast and slow.

Feeling the tide sweep her out then wash her back in for more of the rigorous torment Vegas was inflicting upon her. "Want you now," she gasped, spreading her legs as wide as she could.

"Not yet, baby," Vegas drawled, taking her right breast into his mouth. Sucking and licking, he toyed with her nipple, making it hard, lashing it with his tongue. He stopped. His fingers moved inside of her then stopped. He rubbed his soft lips over the velvety goodness of left breast, swirling hot kisses over her heaving mound of tasty flesh then he stopped. Moving his fingers inside, back and forth, he continued alternating between her breasts and her vagina in a tribal drumming of a primitive beat. Waiting as she reached her peak, again and again, letting her come down from each high before starting over.

"I need you now," she breathed raggedly.

"I need you too, baby," he said, rolling her onto her stomach.

"What are you doing?" She gasped harder.

Vegas lay on her back, his legs between hers, and entered her from behind.

"Ahh, oh, God," her voice barely audible. He slid his hands over her outstretched arms in front of them. Entwining their fingers, they pulled in their arms to lean up on their elbows.

Vegas kissed her neck, her shoulders, her back, plunging inside, hitting her spot with every movement.

Gasping in ecstasy, Tahlia bucked backward, pushing her crotch at him, giving him more access. "Harder, faster," she rasped.

Grinding with the rawness and hunger they both knew so well, Vegas grunted and drew his legs up further, so he was half kneeling behind her.

With hard final thrusts, he came inside of her, spilling himself into her, knowing his seed flowed through her. Making her *his* and *only* his.

Gasping for breath, they collapsed with Vegas still inside of her, throbbing. Tahlia felt him there, his hard dick, his testes pushing against her clitoris which had made the orgasm better, faster, more explosive. "God what you do to me." Her voice was ragged.

Pushing her hair aside so he could kiss her neck, Vegas grinned. "Baby," he said as his tongue played with her, "you do it to me, too." They lay there awhile, and he stroked her body, their legs entwined, his face beside hers.

"We should eat I suppose, show starts soon," she

said quietly.

"Mmm, I think we already ate, baby," Vegas drawled softly and kissed her skin.

Snickering, Tahlia pushed him away, and he protested. His shaft left her, making her feel empty, yet full of him at the same time. She ordered and dropped the phone back in its cradle. "All right, that's done," she said. "Let's go shower."

"Whoo, baby, I like the sound of that."

"Down boy," she said, slapping his hand away as it reached for her.

*****

So, he thought, watching Vegas' homecoming from his weekend away, he'd had it rough, but taking it out on poor Tahlia was not the done thing, although she definitely gave better than she got.

He chuckled at that, then stopped in disbelief as he saw her give in to him when he'd muttered the words 'I love you'.

The sex was raw and hungry and had been disgusting to watch, but he couldn't turn away as he saw her writhe and buck, his penis hardening at the excitement it felt at seeing her naked, hot flesh. Hot flesh that would mould to him as he rocked back and forth on top of her making her cry for more.

Vegas knew nothing about love, but he definitely knew how to make her scream out in waves of ecstasy.

"I should be the one to doing that to her," he hissed, "screwing her senseless like she's never known. Shoving

it into her with every ounce of strength I have. Feeling her naked body under mine as I rub myself over her, slide myself into her, make her feel the fires burning inside of me as I release them to the wild."

He took a deep breath and exhaled slowly. Watching Tahlia naked and screaming always made him hot under the collar. And in his pants. He waited until his breathing became even before glancing at Tahlia again.

"Oh, yes, my dear. It will be me *doing that to you. One day, very soon."*

*****

For the next two and a half days, in between rehearsals for her show and the set with Vegas, Tahlia was in her suite with the new laptop she'd bought soon after getting her first pay cheque. She searched the internet as much as she could, trying to find information on the murder she might have committed. Unfortunately, it all said the same thing.

That Wayne Brady had been shot to death in his own home and the woman he lived with might either be a witness or the killer.

How do they know I had been living there? she thought. *I didn't have much to my name, an' I barely went out. But the neighbours did see me a few times, an' maybe someone saw me take the car.*

But that didn't jive with her nightmares.

The blood and gun, yeah, sure, but the stranger in the shadows, her running. She had been feeling safe and secure at the hotel. If she were being watched, she wouldn't have known, since so many people saw her show night after night, week after week.

"I don't know," she sighed, "maybe there's only one thing I can do to find out, an' that's hire an investigator to search." She knew Diega had detectives at his disposal, so maybe she should ask him for help since he was the go-to guy for his staff. The thought of Diega and what they had done made her shiver with excitement. Oh, God, his mouth, his hands, his touch. Remembering the way he had felt aroused her.

"Stop this, stop this," she said forcefully just as Vegas walked through the suite door.

"Stop what?" he asked suspiciously.

She jumped, her head spinning around to see him standing there. "Huh, umm, I need to stop jumping on the net, it's making me cross-eyed," she recovered quickly, and her heart pounded nervously. She hoped he didn't notice.

Vegas grinned. "Well, baby, I'm here to take you down for the show." He looked serious all of a sudden. "Or, I could just take you down." The connotation was evident.

Tahlia grinned back, glad the Diega moment had passed. "You cheeky shit," she said, standing, "is that all you think about. Sex. Ha, typical male, you think with the head between your legs not the one between your shoulders." She slapped him lightly on the arm as she walked past him. "We'll go *downstairs* for the show."

*****

That night, the show went well. They had been having theme nights, and tonight's was country. Wearing different shirts, tops, and boots for each set, Tahlia strutted around the stage belting out songs that talked about love. Love and betrayal, love lost and won and love everlasting.

During the third set, she and Vegas wore matching bandannas since he didn't want to ponce around in a country shirt. He looked quite funny in his trademark tight white singlet, even tighter blue jeans, and a bright blue bandanna around his forehead. Not very country, right?

When Tahlia had wrapped it around his neck, he'd ripped it off, saying he felt like he was choking and didn't want to wear it, but relented when she asked him how *he* wanted to wear it. He had promptly wrapped it around his head.

The show went very well, with the crowd loving it so much they started line dancing early on. Many of them had dressed for the evening by wearing cowboy hats or decorative shirts, and they were definitely having a good time.

Tahlia had even suggested hay bales and a bucking bronco to go with the cactus plants and tumbleweeds the props manager had come up with.

The music director applauded them after the show. "That was one of the better theme nights we've had so far guys. It was fantastic. We'll certainly be doing it again!"

*****

Friday night after the show, Tahlia and Vegas ran out to her waiting car. They had planned a weekend away at a spa in the desert and were ready to leave when Diega came rushing out.

"Where are you going?" he demanded upon seeing their bags.

"Like it's any of your business," Vegas sneered.

Casting a dark look at Vegas, Tahlia turned to Diega. "We're going into the desert for the weekend, to one of those spa retreats."

"Why do you need to go there when we have a perfectly fine spa here?" Diega asked, sounding desperate.

Pushing Tahlia into the passenger side of the car and slamming the door, Vegas turned to Diega. "Just because *you* gave her a job doesn' mean *you* own her. So if *I* wan' to go away for the weekend with *my* woman, it ain' none of *your* freakin' business." He shoved his finger into Diega's chest. "Ya got that." He noticed the bodyguards move in and quickly jumped into the car and behind the wheel.

As they drove away, Tahlia looked back. The expression that passed over Diega's face was *not* a happy one.

He was angry. If she went away from the hotel for any amount of time, especially with Vegas, he couldn't protect her. And he had to.

"Did you make sure the GPS unit on her car was installed properly?"

"Yes, sir," one of his bodyguards said.

"Good. Have them followed and watched. Be

discreet. I don't want her knowing you're there. Protect her from everything," he turned to walk into the hotel but stopped and glanced back in the direction they had driven, "and *everyone*."

*****

Coming back from the spa on Monday morning, they felt refreshed and alive, and Tahlia had made a decision. Getting back in time for lunch, they went for rehearsals afterwards. When it was over Vegas wanted to go upstairs.

"I'm tired baby, let's go to bed." That damn sexy grin flirted with her.

"There's something I have to do first, besides, we were in bed all weekend an' never got out in case you've forgotten. Why don't you go on up an' get some hot romance happening, an' I'll be up in about fifteen minutes."

"What do you have to do?" Vegas asked suspiciously. Tahlia gave him a look that told him to back off, and Vegas put his hands up in protest. "Okay, baby, okay, none of my business. As long as it's got somethin' to do with you gettin' more of that fancy underwear I love you in."

Shoving him ahead of her toward the lift, Tahlia laughed at the face he pulled. "I'll be up soon," she said, walking off in a different direction.

"*I'm already up, baby,*" Vegas called after her, pretending to get into the lift as he watched her.

Laughing to herself, she stepped into the lift that

took her up to Diega's office, not seeing Vegas watching her from behind a hotel pot plant.

"Now what's she's goin' up to see him about," Vegas murmured, pulling a branch down to watch and becoming angry. "Looks like I'll just have to find out."

I hope I'm doing the right thing, she thought, standing in the lift, watching the numbers light up as she passed each floor. Walking down the hallway and into Kate's office, she saw the room was empty, so she knocked on his door.

"Come."

She opened the door and took a step into the luxurious office, momentarily blinded by the view. "Wow, this is…wow." She blinked a few times then came back to reality and faced him. "Uh, do you have a few minutes?" she asked, still unsure about doing it.

He had stood at the sight of her, watching her watch him. "Of course. Come in."

Locking the door behind her, so they weren't disturbed, she walked over to the desk.

"Have a seat," Diega said, gesturing to the chair next to her, waiting for her to sit before seating himself. Reaching for his phone, he buzzed Kate, who was now back at her desk. "Hold my calls and tell anyone with an appointment to come back."

He gazed at Tahlia. Except for the shows, and those few moments Friday night, he hadn't spoken to her since that night on the roof. When he had pushed himself on her. She had responded, but then ran…all because of Vegas. *God, I hate that man,* he thought viciously, then softened. *She looks so good. Lightly tanned, refreshed, but there's a look of worry on her very beautiful face.*

She moved uneasily in her chair and opened her mouth to say something, then closed it. She didn't know what to say, especially after the last time they had been together, but this was not about that. She needed his help because she was now becoming desperate.

"Tell me what's wrong," Diega said quietly, resting his elbows on his desk. He put his hands together in front of his face, thumbs crossed, forefingers touching at their tips. His other fingers bent at the knuckles and touching. This was something he always did when concentrating, it was a habit that he did unconsciously. His forefingers touched his lips as he waited patiently for the woman sitting in front of him.

Quietly, without looking at him, she spoke. "I think I killed someone." Finally, she looked up into his eyes. She was scared, but he wasn't.

In fact, he looked unconcerned.

"Tell me, why do you think you killed someone?" he asked.

"I lived with a guy called Wayne Brady for two years," she started, averting her eyes so she couldn't see his deep blue ones. "He beat me, an' one night I finally stood up to him an' hit back. He broke my nose, an' I was back to where I started. Then, suddenly, blank. I can't remember, an' I'm travelling down to New York in a car I don't own, don't know where I got it. I have nightmares about a gun, blood, a stranger in the shadows, an' I'm running. Then a few months ago I heard something on the radio, so this week, I Googled an' found that the police still haven't found his killer. The address an' descriptions of me an' the car all fits." Tears flowed down her face. "I think I killed him."

Diega walked around his desk and pulled her up into his arms. Holding her tightly, he stroked her hair while she cried.

Finally pulling back, she looked at him. "I know you have private detectives an' I thought you could help me an' dig around a bit. Find out what really happened." She was expectant, and he was more than happy to oblige.

"Of course I'll help," he said and kissed her forehead. "Don't you worry about it. You go and have a great week of shows. Know that you are safe and secure here. That I'll protect you and sort this out. Okay?"

Tahlia nodded, relieved. "Okay." She wiped her face and walked out of his office, closing the door behind her, knowing the man she loved was upstairs waiting for her.

Removing a folder from his cabinet, Diega sat down behind his desk, and opening the file, he looked over it. Wayne Brady, forty, married once, not for long. His wife left and divorced him citing violence and abuse. Several girlfriends had TROs out against him. His parents were dead, and he was an only child. He had a dead-end job, but seemed to spend a lot of money on women, booze, and drugs. Women weren't the only ones he abused, and the police had been keeping an eye on him. That's how they knew Tahlia had lived there. There was possible mob activity, but she was definitely the only suspect to date. His car disappeared with her, and there was no evidence of anyone else being in the house. That the police had found anyway.

Diega's investigators had dug up more on Wayne's illegal mob activities. Stealing, gun running, drug dealing, assault, not so minor, but enough to warrant the police checking up on him. They had found he was working for someone who worked for a big crime boss. A boss Diega knew well, having gone up against him before. One he would go up against again for the safety of the woman he loved.

If only Vegas knew who he'd gotten himself involved with because that was going to make it a million times worse.

Contemplating how to proceed, Diega closed the file and leaned back in his chair, gazing out the window over the city of Las Vegas.

*****

Interesting, he thought, leaning back in his chair. First Vegas had glued himself to her all week, never leaving her alone, even doing a set together on country night wearing matching bandannas. And now, he was curious about her meeting, scared she might find some answers to her predicament.

He hated seeing the two of them together on stage, that was bad enough, but then they'd left town Friday night to spend the weekend at a desert spa. And, of course, he'd watched her there too. Seeing every movement she made as she slithered and writhed around, screaming at the torrential torment Vegas inflicted upon her.

God, he'd wanted to do that to her. Feel her soft,

supple body under his as he ground back and forth on top of her, screwing her like she'd never been screwed before. Ram his hard dick inside of her until she begged him to stop. And even then he wouldn't. Thrusting harder and harder until she could no longer come, until he would explode inside of her, all over her, as his seed sought their magical release. God, she loved it rough, which surprised him, considering her past as the poor abused girlfriend.

Now, coming home, she wanted to know all about her ex-boyfriend, wanted help, reassurance, something or someone to tell her she didn't do it. She didn't kill him.

But little does she know…help is not on the way.

Chapter 14

During the week, Tahlia stopped by Diega's office every day to see if he had found anything.

"Not yet," he told her, "but I'm sure there will be news soon." His assurances, while somewhat comforting, made Vegas highly suspicious. And worried.

"You'd think with all his money he would've found out somethin' by now," he sneered Thursday afternoon before the show, wondering if he too was under investigation.

"I know," she sighed, wishing she hadn't told Vegas what she'd done, "but it's only been three days. He needs time."

The theme for the show was rock night, and they had decided to sing two songs Vegas had written. The songs were a big hit with the women in the audience who stood at the front of the stage screaming and reaching for him as he sang. Some even cried! And he lapped it up, like a dog dying of thirst. Reaching for *them*, holding *their* hands as he crooned to them. How sickening!

A couple of women even crawled up on stage and jumped all over him before security dragged them off.

One woman nearly ripped his top right off his body, and all the females screamed and surged forward as it hung at an odd angle, revealing his rock-hard six-pack with its snaky trail of golden-brown hair that weaved into his low slung jeans.

It made Tahlia sick with jealousy, but the rest of the crowd loved it, so what could she do. This was *her* show, but it seemed the women were only coming for Vegas, not her. *Well,* she thought later, *at least he's only on Thursday nights for one set. I am still the star of this show, and every night the crowd comes for* me.

Her jealousy was very unnerving as it was so unlike her. She'd never felt these feelings before, having never had anyone to be jealous of. It was obviously something she was going to have to get used to. Unless she told Vegas they wouldn't be doing any more sets together. Could she do that to him? Why not?

Vegas was very happy with the reception of his songs and decided to write more for upcoming shows. They talked about it as they stumbled into their suite afterwards, managing to be in and out of the shower in ten minutes.

"Wow, that's the first time we've showered together an' not had sex." Vegas was disappointed and raised a brow in concern.

Tahlia was still reeling from her jealousy, and while having sex with Vegas would have been a reassurance of her love for him, and his for her, she didn't know if she could, because of the way *he'd* acted toward the women in the audience. *Would he have sex with them?* she wondered. *Would he want them an' not me anymore? After all, there are so many gorgeous women in this place, why* wouldn't *he want to have sex with them?* Maybe she should have used her pent up sexual energy from the show and taken her anger over the women out on Vegas in the shower. Shown him that it was *her* that was the only one he would need to satisfy him. *God, what am I thinking, this is nuts.*

"I know," she said in reply to his question. "But I want to watch some TV. I've gotten into those CSI shows an' they're repeating eps, so I've been watching." Turning the TV on, she dove onto the bed just as the show started.

"Mmm," she murmured as one of the male actors flashed onto the screen.

"What do ya mean, mmm?" Vegas demanded, climbing onto the bed beside her and crossing his arms in anger.

"Shhh," she said, poking him, "I want to watch."

After fifteen minutes, the actor she was watching stripped his jacket and shirt off to reveal a tight white singlet.

"Aw what a body," she drooled, feeling her sexual energy growing again.

The actor's muscles bulged, his hard, lean torso making her heart pound furiously.

"What are ya droolin' over?" Vegas cried. "He's a four-eyed freak. Big deal, he has a tatt an' a chain round his neck, so do I. An' I noticed from the openin' credits, he's got some poncy foreign name."

"He's Italian an' gorgeous. Just look at him, ooohhh, what an' ass, tight an' perfect. An' his name's Carmine, not four-eyed freak," she said, glaring at Vegas.

Going over to the TV and crouching down beside it, he pointed to the actor on screen. "What's he got that I don'?" He flexed his arm muscles. "I got the muscles, I got the tatt. I got a better lookin' ass, an' I don' need glasses." Bouncing onto the bed, he jumped on top of her. "An' you tell me if that Carmine guy can do this?"

Vegas took her to the brink and back. Touching and tasting. His mouth, tongue and fingers toying with her breasts and nipples, her hot wetness. Thrusting himself inside of her, he made her shudder with a delicious orgasm.

Sighing in a contented tangle of arms and legs, Tahlia glanced at the screen. The show was just finishing, with the actor now re-dressed in his shirt and jacket. The scene faded as the credits rolled.

"Well, I don't know if Carmine can do that, but I'm willing to hunt him down an' find out," she declared, grinning wickedly at the man on top of her.

Vegas was disgusted as he leant up on his elbow and glared at her. "Aw baby, how could you?" His delicious lips turned into a grin. "There's *no way* he could do it like I do," he declared, taking her over the edge again.

*****

Friday night, after the show, Vegas left for his weekend with Manny. Tahlia was starting to feel highly suspicious of his weekends, wondering what he was getting up to. Now that summer was here, she considered following him. *Mmm, maybe I will, I'll read up on it an' start an' investigation myself.*

There was a knock at the door.

Looking through the peephole, she made sure her robe was tightly wrapped before she opened it. "Hi," she said shyly.

"Hello," he said softly. "May I come in?"

"Sure."

Diega walked into her suite and turned to look at her. "I've found out some things. I thought you would like to know." He handed her a manila folder.

She sat down and opened it. There were two A4 pieces of paper and several photos. The information was surprising. She didn't know Wayne had been married or had TROs out against him. The photos were of neighbours and inside the house.

"This just tells me about his past, not my time with him. How'd you get these photos?"

Diega sat down beside her. "This is the only information we've gotten so far. The photos were taken of your neighbours because they were the ones who told the police about you. And I won't mention how my PIs got inside the house." He grinned slightly.

"I remember these people. The old woman was a busybody, always being nosy." She looked at Diega. "You won't stop digging will you?"

"No. No, I won't." Diega's look was of concern. "How have you been? Are you okay? Staying safe and being happy?"

Looking at him she saw his worry, and it made her feel wanted. "I'm okay," she said, smiling softly, "hanging in there."

"That's good," he said, standing and buttoning his suit jacket. "I want you to remain in a positive state of mind. No negativity. I'll let you get your beauty sleep. Would you like to do something tomorrow? I know Vegas has left again."

She glanced at the floor and then around the room. "Ahh, I don't know, considering last time, I, I don't think it's a good idea."

"You're right, of course. I'm sorry." Diega walked out the door and closed it behind him without a backward glance.

That's strange, she thought, shaking her head in bewilderment, *but then I did just turn him down.* Her shoulders drooped in disappointment. Sighing, she re-read the file. *Well, I obviously didn't know anything about Wayne. An' I wonder what I don't know now.* She thought about Vegas and his strange behaviour.

Tomorrow I'll go shopping an' get some things, make up my own sleuth kit, so I can be ready next time Vegas leaves.

*****

Saturday morning dawned bright and warm, and Tahlia was ready for her shopping expedition. Making a list of what she thought she might need, she checked her purse. "Nope, gonna need money 'cause I can't use the credit card Diega gave me."

Driving through town, she stopped at an ATM then drove to the first store on her list. The manager was able to help her find the right cameras she needed. An infrared with a zoom lens, and a small one for being discreet. She also bought a bag for all the other things she would be buying.

The second store supplied her with several flashlights, binoculars, and a great Swiss army knife, just right for getting out of those tight situations. Or picking a lock.

"You know," the assistant, whose name tag read Junior, said, feeling all self-important because he knew something, "the Swiss army knife was imported into America by the father of that guy, you know, that guy from that TV show, ah, what is it, you know, that one with all the initials." He thought for a moment, staring into space as Tahlia pulled money out of her purse. "That NCIS thing, yep that's it, he was one of the first to give this great country of ours the Swiss army knife," he stopped for a breath, taking Tahlia's money and giving her change, "who woulda known Tony DiNozzo's Dad did that," he chuckled.

"You mean Michael Weatherly," Tahlia said, fitting her purchases into the bag she'd bought in the camera store. "Fits perfectly," she told the guy and quickly walked toward the door.

"Um, yeah, I meant Michael Weatherly…" the man called after her, but she was already gone.

Throwing the bag into the car, she drove back to the hotel to Google 'sneaky ways of detecting'.

*****

That night, Diega knocked on her door again. "Will you have dinner with me?" he asked quietly after she'd opened it.

"Why should I after what happened last weekend? You took advantage of me an' that's not right. You know I'm with Vegas," she paused, "an' I won't cheat on him.

"You're right," Diega said, and breathed deeply, "believe me I am so very sorry that you think I took advantage. I didn't mean for anything bad to happen. And it wasn't bad. It was beautiful. *You're* beautiful. And I so desperately needed to touch you and feel you and show you how I felt. How much I want you." He wanted to show her how much he loved her, but knew he needed to back off. "I'm sorry," he whispered, "but I can't help the way I feel."

Tahlia sighed, tears welled up in her eyes, and she thought about his words. She gave in. "What were you thinking of?" she asked, leaning on the door.

"Maybe here in your suite, just something casual."

"Uhhh, I don't think we should be anywhere near a bed or couch," she said slowly, feeling nervous, remembering his touch on her skin, his lips on hers.

Embarrassed, Diega laughed softly. "Ah, you're right, I didn't think." He gazed at her, wanting her, aching for her. His face crumpled. "I just want to be with you. I stay away while Vegas is here, so it doesn't cause problems for you. But when he's away I cherish our time together. Please have dinner with me. We can go downstairs." He was waiting expectantly, hopefully, like a puppy longing for adoption. Waiting there with his big blue eyes gazing at her adoringly, waiting for her to say, *'I'll take that one'.*

Her heart melted at his words. A part of her so

desperately wanted to be with him even though she was with Vegas. Diega was a man she just couldn't refuse. *Didn't want* to refuse as her feelings for him overwhelmed her, made her feel love, and joy…and with Vegas gone, she was feeling lonely. "Okay," she said, "we'll go downstairs."

Sighing in relief, Diega's smile was ear to ear. "Great, that's great. Shall we?" He held out his arm, but she brushed right past him as she closed the door.

Walking ahead of him to the lift, she knew she didn't want him touching her. She didn't know what would happen if she couldn't control her desires. Or if she'd even want to. And God, she didn't want to.

They dined in one of the casual restaurants, eating enchiladas and drinking sodas. Diega tried not to scare her by keeping to safe, casual topics of conversation.

Tahlia was enjoying herself, feeling relaxed and safe. Laughing at his jokes, she wondered what it would be like to have a relationship with the man sitting across from her.

He was so amazing, such a charming gentleman. A world traveller, educated, and well read. Could speak five languages, which he ordered in, making her laugh.

Mandy, who was lucky enough to be serving them, looked at him like he was mad, and pretended to get angry, but she knew he was her boss and none of the hotel's employees could stay angry at Diega Montiamo.

Remembering his arms around her body and his lips on her mouth, Tahlia imagined what it would be like to make love with him. She knew it would be even more incredible than that night on the roof, though she had stopped him before they'd gone too far. Was her heart falling for him? Maybe. Was *she* falling for him? Yes.

"Tahlia. Tahlia."

She looked up.

Diega had been calling her name, looking at her with a concerned, but aroused look in his eyes.

"What! I'm fine. Sorry, I…my mind wandered," she said.

"It certainly did. Where did it go?" he asked. He'd seen the expressions move over her face as she'd thought. Were they about him? He knew it was of something good because her pupils had dilated and her lips had become full and red. *I hope she's not thinking about Vegas,* he thought vehemently.

She blushed and didn't answer.

"How about dessert?" Diega asked, signalling to someone.

"No. I don't think I could eat another—"

Mandy put a bowl down in front of her. "We have *got* to see each other tomorrow," she whispered quickly in Tahlia's ear, flashing her a wicked grin, and Diega a sexy glance.

In the bowl was a huge mound of rich chocolate ice cream, with hot chocolate sauce flowing down the sides in thick chocolatey rivers, nuts sprinkled all over floating along with the tide. "Ohhh, how could you tease a girl with so much chocolate?" she asked, grinning from ear to ear.

"Well, if I knew this was the way to your heart I would have offered it up the first time we met." He gazed at her, waiting.

Tahlia rolled her eyes and scoffed. "You mean the first time when you barged into my dressing room? I could have been naked you know."

"I know. I was counting on it." He was still looking at her and waiting for a reaction.

Tahlia grinned softly. "I bet you were," she said, and Diega returned her grin.

Finally, looking at her watch, she decided to go. Standing up, she thanked him for his company, a wonderful dinner, and a wickedly delicious dessert.

"Are you sure you don't want to stay?" Diega asked, standing as well. He didn't want to let her go just yet.

"Yeah, I'm tired. I might just watch some TV or something."

Feeling resigned, Diega nodded. "Okay. Get a good night's sleep."

"I will."

In her suite, she turned on the TV and listened to it while she changed. Crawling into bed, she found a crime drama on one of the channels. As she drifted off to sleep, she dreamt of guns, thugs and Vegas.

*****

The phone rang at eight the next morning, and Tahlia lazily rolled over and picked it up. "Hey, baby," she murmured, thinking Vegas was at the other end.

"Hey, baby, yourself," Mandy replied, "I'm on my way up, girl, so get out of bed."

She arrived fifteen minutes later as Tahlia finished dressing. "So," she said, walking into the suite, "what happened last night? In fact, what's happened since we last spoke 'cause like, I haven't seen you in ages."

Tahlia closed the door, followed her to the living room, and plonked down on one of the sofas. She had a lot to tell Mandy, although she wasn't sure she should. She did need a friend to talk to though since her feelings were so confused.

"Well," Mandy demanded, "spit it out, after all, I was your waitress last night. I did *see* things…"

"It's been weeks since we talked," Tahlia started, "an' a lot has happened."

"Obviously," Mandy said, "*like, hello*, you didn't even tell me you had another date with Mr Gorgeous," she mumbled, getting comfortable. She was wearing a pretty summer dress and had a glow about her.

"Have you, um, had a date lately," Tahlia said, trying to change the subject, "you're glowing."

Mandy blushed. "Yeah, he's gorgeous, muscles bulging in all the right places if ya know what I mean. Please, what am I saying," she said, "*of course* you know what I mean. You have *two* gorgeous men after you." She paused, and a grin slid across her face. "I am *sooo* jealous and hate you *sooo* much."

"Believe me," Tahlia said, "you have nothing to be jealous of. In fact, I wish there *weren't* two men in my life. Ahh," she cried, grasping her hair and pretending to pull it out. "I can't do this, not after what Diega did. But then I have no idea what Vegas is up to either an' I really think I need to find out."

Mandy leaned forward, her eyes gleaming in suspense. "What do you mean, *after what Diega did?*"

She was extremely curious now, knowing how Tahlia felt about Diega, and after seeing them together last night, she definitely knew Diega wanted Tahlia.

Tahlia sighed and brought Mandy up to date with all the details leading to her night on the roof with Diega. "An' then I ran…" she finished, looking over at Mandy who was sitting there all glassy-eyed in surprise. "I don't know what to do," she continued, "seriously. Then last night he comes to my door an' apologises for what he'd done, an' my feelings are so overwhelming that I give in an' have dinner with him, an' you know the rest." Tahlia sat back in her seat and sighed again, completely worn out.

Mandy got to her feet and slowly wandered around the room in a daze trying to take it all in. Wow, her best friend might be in love with their boss. And he wants her, it was so obvious last night. She finally sat down beside Tahlia. "The only thing you need to do is decide which man you want to be with. My mama always said, 'now girly, you can have feelin's for two men, but only one will bring home the bacon an' support you.' Now, I know about Vegas and all 'cause you told me, but," she looked away, "I gotta tell ya, I'd be picking Diega." She slyly glanced at Tahlia.

"Your mother really told you that?" Tahlia asked, stifling a grin.

Mandy grinned back. "Yeah, but then hey, I grew up *over that side* of the country," she said, breaking into a giggle.

Tahlia sighed again. "I met Vegas at a time when I didn't need a man," she said, walking over to the expansive window and gazing out over the city, marvelling at the number of hotels and casinos. And now here she was staying in one. "But," she continued as Mandy joined her, "the attraction was instant, an' I'd never felt that way about *any* man before. An' now, since being here, I've met Diega an' he's the sort of man I *never* thought I'd be with. They're both *so* different," she said, pushing her hair back. "I *really* don't know what to do." She looked at Mandy.

"Sweetie, you really have to decide. I mean hey, I'd love two men throwing themselves at me—"

"They do now," Tahlia interrupted.

Mandy blushed. "Yeah, okay, they do." She grinned and became serious. "Have you considered writing up the pros and cons of each of them?"

Tahlia frowned. "You mean making lists on each of them, of their good an' bad points? I can't do that. The lists would be so long," she joked.

Mandy laughed. "At least you might finally realise how you feel, and which one it is that you feel about." She scratched her chin thoughtfully. "As much as Vegas is all sexy and rough, which some girls like and you certainly seem to…" That made Tahlia blush. "Personally, he's not my type. I like my men lean and clean shaven. Mature, respectful. A man who knows how to treat a woman well and hey, if he's got a lot of dough, great, I'll take him. Diega is definitely the one for me. Besides," she paused, looking at Tahlia, "didn't you say Vegas was getting up to suspicious things. He does leave every fortnight. Do *you* know what he gets up to?" she asked.

"No," Tahlia said, "I don't." She told Mandy about

her shopping trip the day before and showed her the things she'd bought. "I plan on following him when I can," she said. "But I don't know when that will be."

"Well," Mandy said, "you're certainly prepared. One thing, though."

"What?" Tahlia asked.

"If you need help, let me know, and I'll do what I can," Mandy said, hugging her.

Tahlia grinned. Mandy was definitely becoming her best friend.

*****

When Tahlia walked into her suite late Monday afternoon, she found Vegas home from his weekend jaunt. "You're back I see," she said.

He answered with a scowl and kept on smoking his cigarette as he lay on the sofa.

"Do you want to eat here or go downstairs?" she asked as she walked into the bedroom.

"Doesn' matter," he mumbled.

Ordering room service, they ate in silence, with Vegas sitting there all moody and dark.

She watched him, suspicious, wondering how to proceed. "You know," she started, "you promised not to come home all grouchy. Looks like you don't keep your promises." She looked at him defiantly, waiting for some excuse. Preparing for him to lash out.

His eyes were dark, angry, and he looked like he was going to strangle her. Then suddenly, his expression changed, and that damn sexy grin was in its place.

"Mmm, you're right, baby, I did promise." He leaned across the table, took her hand and squeezed it.

Not feeling reassured, Tahlia squeezed back. "Let's go downstairs."

*****

Interesting. Vegas was hiding something, and it was becoming evident, so evident that Tahlia was more and more suspicious with each and every day.

Chuckling to himself, he wondered how much longer it would take for her to find out his secrets. His dirty little secrets. The secrets he thinks are so well hidden in the past, never to be revealed to anyone, let alone Tahlia.

Well, she was certainly on her way, having purchased her 'detecting kit' last weekend. I wonder if she'll find out about her ex and the man she's now sleeping with?

That he's no saint.

But the man she needs to get away from.

*****

The shows that week went so incredibly well that on Thursday the director let them do two sets instead of one. They were getting on well, with Vegas being loving and attentive as if trying to prove something.

Or keep my suspicions at bay, she thought on Friday when he suggested riding out into the desert. "Vegas, tell me again that you actually thanked Manny an'

Maria for keeping us for a month, or is your work for him really enough. I'd like to do something for them. Maybe get something to show we appreciate them keeping us all that time."

"No, no, that's awright, baby, you don' have to do anythin'. I did thank 'em, personally, an' me workin' with Manny on our weekends more than helps. So, it's okay." He grabbed her arms, pulled her to him and kissed her.

Or shut me up, she thought, pulling away. "So where did you think of going?" she asked, trying to gauge his thoughts.

"Well," he drawled, "I thought we could pack up the bike an' head out into the desert, camp out for the night. Maybe…relive our first night together?" That damn sexy grin was still there, and he raised his brows comically.

Even though she was still feeling suspicious she started grinning, she couldn't help herself. "I definitely wouldn't mind reliving our first night together, but shouldn't we take the car?"

"Well, it's not suppose to rain, an' besides, I thought you loved the feelin' of somethin' hard an' throbbin' between your legs?"

Blushing deeply and giggling like a girl, Tahlia gazed into his deep blue eyes, stroking his face as she became serious. "I do love the feeling of something hard an' throbbing between my legs. But it's not the bike." She met his mouth, her tongue delving inside.

They kissed passionately, running their hands everywhere. Picking her up, Vegas carried her to the bed and threw her onto it. Ripping each other's clothes off, they touched every inch of each other. First with their hands, then with their mouths and tongues, as they grunted and gasped and writhed around.

They ground together.

Hard and fast.

Back and forth.

Crying out in unison.

That's the way it always was with them.

The way it always would be.

Afterward, lying still entwined, she ran her hands over his back. "Sooo, when did you want to go?"

Leaning on his elbow, Vegas looked at her as he ran his hand through her hair. "How 'bout tomorrow night, baby? We can relive all the times we did it before gettin' here. The campsite, out in the rain, in the shower, though in the shower an' in the rain would be the same. Maybe we could set up one of those campin' shower things? An' then, we could make new memories. Well, baby, does that sound good?" he drawled, letting that grin spread across his luscious lips as his fingers toyed with her left nipple.

"Mmm," she murmured, aroused again, "I say that's definitely a plan," she purred, pulling his mouth to hers.

Chapter 15

Saturday, they rode the bike out into the desert, far enough away to be out of the hustle and bustle, but where they could still see the city lights. Sitting behind Vegas on the bike was one of the most incredible feelings. Her arms around his waist, the wind rushing by, the sun warming her skin. Tahlia felt free and alive, with no worries to fill her mind that was normally so full of things to worry about.

They pulled into the campsite, found a spot, and built a fire. Laying out the sleeping bags, they settled in and roasted hot dogs for dinner and marshmallows for dessert which they fed each other.

Afterwards, leaning back against Vegas in his arms, revelling in the quiet, Tahlia spoke. "We don't have a shower, so what are we going to do?"

Grinning, Vegas slowly slid his right hand under her top and caressed her left breast. "We'll find somethin' to do baby, or should I say, *someone*?" He pulled her to the side, so she was leaning back, and she twisted her body to face him as his mouth met hers.

Expecting passion, she was surprised when his tongue

didn't enter her mouth. Instead, his lips teased hers, slowly moving over them, then her face and neck. Moving back to her mouth, his soft pink tongue peeked out between his lush, full lips and gently pushed between her lips to tease her tongue.

Opening her mouth, she took his tongue inside. Stroking it with hers, slowly, rhythmically, tasting it, tasting him. His hands, now under her top, slid it over her breasts then her head as he stopped kissing her for the second it took to get it off.

Moving into a kneeling position and facing each other, they continued kissing, slowly as their hands caressed. Tahlia ran her own hands up his torso, his muscles hard under her fingers. She pushed his white singlet over his head, her mouth and tongue running over his hard lean chest. Exploring him, tasting his soft, warm skin. She reached for his belt. He wasn't wearing one.

Gazing deep into his eyes, her hands moved down to undo each button on his jeans, one by one, feeling him harden at her touch. She slid her hands into the back of his jeans under the band of his shorts, shoving them down. Bringing her hands around to his front she set him free, and he removed his clothes slowly as she watched him.

Naked. Raw. Hungry.

Just like that first night.

Stroking his hardened penis, she heard him groan in pleasure and his eyes closed, savouring the feeling of her hands around him.

Vegas reached up and slid her bra strap slowly over

her shoulder, following its path with his mouth. His soft lips on her skin made her shudder as her arms slithered around him and she leaned against his body. He slid the other strap down and gazed intently into her eyes, slid his hands over her breasts, pushing his eager thumbs inside the material to rub her hardened nipples.

Groaning, she collapsed against him, barely hanging on. He pushed her bra down and took her left nipple into his mouth, sucking gently, making her writhe and gasp. His left hand played with her right breast, making it even harder. Lifting his head and gazing into her eyes, he put his arms around her, and finding the bra clasp, unhooked it. Reaching for her jeans, he unzipped them. Not wanting to wait, she thrust her jeans and panties down and off until she was kneeling in front of him as naked as he was.

"Take me," she whispered, grabbing his arms, "take me now." They had laid the sleeping bags in front of a large rock, so he turned her around to face it and pushed her down. Leaning against it, still on her knees, Tahlia spread her legs, allowing Vegas to enter.

He didn't.

Kneeling between her legs so she could feel him probing, but not entering, he slid his hands over her back and ass. She bucked at his touch, wanting him. Moving his hands around to her front, Vegas toyed with her breasts, tweaking them, making her push back against him, feeling him poking her, teasing her. Tantalisingly, he slid his hands between her legs, touching her, penetrating her.

"Aaaahhh," she gasped softly. He found her spot and

brought her to the edge. Instead of taking her over, he slid his fingers out, grabbed her hips, and thrust himself inside.

Back and forth. In and out.

His hands played with her, she bucked against him, opened her legs wider to fully let him in. Pushing her down onto the rock, he took her hard and fast.

Over and over. Back and forth.

Imprinting himself so completely, all restraint faded as he pursued his own climax, fusing them together, burning them into one.

Crying out in both pleasure and pain, Tahlia was glad her arms were tucked under her, so her breasts weren't scarred by the roughness of the rock.

Vegas was still thrusting.

Harder. Faster. Than ever before.

Like a wild animal taking its prey, getting its fill. His hand was in her hair pulling her head back. He was half leaning on her.

With final, grunting, thrusts, he drove his penetration home, spilling his seed, flowing into her, branding her, both of them gasping, climaxing at the same moment…

They fell against each other and collapsed onto the sleeping bags, breathing hard. For a long time they lay there, not speaking, then Tahlia gazed up at him intently.

"You've never been that wild before. I know that our times are raw an' hungry, but there was something different tonight. Something…" She shrugged, unable to find the right word to describe his behaviour.

Looking at her with power in his eyes he spoke softly, with intense control. "I was brandin' you. Every time my seed flows through you, I brand you. You belong to me. You are mine an' no one else's. I own you." His face was dark, emotionless.

She shivered, despite her body still being on fire, and the heat shimmering off her skin in waves. All of her memories came flooding back. Bad memories. Memories she thought were gone. Hoped and prayed were gone.

She'd heard some of those words before, and never wanted to hear them again. Feeling empowered, she sat up, threw him a look of disgust, and crossed her arms in front of her before turning away. "You don't own me," she spat in anger. "So many men have said that to me before, an' finally I know it's not true. You *don't* own me. I am *not* yours, an' the only person I *belong* to, is *myself!*"

Tahlia got up and sat on the rock, seething. She didn't want to go back to what she had left, and after meeting Vegas, she'd thought it was different. Over. But he was changing, and she didn't like what she saw.

Kneeling in front of her, Vegas grinned softly. "I was only jokin', baby. It's been so long since we met that I forgot what happened to you before." He seemed to be pleading in some way as he held her hands in his. "I know I didn' say it for a long time, an' I never said it to any woman before but...I love you. An' since I, I, haven' felt this way before, it scares me. I don' know what to do in these situations. When we have sex the passion is raw an' real an' there's a hunger deep inside me, an' I have to have you, be deep inside you, as far as I can be. I, I, I can' explain it any other way, baby. I just can'." He struggled, looking for words.

"I love you, too," Tahlia told him, stroking his face. Lying down in their sleeping bag, they wrapped their arms around each other and looked at the city lights.

She felt a tickle in her throat and coughed. And unable to stop, she had a fit.

"You okay, baby?" Vegas asked, slapping her gently on the back.

"Got a fur ball," she gasped, then broke out in laughter, "from all the times I put my head on your chest. I think I inhaled half your chest hair. You still got any?" she jokingly asked.

Grinning at each other, they lay back down, her head on his shoulder. Looking up at him, and gazing into his eyes, she kissed him. Softly, gently, she kissed him, playing her tongue over his lips, stroking his face.

Her mouth planted kisses all over his face and travelled down his neck. Biting him, she gave him a hickey, sucking hard. She moved down his body, biting, lashing his nipples with her tongue, leaving teeth marks. Making her way down, she came to his abdomen, the place between his navel and pelvis, she ran her tongue over the trail of hair that ran down there before taking his hard erection into her mouth.

This was the first time she had done this, taken him this way. Sucking him, she made him groan. Sliding her mouth up and down, and rubbing her tongue over it as it hardened even more. She touched his testes and stroked his sensitive skin, making him cry out.

He grabbed her head and pulled her off him, and as she fell toward him, he grabbed her hips and thrust her down onto him, feeling her wetness enclose around him. Grinding in circles and thrusting up and down, Vegas raised his thighs behind her to keep her in place. Tahlia leaned against them as he hung on to her, moving her around, her head falling back, the blood rushing, sending her to dizzying heights.

She'd sat on top of him before, and every time his penis felt larger, harder, like it was going further inside of her. Taking her to new heights, new stratospheres, new boundaries she'd never been to before.

It was exciting. Adventurous. She rocked back and forth, bending her body back over his legs, letting them support her weight as she let him do what he wanted.

Do what she wanted.

Climaxing, the orgasm made them scream into the night, thrusting over the brink.

*****

He was there, out in the desert, and he wanted to kill Vegas the first time he hurt her. Wanted to put a bullet through that bastard's head to make him stop. How could he do that to her, take her that way? So violent and hostile.

But it was extremely exciting, and the hardening in his groin made it hard for him to resist release.

Seeing Tahlia screaming in pleasure and pain as she was thrown against the rock, over and over, making him cry out too as his seed spilled all over his hand as it moved faster and faster, up and down. His grip hard and tight and sure.

Sure it could do the job. Sure it wouldn't be long

before it was replaced by the tempting pussy of the desirable Tahlia and all that she could do for him. All that she would do for him.

He watched her take his penis into her mouth. Licking, sucking, eating hungrily as she devoured him before slamming that wonderful ripe pussy onto his very hard dick that was screaming for release of its seed as it thrust up and down, pumping into her, flowing at an amazing speed.

He lay back, gasping, shaking. He had never felt so satisfied. So fulfilled. So free.

He sighed. "Ah, my dear, sweet Tahlia, how you love me so." His thoughts floated back to Vegas and how he'd hurt Tahlia. That's not the way you make a woman want you. By hurting her, charging ahead when she wants you to stop.

And stop you I will.

Then, I'll have it my way.

All of it, my way.

*****

Monday morning, Tahlia knocked on Diega's door.

"Come."

She walked in, closed the door behind her, and sat in the chair in front of his desk. "Have you found out anything else?" she asked hopefully.

Not sure how much to tell her, Diega thought for a moment before speaking. "My PIs have found out that Wayne was working with a lower ranking member of a crime syndicate. We're not sure about how much he did, but we think it was something like collecting money, transferring goods, theft, assaults, things like that."

She thought for a moment. "Well, no one ever came to the house. He didn't invite anyone in, didn't want anyone to see me, I suppose. I never knew about anything. He kept his affairs to himself an' just used me for gratifying his needs." She flushed with embarrassment and disgust.

Diega let the moment go, not wanting to make her more uncomfortable. "You said you had a car. Do you think it was Wayne's? The police say it was. How did you acquire it and where is it now?" He leaned forward on his desk eager for her answers.

"I don't know how I ended up with it." She shrugged and glanced around the office. "My dreams are still hazy, like my mind doesn't want to remember, but every time I dream, I see a little bit more. I was running, so I don't know why I went back for the car unless it's 'cause I could. I drove it all over the country just about. To New York, down the east coast, then across to Las Vegas. I met Vegas on the way an' he said he'd heard it on the radio. That the police were out looking for the car an' a woman fitting my description. So he suggested we get rid of it."

"Where?" Diega needed to know.

"About a hundred miles out of Vegas. We drove off the highway an' stopped near an' old ravine. Vegas an' his friend pushed it in an' set it on fire. Then his friend drove us to his house, an' we stayed with him an' his wife for a month till I got this job."

"What's the friend's name?" Diega asked, a pen poised in his hand.

"Manny. I don't know his surname."

"Where did you dump the car? Can you show me on a map?" He led her to the map of Nevada and its surrounding states on his wall.

She looked closely at the map. "Umm, we came along here, turned off about fifty miles from this town," she said, pointing to a spot.

Figuring the distance, Diega made a safe bet where they had gone. "Do you have Manny's address?" he asked and wrote it down as she told him.

"Do you think Wayne was killed by the mob member?" she asked.

"Maybe. Let me do some more digging." Seeing the worried look on her face, he quickly added, "Don't worry, I won't let you be blamed for this."

She stared at him, feeling her shoulders sag. "Okay," she said and walked out the door feeling a little scared, a little relieved.

Diega picked up the phone and dialled a number. "I want you to take a team out to the desert." He gave the details. "Find that car and haul it out. Go over it with a fine-tooth comb then destroy it completely. I want absolutely no evidence left. Do you understand me? And get back to me ASAP."

Now that he had more information he would be able to help her better. He wasn't going to let her be hurt or go to jail for a crime he knew she hadn't committed.

He spoke to someone else. "Go to 229 Juliet Way, watch it every night this week, especially this coming weekend."

***

The week flew by with Vegas being extra attentive. The shows were still going strong, but as usual, Vegas was gone before Friday night's show. So, when it was over, Tahlia showered and dressed in black jeans, a long sleeve top and boots. After brushing her hair into a ponytail, she grabbed her bag full of detecting gear and took the lift down to the parking garage.

She drove out to the suburbs and pulled to a stop down the road from Manny's. She was glad the hotel had given her another car because she didn't want Vegas to notice her 'Stang. The problem was, no one seemed to be home.

Crawling past with the headlights off, she saw no lights on anywhere. No cars or the bike in the driveway. *Mmm, where could they be?* she pondered. Driving around, she was hoping to just come across them somewhere.

But after two hours she drew a blank. Sighing in frustration, she decided to come back tomorrow.

***

On Saturday, Tahlia knocked on Manny's door.

Maria answered, first smiling broadly, then looking nervous. "Hello, dear. What can I do for you?"

"Well, I wanted to drop by to ask if there was anything I could do to repay you for letting Vegas an' me stay for a month. I know it's been awhile, but I really want to repay you for your generosity." She waited to see what would happen.

"Don't be silly. We don't want anything, really. Vegas and Manny go way back, and he's been helping on the weekends. So he's more than repaid, really it's okay. So, if that was all?" She started closing the door.

"Um no, that's all." The door closed in Tahlia's face. "Well, that was productive now wasn't it," she muttered as she walked back to her car. "I'll just have to come back tonight."

*****

The sun had set, and it was completely dark when Tahlia drove slowly down the street. Mandy was with her. She had the night off, and when Tahlia had talked to her earlier that day, she'd jumped at the chance to come along.

"I thought I'd dress in black," she said when Tahlia had picked her up. "After all, we are sneaking around playing detective." She'd pulled out a magnifying glass from her backpack and peered through it, pretending to inspect something on the roof of the car.

"Cute," Tahlia had snickered as they drove off.

Now they sat just down the road from the house. There were no cars and no lights.

"No one's home," Mandy whispered, slinking down in her seat and peering over the dashboard.

"Obviously," Tahlia replied, shaking her head in amusement. "I wonder if they even stay here," she said, gazing out her window.

"It doesn't look like it," Mandy said, "but then that

just means whatever he's up to, he doesn't do it here."

"Good point," Tahlia replied. "God, how am I gonna find out where he's going an' what he's up to if he's not here?" She banged the steering wheel in frustration.

"You can always follow him straight after he leaves, that way he'll always be in sight," Mandy suggested.

"Yeah," Tahlia sighed, "that *seems* like a good idea. It's just finding the right time to do it. He leaves on Friday nights before my show. I can't just run off after him an' miss the show. That's not very professional."

"Maybe not," Mandy interrupted, "but if you're desperate to find out, then take a night off. Say you're sick or something, bad throat, whatever. Just do it."

Tahlia knew she was right. If she wanted to find out, she would have to do something. And do it soon.

Driving off into the night, she decided to cruise the city the next day.

*****

Unfortunately, she didn't find him then, either. "Oh, well," she said, walking into her suite, "there's always next fortnight. Maybe I should ask Diega?" She had gone into the bedroom when a knock at the door brought her back. She rushed to answer it.

"Hello. May I come in?" Diega asked.

"Sure," she said, stepping aside to let him in.

He had another folder in his hands.

"Is that more info?"

"Yes. Sit down." They sat next to each other on the couch. Tahlia looked at him intently, waiting to hear what he had to say. "I had my people track down the car. They pulled it out of the ravine, and have gone over it with a fine-tooth comb." He handed her the folder.

Opening it, Tahlia saw pictures of the car. It was nothing but a burnt, crushed wreck. "What did you find?" she asked, glancing at him.

Unsure of how to put it, he decided to just say it. "We found out that the car *was* Wayne's. The plates don't match, but the VIN number did. Which means the plates were changed, sometime, somewhere. And we found some partial prints, surprisingly enough, yours, Vegas and Manny's." He looked at her, waiting for her to digest the information he'd just told her.

"Do you know if I killed him? If I took his car, then I killed him." She was crying, trying to hold it together.

"The police have a gun in their custody. They claim it's the murder weapon and that your fingerprints are on it. They matched them to bloody prints in the house. They're not looking for any other suspects. They're only looking for you." He saw the scared look on her face, and his heart broke. He didn't want to lose the woman he loved, and he would do anything to keep her safe.

"What do I do?" she whispered in despair.

Close to tears himself, Diega swallowed hard. "Stay in Vegas. Don't leave the city. Stay in the hotel if you need to, or I can have a bodyguard tail you."

"No! No. Do the police know who I am, my name? Do they have pictures of me, know what I look like? You said they matched prints. But there were no photos, an' Wayne wanted the house spotless. I never went out. How do they know who I am?" She was sobbing now.

Diega pulled her into his arms, holding her, crying with her. Only speaking when she stopped. "They don't know who you are, and only have descriptions from your neighbours. You'll be okay. I'll protect you with everything I have, and do everything within my power to make this go away. I promise."

"You can't promise. I don't even remember."

They sat in silence for a while longer. "I don't want you going to Manny's house either."

"What makes you think I've been going to Manny's house?" she asked, averting her gaze and holding her breath in anticipation.

"My PIs are watching his house. They saw you drive past. I want you to stop playing Nancy Drew. This could be dangerous."

Worried by his words, she sat up and looked at him. "I was looking for Vegas *not* playing Nancy Drew. An' who are you to tell me?" she asked, raising her brow in humour, *"Frank Hardy?"* She grinned. "I wasn't doing anything."

"*Do not* go to Manny's house," Diega warned, standing up. "If you need anything, let me know." Leaning down and kissing her on the forehead, he turned and walked out the door.

*****

So, she had been trying to find Vegas by playing Nancy Drew, he thought. How cute! Well, she didn't succeed, certainly dressing for the part though. All in black.

Annoyingly, her obsession with the fictional children's character seemed to be getting out of hand.

And the car's been found and hauled out of the ravine. Now it's becoming interesting, from the partial prints found, it seems Vegas and Manny have been very bad boys.

Very bad boys.

She was worried, she was scared.

She should be because danger is on its way.

Looking at the paper in his hand, he read something interesting about Vegas.

Well, I wonder if Tahlia knows about this?

I wonder if Vegas knows about this?

I can definitely use this against him if I need to.

Chapter 16

On Monday, Vegas came home very on edge, his anger simmering on the brink of exploding, so Tahlia chose to ignore him. Which was hard to do since he glared and growled at her for what seemed to be no reason at all. She was absolutely fed up, a sick feeling welled in the pit of her stomach. She didn't want to keep having these feelings, and on Thursday, it was even worse.

Rehearsals for the show were rough, with Vegas yelling at everyone, even her. The songs weren't right, the key was off, the backup singers didn't know what they were singing, and the band couldn't string a melody together.

Boiling inside after one cutting remark, she slapped him clear across the face. "*Never* talk to me that way again," she yelled at him, "I will *not* put up with it anymore, an' if you continue to do so, that's it. We're through. Over. Finished!"

It shocked him that she could *and did* slap him. He changed his attitude in an instant, not wanting to put her offside any more than he had. He begged for her forgiveness, and she reluctantly gave in, spending the weekend with him cruising around Las Vegas.

And every time Tahlia brought up Manny, Vegas changed the subject, making her suspicions grow.

*****

During the next week, Vegas kept an eye on her, never leaving her side for very long. Always there whenever she turned a corner or walked into a room. Standing off to the side of the stage during rehearsals, answering the phone if it rang. Even ordering room service for her, and making decisions she usually made for herself. Which made her even madder.

Tahlia kept an eye on him, too. Monitoring his phone calls which he kept taking in secret. She had to be careful though, to not be noticed, so she pretended to be doing other things when he spoke in whispered tones. She knew he had been up to something, and now she was definite about it. She prayed it wasn't illegal because she just didn't know what she would do if it were.

*****

That weekend, when Vegas left in the afternoon, she was ready. Running to her hotel car, she came out of the parking garage just as he was leaving. Tailing him wasn't difficult, and keeping a few cars between them, she was able to keep him in plain sight.

He arrived at Manny's, and she pulled in down the road to watch him put his bike in the garage out back, then get into Manny's car. She waited until they turned the corner before she followed. Again, keeping a few cars between them, she followed them to a gas station, then a takeout place.

Keeping an eye on the time, she took photos at each stop, tailing them as they drove out into the desert. Seeing them turn off the highway, she pulled over to the side of the road and made notes in her notepad. She glanced at her watch. "Damn, I can't keep following," she muttered, "I need to head back for the show. Well, at least I have some idea where to start tomorrow…or next time."

*****

That night, after the show, Diega walked into her suite. "I have an idea that might help," he said while she closed the door behind him.

"What?" she asked hopefully.

"Hypnotism." He waited for her reply.

Not sure what she should say, Tahlia thought about it for a few moments. "You mean, I get hypnotised an' try to find out what happened that night?" she asked slowly.

"Yes," Diega said, nodding. "It might be the only thing we *can* do to help you remember what happened. If you choose to do it, we can do it tomorrow. How about it?"

Sighing, she looked at him and shook her head. "I don't know. I don't know. Let me think about it tonight an', I'll let you know tomorrow. Okay?"

"Absolutely. That's fine." He seemed relieved.

"Would you be there, while it's happening?" she asked tentatively, glancing everywhere but at him.

"If you want me to, then yes I'll be there." He wanted to hold her, reassure her, drive all of her demons away.

"Can you record it? So I can see it afterwards."

"If that's what you want, of course."

Suddenly needing to be held, and wanting his arms around her, Tahlia stepped over to him. Wrapping her arms around him, she felt his muscular torso, breathed in his manly scent. Every muscle in her body relaxed as she tightened her arms, and she felt his own body relax and mould to hers.

Responding to her, Diega stroked her hair and held her, waiting for her to pull away.

After several minutes, she did, feeling a little embarrassed, a little shy. Gazing up into his deep blue eyes she felt a desperate need.

So she kissed him.

He was surprised. He had always been the one to kiss her, now, suddenly she was the one kissing him.

The kiss was brief, and she pulled back, shocked at her boldness. But with passion and desire pulsating through her, she kissed him again.

And he met her. His lips settled over hers, feeling their softness, resisting the urge to plunder the sweet cavern of delight wide open before him, their tongues slow dancing in a steady rhythm.

They wrapped their arms around each other, and the kiss deepened.

Knowing she had to stop, but not wanting to, she let it go on for several minutes. Soft, lingering kisses tasting of longing and lust as their lips parted, pleading with her to stay before she so reluctantly pulled away.

Breathing hard, they gazed at each other, wanting, needing, lips only millimetres away from joining once again.

"You should go," she whispered, then cleared her throat as she stepped away.

"Okay," Diega said, not wanting to let her go, wanting the kiss to go on forever.

"I'll let you know tomorrow, about being hypnotised," she said, her voice becoming stronger, but she still wasn't able to look at him.

"Okay." He stood still, the quiet weaving around them. He didn't want to go, but knew she needed her space. "I'll let you get some sleep. Good night," he whispered.

"Good night," she whispered back, watching him walk down the hallway to his own suite. She slowly closed the door, smiling softly to herself.

*****

He was there, there in the house, in the house with her and Wayne. A dead Wayne. Dead as a doornail on the floor Wayne. Lying in his own blood. The gun in her hands, warm and heavy as she watched the lingering trail of smoke disappear. The blood all over him. All over her. His blood. His thick, sickly blood that made her gag. She screamed and kept screaming, looking down at the dead body of her boyfriend. The gun in her hand. His blood. The blood that covered her and the gun in her hand.

There was a bang. It was the back door. She stopped

screaming and dropped the gun on the floor beside dead as a doornail Wayne. Oh, no, he's back. He heard me, oh, God, he heard me, what do I do, what do I do? Quickly, I have to get out of here. The bedroom, I can lock the door and get out through the window.

She ran to the room, quietly closing and locking the door behind her. He can't hear me, she panicked, he can't hear me. Running to the window, she tripped over the shoes that she hadn't put on. He can't hear me.

The doorknob rattled.

Oh, no, he's going to get me, I can't let him get me. She pushed the screen off and climbed out, falling as her hands slipped on the sill.

Then, she was running, running, running. Blindly, in fear of her life. Running from something, she didn't know what. She just had to get away. Away from the terror. Away from the man in the shadows…

Tahlia was sobbing, waking, seeing it was morning, and lying curled in a foetal position, she sobbed until she could sob no more. Deciding to be hypnotised so she could finally learn the truth, she picked up the bedside phone and dialled.

"Diega."

"Hey," she said softly, muffled through her tears.

"Tahlia? What's wrong?" He was alarmed. It was still early, and she had never rung him before. She sounded scared, tired, overwhelmed and anxious all in one go.

"I dreamt last night. I think someone was there. I want to be hypnotised."

"Okay. Do you want to do it in your suite, or up on the roof for some privacy?"

"Up on the roof sounds good."

"Okay. I'll come and get you at ten."

"Okay, bye." Hanging up, she looked at the clock. God, it's only six. She groaned and rolled over, looking at the empty pillow beside hers. *I want to find out what Vegas gets up to. Summer's almost over an' he's been doing this for months. Getting more grouchy, more angry. Oh, God, I hope he's not doing drugs.* She started feeling freaked. *If he's doing drugs, can I still be with him?* Should *I still be with him?* She wasn't sure, but knowing Vegas was up to something bad, she knew she had to find out soon.

*****

At ten, Diega knocked on her door. "Are you ready?" he asked when she opened it.

She sighed and felt worn out. "Not really. But I need to do this so, let's go."

Taking Diega's lift upstairs, Tahlia saw that the roof had been moved over to provide shade. A camera was set up all ready to record, and there was someone waiting.

"Let me introduce you, ladies," Diega said as he moved Tahlia over to the couch. "Tahlia, this is Doctor Michelle North. She's a psychologist specializing in dreams and nightmares, and she is also a certified hypnotist. Doctor North, this is Tahlia."

They shook hands. "Call me Michelle. Please, have a seat and get comfortable. We might be here awhile." She flung her long brown braid over her shoulder and adjusted her glasses.

Sitting on the couch, Tahlia saw Diega start the camera.

"Tahlia. Tell me about the dreams. How long you've been having them, what they're like, then we'll go onto the hypnotism."

"Well, um, I see flashes of images. Wayne on the floor, blood everywhere. I'm looking at my hands, there's blood on them too. There's a gun on the floor beside Wayne, or I'm holding it, it changes, running an' running, I don't know where, but I know someone's after me. I don't see him, but I know he's there." She sighed in frustration and ran her hands through her hair.

"It's okay. We'll sort this out. Tell me about Wayne and your relationship."

"I don't know if you can call it a relationship. Since the age of eighteen, I ended up with deadbeat boyfriends. They beat me, I felt worthless. When they couldn't get any more out of me, they moved on to the next victim. I ended up with Wayne for about two years. At first, he wasn't abusive an' I thought he was different. But once I moved in, it started all over again. He would go out till late, demand the house be spotless, his dinner on the table, the usual. I don't know what sort of job he had, but no one came to the house, an' I didn't go anywhere."

"No one ever came to the house?" Doctor North asked.

"No…" Tahlia thought for a moment. "I'm having this strange feeling that someone was suppose to come over one night, but…I don't know."

"Okay. Let's move onto the hypnotism. Would you like to lie down?"

"Um, okay." She lay down, put her feet up, and plumped a cushion behind her head.

Doctor North sat in a chair behind her. "I want you to start counting backward from one hundred. Okay?"

"Okay. 100, 99, 98, 97, 96, 95…"

"Tahlia, can you hear me?"

"Yes."

"Okay. I want you to go back to the night Wayne died. Remember, you are safe, and no one is going to hurt you. Okay?"

"Okay."

"What happened that night? The night Wayne died?"

"I'd been home all day cleaning. That's all he wanted me to do, like a good little housewife. I had his dinner ready when he got home at five-thirty, an' he told me we were going to have a guest that night. He took me into the bedroom an' gave me a dress to wear, an' said I was to get dressed up 'cause I was gonna be a gift for his friend. *'What do you mean a gift? I don't wear clothes like this,'* I said. *'Shut up,'* he said, *'you'll do as I say…'"* A sob caught in her throat. "He hit me."

"Tahlia, remember, you are safe. No one is going to hurt you. Wayne *will not* and *cannot* hurt you. It's okay." Doctor North's voice was soothing.

In a quiet voice, Tahlia continued. "He hit me. Slapped me across the face, an' then, grabbed my hair and pushed me down onto the bed. He said, *'you're my gift to my friend an' you'll do what he wants, but till he's here, you'll do what I want.'"* She stopped, breathing hard. "He raped me," she whispered. "When he was done, he showered an', I lay on the floor crying." Another sob.

"Tahlia, it's okay, it's okay. Wayne can't hurt you anymore. It's okay."

"Wayne made me tidy the room then shower. He told me to get ready an' stay in the bedroom till he called for me. Hours went by, but Wayne didn't call. I fell asleep on the bed an' woke to hear angry voices. It was Wayne an' someone else, a man. They were yelling, something smashed. I think they were fighting. I didn't want to go out there, but, for some reason, I felt compelled to. So I opened the door quietly, an' slowly walked down the hall. They were yelling, fighting, then Wayne said, *hey man, what are you doing, no, come on, don't do that, no, what are you doing. No.*'"She was yelling, raising her voice as Wayne had.

"Tahlia, it's okay. Calm down. It's okay. You're not really there. Pretend it's like a movie or TV program, and you're sitting there watching it," Doctor North suggested.

Calming down, Tahlia started again. "I was scared. I thought something bad was gonna happen an' Wayne was yelling an' then…then there…I was crouching, covering my ears. I think I was screaming. There was a sound, then a thud, an' I heard the back door slam. I don't know how, but suddenly, I'm beside Wayne, an' there's blood everywhere, I'm trying to stop it, but I can't…I think he's dead. The gun is beside him, I pick it up an' scream and drop it. I heard the door slam again an' I turn toward it. I see a shadow, someone's coming, so I run for the bedroom and lock the door. What am I gonna do? What am I gonna do? I run for the window an' push it open. I got out an' ran, just ran."

She swallowed, her breath ragged. "He was coming, he was after me. I don't know where I'm running to. I just run an' run an' run, an' finally, I hid. I don't know where. I just hid. Under someone's trashcan, I think. I heard someone, they were walking around like they were looking for me, but I was quiet, I didn't make a sound. Finally, the person was gone. I don't know how long I hid, till, I don't know. I snuck back to the house, into the window, an' grabbed my stuff, then walked into the living room. Wayne was still there, on the floor, blood, gun. It was so gross. I ran around the house finding food an' money. I found a stash Wayne had then I ran for the car an' took off. I headed to New York 'cause I had a letter saying my mother was dead. I didn't leave anything behind. I didn't have much, but I took it."

"Tahlia, do you remember seeing the person who shot Wayne? Did you see him at all?"

"No. I only saw shadows. I know he was a man by his voice, an' he breathed hard after running after me. I didn't see him."

"Tahlia, tell me how the licence plates on the car were changed."

"I slept in the parking lots of all-night gas stations, an' when no one was looking, I switched the plates. I've learned things over the years, I knew how."

Doctor North glanced over at Diega, who nodded. "Okay, Tahlia, I'm going to count to three, and you will wake up feeling calm and refreshed, remembering everything you've just said. Okay? One…two…three."

Tahlia slowly opened her eyes, feeling calm and relaxed.

"How do you feel?" Diega walked over and sat down beside her as she sat upright on the couch.

"Good. Great. I didn't kill Wayne." She felt relieved

and elated, finally knowing she was not a killer.

Doctor North stood. "Well, my work here is done."

"Thank you, thank you so much," Tahlia said, standing and shaking her hand. As the doctor walked out, Tahlia turned to Diega who was standing beside her. "I didn't kill him, I didn't kill him." A sob caught in her throat and she put her hands over her face as tears came to her eyes.

"No, sweetheart, you didn't kill him. You are *not* a murderer." Diega pulled her into his arms, letting her sob in relief. They sat down on the couch, and he continued to hold her, making her relax, while she let all the months of fear and anguish melt away.

"I can't believe it, I just can't believe it. All these months. So much time I spent worrying about being a killer. A murderer. God, all the nights I had bad dreams, they were definitely nightmares. Images of blood, an' a gun, me running. I couldn't remember if someone else was there, but now I know." She wiped her face.

Her tears had flowed so freely, knowing she wasn't responsible for the death of her previous partner. A man, she realised, she really didn't know anything about. *I have to stop doing that,* she thought, shaking her head. *I really need to sort out my priorities where men are concerned an' get myself together.*

She let herself fall back into Diega's arms, laying her head on his strong shoulder, sighing in relief. A sigh that let go of all her worries, all her problems. A cleansing sigh that washed it all away.

Diega's shoulders are so strong, she thought as the warm summer breeze floated along the rooftop paradise she was sitting in. She felt comfortable there, wrapped in his arms that were still around her. His chin rested lightly on the top of her head. It felt right. It felt good. *Damn, it felt so good.*

"How do we find out who did kill Wayne?" she asked, looking up at him.

"Well," he sighed, "whoever it was, was a professional. No fingerprints anywhere in the house. The gun was covered in Wayne's blood and your fingerprints, prints that were on the wall and in the bedroom on the windowsill. That's how you've been blamed. But I'll do what I can to make this go away." He gazed into her eyes. "I will *never* allow anyone to hurt you ever again. I will do everything in my power, everything in my control to keep you out of danger. Out of jail. You didn't do anything wrong. And I *will not* let any harm come to you." He traced his right forefinger gently along her jaw as she watched him. He wanted to kiss her and do so much more, but he needed to keep his distance until he could woo her away from Vegas. *Now isn't the time,* he thought. "How about some lunch?" he asked lightly.

"Is it lunchtime already?" she asked, surprised that so many hours had passed. She stretched out her weary body then lay back as Diega called down for the waiter.

She was so relaxed she could've fallen asleep right there in the warm glow of paradise had Diega not been eyeing off her reclining figure on the sofa that turned into a bed.

Remembering that it was the same sofa he'd ravished her on, she jumped up, wide awake, and poured herself a drink to cool off while Diega smiled knowingly behind her.

Over lunch, he asked what she would like to do that afternoon.

"I don't know," she said, stabbing at a piece of fish. "I thought I might go for a drive somewhere, maybe out in the desert, see what's there."

"Not on your own you won't!" Diega exclaimed, glaring at her.

"I'll be all right," she replied, smiling at him. "I'm not a killer, so I don't need to be scared anymore, or worry about things. You don't need to protect me."

His gaze was still on her. "That's *not* the point. The police still think you *are* a killer, and I don't want you out there on your own. Besides, someone *did* kill Wayne, and you said yourself that you were followed everywhere. You had a stalker, and you don't know if he's gone or given up on searching for you. *Or* still following you."

"Crap, I hadn't even thought about him still being after me," Tahlia interrupted, her fork stopping in mid-air. "I've just been worrying about the police finding me." She looked at Diega, concerned.

Diega picked up his wine glass. "He could be waiting for the right time to grab you and take you, and I won't rest until he's been found. I don't want you to worry about it while I try to find out who *did* kill Wayne. I'll protect you. There's more than enough security in and around the hotel. You'll be fine if you just stay close." He drank a mouthful of wine. "How about I drive?"

After considering the situation for a few moments, she agreed.

Chapter 17

As they drove north out of Las Vegas on the main highway, they came up to the exit Vegas and Manny had taken.

"Turn off here," Tahlia said, pointing.

"Anything in particular you want to see out here?" Diega asked, keeping his suspicions in check.

"No. Just haven't been out here is all. I want to see what it looks like." She ignored his tone, and as they drove, she saw there wasn't much of anything. Taking notice of the barren surroundings, she made mental notes.

After an hour, Diega stopped and turned around. "Time to head home?"

"What do people do out here?" she asked, "there seems to be…nothing."

"Well, Nevada is a desert."

"Yeah, I know." They sat in silence for the rest of the trip home, keeping to themselves, thinking their own thoughts.

That night, Tahlia had the most peaceful sleep ever. No Wayne. No gun. No blood.

*****

"If you don't change your attitude then I don't want to be with you. It's *that* plain an' simple. I will no longer put up with abuse of any kind, let alone the abuse I'm getting from *you* every time you come home from your weekends with Manny."

It was Monday, and Vegas had come back angry and abusive, so Tahlia was abusing him right back.

He didn't like it. The way she was standing up to him, trying to set him in his place. "What have you been up to while I been gone?" he asked. "'Cause somethin's happened to make ya this different." He knew Diega was to blame for the change in her. Tahlia. *His* woman, *not* Diega's. Something needed to be done, not yet, but very soon. "It's Diega in'it?" he demanded, "you sleepin' with him?" He looked at her shocked face. "Well, are you? 'Cause I won' stand for it, baby. You lettin' him stick it to ya when I'm not here."

"Don't be ridiculous," she cried, "I'm with you an' *I* don't cheat. But hey, if that's the way you feel, you're free to pack your shit an' leave. I'm not stopping you. I won't put up with your crap, Vegas. *Not* anymore. Change, or we're through."

The thought of losing her snapped him out of it. After all, he knew he had a good thing going and didn't want to spoil it. *Damn,* he thought, *he* is *stickin' to her. That filthy pig just can' wait for me to leave to get his dick inta her an' I gotta put up with it. Damn! He will pay for interferin' with my woman.* My *woman. Man… time for apologies.*

He was extremely apologetic. Again.

*****

Sex was different that week, with Vegas trying to show her that he loved her. It wasn't working. He was smoking more, seemed on edge all the time, constantly looked around, and their weekend together was in the hotel. As if he didn't want her out of his line of sight in case she tried to see Diega, or do something he didn't want her doing.

Just as the following week was the same, until Friday when he became over anxious. "You'll be stayin' in the hotel this weekend won' you, baby?"

"Don't know, I might go out on the town, live it up," she said, seeing if he took the bait.

"I don' think that's a good idea, baby. The cops might be closin' in, an' you don' wan' 'em findin' you, do you?" Vegas nervously stood in front of her.

She sighed and pushed her hair behind her ears. "I doubt the cops are after me. After all, they haven't found me." She wasn't about to let Vegas know how nervous she still was.

"Doesn' mean they're not after you, baby. I don' wan' you bein' found." He grabbed her face and kissed her, plunging his tongue into her mouth.

Tahlia pulled back and stared at him, seeing a strange look in his eyes. The same look he had given her at the campsite when he'd said he owned her. A look of power, control, telling her she was his and no one else's, that he wouldn't tolerate any other men taking her from him, having her, making her theirs instead. The look scared her, and she freaked out a little, her insides quivering at the power she saw in those deep pools of blue.

Picking her up and throwing her onto the bed, he yanked her shorts down, taking her panties with them. He slowly massaged her abdomen and thighs, toying with her vagina that had become wet instantly. Moving his hands up under her top, he found her nipples and started rubbing, making her groan despite her feelings and trepidations.

Her fears melted away as she did. Spreading her legs, she reached for his jeans, and unzipping them, let his hard-on free. Pushing her hands down, she clenched his taut ass and pulled him toward her, letting him into her private spot that was only for him. Their mouths joined, their tongues entwined, her hands still grabbed his backside, pulling him into her every time he pulled out.

His mouth moved down her neck to her breastbone, then took each breast in turn. Sucking her nipples and making her groan. Thrusting, they came together, making small grunting sounds. When it was over Vegas rolled off and lay on his back breathing hard.

Tahlia was now feeling uneasy, almost dirty. She hadn't wanted to have sex, but when he touched her, she was gone. She got up and dressed. "I'm going downstairs. See you next week." She left, leaving Vegas wondering what the hell had just happened.

*****

Saturday evening, Tahlia drove past Manny's place, but no one was home. Not even Maria. There were no lights on, except for the one on the porch, and no cars and no bike. Parking down the road, she watched for a while, slouched down in her seat. Nothing happened.

Resigned, she drove back to the hotel to do it all again Sunday.

*****

He watched her, intrigued, angry.

She had been following Vegas, parking outside of Manny's, taken photos even.

We can't have that, he thought, his mind turning to images of Vegas and Tahlia and how their sex life seemed to be going down the drain since their hot and wild night out in the desert. Which had been so titillating, so arousing.

He was worried that she was getting too close, even going under hypnosis to find out about her past. And my God did she find out. Well, she may know she didn't kill Wayne, but she doesn't know who did.

He looked at the file on his desk.

He knew things about Vegas no one else would.

Especially the woman he claimed he loved.

*****

Putting up with crap from Vegas was the last thing she wanted to do, and when he walked into the suite on Monday afternoon, she was ready. Then surprised.

"Hey, baby, these are for you." He handed her a huge bunch of roses. "I'm sorry for all the crap I've been givin' you, baby. I've been a bad boy. Please forgive me."

Tahlia looked up and down at the man in front of her. He looked like Vegas, tight jeans, white singlet. But he seemed tired, worn out, and had a strange scent about him.

"What have you gotten up to?" she asked, her left brow cocked.

"Just helpin' Manny out, baby, I'm gonna have a shower. Wanna join me?" His sexy grin spread slowly across his face.

"No. You go ahead. I'll see you downstairs."

"Okay, baby, see you then."

Walking out the door, Tahlia absolutely knew something was going on, and with summer ending, she didn't have much time left. She was determined to find out what Vegas was getting up to. And if that meant them no longer being together, and Vegas no longer being in her life as her partner, then so be it.

"Is that what I really want?" she asked herself, gliding down in the lift. "God, I don't know what the hell Vegas is up to, but I'll definitely be ready."

*****

Two weeks later, she had her chance. Waiting for Vegas to leave, she took off after him in the car she'd hired from a rental shop and kept in the employees parking lot so no one would know she had gone. Mandy had jumped at the chance to help her out and pretended the vehicle was hers if anyone asked why there was a strange car in the lot.

Keeping a good distance behind, she followed him to Manny's then a fast food outlet. Calling the music director on her cell, she told him she wouldn't be doing the show as something personal had come up.

As Tahlia followed Vegas out into the desert, night-time fell. She had no idea where they were going, but was glad to have a full tank and a spare tin of gas in the trunk.

After two hours of driving, they pulled off the highway toward a small town, then took a narrow track in another direction. Feeling a little suspicious, and very scared, Tahlia followed, by this time having pulled far back and turned off her lights. They drove toward a faint glow in the distance, and she drove slowly, thanking the rental shop for giving her a quiet car.

Parking a safe distance away, she grabbed her camera bag and slowly started walking, glad for her dark clothing. Finding a high, grass-covered dirt mound that seemed to go around the circumference, she quietly crawled up to the top and peeked over.

What she saw made her gasp. Ducking down in case someone had heard her, she waited, pulling her binoculars out of her bag when no one grabbed her.

She peeked over the edge again. The place looked like a compound. Several large warehouses, bright lights, cars and trucks, people walking around. Training her binoculars, glad they were the best kind available, she slowly scanned the area and found Vegas and Manny in the largest warehouse. She watched them for the next hour and took plenty of photos so she would have proof to throw at him if she needed to.

Because what she saw was unbelievable.

Vegas was dealing in guns!

Tahlia saw him and Manny taking them out of crates and putting them into boxes, then loading the boxes into vans. When it was done, most of the men left with their loads, but a few stayed behind with Vegas and Manny.

Beer started to flow, and they seemed to be celebrating as a car full of women pulled up to the gleeful delight of the men. Escorting the women into the shed, the men gave them drinks and started handing a small clear bag around. Vegas leant down and seemed to sniff something. Leaning back, he wiped his nose and gave a thumbs up.

Oh, my God, he *is* doing drugs!

She felt sick. The man she loved was becoming something she didn't like, had never wanted to be with again. Looking back at the scene, she saw both the men and women were snorting, and other bottles of alcohol were making the rounds.

The women were obviously hookers because they were kissing and groping the men who seemed to enjoy it, especially Vegas.

Oh, God, I'm gonna be sick, she thought, her hand covering her mouth, not wanting to believe what she was seeing. She saw Vegas stagger out of the warehouse and over to the wall of another where he relieved himself freely.

A blonde woman followed him, and rubbed herself against his back, wrapping her arms around him and stroking his penis.

And he was enjoying it!

What the…how dare he!

The woman was now in front of him, kissing him. He pushed her against the wall and touched her, feeling her. She kneeled in front of him and stroked him until he was hard, erect, taking him into her mouth she sucked.

OH, MY, GOD, oh, God, how could he? How could he do that to me? How could he? A sob caught in her throat and she saw a brunette woman join them.

Tahlia stared in shock and disbelief, unable to tear her eyes away as the brunette ground with him, lifting his top to rub his body. He leaned over his shoulder to kiss her and moved his arms behind him to grope her big ass as she pushed against him.

The blonde stopped and dragged her tongue up his torso as she stood. The women changed places, so the brunette was now in front, and Vegas pushed her against the wall, pulling her dress up to reveal no underwear.

Spreading her legs the woman took him inside of her, and while Vegas thrust, the blonde pulled her dress up and rubbed her body over his as if joining in. The two women were now kissing each other, and Vegas.

It was a full-on orgy!

Not wanting to see any more, and feeling violently ill, Tahlia grabbed her bag and ran. Racing back to her car, she fell to the ground and threw up, seemingly unable to stop. Minutes later, sitting in the front seat, she sobbed uncontrollably in disgust and shock.

Realising she needed to get out of there, she left, driving blindly through her pain-racked tears, feeling every ounce of anger and hatred for the man she loved.

She screeched to a stop in the hotel basement, and not even bothering to park the car, ran for the lift. On the way up, she cried even harder, having no idea of what she should do.

Watching the whole scene in surprise and worry, the parking garage attendant rang upstairs and informed Kate of what had happened. She hurried into her boss's office to tell him. Anxious and out of his mind, he turned a wall full of monitors on to see for himself.

Tahlia ran into her suite, angry, sick, not knowing what to do until she saw some clothes lying on the bed. A thought came to her mind. Grabbing a pair of scissors from her desk, she proceeded to slash the clothes, and running into the closet, she grabbed the rest of Vegas' stuff, and before she knew it, they were destroyed.

She was so angry. Felt so abused and used she started trashing the suite until she collapsed into a sobbing heap on the floor.

Diega barged through the door, running to her, pulling her into his arms. "Tahlia, sweetheart. What happened? Tell me what happened." He was full of worry and fear, and it showed clearly on his face.

She shook her head and just clung to him, only able to say one word. "Vegas."

Diega turned to Kate. "Pack a case for her. I'm getting her out of here." Pulling his phone from his pocket, he called down to the garage. "Get my car ready. We'll be down shortly."

Holding her tightly, he wondered what the hell happened. When she called in to say she wouldn't be doing the show, everything had become mayhem. She had disappeared, and no one knew where. She hadn't taken her car, and nobody knew what she was driving so they couldn't check her GPS.

Kate came into the living room with a case.

"All right, sweetheart, I'm getting you out of here. Let's go." He pulled her to her feet and walked her around to his private lift. On the way down, he told Kate to let the manager, Rick Sanders, know he was in charge. "I don't know how long we'll be gone, so I want you to change the security code on her suite. Get all of his crap out of there, he's banned from the hotel. Let all the staff know. He's not allowed to set foot on this property. As for the show, the reason will be that she has fallen ill, and has been taken to the best clinic for treatment."

"Sir."

The lift doors opened, and Diega walked Tahlia to his car and gently strapped her in. She seemed to be in a stupor, and he was worried. Getting into the driver's seat, he looked at her forlorn expression and felt disgusted at whatever had happened to put her in this state. Stepping on the gas, he drove out of the garage and into the dark black night, two cars of bodyguards following behind.

Chapter 18

Tahlia sobbed quietly for the first half of the trip and fell asleep for the other.

Diega felt sick. He had never seen her this upset and knew it had something to do with Vegas. *I'll kill the bastard if he hurt her,* he thought, slamming the steering wheel with his hand. Never had he felt so angry over the abuse of a woman. But this woman was Tahlia. And he wanted to be with her in every way. *Vegas, I promise you, I will destroy you if you've hurt her in any way. I will tear you limb from limb and watch you die slowly. And believe me, you will suffer.*

Turning off the main road onto a smaller one, they drove for some time before passing through the high steel gates of a compound. Pulling up to a large, spacious house, he drove into the garage, and alighting, ran around to the passenger door and gently lifted Tahlia out. Carrying her inside, he took her upstairs to the master suite.

A guard had followed, and while he pulled the covers back, Diega gently laid her on the bed and removed her shoes. Tucking the covers around her, he watched her sleep. She looked exhausted. And sick.

Motioning the guard over to the door, Diega leant in close. "I want Vegas hunted down. Follow his every movement. And make sure this place is secure. I want no one coming here. And I mean, *no one.*"

"Sir." The guard left his boss sitting in an easy chair beside the bed, watching over her, falling into an exhausted sleep himself.

*****

Diega woke Saturday morning to see she was still asleep. Not wanting to leave her, but knowing he needed to shower and change, he made it quick, checking in on her before going down to the kitchen to make some breakfast.

All day it was the same. Either Tahlia woke up sobbing, and Diega held her until she fell asleep, or she slept with Diega watching over her.

*****

Sunday was the more of the same, and Diega became even more worried. Pacing the floor, barely leaving her, he slept beside her after she sobbed herself to sleep. He had never seen any woman like this before, let alone Tahlia, so he knew it definitely had *something* to do with Vegas.

Damn him, he thought, pacing across the room and back. *What did he do to make her so morose? Did he hit her? Hurt her? Rape her?* The thought made him sick with grief and anger at the bastard who had done something to make her so upset. *How could he do something like that to the woman he claimed to love? Violate her so badly. If he raped her, I'll kill him. I'll kill him, and then he won't be in our lives anymore. He'll be out of the way, and I'll have Tahlia all to myself. Just me. Just Tahlia and me. We'll be together, and we'll be happy and have a life together just the two of us and no Vegas!*

*****

Monday was overcast, with the threat of a storm, and Diega was standing in the doorway when she woke. "Are you okay? I've been worried." He was immensely relieved, but didn't know if he should go to her, so he only ventured in a few steps.

"I'm fine," she replied, sitting up. She had no idea of where they were, but the room was amazing, with rich red bedding, antiques, art and paintings.

"Have a shower. Your clothes are in the closet. Then you can come down and have some breakfast. Sound good?"

Tahlia smiled softly. "Sounds great."

"Okay. I'll see you downstairs," Diega said, and closed the door behind him.

Getting out of bed, she walked into the bathroom. *Wow,* she thought, *it's fancier than my suite, an' so ornate.* Gold taps, frosted glass, and a huge bathtub made of black marble.

A hot shower felt good and refreshed her. Dressing,

she was surprised to see her clothes hanging up, even though Diega had mentioned them.

Walking along the upstairs hallway, she admired the various artworks and ornaments, and as she came to the backless wood stairs, she could see the open floor plan as she descended. The high cathedral roof with exposed beams, the slate flooring that led to the wide kitchen ahead of her with Diega standing at the island bench in the middle with his back to her.

The living room was to her left with two long leather sofas facing each other in front of a massive black marble fireplace and fur rug. Decorative white organza curtains ran down the length of the huge floor-to-ceiling window that also stretched the entire length of the living room.

Seeing the view, she gasped and ran over to the large French doors leading to the patio. "Ohhh, the view," she gushed, gazing out over the landscape.

"Gorgeous, isn't it," Diega said. Standing beside her, he handed her a glass of juice.

"Wait, where are we?" she inquired, looking at him as she took the glass.

"We're at my retreat. Several hours out of Vegas. Surrounded by thick forests and a high steel wall. You're safe here."

Looking over the wide slate deck and down a few steps, she saw a large rectangular pool, a spa to the right, and what looked to be an outdoor sauna to the far left. Down from that was a grassy green knoll leading to a very large oval shaped lake with a dock. The lake gave her a strange feeling as she looked at it. Its darkness seemed to call to some deep emotion inside of her, making her shiver. She looked away at the thick luscious green tree-filled forest that seemed to surround them.

"It's gorgeous, definitely," she agreed as Diega opened the doors. They stepped out onto the terrace and she breathed deeply. "Ahh, the air is so fresh here."

"That's why I love it here. It's fresh, it's private, it's perfect."

Walking to a small slate railing that ran along the deck, they sat down and looked over the property. Turning to look at the house, she gasped again. "Wow," she said, her eyes widening in shock. "This is gorgeous too. Is it made of actual logs?" Her gaze roamed back and forth along the building.

Diega grinned, looking over the house himself. "Not real ones. I had the place built to be environmentally sound, but to still look like a log cabin."

"A hugely massive two-storey log cabin," she replied.

Diega was still grinning. "It's not *that* huge. Four bedrooms with personal baths upstairs. Kitchen, laundry, living, den and office downstairs."

"That's not huge?" Tahlia laughingly interrupted.

Diega laughed back. "There's a five car garage just behind the house, and underneath is a huge basement that's for storage. I keep jet skis, water skis, buggies, sleds, anything to do with sports in there. Even a small motorboat."

"A motorboat?" Her eyes widened again.

"Yes, a motorboat. We might take it out on the lake while we're here. Would you like to do that?"

Looking at him and seeing his eagerness, she couldn't

help but grin again. "I'd love to. But how long are we staying? An' when did we come here? Oh, my God, what's today? I have a show, we can't stay."

Diega stopped her by putting his forefinger gently on her lips. "Today is Monday, and you are officially on holiday for at least two weeks. So don't worry. We'll have someone or something fill in for you while you're here." He watched her. "I brought you here late Friday night. After disappearing, then calling in to say you weren't going to do the show, everyone freaked out. Including me. We couldn't find you, and then you came tearing into the hotel and trashed your suite and *his* things. You were so worked up I decided to get you out of there, so I brought you here. I could see something was terribly wrong." His eyes searched hers.

Tahlia gazed over the lake, remembering. "My bag. Where's my bag?" she asked, panicking.

"Which bag?" he asked.

"My camera bag in my rental car. Where is it?"

He shook his head. "We didn't bring it. I'll call Kate to find it, okay?"

"I took some photos. I don't want anyone seeing," she said in a small voice.

"Okay. Kate will put it in my safe until you return. Is that okay?"

Nodding slightly, she agreed, feeling a little calmer.

"Do you want to talk about what happened?" he asked gently.

Shaking her head, she said nothing.

"Do you want some breakfast?"

She sighed. "Sure."

After breakfast, and for the rest of the day, Tahlia sat out on the deck, reliving every moment of what she'd seen. *What am I gonna do,* she thought desperately, panicking as she cried, *what am I gonna do? Do I stay with him? Do I leave him? Do I confront him when I get home? God, I don't know what to do, what am I gonna do? Why is he doing those things? Did he do them before he met me? Is that the kind of person he is? Someone that snorts drugs an' cheats on the woman he's with at the time? Can I still be with him knowing what I know?*

She gazed across the lake and thought she heard her name being called. "What?" she replied. *Wait, did Diega call me?* She looked through the huge windows and saw him sitting on one of the sofas reading a book.

He looked up and smiled, giving a small wave.

She smiled back and turned to look at the lake again, a weird and eerie feeling washing over her.

*****

At the hotel, Vegas rode up on his bike and arrogantly strode inside. Ten guards came running up and escorted him back the way he'd came. "What are ya doin'? Get your filthy hands off me, hey." Vegas started fighting, but the guards restrained him.

"Sir, you are no longer a guest of *The Montiamo,* and are not welcome on this property," Mark Dalton, head of security told him.

Another guard had carried out a garbage bag and threw it at Vegas as the others pushed him out the door.

"Here are your clothes. Now leave." The bag lay where it landed.

"What do ya mean, I'm no longer a guest an' not welcome," Vegas bellowed and straightened his clothes. "I'm not leavin'. *Do you know who I am? Do you know who I live with?* The star of this hotel is *my woman.* Where is she? Get her down here, she'll sort it out." He waved his arms around in emphasis.

Mark glared at him. "Sir, Miss Tahlia isn't here."

Vegas was pissed off, surprised, and suspicious all at once. "What do ya mean, she isn' here? She has a show tonight."

Mark stood firm. "Sir, she's not here. She's taken ill and has gone to receive treatment."

Vegas fronted him. "What do ya mean, she's sick? Where is she? I don' believe you, she hasn' been sick since I met her. Where is she, where is she?" The guards grabbed him, twisted his arm behind his back, and restrained him on the ground while people stopped and stared.

Mark leaned down to speak into his ear. "Sir, Miss Tahlia isn't here, and unless you want to be arrested, I suggest you leave and don't come back."

Vegas shut up, knowing that being arrested was the last thing he needed. "Awright, awright," he growled, ripping his arm from the grasp of the guard. "I'll go, I'll go. But I wanna leave a message for Tahlia. Gimme a pad n' pen."

Allowing Vegas to write his message, Mark and the guards stayed wary in case he tried something.

Handing the pad back, Vegas gave them a sneer,

grabbed the bag, mounted his bike, and roared away.

Where the hell is she? he thought, furious at the treatment he'd just received. *An' what the hell just happened?* Gunning his bike, he roared down the street and headed back to Manny's for a place to stay.

As Vegas rode away, Mark looked at the note. Calling his boss, he relayed the message, listening to his orders. Hanging up, he screwed the paper into a ball and threw it into a trashcan.

*****

At six p.m. the rainclouds poured forth, and standing in her bedroom, Tahlia watched the rain come down outside the French doors. She had worried all day, coming upstairs for a nap, even after sleeping all weekend she was still emotionally exhausted.

When she woke, there was a heavy depressive weight bearing down on her. She had known a lighter version of this feeling. A feeling that had come whenever a man had hit her, lied to her, cheated on her.

But this was different.

Heavier. Darker. Deeper. Smothering.

Unable to breathe, she opened the doors and stepped onto the balcony. Although it was raining, she was still able to see down to the lake, which strangely seemed to be calling to her.

"Tah-li-a," the singsong voice called, "Tah-li-a."

Walking down the balcony stairs, Tahlia stepped across the deck and past the pool. She was soaked to the skin, but didn't notice.

"Come-to-me, come-to-me…"

She walked down the grassy knoll and stopped in front of the dock. Still feeling the heavy, depressed burden, she put one foot on the dock, then the other. Walking slowly, one foot at a time, she stopped at the end and looked down into the deep, dark water.

"Tah-li-a," the voice called again, "come-to-me."

Mixing the hot chicken broth, Diega watched it simmer and leant over the pot. *Mmm, smells good. Time to get Tahlia.* Turning off the stove, he walked out of the kitchen, into the living room, and headed for the stairs. Glancing out the door at the rain, he saw a dark shape standing down on the dock and stopped. "No, it can't be. Oh, no, oh, no." He ran for the doors and flung them open, ran across the deck and past the pool. He slid down the knoll, stopping at the dock. "Tahlia," he called softly, not wanting to scare her. "Tahlia," he called louder, before seeing her fall in.

Tahlia heard the lake call her, and not thinking she had anything to live for, allowed herself to fall.

"Tahlia," he screamed. Running across the dock, he dove into the deep, dark water.

The water flowed over her. Cold and black. Sinking further, deeper.

Deeper into the depths of darkness.

Deeper into the depths of blackness.

Down, down, down.

Letting herself go, she could feel all the pain and anguish float away.

No more anger. No more hate.

Down, down, down.

No more pain for the parents she'd lost. No more pain for the boyfriends that had abused her.

Down, down, down.

She felt relief. A release of all things bad. An acceptance of all things good and wonderful. Warm and loving. Bright and vibrant.

Down, down, down.

This is so nice, she thought hazily. So peaceful. So pain-free…

So she was surprised to feel herself being grabbed and dragged back to the surface.

"Let me, uh, go, uh, let me, uh, go," she tried to scream through gasps of air as she struggled against Diega, but exhaustion overtook her, and she stopped fighting.

Diega pulled them both out of the lake, and picking her up, carried her into the house to the laundry where he set her down and pulled off his sweater and then hers. "Take your jeans off," he said and grabbed a big fluffy towel. He rubbed her down and pushed her jeans off himself when she didn't move. Taking off his own pants, he threw the clothes over a rack to dry.

He wrapped a warm robe around her, then towelled himself down before putting on his own robe. Carrying her into the living room, he sat her down in front of the roaring fire. Rubbing her hair with a towel, he spoke roughly. "What were you thinking going out into the rain? Were you trying to kill yourself by jumping into the lake, hoping you'll drown?"

He looked at her and saw the tears flowing down her face. She was racked with sobs, and he held her tightly as she cried. When it was over, he got them both mugs of soup. "Drink this, it will warm you up."

She took the mug and drank. Sitting on the fur rug in front of the fire, they leaned against a big pile of soft, comfy pillows Diega had put against the sofa.

He watched patiently as she finished her soup, and started pacing around the room, waiting for her to talk in her own time.

"He cheated on me," she said finally, shrugging in defeat. Wiping away more tears, she stopped pacing and faced Diega. "He's been cheating on me, an' God knows what germs he's been passing on." She didn't know what else to say.

He didn't move. "How do you know?"

"Well…I know that you know that I've been tailing him. Or trying to. Well, I followed him Friday night. Out to a compound way out in the boonies, an' I watched as he an' Manny repacked guns in boxes an' got pissed an' snorted drugs." She was flinging her arms around to emphasise her words. "Then Vegas went out to take a leak, an' a woman followed him an' gave him a head job. Then a second woman came out an' he screwed her up against the wall. That's when I got out of there an' came back to the hotel. He cheated on me, an' now I don't know what to do." She sat on the arm of the sofa opposite Diega, gasping for breath and wiping away her tears.

He was extremely interested in what she'd told him, realising that there must be photos in the camera in her bag. He made a mental note to call Kate. "Tahlia," he said softly, "do you still want to be with him, knowing what you know?"

"No. No, I don't. But I love him…" Her face fell and crumpled.

"Tahlia. I love you. I want to make you happy. I want to give you everything your heart desires. Do you love me?" He knew what her answer would be.

She looked at him sadly, wiping away more tears. "Yes, oh, God, yes. But I love him too, an' since I met him first, it makes it all complicated." She ran for the kitchen to get away from his gaze, and removing a jug of juice from the fridge, she poured herself a drink.

Diega followed her. Putting the mugs in the sink, he turned around and leaned against it. "I know it's complicated right now. But you can make it simple. Do you want to be with a man who deals in guns, snorts drugs, and cheats on you? The answer is yes or no." He waited for her.

"No, I don't." Sighing, she went on. "But I'm not going to run to you an' jump into a relationship either. That's all I've done since I was eighteen, from one man to another. I've barely been on my own. Except for between Wayne an' Vegas. An' if it wasn't for Vegas I wouldn't feel more empowered. I wouldn't have my job. I wouldn't have my life." She ran her hands through her hair in exasperation.

"I wouldn't give him that much credit," Diega said under his breath.

"I don't know what to do. Do I just dump him? Decide here an' now to never see him or have contact with him again. I had a feeling he was on drugs as his behaviour was getting worse. An' I figured he was doing something bad with Manny, but not gun running if that's what it's still called these days." She glanced at him then quickly looked away. "An' yes, I will admit that I was attracted to you from the moment I saw you across the casino. I'd never seen any man with the confidence you exude, an' since meeting you I… developed feelings an'…no man like you has ever been interested. All my life you were the sort of man I prayed for, begged to God for. I wanted to be happy like my parents were before Dad died. I just wanted to be loved an' never was. Not really." She looked around the kitchen, tears welling in her eyes.

"When I saw you an' then met you, I thought, is he it? Is he the man I've been waiting for? The one man that will make all the pain go way, the one man who will love me, *truly* love me, an' never hurt me, or hate me, or cheat on me. Is he the one?"

She sighed. "You know I've been responding to you more an' more as we spend time together. A part of me wants you so much," her voice trailed off, and unable to look him in the eye, she walked into the living room.

Diega's heart was singing. He wanted to run after her, take her into his arms and never let go. To hold her and love her, cherish her as she'd never been, never had with any other man. His mind was racing. *I need to tread carefully,* he thought. *I need to let her know how I feel, but not push her or she might run again. And I can't have her doing that. I need to be careful, take it slow, one step at a time.* He took a deep breath and followed her into the living room. "When you go back to Las Vegas, do you want to see Vegas again? Live with him, sleep with him…make love with him?" He made sure he had chosen his words carefully.

Feeling sick at the thought, she turned to him. "No. No, I don't. The thought of that makes me sick an' makes my skin crawl." Walking over to the fireplace to warm herself, Diega stood behind her.

Resting his hands gently on her shoulders, he spoke softly in her right ear. "Then let me show you what *real* love is. I will never hurt you. I will never cheat on you. I will love you with the whole of my heart, body and soul. With every fibre of my being. And I really don't mind you leaving Vegas for me. Believe me. Believe me, when I say to you, I love you. I love you, and I want you. Now." Turning her around, he stroked the soft, smooth skin of her cheek. Seeing the look in her eyes he leaned toward her, stopping just before their mouths met.

Feeling unsure, she moved her head away before resting her forehead against his lips. Lips that felt so soft. So full. *So* tempting.

Diega kissed her forehead gently and held her in his arms. "It's okay," he whispered against her skin, "it's okay. You can do this." He looked down at her. So lovingly. So tenderly. A small smile on his lips.

"I can't, I can't," she whispered, closing her eyes and shaking her head slowly. Her brain was full of fog, and she couldn't think, didn't *want* to think. "I can't." But the passion and desire were overwhelming and gazing into his eyes, she touched her lips to his.

A million volts of electricity blew through her, and she wrapped her arms around him, holding him close. Their tongues danced in slow motion, tasting each other's sweetness, sliding deep, sensually mating. Feeling alive, she grabbed for his robe.

"No," he said, stopping her and taking her hands in his. "We're going to take this nice and slow, savour every moment." His eyes were dark, glittering with passion and desire.

Being used to raw, hungry sex, this excited her even more.

Gazing deeply into her eyes, Diega slowly opened her robe, sliding it over her shoulders to let it fall to the floor.

Tahlia shuddered in pleasure at his touch, groaning as his fingers caressed her hot flesh. Unable to hold on, she undid his robe, and sliding her hands over his muscular torso, pushed it over his shoulders. Falling against him, their mouths met then made their way down each other's body.

He slid her bra straps down, tasting the hollow of her neck and stroking the soft silkiness of her shoulders, sending a stream of fire racing up and down her spine.

Groaning, she locked her arms around him, kissed his chest, felt the soft hair against her face.

Diega's hands skated down the curve of her lower spine, caressing it, making her arch into him as he cupped the soft globes of her bottom. His lush lips moved across her body slowly, teasingly, making their way to her breasts as his hands came around to her front, massaging her abdomen.

She slid her hands over his hard body, feasting on every inch of him, her hands greedily grabbing at his flesh. Moving her mouth over him, she gently bit him, tearing a groan from his throat, before bringing her lips back to his for a passionate kiss.

Both of them were breathless.

Diega slid his hands around to her back, unhooked her bra, and slowly, slowly, brought his hands back around to her breasts, sliding the material off, letting it fall onto her robe.

Gripping his arms to hold herself up, she arched in pleasure. His large manly hands encompassed her voluptuous breasts, gently kneading, feeling her soft velvety nipples under his thumbs. Leaning against him, unable to hold on, she felt herself come to the brink as Diega's mouth latched onto her right nipple, playing his lips over it, his tongue teasing it, tasting its velvety goodness. "Aaaahhh," she gasped, his right hand still playing with her left breast. The room was spinning, and she was losing all sense of reality. His hands slid slowly down her curves, finding their way into her panties and slowly pushed them down until they fell.

He gazed at her, hearing his heart hammer in his chest, feeling his blood race. "God you're beautiful," he whispered. She was the most incredible woman he'd ever seen. Whatever imperfections she thought she had, made no impact. Tahlia was the woman he wanted to love for the rest of his life. He wanted to show her all a man and a woman could experience together, a feast of sensuality that would last all night and for the rest of their lifetime. It was a full, total, and all empowering, tenderly emotional level no other woman had taken him to.

Tahlia stood there smiling shyly, and her hands reached for his shorts. Sliding them down over his taut ass, she brought her hands around to set him free. Pushing his shorts down she stared at him. His hard shaft stood proudly. *My God, he's huge,* she thought, blushing. *He's not going to fit inside of me. I've never been with a man this big before, what if I can't accept him. God, what if I never want him to leave. Just stay in there forever.* She blushed harder, embarrassed, noticing he was watching her intently, a knowing smile on his face. Reaching out her hand, she stroked him, making him groan and reach for her.

His eyes were dark pools of desire that burned into hers. He picked her up and lay her down on the fur rug in front of the fire. Lying against her. Kissing her. His right hand explored.

Groaning, Tahlia wrapped her left leg around him while his hand slid over her. Up and down. Back up to her left breast, tormenting her with his kisses. "I can't wait, I want you now," she rasped, tearing her mouth away from his. His body felt amazing against hers and made her blood pulsate through every pore.

"We're taking this slowly," Diega said.

"No. I don't want to go slow. I want you now." She pulled him onto her, wrapping herself around him. "I want you now," she repeated, grabbing his ass. Feeling him between her legs, she moved into position to accept him.

Pulling his knees up beside her hips, he set himself to enter, then plunged deep into her rich, intoxicating passage, which fused around him like a second skin as he probed her innermost self and kept going.

Gasping, she gazed into his eyes, his face now above

hers, and in slow, deliberate movements, he slid in and out. Hot flesh inside hot flesh, burning an imprint onto his brain, making him crave every possible sensation, every level of intimacy, penetrating every part of her. His mouth crashed down on hers. His tongue stroked in sync with his manhood. The dual invasion drove a passionate force inside, driving both of them insane, swelling inside of her as he did, thrusting back and forth. Their hands ran all over each other.

Her nipples were hard against his chest, being aroused by the soft hair that had set her breasts on fire. "Uhh, ahh." She was giddy at the intensity, ravenous for his mouth, falling into a deep well of fierce desire as her body received him over and over again, entirely focussed on the erotic motions he was making. Holding him there, never wanting to let go, arching her hips, rising to meet his never-ending need as he moved into the position to give her his all.

His rampant desire commanded her to feel him, rippling through her as she came and kept coming, unable to be sated. The erotic throaty cries of her untamed need and passion spurred him on even more, and he buried himself inside of her, coming at her with all of the urgency she felt, her erotic scent and heat invaded him, an invasion he welcomed with his entire body and soul. He stopped, still intimately joined to her, allowing her to come down from the electric high she was riding before starting the sweet torture again.

Groaning in pleasure, Tahlia spread her legs as wide as she could, digging her fingers into his back, pulling him into her as far as possible. His hot, wet mouth found her breast, drawing her hard peak into it.

He had to show her how much he loved her. How much he wanted her. Wanted this, needed this, needed to show her what real love was from the first moment he saw her, his flesh to collide with hers, her breasts against his chest, her legs around him. His fierce erection pounded inside her and found its way home.

He had never felt so masculine as he met and answered her pleas for more. The soar of his own pleasure and driving need could no longer be contained as he indulged in the desires that demanded release. His hard shaft seized fiercely as he pushed Tahlia through climax after climax, rolling over the swirling turbulent waves of heat that spilled from him in the last sensual act of mating. She cried out ecstatically, and moments later, he joined her as they came together. Falling over the brink…

*****

He had followed her. He was watching her.

Watching them as he peered through the French doors of the retreat into the living area where he could see Diega on top of Tahlia. Thrusting back and forth as she made throaty little cries, her legs spread wide. Her body so voluptuous on the fur rug in front of the fireplace as she writhed away, arching and groaning.

He exhaled a deep sigh.

What a whore! What did she think she was doing running into another man's arms? Did she think she was in love? Did she think he was the man of her dreams? *What about the one she left behind? What about me!*

He stared at them again, her cries louder than the rain he was standing in, soaking him right through to the skin.

It wasn't the rain.

He glanced down and saw his naked hard-on, fully erect and releasing itself of the seed that flowed from his body. It was all over him.

Like I care!

Looking at Tahlia on the floor climaxing, he knew one thing was certain. That would be him soon, lying there on top of her, taking her again and again as he rammed his dick so far inside of her that she wouldn't be able to stop crying out in pain.

The pain she'll feel for cheating on him with another man. The pain she'll feel when he punishes her for what she's done. The pain she'll feel for being the lying tramp of a whore that she is.

She will be mine!

Chapter 19

Hours later, Tahlia woke, wrapped in Diega's arms under a blanket in front of the fire. Looking up at him, she saw he was awake and watching her. "Hey," she said softly, a small smile playing across her lips.

"Hello," he said, smiling back.

"How long have you been awake?" She nestled into his chest and breathed deeply.

"Awhile. I've been watching you, contented, just lying here with you in my arms, embracing your softness and how you mould to me. Feeling incredibly lucky to have you by my side. Finally. After all these months of watching you from afar, dreaming about you every night, coming up with new ways of making love to you." He kissed her forehead gently.

She flushed, embarrassed by his words. "I, ah, don't know what to say to that, really. Um, thank you."

"For what?" he asked, a little confused.

She sat up beside him and snuggled into his side. "For this. Before Vegas, I had never experienced an orgasm. He was the first man to make me feel alive an' like a woman. Then, I met you, an' you made me feel different to the way Vegas did. You are so different to him, the way you make me feel, the way I react. This… this was amazing. Incredible. I feel lucky too, after all the crappy men I've had in my life, that I've had two incredible men love me an' want me. I can't believe it's ended up here, with you."

"Sweetheart, you don't ever have to worry about ending up with horrible men again," he said, stroking her face and feeling the softness of her skin. "I will be the one you can rely on, to love you, want you, support you through everything you go through during the rest of your life. I will be here for you. Always." Diega kissed her, and the electricity flowed again.

✶✶✶✶✶

Tuesday, they spent relaxing by the pool, laying on a double lounge, their arms around each other. Since the sun was bright and warm, Diega rubbed sunscreen all over her body. He teased her with slow movements, his hands moving over her, making her groan, sliding them into her bikini, touching her, before his tongue chose to get in on the act.

Deciding it was time to play dot-to-dot, Diega joined Tahlia's beauty spots together using his tongue instead of a marker. But his wicked tongue had a wicked mind of its own and joined spots where there were no spots to join. Pulling a towel over them, Diega lay on top of her and slid between her legs.

Kissing and touching they cried out in pleasure as they pleased each other.

*****

He sat back in his seat. How dare she allow him to do those things to her, especially outside where people could see. Retreat or not it was still out in public.

I don't like this, he thought, vehemently. Not one bit. First, she leaves me and then screws him out in public, although she did that with that other animal she's been with. But that's not the point. The point is she shouldn't be doing those things with any other man except me.

I'll make sure of that!

*****

Wednesday, they went horse riding. It was a new experience for Tahlia, having never been near a horse, and she was surprised there was a stable on the property. "You didn't tell me you had horses."

"Well, I haven't told you much about this place. I wanted to keep a few things secret, so I could surprise you every day," Diega said, smiling down at her.

"You certainly have, but you know I don't know how to ride," she said, looking back at him.

"That's okay. I'll give you a few pointers."

He showed her how to mount and dismount on an old horse named Ted, and to hold the reins to make Ted stop and go. When they were ready, Diega had her mount and jumped up behind her.

"Aren't we taking two horses?" she asked, surprised.

"No. I want to be close to you. Lunch is packed, and

we have all we need. Ready?" Diega was still smiling as he adjusted himself.

"Ready." She grinned back.

Walking away from the stables and down a riding path, they went through the thick green forest surrounding them. They walked around the property, with Ted being the perfect gentleman, taking their time and enjoying the day. Tahlia loved the feel of Diega's embrace. So loving and warm. She felt safe and relaxed, refusing to think bad thoughts. They trotted past the house and around the lake to where they could see the house in the distance and they dismounted for lunch.

"How big is this place?" she asked, amazed.

"Two thousand acres," Diega replied, laying a blanket down on a grassy, shady knoll under a tall, wide tree.

Lunch was delicious beef sandwiches with fruit for dessert, and afterwards, they lay on the blanket wrapped in each other's arms watching the clouds float by.

Running her hand over Diega's torso, Tahlia purred. "God you feel good."

"I taste good too," he replied, laughing lightly.

She leaned up on her elbow to gaze into his eyes. "Mmm, you've said that before, so…let's see if it's true." She kissed him, letting her tongue explore the inside of his mouth, tasting him. "Mmm, you're right. You do taste good, like fruit."

Diega rolled her onto her back and lay on top of her, looking serious. "Of course I'm right. And *you* taste amazing."

His mouth met hers in a passionate kiss, his tongue plunging into her mouth. Their hands were all over each other feeling, arousing. Tahlia wrapped her legs around Diega, keeping him close. Sliding his hands under her top, he pushed it up.

"Wait, we can't here," she cried, quickly glancing around.

"Why not. We did it by the pool yesterday. Besides, I have a spare blanket," he said, grinning wickedly as he pulled it over them. Diega pushed her top up and over her head, then proceeded to kiss every inch of her.

Making his way down, he unzipped her jeans and pulled them off, leaving her to lie there in her bra and panties. "God you're beautiful," he said, touching and kissing her.

Gasping and shuddering, she reached for his polo shirt and yanked it over his head. Feeling his chest hair against her, she shuddered again. The excitement was definitely building. Undoing his jeans she pushed them down, letting him take them off, and lying under the blanket their bodies touched, pleasure pulsating through both of them.

Diega removed her bra and began massaging her breasts.

Groaning, she arched into him as she held his head to her right breast, he sucked gently, moving his mouth over her soft flesh. "Nuhhh, ahh," she gasped as he held both breasts. "I, can't, wait, want, you, now."

Sliding his mouth down her body, he pulled her panties off, leaving a trail of hot wet kisses on her skin.

Spreading her legs to give him access, she waited while he took his shorts off.

Lying between her legs, his body against hers, he

entered.

"Aaaahhh," she gasped again, feeling him inside of her. He seemed to slide in forever as if he would never stop.

Diega smothered her in kisses and slowly moved.

Tahlia slid her hands all over him feeling every muscle work to pleasure her. Grabbing his ass, she pulled him inside and clenched her muscles, making him grunt and gasp. "Harder, faster," she begged.

"No. We're taking this nice and easy." Diega continued to move in slow, gentle thrusts as his mouth devoured her.

Feeling his manhood inside of her, Tahlia thought she would explode. Only Vegas had been this far, this deep. But this was different. Diega was even further, deeper, and it excited her even more, knowing he was totally, fully, all the way inside of her.

Seeing the passion and desire in each other's eyes made the orgasm even more powerful…

Something was tickling her face, and she moved her hand to swat it away. But it was still there, annoying her. "Stop it, go way," she muttered, waking up. Opening her eyes, she saw that Diega had been teasing her with a wildflower as she slept.

He was lying on his side watching her, leaning on his elbow, his head in his hand.

Rolling onto her left side so she could snuggle into him, Tahlia pulled the blanket around her. "Hey," she said lightly, smiling as he still tickled her.

"Hello," Diega replied, grinning in return.

She moved her head toward him, so it nestled against

his chest.

He stroked her hair and kissed her face and neck as they lay there, taking their time to enjoy the moment before riding back.

*****

"You filthy little whore," he hissed at her. "How dare you take him into you as you lie there with your legs spread all over the place. How dare you let him, and not me, into you making you scream and cry out. Making you come everywhere while I suck the life out of you. Drink your juices as they pour into my mouth." He wiped his hand over his chin, wiping away the fluid dribbling there. "You filthy vile tramp. This will be the last time you do it."

*****

Thursday they spent inside watching movies. Diega had a large range of DVDs so there was plenty to see. Astounding her with his movie knowledge, he kept her in fits of laughter with his impersonations, until he grabbed her and carried her upstairs to relive that famous scene from Gone With the Wind, where Rhett, in his drunken rage, carries a hysterical Scarlett up the staircase to have his wicked way with her. Although sex had definitely been implied, but not shown, Diega certainly made up for it. Becoming Rhett to her Scarlett, they invented the scene for themselves.

Many times over.

*****

Friday was spent by the pool, until Diega became bored. "Let's go into the sauna."

"I don't know. I don't want to dehydrate," Tahlia said, "an' I don't like being all sweaty, it's gross."

"We can take water in with us and not set the temperature too high. Come on." Standing, he pulled her over to the sauna, and setting a reasonable temp, they took in bottled water and sat down on the wide, cushioned seat.

After fifteen minutes, she grumbled. "Ugh, I'm already sweaty an' gross."

Diega opened a bottle of cold water and poured it over her.

"Ahhhh, what'd you do that for?" she cried, wiping her face.

Diega grinned wickedly. "You said you were feeling sweaty and gross. So, I thought I'd cool you down before I heat you up."

"Heat me up?" She looked at him, and he dove for her and pushed her down onto the seat. "Ohhh, ooohhh, you wanna do it in here."

He lay on top of her, his hot sweaty body sliding against hers. Moving into a more comfortable position, they wrapped themselves around each other. Lying there, they gazed into the other's eyes, before Diega slipped her bikini top off.

"Mmm," she breathed, his mouth and tongue licking the salty sweat from her body.

Sucking her right nipple, he made her groan delicately

as he savoured the pleasurable taste of her breasts and wallowed in their lushness. Sliding down her body, he pulled her bikini bottom off and slipped out of his swim trunks. He lay lightly on top of her, kissing her slowly… deliciously.

The heat from the sauna became oppressive, but it added to the eroticism of the moment as their bodies moved back and forth. Finally possessing the space waiting for him, he let her adjust to his fullness, then slowly slid in and out, keeping his passion in check. He wanted to go slow, to make it more powerful.

It was working.

Tahlia pulled her legs up toward her, her feet planted firmly on the seat so she could move easily. Diega pulled his own legs up to position, pushing himself further inside of her, making her cry out.

Slowly moving back and forth, they climaxed, gasping hard in the heat and resting. Staying inside of her, Diega didn't move, but within moments started plunging into her tight cavern of delight, bringing her to the edge.

The orgasms came one after the other, and as she came down from each climax, Diega slid in and out making her cry out over and over. It was explosive, both pleasurable and painful. But she wanted it, wanted him, not wanting him to stop, not wanting him to leave the secret deep spot that he had found. That was now only for him.

After hours of erotic lovemaking, Diega carried her out of the sauna. They were naked, exhausted, spent. Walking toward the pool, Diega did something wicked.

He jumped into the water, the coldness rushing over them like an ice wave.

Coming up spluttering, Tahlia cried out. "What'd you do that for?"

Diega was still grinning.

"I thought we needed to cool down before heating up again." Grabbing her, he pulled her toward him to do it all over again.

*****

He spluttered angrily and lowered his binoculars. He'd been sitting there watching them, knowing they were in the sauna. Now Diega was screwing her senseless in the pool and spa, holding her down on him even though she was crying out.

He saw her bouncing in the water, her breasts flopping around as she went up and down on him. As long as she doesn't suck him, he thought viciously, hearing her scream. Why can't it be my name she screams out as I shove my dick into her hard and fast.

He saw Diega carry her into the house.

"Damn you, you bastard," he spat, "you will learn to never screw my woman again."

*****

It was Saturday morning, and Vegas was going mental. Staying at Manny's was driving him nuts, and he'd been staking out the hotel in case Tahlia was there after all.

"Where the hell is she?" he yelled, pacing around his

bedroom and puffing on a cigarette. He'd been smoking several packs a day, stressing out over Tahlia's disappearance, and not knowing where she was. Although, he had noticed Diega was nowhere to be seen, and some other prick was in charge of the hotel. The hotel *he'd* been thrown out of.

"What the hell is goin' on?" he'd demanded when he'd tried to get in to see Mandy, Tahlia's so-called best friend. She'd run to call security, but they were already there to throw him out. Again.

He didn't like being thrown out of anywhere and was pissed about a lot of things. Tahlia slashing his clothes to shreds, security threatening him with arrest, even the music director avoided him. "What the hell is goin' on?" he'd yelled at the director over the phone, "I work here too, or have you conveniently forgotten that. I'm on stage with Tahlia Thursday nights, an' the women come to see *me,* not *her. I'm* becomin' the star of Thursday night, *not* Tahlia."

Crap, he thought, *I'm really makin' myself loved ain' I.* "God, what else can I do to find Tahlia?" he asked, falling onto his bed and staring at the ceiling. He put his hands under his head and tried to think.

Day after day he'd rung her suite, her cell, even sneaking back into the hotel. He rode around the city in the hope of seeing her somewhere, but that was useless as well, and there was no sign of her car. But there was a sick feeling in the pit of his stomach that just wouldn't go away.

"Well," he said, a thought coming to mind, "there is somethin' I *can* do. Somethin' I've done before to get what I wan'." His memory wandered back to that night. "Yeah," he said, "I *can* do that."

*****

It was Saturday night, and was the first one Mandy had had off in weeks. She lounged on her two seater sofa in her small one bedroom apartment watching TV and glanced around the room. She was glad she'd been lucky enough to get her job at *The Montiamo*, as the hotel owned the apartment building she was living in, so her rent was *very cheap.*

That was definitely a perk to the job, she thought. So had been meeting Tahlia. Even though she'd been working at the hotel for six months before Tahlia turned up, it was still nice, finally finding another female she could call a friend.

She relished the relaxing day she'd had, spending it in the hotel spa and pool. Before Tahlia, she hadn't done such things, but after they'd become friends, she'd managed to get a few freebies, going with Tahlia when she went. She'd also done a bit of shopping that morning, buying the latest party dress and a small thank you gift for Tahlia. For being such a great friend.

Pity she isn't here to join me, she thought. But then the hot rumours for the last week had been that she had taken off with Diega Montiamo. "Try Mr Fantastically Gorgeous," she muttered, feeling herself blush. "Wonder what they're getting up to?" A giggle escaped her. "Have to have a good gossip session about *that* when she gets back."

She sighed and looked at the TV. Alone for the night, and not having a date with any man in particular, she was feeling a bit lonely. No one had been able to call Tahlia, and Diega was out of range. She hadn't even been able to let them know Vegas was looking for them, but security had taken care of that.

"I can't believe she took off with him," she said, changing the channel with the remote. Flicking through the channels, she couldn't find anything to watch, so left it on a sitcom about some family. "Always the same concept, regardless of the name change," she muttered, watching the father give a lecture about safety to his children who sat there looking bored.

She wondered what happened that night, one week ago. Had Tahlia finally found out what Vegas was getting up to? She remembered how Diega and his security team had questioned her about Tahlia, and what she might have been doing that night. "God, that was a week ago already," she murmured, "mmm, I wonder when they're coming back."

There was a sound outside on the pathway.

What was that? She felt a little jumpy, living on her own, but knowing there were security gates and guards, she settled back when she heard a couple of people walk past her door, laughing and talking loudly. *Ah, just the neighbours,* she thought, getting up to make herself a herbal tea.

He had followed her.

He was watching her.

Waiting in the shadows until someone buzzed themselves in, then racing for the gate before it closed, being lucky enough to get through all the security. The guard had been busy checking the other person's ID so he was able to sneak into the bushes.

And wait.

He stood outside of her ground floor apartment sucking on a cigarette, watching her through the window. She hadn't pulled the curtains all the way, so he had a good view.

Not bad, he thought. But not what I'm here for.

He heard people coming and moved down the pathway, tripping over something as he went, managing to hide behind a tree at the end of the building.

He waited for them to leave, making sure no one else was around before walking back to her apartment.

The kitchen was joined to the living room, and he watched her through the window as she poured boiling water into her mug, then carried it into the living room.

Not gonna have a lot of options, he thought, disappointed that her apartment was in the middle of the building.

He took one last drag, then flicked his cigarette to the ground and glanced around one last time.

Well, here goes.

Bang, bang, bang.

Mandy jumped in her seat as the door vibrated on its hinges.

Bang, bang, bang.

She started panicking. *Oh, my God, who can that be?*

Bang, bang, bang.

She reached for the phone to call security.

Bang, bang, bang.

"Mandy, you in there? It's Vegas."

She slowly dropped the phone in its cradle, not sure if she wanted to answer the door.

Bang, bang, bang.

"Mandy. I know you're in there. Answer the door."

She peeked out through the window. He didn't look happy. Biting her lip, she wondered if she should answer or call security after all.

Bang, bang, bang.

"Mandy. I saw you in the window. Open the damn door an' lemme in."

Reluctantly, she opened the door a crack, keeping the chain on. "What do you want, Vegas?" she asked quietly.

"Lemme in," he demanded, not waiting for an invitation.

Mandy saw him raise his foot and stumbled backward as he kicked the door in. The chain went flying as the door banged back against the wall. He stalked into the room.

"You can't do that," Mandy cried, "get out. Get out of here and don't come back." She moved to the phone. "Get out, or I'll call security."

Vegas slammed the door shut and took two steps toward her. The room was small, so that was all it took. He grabbed her arm viciously and spun her around, gripping her arms tightly.

She squealed in pain. "Let me go," she cried, "you're hurting me."

"Where is she?" Vegas demanded.

"I don't know," Mandy squeaked.

"I don' believe you," Vegas said, tightening his grip.

"Ow, stop it, you're hurting me." She was crying, big fat tears rolling down her plump freckle covered cheeks.

"I don' care," Vegas spat, "tell me where she is Mandy an' I'll let you go."

"I don't know." She was crying hard now, big sobs racking her body. "Please stop, you're hurting me."

He pulled her five foot five body to him, his face above hers. They were staring eye to eye. "You better tell me, Mandy," he said in a low, threatening tone. "Or you will be *very, sorry.*"

She cried harder. The crazed look in his eyes was scaring her badly, and his imposing frame towered over her. She felt so small and vulnerable, having never met such a freaked out nutjob before, and wondered what Tahlia had seen in him. "I told you," her voice quivered, "I don't know." His fingers dug harder into her arms, making her cry out. "I don't know," she sobbed, "I don't know. She didn't tell me anything, and I haven't had a call from her, so I don't know."

"Where's Diega?"

"I don't know that either," she said, "he disappeared the same night Tahlia did—"

"Are they together?"

"I don't know."

"Of course you do, Mandy," he spat, "you work at the damn hotel, you know everythin', so tell me where they are, an' are they together?" His fingers dug deeper.

"Ahh," she screamed, "stop it, stop it, please."

"Tell me."

"The rumours are that they've gone off together," she

sobbed, "but I don't know if it's true, because I haven't spoken to her in a couple of weeks." She gasped for breath, feeling faint from the pain.

"More."

"I don't know any more," she breathed, her head spinning, her eyes rolling back in her head.

He threw her onto the sofa, but she slid to the floor instead, into a crying weak heap. "Well, Mandy," Vegas said quietly, "it looks like I'll have to teach you not to lie to me, now doesn' it."

He removed his belt with the brass knuckle buckle.

Her eyes widened in fear at the crazed, sadistic look on his face.

He unzipped his jeans.

She screamed.

Chapter 20

On Monday, Diega took Tahlia down to the basement. "I thought we could take the boat or jet skis out on the lake." He saw her distasteful expression.

"I don't like deep water. It scares me. I feel like I'll drown." She stopped and realised what a stupid thing that was to say. Remembering what she had tried to do the week before, all she wanted to do was to forget it. "I uh, guess I should get over my fear, an' I've never water skied, so I guess we could." She felt eager now.

Diega was excited too, and using a small buggy, they towed the boat down to the lake. He showed her how to balance on the skis, and hold the rope, before making sure she was suited up with a life jacket.

He started up the engine, and it grunted to life as the craft bobbed on the water. It was a small, sleek motorboat, all shiny and new. Sitting on the edge of the dock, swallowing her fears, Tahlia got ready. Gunning the boat, Diega pulled away, and the hard jolt on her arms made her topple face first into the water. Thankful for her safety vest, she laughed and tried again. The lake was the size of two football fields, and on her fifth go, she stayed up for one lap before falling in again.

Pulling to a stop next to her, Diega leaned over the side of the boat. "Have you had enough or do you want to keep going?"

"Keep going," she said, with a big grin.

For the next hour, she skied around the lake thoroughly enjoying herself, becoming quite a pro. Anchoring the boat in the middle of the lake, and putting up the sunshade, they ate lunch while the fall breeze played around them. Once finished, they pushed the bench seats down and together to form a bed to lay in each other's arms, letting the warmth drift them off to sleep.

The boat rocked against the choppy water and jolted them awake. They noticed the breeze was now a stiff wind.

Diega sat up to have a good look at the sky. "We should go in. There are clouds coming in, and the water's getting rough."

Aroused by the boat's motions, Tahlia pulled him toward her. "We'll go in later," she purred, taking his tongue into her mouth.

Passions rose, and they writhed together, allowing the boat's rocking motion to build the sensations. Hands grabbed and groped as they let their lust take them to heights beyond the stars. Diega's mouth tasted her, and his arousal hardened. Aching for her, he plunged into her womanhood, groaning in absolute pleasure as her wetness enclosed around him and trapped him there. Sliding inside of her went on forever, as if he was entering her completely. Body and soul.

Their mouths mashed together and Tahlia bent her legs, her feet pushing on the bench seat, bucking up against him meeting him at every thrust.

The wind rose.

The boat rocked even more.

The movements made them cry out as the orgasm hit.

The wind howled.

The boat bucked against the current.

The electricity of the climax bolted through them as lightning lit the dark sky, and the wave of pleasure pounded over them again and again…

*****

Tuesday was raining, so they stayed inside. After beating Diega several times at pool, Tahlia told him about the night in the bar when she and Vegas had started the fight.

"Where did you learn to fight that way?" he asked her.

She shrugged. "Nowhere. Being with Vegas has made me empowered, an' in feeling that way I just defended myself finally, an' copied what I had seen on TV. Kicked the crap out of them." She laughed. "I took up the self-defence classes you offer us staff members. Twice a week. I'm becoming very efficient." She was proud of her accomplishments.

So was Diega. "Well, I'm very impressed," he said with a nod of his head.

"So am I," she replied and racked the balls up again.

"Remind me not to get into a fight with you," he added and leant down to strike the ball, knowing he could easily take her on as he had black belts in several martial arts.

"A fight, huh." She decided to tell him something else. "Do you remember that night we saw that Australian group in the club, the night you asked me to supper?"

"Yes." He straightened, gazing at her.

"When I had gasped an' covered my face." She nervously fiddled with her pool cue.

"Yes." He felt the start of a grin.

"Well, I'd, had a thought about you."

"Really?" Diega's grin slid from ear to ear, and he walked around the pool table to stand in front of her.

"Well," she blushed, "one day in the casino I was watching you. You were schmoozing with your guests an' I was thinking how great you looked in your suit. All hot an' suave." She blushed harder.

"Go on." He was enjoying the moment.

"Well, I had thought you looked very…James Bond-ish."

"Really? I look like James Bond?" Another huge grin crossed his face.

"Yeah, you did. But in the club, when I was thinking about it, oh, my God, this is so embarrassing," she said. "My mind slipped an' said, James Bond-age instead." She glanced away completely embarrassed.

"Really?" Diega said sultrily, slipping into character, "Bondage, James Bondage."

Tahlia giggled at his impersonation.

"Bondage, huh. I can go for that." He grinned wickedly at the shocked expression that came over her face.

*****

Wednesday was still raining, so Diega challenged her to several games. "Now, let's see. If you win…you get to have your wicked way with me. And if I win…I get to have my wicked way with you."

"That's not fair," Tahlia complained, "either way you win."

"And either way you win," Diega shot back.

"Mmm," she grumbled, resigned.

Many rounds later, she won, and after minutes of musing, grabbed two blankets and pulled Diega outside into the rain.

"What are we doing? We'll get soaked."

"Shhh, just enjoy," she said, leading him to the grassy knoll between the pool and the lake. Laying a blanket down, she turned to him, both of them now soaked. Pulling his sweater off, she slowly ran her hands over his torso, arousing him, then she pushed his t-shirt up and over his head, letting the rain run over his naked skin.

Diega removed her sweater, and taking their pants off, they were soon naked and facing each other while the rain poured down their bodies. Picking her up so her legs wrapped around his waist, Diega kneeled on the blanket and gently laid her down. Pulling the second blanket over them, they entwined in the rain.

He sucked the water from her skin, drinking her essence. She tasted sweet, like honey, and he desperately needed her sugar fix. Taking her breast into his mouth, he sucked slowly, deliberately, making her groan in pleasure. He knew what she liked, and it was having her nipples played with.

Planting kisses across her chest, he toyed with her left nipple, slowly encircling it with his tongue. Tahlia moved against him, feeling him probing, pushing. He slid down her body lazily, rubbing his lips over her wet skin until he came to her womanhood.

His mouth enclosed around her as his tongue slid inside, caressing her, probing, so incredibly intimate, so sensual, so artful, tasting her. Just as sweet as the rest of her. This was the first time he'd done this, and he was definitely going to do it again. He slid around, rubbing against her spot, making her cry out as she rode the tide of passion.

Opening her legs, she pulled him toward her, and taking him into her hand, she guided him inside and gripped him to hold him there. The feel of the rain pounding down on their naked flesh heightened the arousal, making them writhe together in an erotic mating of flesh.

Diega tormented her with the exotic dance of love. Making her buck wildly, crying out as the orgasm took over her body, unable to move her arms that were lying limply by her side. He slid his left hand under her right leg and lifted it so it was over his left shoulder. He gripped her thigh tightly as he thrust, almost kneeling between her legs. She cried out even louder. He was blowing her mind over and over, it didn't stop, a seemingly never-ending tidal wave of emotion, passion, and lusty desire.

Then it did stop.

Opening her eyes groggily, she gazed at him.

With a look of power and control, he took the final plunge.

Hours later, they were lying in front of the roaring fire Diega had built in the living room fireplace. Under a warm blanket, they held each other, listening to the comforting sound of each other's heartbeat. Feeling all warm and toasty, they stayed there until morning.

*****

Thursday was sunny, but everything was soaked outside, so they decided to stay indoors for the day, only having lunch out on the deck. Afterwards, Tahlia walked around the den, her gaze wandering over the books on the shelves. It was a library with a vast array of choice, and choosing one, she took some time to relax and read while Diega made some calls.

She was gazing out of the window when he walked into the room. "You know," she said, looking at him, "we haven't really talked about ourselves. Gotten to know each other. I only know bits an' pieces about you from what the staff has told me, an' the few Wayne bits you know."

"You're right," Diega said, "we haven't. I didn't want to push you. You didn't seem to want to talk about your past." He sat down beside her, put his arms around her, and held her tightly.

"Yeah, I know. But now that we're here, an' we've been intimate, um, many times," she blushed, "since that's kinda *all* we've been doing. We should talk an' get to know one another. You know about Vegas, an' Wayne. Everything that happened with him. I only know a bit about you, an' that your parents have passed an' you named the hotel after them. But that's pretty much it."

"I don't really talk about myself." Diega sighed and realised he wanted to divulge his whole life story to the incredible woman wrapped in his arms. "I was an only child until I was about five. That's when my mom became pregnant with my baby brother. She was so happy to be having another child. At first, I was jealous, but Mom involved me in the process, telling me I would be teaching him to play football and baseball. Showing him how to do things. I got excited and couldn't wait. Mom went into labor and Dad took her to the hospital while my aunt watched me." A look came over Diega's face that showed pain and misery.

Tahlia held him close. "I didn't know you had an aunt."

"She's not my blood aunt, just a close friend of my parents. A week later they came home without him. Without my baby brother." He frowned. "Mom was devastated and locked herself in her room. Dad tried to hold it together for my sake. It wasn't until years later I, I finally understood what had happened." He took a deep breath. "My brother was stillborn."

"Oh, no, I'm so sorry," Tahlia whispered, wanting to make his pain go away.

"Mom finally got it together by throwing herself into raising me. She made me her whole life, but never really recovered. One day, when I was fifteen, Mom was driving down a street and ran a stop sign. The truck ploughed straight into her. She died instantly."

"Oh, my God, Diega," Tahlia said, wiping away the tears that were flowing in rivers down his face.

"It turned out," he took a breath, "that the doctor who was looking after Mom during her pregnancy was selling babies to couples who couldn't have children themselves. Mom believed that he had sold my brother. That he hadn't died like she'd been told, and there still might be a chance that he was alive. She had been busy sifting through papers on the passenger seat when she was hit. It was just before summer and, and it changed me…" He gazed off into the distance.

"How do you mean?"

He looked at her. "I withdrew into myself, hardened, couldn't cry. Didn't talk to my friends or hang out with them over the holiday. I read my Hardy Boys, started my first job. Drowned myself in music, picking up as many instruments as I could learn. I couldn't just sit and think about it. I had to be doing something."

Diega sighed again, letting it all flow out. "Then, Dad died. He was so proud of my accomplishments. So happy that I had done something good with my life instead of letting Mom's death eat at me. He's with her."

"Have you found out anything about your brother?" Tahlia asked, wiping away her own tears.

He shook his head sadly. "No. I've tried to keep it out of my mind. Dad said, that although the doctor had been selling babies, it wasn't at the time my brother was born, so, he did die after all."

"I'm so sorry," Tahlia said, kissing his cheek and

resting her head on his shoulder.

They sat that way for a while, Diega's pain easing after so many years. It had been good to let it all out, having never spoken to anyone about it before. Tahlia was different from the other women he'd dated. She was special, the one woman he wanted to spend his life with. The one woman he'd opened up to, and it had been so easy.

"You never married? Have you thought about starting a family of your own?" she asked him.

Diega gazed at her. "Not until you." A slow quiver moved up her spine. "I've had relationships. Some serious, where we've been a couple for a while. Some not, where we've just dated. But not once did I ever feel that I wanted to marry or have a family with any of them. And now, my life has led me to you." He looked at her with such love that Tahlia started crying again. Holding each other close, they ended up laughing.

"God we're a pair of crybabies," she said, "looks like we're both orphans."

"Tell me," Diega said quietly.

"Well, as you know, my Dad died when I was ten. My mom fell apart, I was abused for years. My relationships didn't work out, an' I thank God I haven't brought children into the world. She died earlier this year from cancer. I was sent a letter just before all that crap with Wayne. We hadn't been close since Dad died. I went to New York to see that she was buried, continued on to Miami. Then I was being followed an' he tried to get into my trailer, so I fled again. I don't think I've been followed here, nothing's happened. I met Vegas on the way, an' then, here I was. You know what happened after that."

"So, none of your relationships were good?" Diega asked gently.

"No. None. They were all the same. Dogs just out for a quick screw or to control me. None were good till Vegas. But, God, look how that turned out." She sighed, laying her head on his shoulder again.

"I can change all that," Diega said, kissing her gently.

"I don't know. I'm so use to being abused in one way or another that I just can't get use to a decent guy. I thought Vegas was decent, but he cheated on me like all the others. An' now, here we are, sitting here blubbering like babies about our awful pasts. God, we're pathetic," she laughed.

"Not too pathetic," Diega said and looked deeply into her eyes. "Let me love you."

"Don't you already?" Tahlia asked, gazing at him lovingly.

"Yeah. I do."

*****

He sneezed.

"Damn this cold," he slurred, blowing his nose. "If only they'd bloody well stayed inside while it rained I wouldn't be sick now." He sneezed again.

If only he hadn't been so goddamn stupid himself, being out there in the rain. Getting soaked to the skin, time and time again. He couldn't help himself though. Every time they had made love, it was out in the rain. It was beautiful. It was wonderful. And he'd shoved his hard dick in higher and faster every time, crushing her to him, making her cry out.

And now he was suffering for it.

"Damn it." How could she do this to me, take me out in the rain and screw me like she'd never been screwed before? He sneezed a third time.

"Damn that whoring, vile, filthy bitch. She'll pay for this."

*****

Friday, was nice and dry, so they packed a picnic basket and walked through the forest, coming across a stream where they sat down for lunch, listening to the soothing sounds around them. The water from the stream cool and refreshing to drink. With no need for words, they lay together on a blanket, entwined in each other. Their bodies warm and naked, making love in the midday sun.

*****

Sunday morning, Tahlia woke in Diega's strong arms. Snuggling down in their big comfy bed, she curled against him, listening to his heart. It beat slowly, a rhythmic drumming that was comforting. She nestled her head into the soft hair on his chest, just over his heart, so she could hear it better.

She took a deep breath and exhaled gently, slowly, letting her body relax even more, her eyes gazing around the room at the incredible furnishings. Not even her own suite at the hotel had furniture or art like this. They were nice enough and probably expensive, but still, not like this.

She smiled to herself, like the Cheshire cat that not only got the cream but a big fat bird as well. It had been so great being there. Spending time with Diega, getting to know him better, and she didn't want to leave this heaven she'd come to.

Tahlia's smile melted away as her brow furrowed. Her life wasn't about running away anymore. Or sex for that matter, even though she thoroughly enjoyed making love with Diega, and sex with Vegas had been incredible, things were different now. Very different.

Knowing she had to go back scared her because she didn't want to face Vegas. *God, what am I gonna do?* she thought, suddenly miserable. *I really don't want to go back to him.*

"Then don't."

Her head jerked up in surprise, not realising she had spoken out loud.

"Don't go back to him. Why would you need to now that you've accepted me into your heart," Diega said softly, watching her. His arms tightened around her. They were comforting, strong, safe.

Thinking about it, she knew he was right. "I need to tell him though," she said, sighing, "otherwise, he'll think we're still together."

"Call. After the way he treated you, he doesn't deserve anything more."

"No, I need to see him," she replied, knowing she had to end it with Vegas.

Deciding this would be their last day there, they spent

it in bed, always entwined, never leaving each other except for early evening when they stumbled downstairs for dinner.

They were soon back upstairs, however, sharing a hot, sensual shower.

Slowly soaping her skin, Diega lazily slid the washcloth over her body. Standing behind her, his hands slid around to her front, kneading her breasts, making her groan. Pushing back against him, she took one of his hands and led it down between her legs. His fingers slid inside of her, pleasing her, stroking her as his other hand played with her nipple, rubbing his palm over it, rotating it in slow motion, exciting it beyond belief as the water washed down over her. Diega rubbed himself against her, making her come, one hand still inside of her, one still around her breast.

Removing his hands from her body, he pushed her against the wall. Turning the shower nozzles, so they were completely covered in water, Diega came behind her, opening her legs, entering. Being pushed against the shower wall, Tahlia's nipples hardened as they rubbed the tiles. Turning her head, her mouth met Diega's, their tongues toying with each other as he moved up and down inside of her.

There were metal bars on the wall of the shower, and hanging onto them made it extremely erotic. She pushed back against Diega as he thrust, the motion making her cry out. He slid out of her and turned her around so that her back was now to the wall.

Grabbing the metal bars, Tahlia wrapped her legs around Diega's waist as he entered her. This was the most exquisite experience she'd had. As his powerful body thrust his manhood into her, he held onto her so he could drive deeper inside.

Feeling herself explode as he let his seed flow forth, she fell onto him in exhaustion while he finished his grinding release.

*****

Monday morning, Vegas parked his hire car down the road from the staff parking entrance. Around twelve, he saw Diega's car roll down the street and into the basement with Tahlia in the passenger seat. Running over to the entrance, making sure he wasn't seen, Vegas watched them get out and walk toward Diega's personal lift. They had their arms around each other and looked extremely happy. His blood boiled over when he saw Diega kiss her on the lips and her return it with a huge smile on her face.

"There is no way he's gettin' my woman," he spat, running back to his car.

He had tried several times to get into the hotel, and when he finally realised he wasn't getting in looking like himself, he devised a plan. Vegas looked at his reflection in the rear-view. He looked like a different man. He'd shaved, his face clean and smooth, his hair now streaked blond and brushed to the side. He put on a pair of glasses. They weren't magnified, so he didn't have to worry. He smoothed his suit, which was new since Tahlia had slashed his other ones, and he wore a casual polo shirt underneath. A leather belt and shoes finished the ensemble. "I look like a different person," he said to himself, "so no one will know."

Acting cool and calm as if he belonged there, Vegas walked into the hotel and over to the lift. Trying not to draw attention to himself, he smiled at people and played it casual. After all, he didn't want the guards finding him before reaching Tahlia. Gliding up in the lift to the floor her suite was on, he stepped out and looked around before making his way to her door and knocking. He was surprised at how easy it had been.

Stepping out of the shower and wrapping a towel around herself, Tahlia heard the knock and ran to open the door, thinking it was Diega. "Hey," she started brightly then stopped, not knowing who was standing in front of her. But the look that came from those deep pools of blue staring back at her made her realise in an instant. "Vegas," she whispered, and her blood went stone cold.

"Hey, baby," he drawled, pushing his way into her suite. "Ya miss me? I missed you, an' I didn' even know where you were." He slammed the door shut and faced her before removing his glasses.

"How did you get in? You've been banned." Looking at his clothes she had a strange feeling.

"Well, baby, I remember this TV show we once watched. I decided to use the guy you drooled over as inspiration. An' it worked," he said, a big grin on his face as he spread his arms out. "I got in. Ya happy to see me, baby?" He reached for her.

Tahlia angrily slapped his hand away. "Don't you touch me," she spat, "do you really think making yourself into some character from a TV show will stop security from figuring out who you are? They have facial recognition. They're probably on their way up here now, so I suggest you leave." She opened the door, but Vegas slammed it shut with his right hand, and pushed her back with his left.

"I ain' goin' nowhere, baby. Not till you tell me where you been." He stepped toward her, his tone threatening.

Backing up, Tahlia knew she had to do something. Remembering her self-defence class she got ready, positioning herself in the proper way. "Where I've been, is none of your business," she yelled, "'cause we're through. In fact, we've been through for two weeks since I found out you were cheating on me. God knows what diseases you got an' passed on to me. But I'm done. *We're* done. Now it's time for you to leave."

She kicked out her right leg and hit him in the groin. When he doubled over in pain, she aimed for his head, but he moved, and she missed. Vegas dove for her, but she sidestepped quickly, the bedroom now behind her. He was on the floor after crashing into an antique wooden chair with a yelp of pain as the arm hit him above his left eye.

Wishing she could grab the phone and call Diega, she could only pray that he was watching, or that security had picked up footage of Vegas walking into the hotel and had either told Diega, or were on their way themselves to help.

Getting up with a roar, he ran for her, and she lashed out with her foot. He caught it and sent her spinning onto the bed face down.

Jumping onto her back, Vegas grabbed her hair with his left hand and yanked her head back, choking her. "Baby, I take shit from no one. Not even you, an' 'cause of that, I'm gonna teach you a lesson."

He pushed her towel up and unzipped his pants.

She was sobbing, but was not going to beg.

Vegas spread her legs. "A lesson you'll never forget."

Chapter 21

"NO, YOU WON'T."

Tahlia stopped sobbing.

Vegas stopped moving.

Slowly turning his head around, he saw Diega standing in the bedroom doorway, four beefy bodyguards steadfastly pointing their cold looking guns at his head.

"Let her go, and step away," Diega said through clenched teeth.

Vegas rose slowly, his hand still in her hair pulling her with him.

"Let her go," Diega repeated, his four guards steadily taking a step closer.

Vegas turned Tahlia around to face him, releasing her hair, but keeping his hand on her head. He whispered to her, "I'm sorry, baby," and backhanded her across her face. The force was so strong she went sprawling over the bed and off the side. The four guards pounced and beat Vegas down as Diega yelled Tahlia's name.

Lying on the floor stunned, barely hearing six men yelling, Tahlia felt the burning handprint. It had been a long time since that had happened, and she would never forgive Vegas. Diega was beside her asking her if she was all right. She nodded her head in a stupor as he pulled the bedspread over to cover her.

He turned to his guards who now had Vegas subdued and bleeding profusely all over himself. "You know what to do."

"Sir." With that, they were gone, and it was just the two of them.

"Where are you taking him? What are you going to do?" She was crying, her heart broken, torn and trodden all over.

"My men will get him the hell away from here, and from you. They'll make sure he never bothers you again. I promise." Diega was beside himself. Never before had he felt such hatred and anger for someone as he did for Vegas at that moment. He tried to touch her face, but she pushed his hand away.

"No, don't hurt him." She struggled to get up. "If he leaves, I leave. Where are you taking him?" She had no idea what she was saying, and Diega looked at her stupefied, holding her tightly as she collapsed back into his arms sobbing her heart out.

No one had known Vegas was in the building, but when the cameras picked him up knocking on her door, Diega had freaked. Rushing to her suite just in time, he'd seen the woman he loved face down on the bed about to be raped. Vegas had then slapped her, and Diega had wanted to kill the animal himself. But he let his men do their job.

He will be punished, he thought.
Severely.

*****

As he watched Tahlia that night, singing on stage, he thought about the last few weeks.

They had been very eventful. Watching Vegas screw another woman and receive a blowjob had been devastating for her, making her sick. She had left for two weeks, going off with damn Diega to his retreat, but now, she was back, and this show was particularly sad as she sang songs of pain and heartache.

He smiled.

It's no wonder, since the end of her relationship with Vegas had come to quite an explosive end. That was one hell of a beating he'd received out in the desert, being left to die a slow, bloody death.

He deserved it after trying to rape her and slapping her across the room.

He was going to have to teach Vegas a lesson.

In fact, he would have to teach them all a lesson.

He gazed lovingly at her, standing and applauding with everyone else as she accepted bunches of flowers and presents from the audience.

He knew she had no idea.

None of them had any idea.

Of the pain and torment about to be unleashed.

He smiled and straightened his tie.

Let the games begin…

*****

That week, every show was about pain and heartache,

death and despair. It was incredibly depressing, but Tahlia found it somehow enlightening. Singing the lyrics to every song made her feel better as if realising other people had it worse, and that she really was okay.

Diega was begging her to move into his penthouse as it was private and safe, but she refused, telling him that she felt it easier to stay in her suite because as their relationship was just starting, she wanted to be courted. It was time to change how she viewed the relationship between a man and a woman, and though they had been intimate, many times at his retreat, she really wanted to date.

Diega said he completely understood, thinking it unwise, but also endearing at the same time. So every night that week, he escorted her to and from her shows and presented her with a huge bunch of roses. A tradition still going from her very first show.

They weren't intimate that week as Tahlia wanted time to grieve over the end of her relationship with Vegas. And Diega abided by her wishes while hating them, and was barely able to tear himself away from her each night.

But it was the way it had to be.

*****

Backstage after the show on Friday night, Tahlia finally caught up with Mandy. "Oh, my God, there's so much I have to tell you," she gushed, "you are *not* going to believe what happened." She stopped when she saw the look on Mandy's face. "You, know," she went on, "I haven't seen or heard from you for the last week, since being back." Mandy's smile crumpled. "Mandy, oh, my God, what's wrong?" Tahlia cried, hugging her.

"Can we go up to your suite?" she asked through her tears.

"Of course we can," Tahlia said just as Diega walked through the door.

"Ladies," he started, then stopped when he saw Mandy's tear-stained face.

"Do you mind if we don't spend tonight together?" Tahlia asked him.

"No, that's fine," Diega said, believing he knew what it was about. He'd been informed the day they returned about the happenings at the hotel and with his staff. He'd been so disgusted with everything and praised his manager and security team for the way they handled it. Now, he realised, it was time for the girls to catch up. "Why don't I escort you lovely ladies upstairs and I'll leave you to chat."

"Thanks for understanding," Tahlia said as Diega led them to her door.

"I completely understand." He opened the door and watched Mandy walk inside then turned to Tahlia. "I'll have someone escort her home when she's ready to leave." He kissed her sweetly. "Goodnight, my love."

"Goodnight," she whispered, a huge smile on her face as she watched him walk away. Shutting the door behind her, she walked over to Mandy who was sitting stone-faced on the sofa. "Tell me what's wrong," she said, and Mandy promptly burst into tears.

Tahlia listened in horror as Mandy recounted her

harrowing night at the hands of Vegas. The man she'd once, and maybe still did, love. She felt sick to the core as she was told about the pain and torment he had inflicted, and shook her head sadly.

"When he got on top of me," Mandy whispered, "I tried to stop him, but he was so strong. I'm so grateful that someone heard my screams and alerted the security guards. Otherwise, it would be so much worse."

"Oh, Mandy, I'm so sorry you had to go through that," Tahlia said, hugging her friend closely. "He tried the same thing when I got back. Even though he'd been banned, he still managed to get past security an' make it to the suite. I thought it was Diega knocking, but Vegas was at the door instead. He forced his way in, an' after fighting, he got me on the bed an' was about to rape me. Thankfully security found out, an' Diega got here in time to stop him." She sighed and shuddered at the memory. "Thank God for Diega. I knew Vegas had a mean streak, but I certainly didn't think he'd do what he was about to." She turned to Mandy. "What did the guards do?"

"When the guard knocked on the door, Vegas moved, and I managed to grab my mug of hot tea and throw it over him. He yelled, and they came in, the door didn't have a lock anymore, so they were able to get in easily."

"What happened next?"

"Vegas tore out of there. He pushed the guards out of the way and ran. They tried to follow, but lost him."

"So what's happened since? Where have you been?" Tahlia asked, worried about her friend as she stroked her hair.

"Once the hotel security was notified, the manager moved me into a suite in another of Diega's hotels. I didn't want to see or talk to anyone. I felt safe there, but still. I didn't know you were back," she said, gazing forlornly at Tahlia. "I finally called one of the other waitresses, and she told me, that's why I came tonight. To see you."

"That's sweet," Tahlia said, looking earnestly at her friend. "Have you seen someone?"

"You mean a shrink?" Mandy wiped her face with her crumpled tissue.

"I mean one of the doctors here at the hotel. They have counsellors you know. It might help."

"I can't see a shrink," Mandy whispered, "I just can't."

"I do."

Mandy looked at her. "You see a shrink?" she asked curiously.

"I've seen the doctor here, yes," Tahlia said. "It's not so bad you know. Believe me, I needed it."

Mandy glanced away. "Maybe it wouldn't be so bad then," she said. "If you can do it, maybe I can too."

"No, it wouldn't be so bad," Tahlia replied, "it's helped me. Especially this week."

"Okay," Mandy sighed, seeming like her old self. "I'll go see the shrink if you tell me *every* juicy detail about the little vacation you didn't tell me you were having."

"Deal," Tahlia said, and they both started giggling.

*****

Saturday was overcast, and Tahlia felt sick when she

woke. She knew the emotions she'd experienced over the last week, and last night after hearing about Mandy, were now showing in physical signs, and she felt exhausted and unable to move. Knowing she should go to the doctor, she rang and made an appointment for that morning, deciding to head out for some shopping beforehand. She was dressed when there was a knock at the door.

"Hello. Breakfast?"

"Ugh, I'm not hungry," she replied as Diega wheeled the breakfast trolley into her suite.

"Why not? Is everything all right? You're not sick are you?" Diega held her by her arms, his eyes searching her face for signs of illness.

"No, I'm not, I don't think. It's just that this week has been one of the worst, an' I'm just not hungry." She pulled away from him and walked toward the dining area.

"You should see the doctor. When was the last time you saw her?" he asked in a concerned tone, wheeling the trolley after her.

"A couple of months ago, but I rang this morning an' made an appointment. I think it's just stress. I'll be okay." She sat down and nibbled on a piece of toast from the plate that Diega had placed on the table.

"Well, then, what would you like to do today?" he asked.

"Ah, I need to go shopping, so I thought I might go before the doctor's."

"Okay, I'll take you where you need to go. What sort of shopping?"

She felt a little weirded out by his sudden possessiveness and need to know what she was buying. "I don't want you taking me anywhere. I'd rather go alone."

"There's no way I'm letting you go anywhere on your own," Diega reprimanded. "Vegas is still out there, and I won't risk your safety just because you want to go shopping. Is it *that* important?"

She riled at his words. "I need to shop for *women's personal products*," she almost spat, letting the words sink in.

"What do you mean women's personal...oh...?" Diega let the sentence go as he blushed. "Okay, then, Janine can go with you so that you're safe. Is that reasonable?"

Sighing at the thought of the personal bodyguard Diega had hired to protect her, shadowing her every move, she agreed.

And Janine was waiting for her when she got downstairs. "Ma'am." She nodded as Tahlia sat in the new bulletproof four-wheel drive Diega had bought that week just for her.

"Janine."

"Where to ma'am?" she asked when she got into the driver's seat.

"The doctor's, then the local mall thanks. I need to pick up a few things."

Being driven around by a woman was strange, as Tahlia was used to men doing the driving. But Diega had insisted on a bodyguard and wouldn't relent. So, finally agreeing to it, she'd asked for a woman.

Janine was a black belt in several martial arts, an expert shooter, and excellent in driver safety. Diega knew she was in safe hands.

Parking and getting out, Janine followed several steps behind always on the lookout. The visit to the doctor took half an hour, then it was off to the mall. Going to some clothing stores first, she bought a few tops before walking to the drug store.

"Um, do you mind waiting by the door. I want to buy something for Diega, an' don't want you seeing in case he tries to get it out of you." The lie was quick and easy and all she could think of.

"Ma'am," Janine said and stood just inside the doorway.

Grabbing what she needed and quickly paying, Tahlia was ready to leave. "We can go back to the hotel now."

It was well after noon when Tahlia walked into her suite with her shopping. Not feeling hungry, she went into the bathroom with her parcels from the drug store.

Ten minutes later she threw up.

"Oh, my God, oh, my God," she choked, flinging open the door and stumbling into the living room. "This can't be happening. What am I gonna do?"

She'd received a phone call while in the bathroom and taken it on the extension.

"Nooo," she screamed, "this can't be happening, this can't be happening." Picking up a crystal vase she threw it across the room and watched it smashed into a million pieces.

The shock fell away, and she took a few deep breaths to calm herself before walking over to the mess. She was thinking about calling a maid when she saw a small black thing on the floor. Picking it up and examining it, she realised what it was, as she'd seen it on a TV show. A small hidden microphone had been in the statue the vase had smashed into. Wondering why one would be in her suite, and who the hell had invaded her privacy that way, Tahlia started searching, smashing really, as she came across more recording devices.

Not caring how expensive the art was, she smashed all statues, vases and sculptures. Pulled every painting and mirror from the wall, tipped over every pot plant. Searching every inch of the walls, ceiling and light fixtures, Tahlia found miniature cameras.

Walking around, she figured out what would have been seen. *Oh, my God, they saw everything.* She felt sick. The bedroom, the living room, even the bathroom. *They would have seen everything, when I showered, when Vegas an' I...oh, God.* She made it back to the bathroom before throwing up again.

Sick to her stomach, she rang Diega's office to talk to him.

"Hello, Kate Marshall."

"Where's Diega?"

"Hi, Tahlia. He's on his way up to change for a last minute meeting."

"Thanks." Rushing out of her suite and around the corner, she punched in the four-digit code on the stairwell leading to his penthouse.

Running through the door, which was always unlocked, she yelled his name. Going from room to room, she couldn't find him, and finally stopped in his study. One wall was covered in large size monitors, and looking closely, she saw that the pictures on the screens were of her suite.

"Oh, my God, no." She was horrified. The man she had given herself to had been spying on her and Vegas. Sobbing, she moved her head in different directions, since she had thrown the cameras on the floor, making out her bedroom and bathroom. "Oh, God, how could he? How could he do this to me? Spy on me. Watch me being with Vegas. Oh, God how could he?"

Grabbing one of the monitors, she let it fall to the floor and smash. Doing the same to the others, she trashed his study looking for recordings in case he made copies of what he'd seen.

"Nooo," she screamed, breaking down and sobbing, falling apart on the floor for a few moments. Stopping, she knew she had to get out of there. Wiping her face, she ran down to her suite. Shoving some clothes into a tote, she grabbed her car keys and handbag, and after a painfully long lift ride down to the car park, she jumped in her car and left, with no idea of what to do.

5:45 p.m.

Tahlia parked her car at a lookout above the city. It was becoming dusk, but she didn't care.

She had to think.

She had to make a plan.

But all she could do was cry.

Chapter 22

At the same time Tahlia was at the lookout, Diega walked into his suite to change. Thinking about his plans for the evening and the surprise he had for her, he pulled jeans and a t-shirt on, then strode into his study to retrieve a file for Kate.

All he saw was wreckage.

"What the hell!" Diega rang his security chief, Mark Dalton, and demanded to know who'd been in his suite. While they made checks, his cell rang. "Yes," he barked.

It was Kate. "Sir, did Tahlia catch up with you? She called to ask where you were. I told her you'd gone up to change for an appointment."

"No, she didn't." The truth dawned on him. "I want you to go and check Tahlia's suite. I think something's happened. Call me when you're there."

"Sir."

Mark came back on the line. "Sir. The cameras picked up Miss Tahlia punching in the code to the stairwell then going into your suite."

"When was that?"

"About two hours ago."

Diega hung up as his cell rang.

"Sir, the suite is trashed. Every piece of artwork, paintings, mirrors. It's like a huge tornado's ripped through."

"Is she there?"

"No, sir. I checked her things, some clothes and a bag are missing, and there's no note."

Diega rang down to the parking garage. "Is Tahlia's car there?"

"No, sir. Miss Tahlia tore out of here over two hours ago."

Diega called his security chief back. "Pull up the GPS on Tahlia's Mustang. I want her found. Now!"

"Sir."

Pacing around what was left of his study, he tried to put a timeline together. She had gone shopping, Janine had driven her. Coming back and spending some time in her suite, what had she done to discover the cameras and microphones. And if she had rung looking for him, coming up to the suite to find him, she would have found that he'd been watching her, and everything she and Vegas had done.

Oh, God. Oh, God. Diega fell into the chair behind his desk feeling sickened.

The phone rang.

"Sir, she's at the lookout near Boulder Canyon. She's not moving."

"Get my car ready, I'm going to get her."

"Sir."

Hanging up, Diega looked at his watch as he ran out of his study.

6:00 p.m.

*****

For some strange reason that day, Vegas was on edge. He'd been unable to get near Tahlia during the week to apologise for hurting her. Although he'd forced himself on women before, he never needed to do that with her. She was different, special, always wanting him, needing him. Sex was explosive and extremely enjoyable. Never had it been that way with other women. He enjoyed sex sure, but it was the feeling of power over the woman that gave him a buzz. It was never deep, never emotional. Tahlia made him feel alive, from the moment at the gas station until their last time together.

Thinking back over the last three weeks, Vegas tried to figure out what had gone wrong as he prowled around his bedroom in Manny's house. "We made love before I came to Manny's, but when I got home on Monday, I was thrown out an' told never to return. When I did, I found Tahlia with Diega." He snarled at the name. "She didn' look sick."

He didn't believe that lie, but was overwhelmed with the feeling they'd been together for the last two weeks. When he got in to see her, she told him it was over and kicked him in the groin.

He sat down heavily on the side of his bed and hung his head in his hands. What happened next disgusted him beyond belief.

He'd tried to rape her.

Diega showed up with his goons, and he'd slapped

her just to piss him off.

"An' got a severe beatin' for it," he said, sitting up. He was still sore and bruised, but didn't hate Diega for it. "I deserved it. Hurtin' Tahlia that way makes me sick." He leaned over and grabbed a pack of cigarettes from the bedside table. Pulling one out, he lit it and took a long drag.

Cruising around on his bike, he'd seen her go out with a bodyguard and followed her to the doctor's, then the mall, watching from across the road. God, he loved her, wanted her, needed and ached for her. He thought back to what she'd said.

"We're through. In fact, we've been through for the last two weeks since I found out you were cheating on me."

Yeah, I cheated on her, with two women an' I regret it, so desperately. I wan' to make it up to her. My excuse…well, I was drunk an' on drugs. But how the hell did she find out? He still hadn't figured that one out.

He'd followed them back to the hotel and watched as they entered the parking garage, then gunning his bike, had ridden away.

6:19 p.m.

He looked out the window and had a strange feeling that something was terribly, terribly wrong.

*****

It was almost dark now, and the casinos and hotels were lighting up the skyline. Tahlia knew she needed to make a decision, but couldn't clear her mind long enough.

She looked at her watch.

6:20 p.m.

Wiping her face, she reached into her handbag on the passenger seat. Digging around, she found a tissue, and as she sat up, she heard the sound of a gun being cocked in her left ear.

*****

6:45 p.m.

Diega pulled into the lookout parking lot and screeched to a halt behind the Mustang. Seeing the driver's door open, he rushed to the car to find her gone.

"Tahlia, Tahlia. Where are you? It's Diega," he called loudly. He looked through the car but didn't see much. Her bag was still in the passenger seat, and the keys still in the ignition. Pulling out his cell, he rang his security team. "She's gone. Get out here and start searching, bring the sniffer dogs."

While waiting for his team, Diega and his bodyguards searched as far as they could, but found no sign of her. The team arrived quickly, having already been on the way, and turned on powerful spotlights so they could spread out to search. The sniffer dogs caught her scent, but didn't go far. It ended ten feet from her car.

"What the hell happened here?" Diega yelled at his chief officer. "Find her."

"Sir, she's not here," Mark replied.

"What do you mean she's not here? She has to be…" A sob caught in his throat. Pulling himself together, he started devising a list of people who would want to hurt her, kidnap her. There was only one name.

Vegas.

"Find me, Vegas," he spat. "I want to know where he is and what he's doing. Now."

"Sir."

Diega looked at his watch.

9:00 p.m.

*****

When Tahlia had heard the gun, she dove for the passenger side, but he was too fast and grabbed her. Pulling her out of the car, he put a handkerchief over her mouth and nose. She struggled and knowing what the smell was, had tried not to breathe.

The vapours got her anyway.

Now she was coming to and was very groggy. Breathing deeply, she smelt fresh clean air and took long deep breaths to try and blow away the cotton wool in her head. Moving slightly, she realised she was bound. Her hands behind her back, her feet together. She was lying down on something soft, so she assumed it was a bed since she was blindfolded and couldn't see.

Straining her ears for the slightest sound, she vaguely heard talking in another room. Struggling against her bonds, a wave of nausea washed over her, and she rested a moment, trying to remember how to get out of the ties around her. Feeling okay again, she moved her arms down and under her knees as she rolled onto her back. Moving her legs through the circle of her arms, she brought them to her front.

A door opened and someone burst in. "She's trying to undo her bonds," a man yelled and grabbed her in a vice-like grip.

Screaming was impossible as there was tape over her mouth, so she kicked out her bound legs, managing to hit one of them.

"Stop it." The voice was commanding, and everyone stopped, making no sound.

"She is to be treated carefully. *Do not* hurt her, or I will shoot you myself." There was silence. "Is that understood?"

"Yes, sir," came a chorus of voices.

Tahlia's hands were bound to the wall above her head, pulling her into a sitting position. Footsteps walked over to her, and a hand touched her face.

She yanked her head away.

"You've caused me a lot of problems, my dear. But you'll soon learn to never mess with me again."

*****

Vegas leaned back in his seat. He was sitting at Manny's dining table, and as Manny walked in with beers, the doors burst open. Security teams swarmed the house, yelling orders, pointing rifles. Standing and holding their hands in the air, Vegas and Manny were pushed against the wall and patted down.

The house and property were searched and secured. No one else was there.

Diega stormed into the house and ran for Vegas,

slamming him up against the wall. "Where is she, where is she?" His left arm held Vegas across his chest, trapping him while his right hand held a gun to his throat.

"Where's who?" Vegas croaked, gripping the arm across his chest.

Diega leaned in close. "Tahlia. Where is she? I know you have her. After last week, of course you would. You were pissed off that she dumped you for me. So, where is she?"

Vegas stared wide-eyed. "Tahlia? Gone? What do ya mean, where is she? I didn' take her, she was with *your* bodyguard. Where's she gone? How do ya know she's missin'?" He was starting to freak out.

"How do you know she was with my bodyguard unless you followed her, huh." Diega lowered his voice, thrusting his arm against Vegas's chest. "If I find out you've taken her, I will kill you. She went missing from the Boulder Canyon lookout between 6 and 6:45 p.m. I'll say it again, if you've taken her, I, will, kill you." Diega took a step backward as if to leave, but then swung his hand around and smashed the gun butt over Vegas' head, knocking him unconscious.

10:30 p.m.

*****

Tahlia didn't know whether she'd been asleep or unconscious. All she knew was that she was still bound and attached to the bed. Sick to her stomach and wanting to throw up, she struggled to keep herself from retching. She knew she needed food and water, but since she was gagged, making groaning sounds was all she could do.

Finally, someone came in and removed the tape from her mouth. "Here, drink this." A woman held a glass of water to her lips.

Tahlia drank thirstily. It tasted good. Nice and cold to help her sore, parched throat. "Food," she rasped, "I need food."

"I know," the woman said, "I have some soup for you. I'll put the spoon to your mouth."

For the next few minutes, she ate hungrily and wanted more.

"I'll see what I can bring you," the woman said, leaving without putting the tape back over her mouth.

Breathing deeply to try and get rid of the fuzziness, Tahlia calmed herself. But she was scared. Terrified. She'd gone through a lot with different men, especially Wayne, but there was something seriously wrong here. The woman came back and fed her a plain sandwich and said nothing.

"What's happening? Where am I? What's going on?" Tahlia pleaded with the woman. "What day is it?"

"Sunday, I can't tell you anything else, I'm sorry."

"Wait," Tahlia cried, hearing retreating footsteps and a closing door.

The woman was gone.

*****

6:00 a.m.

Sunday morning saw Diega pacing in his office. He'd

been racking his brain to come up with a kidnapper, and now had quite a few names. Any associate of Wayne Brady's, the mob member he worked for, and the mobster he worked for. Enemies of Vegas, enemies of Diega himself. He had even been through Tahlia's mail in case she had a stalker.

All to no avail.

"God, tell me where she is? Please," Diega begged out loud, on the verge of falling apart, only pulling himself together when his security chief walked in.

"Sir. We've been over the car with a fine-tooth comb. There's nothing. No hair, no fingerprints, no footprints outside the car, nothing. She either disappeared of her own accord or…" Mark weighed up his next sentence.

"Or?" Diega demanded, leaning forward over his desk.

"Or a professional took her. Making sure he wore gloves, brushing away all footprints and tyre tracks."

Diega knew he was right, and that could only mean mobsters were involved. He sighed. "Okay. That narrows down the list. I want to know where these people were at the time she disappeared. Whether there's been any unusual activity where they're concerned." He handed a list of suspects to Mark who walked out and closed the door behind him.

Diega wearily sat down in his chair and gazed out the window at the city. "Tahlia, where are you?" he whispered.

*****

Vegas had helped Manny and Maria clean up the house after he came to. He thought about what had happened and was totally freaking out about Tahlia disappearing. Sitting on his bed smoking a cigarette, he had no idea of what to do. Thinking about his part-time job he knew he hadn't pissed anyone off, so, none of them would have taken her.

He thought about his old boss and the circumstances in which they had parted. *No,* he thought, *he wouldn'... would he?* Vegas realised he didn't have the resources to track her down, but he did have the experience.

Thinking of someone who *did* have the resources, he tried to swallow his pride. It was going to be hard, very hard, but he had to do it to find his Tahlia.

He picked up the phone and dialled.

7:00 a.m.

*****

Continually drifting off to sleep wasn't helping, but Tahlia knew it was the leftover chloroform mixed with exhaustion. Hearing voices outside the door, she strained to listen but still couldn't hear clearly. The door opened, and two sets of footsteps walked in.

"We're gonna take you for a little walk," one voice said as its owner unlocked her hands from the wall then untied her ankles. Dragging her to her feet, they walked her down a hallway, around a corner, and into another room. Sitting her down on a chair, they shoved something into her hands.

"Hold that up," the voice said, and her blindfold was

yanked off.

A flash went off in her eyes, blinding her momentarily. Not that it mattered as they blindfolded her again. Being walked back to the room, she thought she'd come from, she was shoved onto the bed and retied before being left alone.

*****

The phone call Diega received had been interesting, but a joke. *How the hell could he help?* he thought as Mark came into the office.

"Sir, we've accounted for everyone's whereabouts. Especially his," he said, pointing to a name on the list he put on the desk.

"Where was he?" Diega asked.

"Exactly where we found him, sir."

"All right, thank you." He watched Mark leave then leaned back in his chair and reconsidered the phone call. "I don't need him," he said viciously. Calming down, he realised this person had known Tahlia for some time before he'd met her. And besides, considering what this person has been getting up to, it might be a good idea to bring him into the fold.

What's that old saying? *Keep your friends close and your enemies even closer.*

He picked up the phone and dialled a number.

7:30 a.m.

*****

Vegas listened intently to the voice at the other end of the phone line before hanging up. Walking out to his bike, he headed along the strip to the place he needed to go, and pulling up, strode through the entrance and stepped into a lift. Getting out, he walked down a hallway and through an office door.

"So, what are we gonna do to get Tahlia back?" he asked Diega, who looked up from something in his hand.

"I just received this," he replied and held it out for Vegas to see.

Walking over to Diega, he saw it was a photo, and taking it, stared at it. It was Tahlia, holding a copy of today's paper, looking tired, worn out, and completely stunned. "So what are we gonna do?" he asked again, glancing up at Diega.

"Who do you know that would do this?" Diega asked, crossing his arms over his chest.

Vegas shook his head. "No one. I haven' pissed anyone off. There's no one after me or Tahlia 'cept for the cops back in Maine, but I doubt it's them." He threw the photo down on the desk, moved over to the window, and looked out over the city.

Diega started pacing. "There are only a few people I've narrowed it down to, and this," he pointed to the photo, "is one of their favourite things to do."

The phone rang, and Mark Dalton came running in as Diega picked it up. "Diega."

"Hello, Diega."

Hitting the speaker button, Diega dropped the phone into its cradle. "Santiago. I don't have time for you. What do you want?"

Diega knew Carlo Santiago well.

"Now, Diega, there's no need to be snippy, and that's no way to speak to an old friend."

"We're not friends," Diega spat at the phone.

"Anyway, I just thought I'd give you a friendly call to see how you are and to say hello. Hello, Vegas. How are you?"

Vegas stood rooted to the spot. *How the hell does he know I'm here?* His eyes widened, the panic rose, but he stayed silent.

"What makes you think Vegas is here?" Diega asked, curiously gazing at Vegas.

"Because I've been keeping an eye on both of you. Watching you and that *lovely* lady you're both involved with." There was a dramatic pause. "Did you...*like*... your little present?"

Realising what he meant, Diega blew up. "Santiago, you bastard," he yelled, slamming his hands on the desk and leaning toward the phone, "where is she? What have you done with her? If you hurt her, I will hunt you down and kill you. *That* is a *promise.*"

"Diega, Diega, Diega. Calm down, my friend."

"*I am not your friend,*" Diega yelled, straightening.

"Well then, calm down anyway. Now, as you can see from the photo, she is alive and well. And all mine. So, I'll say goodbye, for now, to both of you, and I might call again sometime soon."

"Santi—" Diega started.

The dial tone sounded.

"Damn it," Diega slammed his hands down onto his

desk again. *"How dare he. How dare he do this."*

Mark nodded as something came through on his earpiece. "We were unable to trace the call, sir."

"Damn it," Diega said again, angrily pacing back and forth with his hands on his hips. He stopped and looked curiously, suspiciously at Vegas. "You haven't said anything. How do *you* know Santiago?"

Shifting uncomfortably, Vegas couldn't look Diega in the eye. "I don' know him personally, but I have heard of him."

"Uh-huh." Diega wasn't convinced, and he turned to Mark. "So what do we do now? I can't sit around and wait. I won't."

"Sir. We will do all we can. But you know from personal experience what he's like." He spread his hands. "And now, someone else is involved."

"All right, do what you can." Diega sighed, resigned to fate.

"Sir."

Diega turned to Vegas. "You asked before what are we going to do. Well, we're going to find her." Going behind his desk, he pored over the maps laid out. He knew Nevada well, having been born and raised, and now he was going to use his knowledge to help him find the woman he loved.

8:30 a.m.

*****

Tahlia was really scared. Crying so much that her tears had soaked her blindfold. She had no idea of what was going on, or who was behind it, but she knew it was bad. Thinking about her life, and everything that had happened in the last year, she wondered who it had to do with.

Was it someone who hated Vegas, or someone who was after Diega? God, what if it's Wayne's killer? No, it couldn't possibly be.

The door opened and someone walked in. Pulling her knees up to her chest to protect herself in some way, she waited. She could sense the person standing there, watching her.

"Well, my dear," he finally said, "it seems the men in your life now know you're missing." He chuckled, more to himself. "Except you're *not* missing because I know where you are. You're *here*, with *me*. And now they know you're never coming back. You're all mine. Forever." He touched her face and stroked her hair. "I can see why they both love you. Why your audience loves you. Why *I* love you." His hand slid down her neck, into her shirt, and caressed her breast.

Pulling away, she curled up as much as she could. "Who are you? What the hell do you want?" Her voice not as strong as she wanted it to be.

"I'm your future, Tahlia, and I want you. I want what Vegas had, then Diega. I want to touch you and kiss you and come inside of you. I want to make you scream like they did," he paused for dramatic effect, "it would really make the moment if they were watching when I had my way with you. The pain in their eyes as I make you mine. As I thrust inside of you, take your breast into my mouth, screw you the way they did." He touched her face again.

"Stop it," she cried out, "don't touch me."

"Oh, one day, my dear, I'm going to touch you all I like."

*****

He watched her as she huddled on the bed.

No one knew he was there. No one had seen him enter. And Tahlia couldn't see him now, so that didn't matter anyway. She could sense him though, so she knew. That her past had finally caught up with her and was making her pay for all of her dirty little deeds. Dirty little deeds of a dirty little whore. Dirty little deeds she needed punishing for. Punishment for a dirty little whore.

Oh, yes, my sweet Tahlia. You will be punished. Severely.

He straightened his tie.

The games have now begun!

Chapter 23

Diega and Vegas pored over every map of Nevada and Las Vegas they had, while the security team went through every file on Santiago and his cohorts that they could find, even making unplanned visits and raids to find out what they knew. But they all knew nothing, had no idea what Santiago was up to, and Diega wasn't happy, yelling at everyone that didn't bring him good news.

The sun was setting, and it was now twenty-four hours from when Tahlia had been taken, and he wanted her found. Now. Even Vegas had gone to see people he knew to see what they could tell him, but that too was a dead end.

"So what the hell do we do now? No one seems to know what Santiago is up to, an' how the hell do we find him?" Vegas was looking at Diega from across his desk.

"I don't know what we do now except to keep looking. Either everyone is lying, or they actually don't know anything. And even though I've gone up against Santiago before…this…*is different*." Diega glanced at Vegas. They were both worn out and tired, having not slept or eaten in almost two days, and had dark circles and bags under their eyes.

Running his hands over his face and through his hair, he sighed. *I don't know what to do. Oh, God, I don't know what to do,* he thought. Leaning back in his chair he closed his eyes, picturing Tahlia's smiling happy face and their time together at his retreat. His thoughts were interrupted by the ringing of the phone. Opening his eyes, he saw Vegas scowling at him as he hit the speaker button.

"Diega."

"Hello, again, my friend. It's now 6:20 p.m., the exact time Tahlia was taken out of your life and brought into mine. How have you been?"

"Santiago, you bastard," Diega started, leaping out of his seat and leaning toward the phone, "where is she? I want to speak to her so I know she's all right, and if you've touched her—"

"Diega, my friend. She's just fine, and as a show of good faith, she's right here…say hello, my dear." There was a jumbling sound.

"Diega, help me," Tahlia said in a tiny voice.

"Tahlia—"

"So you see, Diega, Vegas, she's just fine. And to prove it even more, I'll send you another present tomorrow. Goodbye, for now."

"Damn it, damn it," Diega yelled, picking up a paperweight and throwing it across the room. Vegas dove out of the way, seeing that Diega was a force to be reckoned with.

Mark walked in and casually glanced at the smashed

ruins. "Sir, we still can't trace the call."

"Find him," Diega demanded through clenched teeth. Standing at the full-length window, hot tears began to well in his eyes, but he didn't want to fall apart in front of Vegas. "There's absolutely nothing we can do," he whispered, "I don't know how to find her…"

Vegas stood beside Diega. "We have to find her," he choked. "Even if we look under every rock an' stone in Nevada. We have to find her."

Diega looked at him. "I know."

*****

Someone walked into the room and untied her hands from the wall. "Come with me." It was the woman from yesterday, leading Tahlia into a small room where she untied her. "Please do not remove the blindfold until you hear the door close. You are to have a shower and dress in the clothes provided. Once done, put the blindfold back on and knock on the door. Understood?"

Nodding, Tahlia heard the door close behind her. Ripping off the blindfold, she saw she was in a bathroom. The window too high and too small to climb through. The room bare, except for some toiletries and clothes.

Sighing, she took off her clothes and stepped into the shower. The hot spray felt good on her skin, and she stood there for a few moments savouring the feeling. Quickly washing her hair and body, Tahlia got out and grabbed a towel. After drying herself, she picked up the clothes that had been left for her. Bra, panties, and a red dress. Self-conscious, she dressed quickly, and dried and brushed her hair.

Standing next to the door, she put the blindfold back on and knocked on the door, waiting. The door opened, and the woman came back in and retied her hands. Tahlia was led to another room and placed at a table.

She could smell food, and her mouth watered as the woman walked out, closing the door behind her. Listening for a sound, Tahlia sensed that someone else was in the room. Footsteps slowly walked around the table and stopped behind her. Her blindfold was removed, and she saw the table before her was laden with the most amazing food.

"I won't untie your hands, in case you try something where you'll end up being hurt." It was the voice of the man who had taken her, standing behind her, his hands lying heavily on her shoulders as his fingers gripped them tightly.

She shuddered at the pain and her heart pounded. She was scared.

The man walked around the table to sit in the chair opposite her. He was tall and muscular, well built, with short, curly black hair, and eyes so dark blue she couldn't see his pupils.

"You, my dear, may call me Carlo. But very soon, you will call me your husband. For now, eat up, you must be hungry." He picked up his cutlery and started slicing.

What a creep, she thought, waiting for him to take the first mouthful before picking up her fork. *Telling me he's going to be my husband. Who the fuck does he think he is?* She was starving and ate hungrily, but as well as she could since her hands were tied. Finishing before he did, she sat back and waited. Saying nothing as she studied him.

Tanned skin, wide brow and square jaw. The smooth European looks of an older man. He looked vaguely familiar, but she couldn't place him. *Have I met you before,* she wondered, trying to put a memory to the face, racking her brain to remember.

"You were hungry, weren't you? You may have more if you like."

"No, thanks," she said, picking up her glass of water and drinking it in one go, wiping her mouth with her napkin when she was done.

"Not very talkative are you?" Santiago asked, watching her.

Gazing around the room, Tahlia saw it was a dining room of sorts. An elaborate tiled floor, glass table and ornate chairs. A crystal chandelier hanging above the table, ornaments and statues placed on shelves.

"Do you like what you see?" he asked, curious as he lifted his wine glass to his lips.

"The dining room, yes."

He didn't like her answer as he had been referring to himself. Finishing his own meal, he leaned back in his chair. "I know quite a lot about you, Tahlia Johnston. In fact, I know your whole life story."

"I highly doubt that," she replied, looking away.

"You were born in Australia. Your parents moved to Los Angeles, then New York, where your father died when you were ten. Your mother went into a downward spiral, and you were assaulted by her boyfriend on your twelfth birthday. From the age of eighteen, you began dead-end relationships, ending up by killing your last boyfriend. No wait, that would be the one *before* Vegas. What was his name…ah yes, Wayne Brady. Then, of course, there was Vegas, then Diega. Need I say more?"

His dark eyes seared into her brain, and his knowledge scared her. Yet she was strangely affected. "I didn't kill Wayne, besides, if you've done this to me how do I know that *you* didn't kill him?" She felt tired and her eyelids were heavy.

"I didn't kill him, my dear. But I do know who did. Are you feeling tired? You look exhausted."

That was all she heard.

*****

8:00 a.m.

Monday morning the parcel arrived.

Ripping it open, Diega and Vegas stared at the photo of Santiago and Tahlia. They were sitting at a dining table, eating. She was wearing a red dress, and her hands were together, possibly tied. She didn't look happy. Reaching back into the envelope, Diega pulled out a bra and panties.

"Oh, my God," Vegas said, putting his hands over his mouth, "they're Tahlia's. I was with her when she bought 'em." He felt sick and turned away.

Diega handed the photo and underwear to Mark Dalton. "Look over every inch of that photo, see if you can tell where it was taken. And test her underwear…in case he touched her."

"Sir." Mark dropped the photo and underwear into separate clear zip bags.

Diega picked up his phone. "Get ready, we're going on a tour of Nevada." Setting the phone in its cradle, he looked at Vegas. "Let's go, we're going to do what we can."

"Where we goin'?" Vegas demanded and followed Diega out of his office and down a hallway.

"We're going up to the roof. I have a private helicopter. We're going to tour the state of Nevada."

Taking Diega's lift up to the roof, Vegas saw a chopper ready for take off.

"Get in the back and buckle up," Diega yelled over the noise, before climbing into the front next to the pilot.

For the next four hours, they scoured the desert, looking for compounds, buildings, places where Santiago might be hiding her. The chopper had plenty of technical devices, but not all of them were for daytime use. Flying back and forth across the state, they finally turned back. When they landed, they headed for Diega's office.

Mark met them there. "Sir. The underwear was fairly clean, like it was brand new. The techs are still working on the photo."

"Not good enough, work harder."

"Sir."

"And get the choppers ready. We're going on a sweep of Nevada at seven p.m. to use the infrared." He turned to Vegas. "You should get some sleep and eat something. We'll be out most of the night."

Nodding, Vegas went to the room he'd been given, and Diega went up to his suite.

Sitting on his bed, Diega looked at the photos of him and Tahlia they'd taken at his retreat. She looked so happy, so carefree, and now, she was trapped. "I have to find you," Diega whispered. "I *will* find you." Setting his clock, he lay down.

1:00 p.m.

*****

Tahlia was groggy and back on the bed, tied up and blindfolded. Hoping to clear her mind by breathing deeply, she tried to formulate a plan. Rubbing her head against her arm, she inched the blindfold up and off, and looking around, saw she was in a bedroom.

It was simply furnished, with the few items of furniture looking like antiques. The windows were bolted shut, with rich blue curtains framing them. The floor was polished wood, a single easy chair next to the window. A bedside table had a small lamp.

Looking at her hands, she saw they were tied together, then chained to a bolt in the wall. Struggling against the bonds, she soon wore out and fell asleep. When she woke it seemed to be late afternoon, and Santiago was sitting on the easy chair. "Hello, Tahlia. Sleep well?"

"What did you do? What did you put in my food?" she demanded groggily.

"Only a sedative my dear. Would you like a drink?" He held a glass of water to her mouth. Drinking it, she eyed him cautiously, and he stared back at her before placing the glass on the bedside table. "I'll see you for dinner at seven. Put something pretty on." He walked out the door.

*****

6:00 p.m.

The woman came in and led Tahlia to the bathroom. She had a quick shower and put on the dress that had been left, then did her hair.

6:55 p.m.

She was led to the dining room.

*****

7:00 p.m.

Diega and Vegas lifted off in the chopper. Using infrared, they scoured the desert of Nevada, looking for underground bunkers and compounds. For hours they flew through the night, along with other choppers, fanning out in formation.

*****

Having dinner with Santiago was a waste of time. Tahlia didn't want to eat a thing, knowing he had drugged her food the night before.

"You need to eat something, my dear, keep up your strength." He sliced through some meat.

"You drugged my food, why would I want to eat again?" She struggled to unbind her hands, but found she couldn't.

"Have some fruit then." He wiped his mouth and took a sip of wine.

"You probly shoved a syringe into it," she grumbled

and grabbed an apple from the fruit basket on the table.

8:00 p.m.

Dinner was finished, and as she was being led back to her room, she heard the sound of choppers overhead. The sound was faint, but she knew they were up there. Hoping for rescue, her heart leapt. But as they faded away, so did her hope.

*****

"Sir, there's nothing else we can do. We only have enough fuel to get back to the hotel," the pilot said.

"All right," Diega yelled over the noise, "turn around."

Feeling resigned and exhausted, Diega and Vegas flew back to the hotel for the night.

11:00 p.m.

*****

8:30 a.m.

Tuesday morning, another parcel arrived.

They found the dress she'd been wearing when she'd dined with Santiago. The photo that came with it made them both sick.

Tahlia lying on a bed in her underwear, a shirtless Santiago was beside her, kissing her, his hand on her leg.

They looked intimate.

Throwing the photo and dress down onto his desk in disgust, Diega paced angrily. "That bastard will die for this. Touching her that way. God, what are we going to do? I feel so useless." He choked back a sob.

"You're not the only one," Vegas replied, slumping into a chair. He was sickened that some bastard was with his Tahlia. Although she had told him they were no longer together, he still loved her, still wanted her, still ached for her. He wanted revenge on Santiago. *No one takes my Tahlia an' gets away with it!*

They could do nothing, except sit by the phone and wait.

*****

Tahlia didn't know whether it was Tuesday or not, she was guessing. Santiago had left her alone all day, and the only visitor was the woman who brought her food. She didn't even dine with him. However, he came into her room to say goodnight.

"Our life will be so different after tomorrow, Tahlia. We will leave this place and live happily ever after."

"I'm goin' nowhere with you. Diega will hunt you down an' kill you," she spat.

At first, it was a chuckle, then a rolling laugh, Santiago threw his head back in delight. "Oh, my dear, while you may not know what Diega or Vegas are capable of, there is no way they are getting you away from me." He was still laughing as he walked out the door.

*****

Wednesday morning, Diega and Vegas received another present.

Holding it in his hands, Diega felt sick. On the one

hand, he needed to know, but on the other, he didn't want to see. Ripping the large envelope open, he pulled out another set of bra and panties.

"They look like what she had on in yesterday's photo," Vegas murmured, starting to feel sick.

Slowly reaching back into the envelope Diega pulled out a photo. "Oh, my God, oh, my God. No, nooo." He screwed the photo up in his hand, and Vegas ran for the ensuite, barely making it before throwing up.

Trying to control his anger, Diega took some deep breaths. It didn't work. Grabbing a small statue from his desk, he threw it across the room with every ounce of anger.

It smashed against the wall as Vegas emerged from the bathroom, barely missing being hit.

Walking over and picking up the photo from the floor, Vegas smoothed it out. It showed Tahlia naked on a bed with Santiago naked on top of her. He was between her legs, her legs around him, his mouth on hers. Vegas felt the urge to be sick again, so he took deep breaths to calm himself.

The phone rang, and Diega hit the speaker button. "What?" he barked.

"Diega, I take your attitude to mean you've seen the photo. Ah, yes, the lovely Tahlia. I finally know what yourself and Vegas find so appealing about her. She's absolutely amazing in bed. I haven't had a better lover. She was hot and wet, and I slid inside of her so easily, as if she were made for me. We're going to be so happy together."

"*You sick son of a bitch!* What is it that you want?

Do you want my money, my casino? You can have it all, I don't care. I want Tahlia back." Diega was pissed off and he'd had enough. He was also close to being heartbroken and collapsing in an emotional heap.

Santiago was laughing, finding it very funny. "I don't want your money, Diega, I have my own, as for your casino…well, I'll have to think about that. There is nothing that I want except Tahlia, and I already have her. We will be very happy. Oh, and we're getting married next week. Maybe we'll invite you both to the wedding." He was laughing as he hung up.

Feeling absolutely sick, Diega collapsed into his chair as Vegas slid to the floor, both in their own thoughts.

Mark walked in. "Sir, we still can't trace him. We can't even pick up noises in the background. We have nothing."

Diega barely looked up as he spoke through gritted teeth. "I want choppers out all day and all night, in every direction, fan out. And when they head back send more out. You will not stop until she is found. Do you understand me?" Diega's look sent him running.

*****

Tahlia was trying to decide what to do. *I have to get myself untied before making a move*, she thought. *An' if I can grab a gun, then I'll shoot. I have to. Otherwise, I'll be stuck here forever.*

She blinked back a few tears. *I will not let him keep me here. I will get back to Diega an' we will be together forever.*

She formulated a plan.

It seemed to take hours, but finally, Santiago walked in.

"Good news, my dear. We're leaving today. And next week we'll be getting married, so we have a wedding to prepare for."

"I'm not going to marry you," she spat.

"Oh, my dear, we have to marry now. Especially since we consummated our relationship."

"What! I didn't sleep with you, you're mental if you think I would." She threw a dirty look his way.

Santiago laughed and walked back to the door. He motioned to someone, and they rolled in a TV and DVD on a trolley then left.

"Oh, Tahlia, we certainly did consummate our relationship." He picked up the remote and pressed play.

What Tahlia saw horrified her, made her so sick she threw up over the side of the bed.

"Now, that's no way to react to our lovemaking. Breathtaking it was too."

She was unable to tear her eyes away. She and Santiago naked on a bed. He was on top of her, thrusting, grinding. And she was moaning. "Oh, God, stop it, stop it," she screamed, sobbing.

"Oh, but I couldn't. We went at it all night." He looked at her. "I've sent a copy to Diega and Vegas, they should be getting it soon. In the meantime, we need to leave."

He got up from the bed and unchained her hands.

Because her feet weren't bound, she made her move.

Grabbing his throat in her hands, she choked him as hard as she could, and kneed him in the groin. Able to get him on the ground, Tahlia smashed his head on the wood floor, making him bleed. She was like a mad woman, punching and scratching at his face. She kept at it until he was unconscious.

Searching him for a gun, she pulled it out of the holster just in time as two men lunged through the door. Aiming, she fired in quick succession, killing them both. Going over to their bodies, she grabbed their guns and ran through the doorway.

Running through the house, not knowing which way to go, Tahlia heard voices shouting. Seeing she was in the kitchen, she opened every door, finding one that led to a hallway. Closing it behind her, she ran, making her way into the garage.

Trying every door on every car, she found an unlocked SUV. Jumping in and quietly closing the door, she searched for the keys, finding them tucked into the visor. Starting the engine, she hit the gas and burst through the garage door.

Coming out into the sun, Tahlia didn't know which way to go, so she veered to the right. Speeding around the compound, she found no road or bridge and slammed on the brakes as she came perilously close to a deep ravine. Hearing men shouting behind her, she turned to see Santiago and about twenty men pointing their guns at her.

"You can't go anywhere, Tahlia, there's no road, no bridge. Just a deep ravine around the whole house. So step out of the car with your hands in the air," Santiago yelled, holding his hand to his head.

"Like hell!" She was going down fighting *not* giving

up. Turning around in her seat, she aimed two guns, one in each hand, and fired. Killing three men, Tahlia picked up the third gun when the others were empty. Finally out of bullets, she ducked down in her seat, only to have Santiago thrust his hand through the window, his gun at her head.

"Go ahead, kill me," she spat.

"Oh, my dear, you have no idea what you've done." He was furious, in fact, he was very pissed off.

"No, you can push the car into the ravine, you can blow my brains out, I'm not going anywhere with you," she yelled back.

He yanked the door open and grabbed her arm viciously, dragging her out while she screeched in pain. "You're right, my dear. You *are* more trouble than you're worth. So, I'll let Diega and Vegas fight it out for you. But not before I get my way."

Pushing her ahead of him, Santiago kept his gun on her all the way back to the house.

*****

The last present arrived for Diega and Vegas.

It was a DVD. Sliding it into the player, they watched the scene from the photo.

"Oh, God, there's no way she'd let him do that," Vegas yelled, feeling sick.

"Does she look awake to you? That's not the Tahlia I know," Diega said, and they both leaned in for a closer look.

"She looks…asleep," Vegas said, shrugging, unsure.

"Drugged," Diega replied, "he drugged her and raped her."

"Oh, my God," Vegas repeated, running both hands through his hair.

"Sir, there have been reports of gunfire in the Black Mountains. The choppers picked it up and have taken footage," Mark said as he ran in.

"Patch it through," Diega said, becoming excited. Moments later, vague images came through on the monitors in Diega's office. "What happened?" he demanded.

"We're not sure sir, gunfire was heard, and a lot of dust was in the air."

They could just make out twenty or so men aiming at a car at the edge of a ravine.

"Oh, my God, is that a house?" Vegas asked, pointing to an outline in the dirt.

"You're right," Diega exclaimed, "a house built into the ground so you can't see it from the air. Oh, my God, no wonder we haven't been able to find anything. Santiago probably has it lined with something so it would cut off any heat."

Watching the screen, they saw a person being marched back to the house by a man who looked to be holding a gun.

"It must be them, it has to be. Get everyone together, we'll raid the place tonight. Get me every bit of information you can. Now," Diega demanded.

Still looking at the screen, he and Vegas were lost in their own thoughts of Tahlia.

*****

"Nooo, stop it, stop it," Tahlia screamed, sobbing. Santiago had dragged her back into the bedroom where he tied her up and was raping her repeatedly. Remembering her past, she tried to block it out. Shutting down her mind, she thought nothing, her mind empty and blank.

After many times, and many hours, he was done and called to his assistant. "Get her dressed, we're leaving soon." Walking into his office ensuite, he washed and cleaned up, making himself presentable. *Time for my plan,* he thought, straightening his tie.

*****

"You sick bastard," he hissed. "How dare you do that to her." He stared venomously at the man he saw before him. "How I hate you. How I detest you. How I will kill you."

His eyes closed, remembering that afternoon when his precious Tahlia had been violated so violently by the man who was standing in front of him. He opened his eyes, gazing at the anger and hatred radiating from every pore of the man's body. The man he would kill. Kill for what he had done. "She may be a dirty filthy whore, but she is not yours to have." He straightened his suit. "SHE IS NOT YOURS TO HAVE!"

*****

Walking into his office, Santiago sat down behind his large oak desk and prepared himself. Taking a deep breath, he picked up the phone and dialled.

"Diega."

"Diega, my friend, I've finally decided that you and Vegas should be reunited with your darling Tahlia."

"Really, why's that?" Diega was extremely suspicious.

Santiago preened himself. "Well, for months now I've watched her, wanted her, mainly because you did. And I had the whole *archrival thing* going on. But out of the goodness of my heart, I'm giving her back to you since I've had my way with her." A sly smile crossed his lips. "Be at Grand Wash Cliffs at midnight. There's a cave about five miles in from the entrance. She'll be in there, waiting for her saviours. Just the two of you, no one else. Remember, midnight." He hung up. *Now, time for some fun.*

5:30 p.m.

Chapter 24

Sitting back in his chair, Diega was suspicious. "He's up to something, I just know it. I *feel* it. This isn't right."

Vegas agreed. "Why would he just give her back? Wait," he was thinking something bad, "unless he took her to get even with you, he said there was the whole archrival thing happenin'. What if he just took her…to try an' make her pregnant…or somethin'?" He closed his eyes and choked back tears.

Thinking about it, Diega knew he could be right. "We did see them…him."

"I'll kill that bastard," Vegas blurted out.

Mark turned up. "We tried to track the range and were able to pinpoint it to the Black Mountains."

"So that compound *is* his," Diega said. "I want two teams. One to the compound, the other to Grand Wash Cliffs. I want the place scoured for devices and lookouts. I want to know every detail. He won't give her up easily."

"If he gives her up at all," Vegas said.

"We *will* get her back," Diega said, sounding more confident than he felt.

*****

9:30 p.m.

Night team one raided the compound. Sneaking up to the ravine, they slid collapsible bridges across and ran toward the house. In a round of gunfire, they burst through every door and window taking down everyone in the house. The problem was, Santiago and Tahlia weren't there, but they killed the five guards who were. Relaying the news to Diega, they made a full sweep.

*****

10:00 p.m.

Night team two swarmed into Grand Wash Cliffs. Using infrared, they scoured every inch within a ten mile radius of the cave, finding nothing, no one. They relayed the news to Diega, then backed off and stood guard.

*****

11:30 p.m.

Diega and Vegas rolled to a stop two hundred yards from the cave. Watching through infrared binoculars, they waited. Sitting in a high tech, bulletproof, black surveillance van, they turned around in their seats to speak to the men in the back.

"Sir, we can see every inch, there's no one there. Nothing."

Vegas looked through the binoculars again. "So,

what do we do an' when do we do it?"

Diega sighed. "I don't know. We wait."

*****

Tahlia was still in a stupor, but had some vague awareness of what was happening. She had been tied, blindfolded, and put into a car. After driving for hours, the movement was making her nauseous. They finally stopped, and she was carried somewhere and placed on the ground, feeling horrible and headachy with no idea what was going on.

*****

11:45 p.m.

Diega's cell rang. "Where is she?"

"She's inside, my friend. I'm surprised you haven't been in yet. You must be eager to get her back. Anyway, she's there waiting. Go and get her."

Turning to his technicians, he waited for an answer.

"We're detecting heat, looks like people. Yes, two are moving, one's lying on the ground. It must be them."

"How come you didn't pick them up before?" Diega demanded, glaring at them.

"We don't know, sir. It's like they just appeared out of thin air," one said, the glow of the monitors in front of him lighting up his face.

"How the hell'd they do that?" Vegas demanded.

"We don't know. Maybe there's another opening we don't know about," the other chimed in.

382

"All right. Keep in contact. Let us know what's happening every second," Diega said.

Putting tiny ear speakers in their ears, and small microphones on their shirts, Diega and Vegas stepped out of the van and waited a moment.

11:50 p.m.

*****

Tahlia was cold and sick and still lying on cold hard ground. Santiago and some other man were whispering, and she strained to hear. Hearing the word *bomb*, she freaked. *Oh, my God,* she thought, *they're going to blow us up an' kill us.* Moving around, she tried to free herself, but stopped when a wave of nausea swept over her. Breathing deeply, she tried again and struggled hard.

"My dear, there's no need to move. Make yourself comfortable, it's almost midnight. Diega and Vegas will be here for you any moment. Until then, Tahlia, try and relax." He turned to his companion. "How much longer?"

"Not long now."

*****

Diega and Vegas stopped at one hundred yards and looked around cautiously. Slowly walking on, they were constantly on the lookout. Stealthily, they moved, one foot in front of the other, making no sound as they stepped forward.

"Sir, three people are still in the cave."

"All right," Diega replied quietly, resting his hand on the holster at his waist. He flicked the top, revealing his gun. "If I don't get her out safely. I will kill you. And *that* is a promise I will definitely keep."

Vegas looked at him, stupefied. "Why would you kill me? I didn' do this." He kept his voice low.

"Yes, you did. I know things about you that Tahlia doesn't." Diega glanced at Vegas. "If it wasn't for you, and what you did, this wouldn't be happening. Tahlia didn't deserve what you did to her. She didn't deserve you in her life."

"I didn' mean to hurt her, an' I regret it deeply. But you should blame yourself. It's Santiago's crusade to outdo you that brought us here to this moment." Vegas was angry, but kept himself in check.

They were nearly at the cave entrance. Diega checked his watch.

11:59 p.m.

*****

Tahlia struggled hard and desperately against her bonds as she panicked. She was about to die and didn't want to. Not when she had finally found the man she wanted to spend the rest of her life with. The one man that would love and cherish her for all time, with passion and desire, and not beat and abuse her. She did not want to die.

"Nooo," she started to sob, escalating into a wailing scream, "nooooo."

"My dear, it's all right." She didn't hear him. "You'll

soon be reunited with your two saviours. In fifteen seconds it's midnight, and you will be with the two men who love you." Santiago turned again to his companion, who nodded.

They both left the room.

10…

Tahlia sobbed. Thank you, God, for bringing Vegas and Diega into my life.

9…

Diega stopped as an eerie feeling washed over him.

8…

"I love you both, so much," she gasped, unable to stop her heart from breaking.

7…

Vegas turned to Diega questioningly, feeling something himself.

6…

"Help me," Tahlia screamed before fainting.

5…

The technician in the van saw something bad.

4…

Diega heard a woman scream then stop.

3…

"Sir, run," the technician screamed into the microphone.

2…

Diega and Vegas ran.

1

Chapter 25

The explosion ripped through Grand Wash Cliffs blasting dirt, trees and rocks miles in every direction. Diega and Vegas had gone flying through the air to land a hundred yards from where they'd been standing and were now covered in debris. The van had been lifted and tossed backward to land on its roof.

Dirt continued to rain down as Diega lifted his head, and team two came swarming in to help their boss. Pulling him out from under the rubble, they helped him stand.

When no one came to his aid, Vegas tried to push himself to his feet. "Ahh," he cried and grabbed his left shoulder which was pointing at an odd angle. He gritted his teeth against the pain and slumped back on his heels.

Turning to look at what was left, Diega went ballistic. "Get in there," he screamed, pointing to what was left of the cave. "Find her, find Santiago."

Vegas stirred himself and tried to stand through the searing red-hot agony of a busted shoulder, only vaguely aware he was being completely ignored.

"Sir." One of the team came running up. "The

technicians are okay. They wanted you to know that there was something ticking. They thought it was a bomb, that's why they warned you."

"Damn that bastard to hell," Diega screamed, "she was in there. Was she in there?"

"Sir, she was in there. But only her, the other two had left. Team one has arrived, and they're going over every inch of the other side of the cliff."

"He escaped?" Diega spat, facing off against his security people. "Santiago escaped?" His anger overwhelmed him as his teams stood there motionless, looking at him. "Find him. Find him. Find him, and I will kill him myself," he screamed.

Vegas finally managed to stumble to his feet and wavered uneasily, unsure if he would even stay standing, or if he'd collapse from the intensity of his injury. Still clutching his shoulder, he wanted to vomit, but held back the desire by swallowing hard and gritting his teeth.

Suddenly, an unnatural eerie quiet settled over the site.

Diega stopped screaming, and his face hardened at the thought that came to him.

Vegas' gaze settled on Diega's back and cleared through the pain-filled fog smothering his brain. The brain that slowly reminded him of what had been said just minutes before.

Remembering his promise to Vegas, Diega pulled his gun out of his holster, turned around, and pulled the trigger.

Chapter 26

Diega opened his eyes to a cold fall day. Rain was trickling down the window, grey clouds hung low in the sky. Not wanting to get out of bed, he lay there, trying to clear his mind of thoughts that now invaded. Day after day they wouldn't stop. Night after night his dreams tormented him. Tortured him in ways he'd never known. Never felt. It was horrible. The feeling of emptiness and loneliness. He had found the woman he'd wanted to spend the rest of his life with.

Now…she was gone.

Damn that Santiago. I will find him, and I will kill him.

Rolling over he looked at the bedside clock.

6:30 a.m.

He couldn't go back to sleep now, even if he wanted to. And he desperately needed sleep, but just not now. He flung the covers back and walked around the suite.

Tahlia's suite.

He'd been sleeping there since the explosion. He couldn't bring himself to say, since her death. A part of him didn't believe that she was gone. It was a sense, deep inside. He couldn't explain it, just knew that it was there, telling him she wasn't dead. Then there was his brain telling him not to be stupid. She had been in the cave, she had died. He'd heard her scream. Hadn't he? He'd heard something that sounded like a woman screaming, but wasn't sure.

Running his hands through his hair, he stood still and gazed around. Everything was where it had been their last morning together. Their last moment in time before… He choked back a sob, but the pain and anguish were too much. Falling into a crumpled heap on the living room floor, he allowed himself cry.

*****

In Las Vegas General Hospital, a man lay in a bed. Tubes and wires were attached everywhere, monitoring his heart rate, his breathing, even his brain function. He'd been in a coma for weeks, doctors believing it might be some time before he came out of it, if ever. And if he did recover, they weren't sure if he would be like he was before. His brain was swollen from a head wound he'd received, but not showing abnormal function. He also needed a blood transfusion during surgery where the doctors battled to save him. Afterwards, when he started coming to, he'd said one word before falling into a coma.

Tahlia.

*****

Diega had moved some of his clothes into Tahlia's suite,

and as he dressed, more images tormented him. Beautiful Tahlia, her sparkling green eyes, her lush pink lips and the way they smiled. Their time together at his retreat. *God, she was so happy. I was so happy. I had the woman I loved, she had finally given herself to me, we were happy and carefree and together. We were back a week before, damn I'll kill him for killing her.*

There was a knock at the door. He opened it to see Kate standing there patiently as she had every other day since his world ended.

"Sir, will you be working today?"

He leaned on the door. "You know, Kate, for the last four weeks you've knocked on the door every day, and when I open it, you ask the exact same question. Will you be working today?" he paused, "and what's my answer?" He waited almost impatiently.

"No. And I don't know when I will be." She repeated his answer word for word.

"Exactly. So why do you insist on asking me if you already know the answer?" He walked into the bedroom and grabbed his jacket off the bed. "For the record, so you don't keep asking every day, and so I don't keep repeating myself, Rick Sanders is in charge," he said, pulling his jacket on. "He's the manager, and he's done very well when I've not been here in the past, so he'll continue to be in charge until I decide if I want to come back to work or not. Now, was there anything else besides asking if I would be working or not?"

"I just wanted to give you a report on how the casino and hotel have been doing. Like I do every week," Kate replied as Diega walked her out.

"Fine. If I feel like looking over it, I will, if not, it doesn't matter." He took the file from her and slapped it down on the small table beside the door before he shut it. They walked around to his private lift.

"Mandy has been asking about Tahlia. If there's going to be a service or not," Kate said. "What do I tell her, and will your schedule be the same today?"

"Yes, it will be. And tell Mandy…I don't know." He sighed, and stepping into the lift, he turned to her. "I'll see you this afternoon."

The doors closed on Diega, leaving Kate to wonder why he did it every day. Why he went to see a man he hated so much that he'd tried to kill him.

*****

He slowly opened his eyes, his vision blurry. Wiping his hand over his face, he glanced around. Where was he? What the hell happened…?

Oh, he thought, horrid memories sliding back into his mind, that's what happened. He walked over to his window and gazed out over the landscape, trying to forget.

I hate this, I absolutely hate this. Hate Tahlia being taken away from me. How dare he take her away from me. How dare he do this to me. How dare he!

I will make him suffer for what he's done. Taking her away from me when I am the man she loves, the man she wants. The only man who really loved her.

I will make him suffer. Make them suffer.

I will kill him. I will kill all of them!

*****

Walking into Las Vegas General, Diega went up to room 302 to see the man in a coma. The doctor was there when he walked in. "How is he?" Diega asked.

"About the same, Mr Montiamo."

Diega nodded, and the doctor left the room. Staring down at the man in the bed, he wondered why he was there. Why he came every day to sit beside the bed of a man he hated. A man he'd never forgive for what he'd done. He knew he must do this for her, even though she was gone.

She would be looking down on him, wanting him to do this.

"Why the hell did she love you?" Diega asked the man. "How *could* she love you, knowing what she knew about you. Yet, she loved you until the end. And me, knowing what I know about you…I know why you loved *her*. The same reason I did."

Diega's thoughts trailed off as he thought about his beautiful Tahlia. Sighing, he sat down in the chair next to the bed, opened the newspaper he'd brought, and began to read the latest news to the man in a coma.

Listening to Diega read the paper was boring as hell, and he did it every day. It annoyed him that he was there. Day after day, week after week. It was always the same, and he wished it would stop.

Why is he here? the man in a coma thought. *He hates me with a passion, an' even says so in his rambling one-way conversations. It's the same every day. He'll come in, say a few nasty things, berate me, tell me he hates me for what I've done, an' then sit an' read the paper out loud. Like it's a normal thing to do. Every morning for two hours he'll be here an' then leaves. I wan' to know what he does when he leaves. Where does he go? What does he do? Does he hunt down that bastard for what he did? Has he killed him yet, 'cause damn it, if he hasn', then I will once I'm out of a coma.*

He knew his left arm was fairly useless, having severely ripped the muscles and tendons, but a physiotherapist had been coming in every day manipulating his arm around trying to help. His head pounded furiously all the time until they pumped the drugs in, and he hated being in a coma, not able to move or talk. He wanted to get out of bed and hunt the bastard down. Torture him and rip him limb from limb, making him die a slow painful death. His thoughts were interrupted as Diega finished up and folded the paper.

Fine'ly, he thought, *now he's goin'. God, I hope he doesn' do that thing again. I hate it when he touches me. Why does he do it when he hates me so much?*

Diega stood, gazing down at the man. Reaching out his left hand, he touched it to the man's cheek then pushed a lock of hair away. Sighing, he walked out the door, ready to conduct business.

*****

Back in his office, Diega sat behind his desk and rang Mark. When he walked in, Diega was gazing at him expectantly.

Sighing, Mark knew what was to come. "Sir, we still don't have anything to go on. It's like Santiago disappeared off the face of the earth. We can't track him by satellite, we couldn't track his flight plans. Nothing. He's just…gone."

"He can't be gone," Diega yelled, thrusting his chair back and walking over to the window. "He did *not* disappear. He was there that night then left. He *must* be *somewhere*. I want every state of every country checked. Even if you have to go through them with a fine-tooth comb. Get the best computer experts you can. Track down the best hackers if you have to. I *want him found*."

"We're doing all we can, sir, but he has money behind him too. If he doesn't want to be found he won't be." Mark shifted uncomfortably.

Diega looked at him mournfully. "Find him." Turning to stare out of the window, he stood still and let the quiet wash over him.

It was too quiet. Had been for too long.

Memories of Tahlia singing floated through his mind. He had watched every show from his seat up in the balcony. Seeing her on stage talking to the audience and belting out a tune. It was amazing. *She* was amazing. And he had wanted her from the moment he saw her and knew she would be his someday. Then that day had arrived, and it was the best day of his life.

No other woman had ever made him feel that way. So high and giddy with love, passion and desire. He'd had relationships, preferring to work hard and set up a life for himself, but they weren't that fulfilling. He was happy enough at the time in them, but knew they were not the one he wanted to share his life with. Have children with.

He had wanted to make Tahlia his wife, even coming up with an idea for a wedding and honeymoon while they were at his retreat. He'd bought a huge ruby engagement ring after they'd come back to surprise her with over a romantic dinner on the roof.

But then she'd been taken, and Satan himself had come into their lives.

"I will kill you, Santiago. That is a promise. I will hunt you down and tie you up, strip your skin from your body inch by inch, making you scream in pain, hurting you the way you hurt my Tahlia. Yes, you hurt her. You thought she was yours, and you could have a life with her. But she didn't want you. She fought you as much as she could. God, you had to drug her and rape her because you knew she didn't want you. She didn't want you, she wanted me. And I *will* kill you. I promise you that."

*****

Somewhere, on a tiny island, a magnificent white mansion stood proudly, surrounded by blue sea and palm trees. In one of the luxuriously decorated rooms on the third floor, a woman lay in a queen-size bed slipping in and out of consciousness.

It had been four weeks now, and she still wasn't well. The man watching her was worried. She had been sick with something, the shaking and sweating, hot one moment, cold the next. She never fully woke, but would mumble things the man couldn't always hear or understand. He'd called in the doctor to examine her last week and was now waiting for him to arrive with the results. The door opened, and his assistant escorted the doctor in.

"Tell me what's wrong with her? Why is she so sick?" he pleaded, wringing his hands.

The doctor pulled a file out of his briefcase and opened it. Reading a few lines, he looked at the man. "She has pneumonia, a bad case of it. Lack of nutrition hasn't helped. Made her immune system weak. So when you had her out late that night, it just made things worse."

"Will she get better?" the man fretted.

"It will take some time since I didn't see her until last week. Had she received some treatment straight away, she would be better now. But it's going to take a while. She will need medication, good nutrition, more sleep, vitamin shots will help. Here, give her these, crush them in food or drink," the doctor said, handing him a small bottle of pills.

"Thank you. My pilot will fly you back. Let me know if there's anything else I can do to help her." He escorted the doctor to the door and opened it, then turned to look at the woman in the bed.

"There's one more thing you should know," the doctor said, stopping in the doorway.

"What's that?" the man asked, looking at the doctor curiously.

"She's pregnant."

The assistant closed the door behind the doctor, leaving her boss completely stunned with his jaw hanging open. He turned to look at the woman in the bed. "Oh, my God…you're pregnant. You're pregnant."

He laughed. First a chuckle, then a rolling throaty laugh. "You're pregnant, you're pregnant." He walked over to the bed and sat beside the woman. Pushing a lock of hair from her forehead, he stroked her face and watched her. Thoughts running through his mind. "A baby. A baby. We're going to have a baby," he said dreamily as his mind wandered. "I want a son. He will carry on our fine upstanding name and tradition. Make his poppa proud. He'll be beautiful, with a good looking father like me, and a beautiful woman for his mother. He'll be perfect. We'll be such proud parents. Oh, my dear, my beautiful, perfect wife. You're giving me a baby." He became alarmed. "Wait, what if it's a little girl?" He relaxed. "Well, she'll be the apple of Daddy's eye, that's for sure. But I want a son, to carry on the name. To run the world one day. I just know his two older brothers will love him too. It may take a while for them to come around to me having married you, and that we're now having a baby, but they will love him. Or her. How could they not?"

Gazing at her, he worried about how her health may be harming the baby. The doctor would have said if anything was wrong. He smiled, so proud and happy. "To think, my dear, my essence flowed into you mating with your seed, they joined in love and made a tiny little person. Now, we're going to be parents."

Oh, my God, she thought, lying back in her bed. *A*

baby! An' here I am stuck with pneumonia. Ugh, this freak is just loving it, me lying here incapacitated an' not being able to get up an' move. Not being able to run away from this madman who has me in his sick clutches. An' God knows where I am. I don't think it's wherever I was before. Oh, God, help me, please help me.

Chapter 27

Diega stood at the window, gazing out over the city. It was a cold, blustery day, but he didn't care. He was happy. Finally. A smile played across his lips as he slid his hands into his pants pockets. He inhaled deeply, slowly. The scent in the room wove all around him, tickling his nose as he breathed. Her perfume, light, fruity, combined with her own womanly scent that held him captivated in a place where all things, all time, just fell away. A place he wanted to stay in forever. With her. The love of his life.

Womanly arms slithered around his waist, and hands slid under his polo shirt to greedily run through the nest of hair they found. His eyes closed slowly, savouring the feeling. She rubbed her face against his back feeling his hard, taut manliness.

"Oh, sweetheart, I knew I'd find you and bring you home," he whispered, pulling Tahlia into his arms, taking her with a fierceness he'd almost forgotten. Touching her. Kissing her.

The kiss went on forever.

She felt so good, so alive, so real…

Diega's eyes slowly opened to another day. Another horrible lonely day. Life without Tahlia was nothing he'd ever experienced. Before he met her life was, *seemed* normal, now, it was like death. His brother, mother, father, now Tahlia. The woman he wanted to spend the rest of his life with.

Walking into the bathroom, he looked at himself in the mirror. God, he looked awful. His face thinner, and in need of a shave. Dull blue bloodshot eyes with bags and dark circles. His hair needed cutting, and knowing Tahlia liked it short in back and long on top, he made a mental note to get it cut later that day. God, good sleep was non-existent, and he looked so haggard.

"Tahlia," he rasped through dry lips and a parched throat. He glanced back at his reflection. *She would hate to see me like this,* he thought, the tears welling in his eyes.

"I won't cry," he choked, swiping at his face and staring himself down. "I will *not* cry. I will *keep* searching for Tahlia until I find her. And I *will find her,*" he said determinedly, defying the morose-looking figure staring back at him.

He took a long hot shower and formulated another plan of attack. Turning off the faucet with a flourish, he grabbed a towel and wrapped it around his muscular waist. Standing in front of the mirror again, he picked up a can of shaving cream and carefully rubbed some in. Taking his razor, he executed a few quick moves before wiping his face.

There, nice and smooth, he thought, *just the way Tahlia likes me.* He slicked his hair back, splashed on the aftershave Tahlia loved to smell on him, and dressed neatly in a black suit. Glancing in the closet mirror, he smoothed his jacket and walked into the living room.

It was still early, and every morning he went to her bookcase and pulled out a Nancy Drew. He felt he had to read the books she loved, as they were a huge part of her and it mattered to him. Every day it was a new one, each one in order. Pulling one from the shelf, he sat on the sofa, and flipping it open to the first page, began to read.

An hour and a half later, he put the book back on its shelf and left for the hospital. Every day he did this too. Went to the hospital to see him. He had to. He owed it to the people he loved.

Twenty minutes later, he stood at the end of the bed, looking down at the man in a coma. It was two months now, and the doctors still didn't know how long it would take for him to come out of it. *God, please let him come out of it. There's something he needs to know.*

Reaching into his jacket pocket, Diega pulled out an envelope. Removing the papers and reading them again, tears welled in his eyes. He had read and re-read those papers every day since receiving them. And every day he felt the same.

Amazed. Unbelieving. Stunned.

He'd sent his private investigators out looking for information, and what they'd come back with shocked him to the core. And he was *still* dealing with the news.

Sitting in the chair beside the bed, he opened the newspaper and began to read.

Oh, God, here we go again, the comatose man

thought. *I am so fed up with this crap. Why can't he leave me the hell alone? At least he's only readin' the paper, unlike the other day when he shaved me. God, get me outta here. Why am I trapped in this useless body? Let me outta here. Now!*

*****

The woman in the bed was tossing and turning. Though she had been getting better, her sleep was fitful. Her husband watched over her, never leaving her side, not sleeping much himself. He was worried about the baby. She hadn't been thoroughly examined yet, and he was wondering if he should take her to the mainland to have a physical and ultrasound.

I can't wait to hear his heartbeat, he thought, standing at the end of the bed, proudly looking down at his wife.

She groggily opened her eyes and stared at him.

They were empty. Void of all emotion.

Just like her.

*****

Diega was in his office when Mark walked in. "Sir, we may have found a lead to Santiago's whereabouts."

Diega's interest perked up. "What is it?"

"He seems to have some offshore bank accounts, we're in the process of tracing them."

"Good," Diega said, feeling excited. "Maybe then we'll find the bastard so I can kill him. Keep searching. *Do not give up under any circumstances.*"

"Sir."

Diega glanced at his watch. *I have time to go visit since I don't have much else on my plate,* he thought, picking up a bunch of roses on his way out of the hotel.

Fifteen minutes later, he pulled to a stop in a car park where he alighted and strode over manicured lawns until he came to the headstone he wanted.

Standing before him was the angel monument he'd put on his mother's grave. Both his parents were in there. Their names, along with his baby brother's, on a plaque highlighted in gold. Diega put the flowers in the holder and reached down to touch the plaque. Sitting on the ground in front of it, he reflected back across the years.

He'd come to his mother's grave often after she died, knowing she was in there, speaking to her like she was still alive. Then, his father. By that time, he had money and was able to put his parents together, making sure they were side by side in death, just as they had been in life.

The angel was his idea when she died, but they were unable to afford it then. He'd only been able to have it specially made and put there years later when he'd saved money from his teenage jobs. He loved that statue. It reminded him of his mother, and he always saw her face when he looked into the angel's eyes. Touching the plaque, he smiled softly at the image of his parents. Smiling, happy. Like the last time he'd seen them together.

"Hi, Mom…Dad. I'm here again." He looked up at the angel. "I miss you both so much, and God I wish you were here with me now. I need your strength and your wisdom. I need you to tell me what to do because I just don't know anymore. I don't eat, I can't sleep. I barely make it through the day. I'm not running the hotel or having a life. All I do is go to the hospital every day for two hours, sit in my office for a while, and mope around Tahlia's suite." He wiped away some tears and felt himself break down.

"God, you would have loved her so much. And if she's up there with you, please look after her. Watch over her, keep her safe. She was the one woman I wanted to spend the rest of my life with. Have children with. I love her…so much." He broke down, sobbing into his hands.

Pulling himself together he wiped his face. "You would have loved her, she was perfect for me. And now, she's gone, and I don't know what to do. Do I go on with my life, forgetting she existed? Find another woman and have children. I guess you both know about everything that happened. Our meeting, finally getting Vegas out of the way and becoming a couple. But that damn Santiago ruined our dream. I will kill that bastard when I find him. And as for Vegas…well, I hope you know about him. You need to know. So… what do I do?" He sighed. "What do I do?"

He kissed his fingers and touched them to the plaque. "I love you both so much, and if you can lead me in the right direction, I'll appreciate it so much."

With one last sob, he walked away and drove back to the casino to see how it was running. Everything seemed to be in good working order, and he greeted patrons he knew, just as he used to, before the pain and killing.

"Diega, darling." Ana Maria came running up to him, throwing her arms around him, and planting a big kiss on his lips. "Darling, I haven't seen you for a while. I was beginning to think something was seriously wrong."

"Something *is* seriously wrong," Diega replied, disentangling himself from her clutches.

Ana Maria Volstead was a woman who got what she wanted. And for the last year, she'd wanted him. For her next husband that is. She'd gone through five already. Old rich men, of course, leaving her with quite a fat bank account. But now it was Diega she had her sights set on.

With her money she'd done herself up. Liposuction, facelift, dermabrasion. Her blonde, wavy hair shone brilliantly, and she knew it turned a man's head. Her figure was to die for, and her clothes fitted snugly, revealing implanted breasts that burst out of everything she wore.

Ana Maria knew men wanted her and used her looks to lure them in. It usually worked, except for this time. When she'd set her sights on Diega, she knew he was the one. The sixth one anyway. And maybe, just maybe, the last one.

"Darling, where have you been? I've been looking everywhere, and no one wanted to tell me where you were. I haven't seen you for months."

"That's because I was dealing with something serious and didn't have time for you." Diega normally wasn't abrasive with people, but he couldn't stand Ana Maria. He knew she was only after him for his money, and he didn't like her, so what was the point. He continued walking through the casino.

She followed. "Diega, darling, there's no need to bite my head off, I was only asking. I've been so worried and looking at you now, you don't look so good."

"Go away, Ana Maria."

"I'm not going anywhere, darling. You're stuck with me. So, why don't I come up to your suite tonight, and we can have a little dinner, a little dancing, *a little romancing?*"

Diega stopped mid-stride and turned to her, his attitude boiling over. "You *are not* coming up to my suite, we're not dining, not dancing, and sure as hell *not* romancing. *I'm not interested in you.* You're only after me for my money, and once again, *I'm not interested in you.* I don't know how to say it any clearer. Go away and leave me alone, or I will have you banned from this hotel. Do you understand?" His eyes were snapping in anger as he turned and stalked toward the lifts.

Ana Maria ran after him. She didn't like his words and how dare he, but she wasn't about to let him get away. "Diega, darling, we're meant to be together, after all, I'm much more appropriate for you than that…that thing you were after a few months ago. What was her name, Tammy, Tamara—?"

"Tahlia," Diega stormed and faced her again. "Don't *you ever* speak her name. She was the love of my life, and now she's dead, so don't you *dare speak her name.* Tahlia was more of a woman than you'll ever hope to be. She was kind and caring and didn't have a selfish bone in her body, *unlike you.* A whore that goes after old rich men to marry so you can push them into their grave and take all their money—"

She slapped him. Hard. "How dare you speak to me that way. She was nothing. She was the dirt in the gutter that I step over, and I am much more of a woman than she was," she spat.

Diega's fury boiled over, and he waved over security guards as his rage came in torrents. "Get out of my hotel. Get out, and don't ever come back. *You* are no longer welcome here."

Four guards came running up, with two taking hold of her arms and pulling her away.

"You filthy animals, get your hands off me. Get your hands off me," she screeched as they led her toward the door and the crowd stared in amazement.

Sighing, Diega realised he'd had enough and decided to retire for the evening. Going upstairs and opening the door, he felt an overwhelming sadness as he stepped inside their suite. It seemed so empty without his Tahlia and the life force she possessed. Her zest for fun and laughter. He closed the door and slowly walked toward the bookcases he'd put in for her.

All of her books and collectables. They made her so happy, with her face always lighting up as she talked about them. Unlatching one of the doors, he picked up the Nancy Drew doll from the sixties he'd bought her. Her face had erupted into a huge smile when she'd opened her present, and she'd flung her arms around him. And the diaries, he'd managed to track down both versions for her. She was so happy, so grateful.

He put the doll back on the shelf and closed the door. Turning to her desk, he looked over it. Pen holder full of pens and pencils, a few snow globes and knick-knacks. He picked up the figurine of a mare and her foal that had been in the den at his retreat. After going horse riding, Tahlia had been so excited by it that she'd noticed the figurine and loved it. He'd given it to her there and then, and now, it sat in a prime position on her desk. To serve as a reminder of their time together.

Diega put it down and wandered to the bedroom and into the closet. He reached for one of her dresses. The blue one he'd bought her, such a beautiful array of shades, and he remembered how the colours lit up the hint of blue in her green eyes. They were sparkling so much they outshone the diamonds in her ears.

She looked so incredible that night. The night she kissed him back for the first time. The way she felt in his arms as he swept her around the dance floor. He buried his face in the dress and breathed in her scent.

"Oh, God, please, tell me if she's really gone. Because I don't know if I can go on living," he whispered, letting the dress slide through his fingers. He picked up a bottle of perfume from the dresser and sprayed some on himself. The fruity scent reminded him of her and helped bring her closer to him.

Walking back into the living room, he put a DVD in the player. Sitting on the sofa, he pressed play on the remote and up came one of Tahlia's performances. Every show had been recorded, and one by one, every night, he watched them. Reliving every song, every movement, every smile.

Tahlia.

His Tahlia.

My beautiful, lovely, amazing Tahlia.

I will never forget you.

Chapter 28

Christmas was a solemn affair. In fact, Diega didn't celebrate it at all, preferring to spend the day in Tahlia's suite, all alone, just himself and his memories of the only woman he ever truly loved. They would have been spending their first Christmas together, maybe as husband and wife. The wedding was planned, just a small ceremony with a tropical island honeymoon.

He opened the ring box. A huge ruby heart surrounded by diamonds. Inside, an engraving, *'I, a heart shape, U A D xx'*, I love you always, Diega, kiss kiss. He held the ring, remembering how he was going to propose. Dinner on the roof, fairy lights all around, their favourite song playing. He would get down on bended knee and bring out the ring. She would scream in delight and say yes as he slipped it on her finger. Then they would spend the night making love, totally wrapped in each other.

Plummeting back to earth and cold, harsh reality, he put the ring back in the box and closed it with a cold, sharp snap.

He would never propose.

She would never accept.

They would never be husband and wife or have children.

God, I hate Christmas!

He decided to visit his parents.

Diega placed a bouquet of roses in the vase attached to the grave. Touching the plaque, he said a small prayer. "Mom, Dad. How are you? Not too cold I hope. How's your Christmas been? Mine's been crappy. As you may know, I planned on proposing to Tahlia months ago, and we would be married now. Maybe with your first grandchild on the way. That would have been so great. To have my beautiful wife, my soul mate, my heart. She means everything to me." He choked. "*Meant,* everything to me. And I still don't know what to do. My men can't find Santiago. I can't find my life. I don't want to go on."

He sobbed, hot tears flowing down his cold cheeks. "I don't know what to do. I don't know what to do." He fell to his knees and broke down. For a few minutes, he let himself ease his pain, hoping his parents were watching over him from above.

"What do I do?" he gasped for breath, "what do I do? I'm lost, I'm lost, and I can't find my way back to the path I'm supposed to be on. I can't find my way." He got a hold of himself and wiped his face. "Mom, Dad, if you're up there, please help me. I need you to guide me back to the path I'm supposed to take. The path that will lead me to where I'm supposed to go, to where I need to be. Whatever my future may be, please, please, lead me there. Please, I'm asking for a Christmas miracle, as much as this Christmas and every Christmas since you both died has sucked badly, I'm asking, no begging, please, please, help me. Bring me a miracle. Please."

He wiped his tears away and took a few deep breaths. "I love you both and hope the rest of your Christmas is merry and bright. And have a drink for me while you're at it."

He stood slowly and walked away from the grave hoping his prayers would be answered.

*****

The woman in the bed lay motionless. She was propped up, with pillows behind her while the soft, warm breeze floated in through the French doors. Her husband was opening her presents since she couldn't.

It was Christmas. And she was pregnant.

In what was seemingly a permanent state of shock.

She didn't move, didn't talk, didn't want to be there. It was Christmas for God's sake, and she was stuck in bed, a madman opening her presents that he'd bought and wrapped himself.

"Oh, look, my dear, a beautiful emerald negligee. It will set your eyes off perfectly." He held it up for her to see. "Oh, there's a matching robe as well. Looks like Santa knew what to get you." He picked up a small brightly wrapped box. "Oooh, I wonder what this is," he said, shaking the box.

Removing the lid, he pulled out a square velvet box about palm size. Opening it, he gasped. "Oh, they're beautiful, look." He turned the box toward her. "Look, my dear, they match your engagement and wedding rings."

The earrings, large, white teardrop diamonds, dangling from large, white round diamond studs, sparkled brilliantly in the afternoon sun, bathing the room. They did match her rings, but she didn't care. He carefully put them in her ears then sat back to admire, and held up a mirror so she could see them.

"My, they are stunning. And so are you." He pulled down the covers and placed his left hand on her stomach. She was showing, and he wished he could feel the baby.

"Not to worry, little one. Santa didn't forget you. He brought you a whole roomful of presents. A beautiful crib and pram. Clothes and toys. You're going to love it. And Daddy loves you. Yes, that's right, I love you, little one, and your mommy. I love you both so much, and I can't wait for you to arrive. It will be wonderful."

He looked at his wife who was staring soullessly at the ceiling. "You know, my dear, we need to come up with a name. I bought a baby name book and have been going through it. I have quite a few picked out and can't decide. I want a strong manly name that will precede him wherever he goes. A name that enemies will fear and women will lust after."

He glanced at the plate of food on the bedside table. "You didn't eat anything. You really do need to keep up your strength for you and the baby. Now, Carol is going to come in and help you change into that lovely negligee Santa got you, and I'm going to freshen up. Try to eat something."

He walked out as his assistant walked in.

*****

Diega walked into the hospital room and saw that the nurses had put a small Christmas tree with little balls and strings of tinsel on the bedside cabinet. "Not much of a Christmas is it. Does this suck as much for you as it does for me?" he asked the man in a coma, knowing he'd get no reply. Sighing, he walked around the room.

It was one of the best rooms in the hospital, and he'd brought a few things in to make it nicer, more homely. Leaning against the windowsill, he watched the man.

"When are you coming out of your coma? You know," he laughed lightly, "I thought you would have come out of it sooner with *your* attitude and all. You're not one to lie around and do nothing. You go out and do what you want, take what you want, to hell with everyone else, and destroy a woman's life in the meantime. Not caring, not giving a crap. What sort of man are you? Oh, wait, you're *not* a man, you're *an animal.* A filthy vile animal who abuses women. You cheat on them, abuse them, and treat them like absolute crap. No, you're *not* a man. Because a *real* man wouldn't do what you did. *I* am a real man. *I* know how to treat a woman. To show respect and dignity. To make her feel like she's the only woman on the whole planet. The only one that's special, wanted, needed."

The man's heart monitor went off, and nurses came rushing in.

"What's happening?" Diega demanded, standing up

and looking at the monitor.

"His heart is racing. We don't know why."

"Is he coming out of his coma?"

"Maybe," the nurse replied. "What were you doing?"

"Talking to him, obviously making him angry."

"Well, it might be working," she said.

Diega walked around to the side of the bed opposite all the machines. Maybe there'd be a Christmas miracle after all. "Look at you, lying there all pathetic and useless. You can't even stand when ladies walk into the room. *You* are *no* man."

The man's heartbeat raced, and his eyes moved back and forth rapidly under their lids.

Diega put his left hand beside the man's head and leaned toward him. "*You're no* man, *you* are an animal. An animal Tahlia didn't even want anymore." Diega leaned back, removing his left hand as the heart monitor beeped like crazy.

The man in a coma was in a coma no more.

His eyelids flew open to reveal deep pools of blue, and his right hand snaked out and gripped Diega's left wrist.

Diega leaned toward him. "Welcome back," he said.

"Good to fine'ly be back," Vegas drawled.

*****

The woman in the bed was freaking out. Carol, her husband's assistant, had washed her and was dressing her in the emerald lace and silk negligee he'd bought her. *God, I hate him,* she thought viciously as the covers were pulled over her. *I really don't want him coming in here. God, make him go away.*

It was late afternoon, and the sun was heading for the horizon when her husband entered the room.

"You know, my dear, you've been sick for so long, and are still sick in some way, that I've refused to get into bed with you. I didn't want to hurt you or make you worse. You needed your rest, not me hounding you for lovemaking. But it's Christmas, so I'm allowing it just this once." He stepped over to the bed and pulled the covers back, his gaze roaming her silk and lace clad body. "You are so beautiful. That colour sets off your eyes perfectly."

He sat down beside her and ran his hand over her stomach. "God, I can't wait until you grow some more. I want to see your belly grow as the baby does. To feel him, or her, move and kick inside you. And the birth, I can't wait for the birth. I want to cut the umbilical cord and hold him in my arms. Give him a bath and dress him in a cute little outfit." He sighed happily, thinking about their future.

God, I hate you, she thought. *I hate you for taking me away from my life, my job, the man I love. I hate you, I hate you, I hate you! An' get your filthy paws off me.*

He pulled the covers down to the end of the bed and removed his robe. He was well built, muscular, and in good shape for his age, mid-sixties, though you wouldn't know it. His hair now with a hint of grey. His dark blue eyes sparkling with the anticipation of what was to come. His shorts clung to him and showed off a sizeable manhood which he was very proud of. And at his age, he could still get it up without the help of artificial substances.

He removed his shorts and sat back down beside her, reaching for the ribbon on her negligee that held it together just under her breasts. He slowly pulled on it, undoing the bow, sliding his hands over her breasts to push it aside.

"God, you're beautiful." His mouth reached for her left breast, gently sucking her nipple, arousing it until it was hard. "Before long our son will be doing this, suckling at your nipple." His mouth moved to her right breast then made its way down to her stomach.

His hands moved all over her. Her breasts, her stomach, into her panties. Pushing them down as his fingers slid through the tight curls into her womanhood. His mouth lazily kissed her belly then he moved his head down to her pelvis, ready to slide his tongue in.

Something snapped inside of her. *I hate you,* she screamed in her mind. *An' I will not take this anymore. I hate you, get your filthy paws off me.* Her left hand reached out and grabbed his penis, to his surprise, twisting it as hard as she could. When his head flew up in shock, she launched her right fist into his face and knocked him off the bed onto the floor. "You sick son of a bitch," Tahlia screamed, getting to her knees on the bed. "Don't you *ever touch me again.*" Ripping her rings off, she threw them at him as hard as she could.

She was back!

Chapter 29

Vegas stretched his lean body slowly as he languished in bed. This was something he was becoming used to and found very appealing. Gazing around the room, he wondered why he wasn't in the suite he'd shared with Tahlia. It was still one of the best in the hotel though, and Diega had told him he could live there as long as he wanted. He'd asked why. *"I have my reasons,"* Diega had said and left him to recuperate on his own.

It was four weeks since he'd woken from his coma, and the doctor had told him he could leave the day after waking. Diega insisted on him staying in a suite, and the hotel nurse saw him every day to make sure he was taking his medication. There was also a trained physiotherapist coming three times a week, as his arm was still shot from it wrenching when he'd landed on it after the bomb, not to mention Diega shooting him in the same shoulder.

"Damn that bastard, why the hell'd he shoot me?" Throwing the covers back, he stalked around the bedroom. "What the hell is goin' on? He shoots me, makes sure I got the best doctors, now puts me up in the hotel. What's he up to?" He wasn't sure but definitely wanted to find out.

With a knock at the door, breakfast arrived, and he dug in. Since being back at *The Montiamo*, he was once again eating the best food. *Would be even better if Tahlia was here. God, I need a smoke!*

He'd detoxed, after being in a coma for three months, but now the craving was back. "No! I will *not* get back into that habit, not to mention the drugs!" He'd been out of existence for so long, and so much seemed different.

Diega wasn't hateful towards him, and his coma had weaned him from his addictions. Unfortunately, his body was a bit the worse for wear, as three months in a bed sucked. He flexed his right arm. *Need to get in the gym, ugh. An' the one thing that sucks most, Tahlia isn' here.* Even having her with Diega was a lot better than her being dead.

Diega.

Vegas leaned back in his chair. *What's he up to? Mmm, I'll just have to go find out.*

*****

Diega was sitting in his office. He hated winter. Had always hated winter. Tahlia and I would be together now, relaxing on a tropical island somewhere warm. Her wearing that blue bikini I like so much, or maybe nothing at all. A smile crossed his lips as the image of Tahlia's curvaceous body came into his mind. He could smell her scent, soft, warm, fruity. Her body so pliant under his expert touch. God, he loved her.

For the past month, he'd been continually having this strange feeling, and it wasn't because Vegas was out of his coma, that would be another problem, but it was one he couldn't put his finger on. It gnawed at him deep inside in a place he'd only found with Tahlia.

He picked up the frame on his desk and gazed at the photo encased within it. Tahlia in one of her stage dresses, her dazzling smile lighting up her face, holding one of the huge bouquets he'd given her. He was standing proudly beside her, his right arm around her waist. God, he loved her.

"Tahlia, it's been four months. I still love you as much as I did the first time I saw you. Your smile, it lights up my life, and your vibrancy and zest for life brightens my world. You are my everything. I don't want to go on without you. I *can't* go on without you. If you are out there, please, *please*, let me know in some way. Please."

He put the frame back in its place and tried to concentrate on the papers in front of him. Tests from the bomb site showed there was a woman in the cave, but the DNA tests proved it wasn't Tahlia.

"What!" Picking up his phone, he dialled Mark. "Get in here, now." When he walked in, Diega pounced. "Why the hell didn't you tell me sooner. You should have told me Tahlia wasn't in the cave."

"Sir, the team only finished two weeks ago. It was a large area to go through, and it's taken time. Then there were the tests. I only got this file to your desk today."

"So, she wasn't in the cave. It wasn't her, so she

could still be alive. That means that bastard still has her." Diega was excited now and pacing around the room. "It wasn't her, it wasn't her."

"No, sir."

"That means she's still alive." He stopped and turned to Mark. "We need to find Santiago, and find him now. If Tahlia is still alive, then he has her. I want him found."

"Sir."

He turned to look out the window and excitedly contemplated the news. She wasn't in there, oh, God, she wasn't in there. *Hang on, Tahlia, I'm coming. I'm coming, baby.*

*****

Tahlia finished brushing her hair and angrily threw the brush across the room. It hit the door as Santiago opened it. "Is something wrong, my dear?"

"Of course there's something wrong, you bastard. You've got me locked up in this prison, an' I can't go anywhere or do anything, an' God knows where we are. I want to go home." She started throwing the things from the bedside table at him. "Let me go home," she screamed.

He ducked and weaved as they smashed around him. "You will *not* be going anywhere. This is your home, *our* home, *our family's* home. You will have the baby here, and we will *raise him* here. That is the end of the story, so get used to it."

"I will *never* get used to it," she growled and walked

up to him. "I will *never* love you, *never* want you, an' God help you if you ever touch me again. You're a rapist an' a kidnapper. I hate you, an' the first chance I get *I will kill you.*"

Santiago glared stonily at her while trying to keep his anger in check. "For the last time, Tahlia, this is where you'll stay—"

She slapped him, with every ounce of strength and power she had.

The blow sent him back two steps, and his right hand flew to his face.

She'd drawn blood.

His fingers touched his lips, and he glared darkly at her. "Well, my dear, you have one hell of a nasty temper. You split my lip. You're lucky you're pregnant because I refuse to hit a pregnant woman. But so help you, if you push me too far, I may be driven to break that rule." He walked out the door and locked it behind him.

"Arghhh," she screamed, "I have to get out of here, I have to get out of here now. Ahh." She gasped and clutched her stomach. Her belly was protruding as she was into her second trimester. Was that a pain or a kick?

Tahlia sat heavily on the bed and stroked her stomach, sliding her hands in circles to calm the tiny person inside of her. "I'm sorry, baby," she whispered, "I'm sorry. I'm trying not to get angry, I know it upsets you. It's okay, baby, it's okay." She slowly walked to the French doors, and flinging them wide, moved onto the balcony.

The view was glorious. A deep blue sea, yellow glowing beach, green palm trees gently swaying in the breeze. Her room was on the third floor, and looking over the balcony, she saw she wouldn't be able to climb over it. No stairs, no lattice, nothing she could use.

Hot stinging tears welled in her eyes and flowed down her cheeks. "Oh, God," she sobbed, "oh, God help me, please. I can't do this, I can't do this. The baby, he can't be born here. Not with that madman running this place like a dictator. I can't do this. Help me, please."

*****

Vegas strode into Diega's office and slammed his hands on the desk, glaring hard and leaning in to confront his enemy as Diega gazed at him warily. "Why?"

"What?"

"Why?"

"Why what?"

"Why are you bein' all nice to me when I know damn well you hate my guts? I had Tahlia first an' you didn' like it, so you had to steal her from me. Then you shoot me an' come to visit me in hospital everyday actin' like a freak. Now you give me a suite an' let me stay here as long as I wan'. Why? Why you bein' nice to me?"

Diega grew warier. "I have my reasons."

"So tell me."

Diega sighed and contemplated the news he needed to tell him. Then copped out. "Tahlia might be alive," was all he said.

Vegas leaned back in surprise. "What?"

"It wasn't her in the cave."

"What?" Vegas was confused by the change of subject and the amazing news. "What do ya mean, she might be alive?"

"It's taken four months to dig through all the wreckage of the cave, and after finding a few pieces of human flesh, they tested it doing DNA tests. A woman was in the cave, but it wasn't Tahlia. She might still be alive."

Diega's words sank slowly into his brain. *Might be alive,* he thought. *Not dead. Might be alive.* He staggered to the window and leaned against it for support. "She might be alive?" he asked, unbelieving.

"Yes," Diega said, standing beside him. "Santiago would still have her. We knew he wouldn't give her up easily, if at all. We were both suspicious about his actions and motives."

"So, what do we do?" Vegas asked, turning his head to look at Diega.

Diega grimaced and sighed again. "I recall another time you were here asking me that same question. It seems like an eon ago."

"So, what do we do?" Vegas asked again, standing up straight to face Diega who stared back.

"Exactly what we've been doing. Everything we can to find her."

*****

Tahlia stroked her bulging belly. She was now in her fifth month, and the baby kicked up a storm. Fortunately, he slept at night when she did, though her sleep was anything but peaceful. Santiago locked the door on her every night, leaving her alone. *Thank God, for small mercies,* she thought, still worried that he could come in the middle of the night and do something horrible. Terrible. Vile.

He walked through the doorway.

Speak of the devil.

"Hello, my dear, how are you today?" He walked over to her and reached out his hand to touch her stomach.

"Don't touch me," she snapped and slapped his hand away.

Santiago sighed and smoothed his suit. "Tahlia, your attitude has been annoying me since you came out of your self-induced coma. But now, it's just pissing me off. Either you play by my rules, or you stay in this room until the baby's born. It's your choice."

Choice, she thought angrily, *not much of one.* She stared him down. "I want to go outside. To sit on the beach or swim in the sea." She felt like a child asking Daddy for permission.

"Well, if that's what you want, then you need to do as I say."

Tahlia crossed her arms defiantly over her chest and took a step back.

"All right," Santiago said, sighing again, "seems like we'll need to take this slowly. You can go outside and sit on the beach, *but in return,*" he pointed his finger at her, "I will touch your stomach. I want to feel my son kick, to feel him grow inside of you. And I will do it when *I* want to do it, not when you *tell me* I can." He gazed at her uncertain look.

She desperately wanted to get out of that room, to see if she could escape in any way, and while the thought of his hands on her repulsed her, she needed to get out. "All right," she said crossly, pointing her finger at him, "but *only* my stomach."

"That's all I'm asking for," he said, reaching for his son. "For now."

*****

Vegas jumped onto his Harley and roared away from the hotel. It felt good to ride along the strip, wind whipping around him and through his hair. He hadn't been on his bike since before that night. The night Tahlia… *Stop it,* he snapped at himself. *She could be alive an' we have to find her. We will find her an' I will win her back. I may not be able to give her much, but she might come back to me.*

He gunned his bike and sped into the desert, his leather jacket keeping the cold away. Riding up to the campsite they'd shared that night, he found the rock he had her against. Vegas parked the bike and stood staring over the city, his hands shoved into his pockets.

Tahlia was so right for him, he'd known it from the moment he saw her at the gas station. But he had secrets, and she might not be able to understand why he kept them from her. It was to protect her and keep her safe. Safe from the man after her. The cops. He had lied to keep her safe, and he'd continue to do so if it meant the difference between her life and death.

Sitting down on the rock, his tears stung his eyes,

and for the first time since his mother's death, he allowed himself to cry.

✳✳✳✳✳

Diega was poring over maps in his office conferring with Mark. "So, where do you think they could be?"

"We've gone through the U.S. and raided South America. There is no sign in Canada. I say he's definitely out of the country, more than likely in a country that we can't drag him back from." Mark scratched his head.

"That's the best scenario?" Diega asked, feeling weary as he glanced at him then back at the maps spread before them.

Mark shrugged. "With his money, he's probably bought his own country."

"Or his own island." Diega looked up at Mark, the light dawning as he stood up. "Islands, why the hell didn't we think of that before?"

"It's very possible that he's on some small island somewhere," Mark said, picking up some maps.

"Start searching," Diega said. "Take boats, planes, whatever you can. Go from island to island in every ocean and sea. Find them."

"Sir." Mark left with an armload of maps, ready for their new plan.

Diega was feeling good about this. "Why didn't you think of this before," he berated himself. "And you call yourself a businessman, please, you should have thought of this months ago." He sat at his desk and busied himself with phone calls, making plans for finding

Tahlia. He was feeling even better than he was the other day when he'd found out she wasn't in the cave.

Kate knocked on the open door and walked in with some files. "You need to sign these, sir."

He beamed up at her. "Kate, how are you today? Are you happy? I am. Tahlia might be alive, and I am feeling good."

Kate smiled. She hadn't seen him this happy in months. "So, something good has happened then?" she asked, placing documents in front of him.

"Absolutely. We discovered it wasn't Tahlia in the cave, so that means she's still alive, and now we're going to raid every island on this planet. We will find her Kate, and when we do, I will bring her home, marry her, have a family, and live happily ever after." He whipped his signature across the papers.

"Santiago?" she asked, replacing signed files with new ones.

Diega stopped what he was doing and gazed up at her, suddenly deadly serious. "I'll kill him. Simple as that. I'll kill him, so he never bothers us again."

"And Vegas?" She wasn't sure that was a question she should have asked.

Diega sighed. Vegas was a subject he didn't want to discuss with other people. "Vegas," he started, "is Vegas. He'll stay in the hotel as long as he wants. Although I don't think he'll want to stay once Tahlia's home with me."

"Why did you go to the hospital every day?" she asked, sorting through more papers. "You never told me, and I never questioned. You hate the man with a passion, and yet you spent two hours every day with him—"

"Kate," Diega interrupted, "I'm not discussing Vegas with you. I had my reasons, end of discussion." He stood and handed the files back to her. "Anything else?"

"Tahlia's fill-in isn't working out. She's making ridiculous demands, and being a general pain in the ass. And Ana Maria keeps calling wanting to speak to you. I keep putting her off, but she's extremely persistent."

"God I can't stand that woman," he said, sighing. "Get a new act for the show, and tell Ana Maria where to go."

"Sir." She grinned and left to deal with things.

Diega had just sat down when there was another knock at the door.

*****

Tahlia ran the last ten feet to the beach and kept running until she was knee deep in the ocean. God, it felt so good to be out of that prison. Out in the warm fresh salty air with the sun shining down, warming her pale skin. She sank to her knees in the water to let it rush over her as it came in, wetting her summer dress, plastering it against her belly and the baby within.

"Well, little one," she said, "this is how you live, floating around in Mommy's ocean all safe and sound."

"He certainly is," Santiago said and stood behind her.

Tahlia's skin crawled at the sound of his voice, hating him for interrupting the moment with her baby. "Here's your hat my dear, you don't want sunstroke."

She snatched it from him and jammed it onto her head. "Go away," she grumbled, "I was having a moment with my baby."

"*Our* baby," Santiago corrected, rolling up the sleeves of the white summer shirt he wore open over his tight navy shorts. He wanted to tan his toned body. "And I have every right to be concerned. I need to keep you in maximum health, so the baby is healthy. Come sit on the blanket. It's in the shade, and you'll be out of the sun."

"I'll do what I damn well want, an' if I want to sit in the water or go for a swim, then I damn well will." Defiantly she got up and waded out into the water.

Santiago watched angrily, but knew she couldn't go anywhere, so he had no need to worry. *She might try to drown herself,* he thought. *No, she wouldn't…*

She might, to spite you for what you've done, his brain said.

No, she wouldn't kill herself and the baby, she loves our baby.

She loves her *baby, not you. You'd better hope you're right.*

He waved to one of his bodyguards who waded in to give her a blow-up ring that she put under her arms and floated around on.

Back and forth she kicked her legs to propel herself through the water. Luckily it was calm, and she made sure Santiago couldn't see her checking out the island. With every turn, her eyes bored into the distance, figuring out the island was large, long even.

The white mansion standing back from the beach

was three storeys high, expansive, and looked incredibly expensive. It stretched out over the island and took up a large portion of beachfront. The tiled roof shone like fire in the sunlight, and forest green palm trees swayed around it with the motion of the warm breeze. It looked like an oasis, a tropical island everyone would want to holiday on and never want to leave. Except she *did* want to leave. *Did* want to get the hell off the island that was now her prison.

After an enjoyable hour in the ocean, she walked up to sit on the blanket that was spread out under a huge sun shade. There were two beach chairs, and Santiago sat in one reading a book.

"Have fun, my dear?" he asked, glancing up.

"Yes, actually I did. The only fun I've had since Las Vegas when I was with Diega. Lying in his arms making mad passionate love." She said it to anger him and was surprised when he didn't blow.

"Well, that was a long time ago. As you know, things have changed. You're with me now, and we're having a baby." He continued reading his book.

Tahlia sat back in her seat and ran her hands over her stomach. The warm breeze was heavenly, and she hadn't felt it since Miami. God that was a long time ago. *Well, baby,* she thought, *we're going to get out of here an' off this island one way or another. Even if I have to kill the man sitting beside me. Oh, yes, I will kill you.*

*****

Diega looked up to see Vegas standing in the doorway.

"That's the first time you've knocked," he said as Vegas closed the door and locked it. Diega became wary. He hadn't done that before either.

Vegas slowly walked toward the desk and silently sat in the chair opposite Diega. Stretching out his legs in front of him, he crossed them and gazed at Diega who looked surprised by his action. For several moments they stared at each other in a showdown of macho testosterone until Diega broke the spell.

"So, what do you want?"

"The truth!" Vegas stared, unblinking.

"The truth?" Diega stared, defiantly.

"Yep."

"The truth about what?"

"The truth about why you came to the hospital. Why you would shave me, an' read the paper, an' why you'd touch me the way you did?" His lip turned into a sneer. "I hated that. I hated you touchin' me that way, an' it freaked me out. You hate me. I hate you. So you tell me why, after everythin' that happened between us an' Tahlia, you tell me *why* you did what you did. An' I'm not leavin' till I get an answer."

Diega sat back in his chair and clasped his hands together, his elbows resting on the chair arms. He contemplated what to say. *Do I tell him the whole truth or only some of it? And what if he does freak out, not believing what he reads, what he hears?* "You may not like what you hear."

"Won' know till ya tell me," Vegas replied.

"You might not like what you read. In fact, I know you won't believe it."

"Yeah, why's that?"

"Because I didn't believe it when I found out."

Vegas became aggravated. "Just tell me," he yelled, leaning forward in his seat.

Sighing, Diega now rested his arms on his desk. "When you were in the hospital you needed a blood transfusion."

Vegas gazed steadily at him. "Awright…so?"

"There was none of your blood type in the whole of Las Vegas, in the whole of Nevada. All the hospitals were out."

"Yeah…so?"

"You were given O negative blood, but supplies were low, and you needed more."

"Just tell me," Vegas demanded.

Diega's gaze met his. "The doctors went through the Nevada registry and found that I have the same blood type as you. They asked me to donate."

Vegas didn't like that one bit. "I have your blood racin' through my veins?" he spat, his eyes narrowing. "Why couldn' they find someone else with the same blood type. Why the hell did it hav'ta be you?"

Diega stared him down. "Because I not only have the same blood type as you, I have the same genetic quirk, and I'm the only other person in Nevada with it. *That's* why it had to be my blood."

Vegas sat back in his chair trying to comprehend the news. "No, no." He stalked over to the window and looked out. "Why you, why you?"

Diega watched him carefully. "I just told you. Besides which, you don't have parents."

Vegas spun around to face him. "What do ya mean, I don' have parents?"

Diega smirked. "Did you really think I wouldn't have you looked into?" He leaned back in his chair. "From the day Tahlia auditioned, and I saw her, choosing her for the job, I had you checked out. My private investigators dug up quite a bit on you. It wasn't hard since the foster care system was easily hacked into."

The look in Vegas' eyes changed from anger to curiosity back to anger. "You had *no* right to check on me." His voice low and threatening.

Diega waved a hand. "Oh, please. I only let you live here because Tahlia was going to leave if you didn't. So, of course, I had you investigated." He paused. "Want to hear more?"

Vegas kept his emotions in check and crossed his arms, now extremely curious. "Go on."

"You were sent to a foster care home when you were fourteen. Your father had beaten your mother to death and tried to do the same to you. He disappeared, and you were in the hospital for some time." Diega watched the wave of emotion wash over Vegas as he closed his eyes and lowered his head. "Did you know that you were adopted?"

Vegas shot his head up in shock. "What? No, I wasn'. What the hell are ya talkin' 'bout? I was *not* adopted." His anger was rising, and he wanted to thrash Diega senseless.

"The foster care system still has your records on file. They found out you were adopted when the doctors at the hospital told them you weren't a blood match to your mother." Diega pushed a piece of paper across his desk. "Your adoption papers."

Wrestling with his emotions, Vegas walked over and snatched it up, his eyes racing over the paper. There, in black and white, were his parents' names. Michelle and Martin Casnova. The adoption date, and the name they'd given him. Vegas. Naming him after the city in which he was adopted. They'd said it was after the city in which he was born. *Well, I guess that's true too.*

His bottom lip quivered and tears welled in his eyes. "No, no!" His head shook. "No, no, I don' believe it." He screwed the paper up and turned back to look out the window.

"It's true. When you were in the hospital and needed a transfusion, having the same genetic quirk as me, I began to wonder. But I had the paper and already knew. I found it strange that you and I had the same quirk. You were adopted, and you obviously didn't know," Diega rambled. "Did no one tell you? The foster system?"

"No, no, no one told me. Not my parents, not the foster system, no one." Vegas wiped his face with the back of his hand. "So, is this all you had to tell me?" he asked, waving the hand that still clutched the adoption paper.

"No."

"Well, then."

"I tracked down your biological parents."

Vegas looked at Diega, stunned. "You…tracked down my parents. Why?"

"I was curious."

Vegas slowly sat down in his chair again. "Who are

they?" he asked hesitantly.

Diega weighed the situation. "Do you really want to know?"

Vegas shook his head. "No. But I need to know why they gave me up. If you so easy give up a kid, you obviously don' love it."

"That's not true," Diega interjected quickly. "Sometimes, there are, extremely extenuating circumstances."

"Such as what? Oh, I got pregnant at seventeen an' can' keep you. Yeah, right." Vegas threw the paper onto the desk and crossed his arms defiantly before leaning back in his seat.

"No, no, that's not it. Sometimes your life is taken out of your hands because someone decides to screw with it," Diega went on almost desperately.

"Oh, please," Vegas cried, throwing his arms up, "why don' you just tell me who my parents are, an' tell me where they live in case I wanna go see 'em an' ask why they gave me up."

"You can't see them," Diega said quietly.

"Why not?"

"They passed away." Diega gazed at him, watching for his reaction.

Vegas' face fell, along with his whole world. "They're… dead?"

"Yes."

Vegas swallowed. "When?"

"Some time ago."

"How do you know?"

"Vegas," Diega said softly, "I have all the birth and death certificates."

Vegas gazed mournfully at Diega. "Just tell me," he almost whimpered.

Diega said nothing, just pushed another paper across his desk.

"What's that?" Vegas asked softly.

"The results of the DNA test that I had performed while you were in your coma. I wanted to make sure you are who I thought you were."

Vegas picked up the paper and read it, not quite understanding the technical terms, but getting enough of it to see his name and two other people's names. Reading them, he knew the surname.

A name he hated so much.

"No! No! This is… No!" He shook his head angrily and looked up. And for the first time, noticed Diega's eyes were the exact same colour as his own.

*****

Tahlia was back in the ocean when Santiago called for her.

"Time to get out, my dear, it's getting late, and after showering, we'll have a nice dinner."

"I don't wanna go in," she yelled back.

"I don't have time for your stubbornness, Tahlia, it's time for dinner."

Reluctantly, she walked out of the water and over to Santiago who placed a robe around her shoulders. "Did you enjoy yourself today?"

"I did. Would have enjoyed myself more if you weren't here," she said, tying her robe and putting her sandals on.

Santiago took her arm and led her back to the house where she was escorted upstairs so she could shower and change. Half an hour later they were having a richly prepared dinner in the second floor dining room. It was lavishly decorated with exquisite furnishings, but Tahlia didn't care, she was ravenous and dug in hungrily.

"You're certainly hungry. It's good to see you eating well. You and the baby obviously built up quite an appetite today."

"Yeah, I guess we did," she said, finishing her meal. Tahlia didn't care for conversations with Santiago, even if he was her husband. She didn't believe him on that part, knowing he could be lying, and she certainly didn't wear her rings or think of him as her husband. Or herself as his wife. "I'm done so I'm going to my room," she said and stood up. "Arghhh." Grabbing her stomach, she fell back into her chair and sat there gasping as Santiago raced around the table to help her.

"Tahlia, what's wrong? Is it the baby? Tell me what's wrong."

"It's okay…it's okay. I think the baby gave an almighty kick. Aaaahhh it really hurts." She was still catching her breath.

"All right, I'm getting you up to your room to rest, and I'll call the doctor in. I want you examined thoroughly."

Tahlia didn't reply, she just let Santiago and his bodyguard take her to her room and tuck her into bed. Her stomach hurt, and she was worried it was more than just the baby.

*****

"No. No," Vegas yelled. "There is no way in hell I'm related…no. No." He screwed up the paper and threw it onto Diega's desk.

"DNA tests don't lie," Diega said evenly.

"But *you* do," Vegas spat, furiously pointing at Diega. "Why should I? Why *would* I believe this, this crap?" he asked, pointing to the paper. "Why should I? *You* are a liar. You probly had this made up to piss me off. I hate you. You hate me. So why would you do it? Huh, why?" He stalked around the office angrily, wanting to belt the absolute crap out of Diega. There was no way in absolute hell that he was related to…no, no way.

"DNA tests don't lie," Diega repeated. "And why would *I*? What would *I* have to gain from lying? Why would *I* need to, what pleasure would *I* get out of lying about this?" Diega was on his feet and coming around his desk to stand in front of Vegas. "Why would *I* need to lie about this?"

"I don' know, I don' know," Vegas yelled, desperately trying to sort his thoughts out.

"I wouldn't lie about this. Does it matter if you believe me…it's up to you if you do or you don't. But I have absolutely no need or reason to lie about this." Diega turned to pick up the file, and stuffing the papers inside, handed it to Vegas. "Take these. Look over them. There's more to the story than you know. And you need to know the truth. You have a *right* to know the truth." He knew he was desperate, and looking at Vegas he saw he was too.

438

Vegas snatched the file angrily and stalked out the door without a backward glance.

*****

The next day, Tahlia was being examined by the doctor Santiago had flown in. He'd taken her temperature and blood pressure, even done an ultrasound with the machine Santiago had bought. Turning the machine off, the doctor stood as he wiped his hands.

"Well, how is she?" Santiago asked.

"Just fine. Her temp is fine, blood pressure a little high, the baby's healthy. No problems whatsoever."

"Oh, thank God," Santiago said, saying a small prayer.

"You need to rest young lady and eat lots of fruits and vegetables. You need to keep your strength up for the baby. A little exercise wouldn't hurt, maybe a walk along the beach twice a day. Fresh air will do you good, but you need your rest. Don't overdo it." He packed up his bag and turned to Santiago.

"Thank you, doctor, thank you so much for coming. My pilot will fly you back. We'll see you next month."

"Of course," the doctor said and was escorted out.

Santiago sat on the bed next to Tahlia. "Oh, my dear, I was so worried. You're five months now, and we need to keep you healthy. So that means three square meals and two snacks a day, and we'll start with one walk a day, building up to two." He touched her stomach and felt the baby move. "He kicked," he whispered, totally elated. "He kicked."

He leaned in to kiss her, but Tahlia turned her head,

and he caught the soft skin behind her ear instead. He gently kissed her as his hand slid from her stomach to her breast.

"Don't," Tahlia commanded. "You touch my stomach *only, nothing* else." She pushed his hand away. "Get out," she spat, pulling the covers over herself.

Santiago let out a long angry sigh as he stood and buttoned his suit jacket. Then, without a backward glance, he walked out of the room and locked the door behind him.

*****

A baby? What do you mean, a baby? He couldn't believe what he'd heard. Oh, God, how long have I been out of circulation? A baby? Can she be pregnant? The doctor said she was, and her stomach is rounded. But here? Now, I haven't seen her in so long, is it possible, or is it a lie? I've only just found her, and now I find out she's pregnant.

He paced the room, thoughts menacing his mind.
My baby?

Could it be mine? Could the baby be mine and not his? What the hell am I going to do with a baby? A living breathing human being.

He glanced at the woman in the bed and remembered their times together. A depraved hotbed of sexual heat and lust. It had been so heavenly being inside of her. Coming inside of her, thrusting and grinding away on top of her as she screamed in orgasm, begging him to do it again and again. To not stop, just keep going and going and going.

What are we going to do with a baby, my darling? he wondered, trying to think of something useful for him to do. He stopped in front of the window and gazed outside. That filthy whore is pregnant?

There's only one thing I need to do, he thought, only one thing I can do.

Make sure that the baby IS mine!

Chapter 30

Vegas had been avoiding Diega since finding out what happened those months he'd been in a coma. He still hated him! Hated him for showing him the papers. "Oh, God…this can' be for real," he said, sitting down on the rock at his and Tahlia's campsite.

He went there often, making it his quiet place to think and be alone. *How can this be happenin'? How? Why?* He looked up into the cold winter sky. It was almost spring, but it didn't matter, the cold had leaked into his heart anyway.

He was lonely. Alone. A desolate feeling inside. "What do I do?" he asked again, anguish washing over him. *What do I do?* His cell rang. "What?"

"You need to come back to the hotel, there's something you need to see," Diega said.

"I wan' nothin' from you, an' you have nothin' to show me."

"It's Tahlia."

Her name hit Vegas hard. "I'm on my way."

Twenty minutes later he ran into Diega's office and saw the monitor was on. "What's goin' on?"

"We received this today," Diega said, holding a DVD in his hand. "I've already seen it." He slid it into the player.

An image of Tahlia lying in a bed wearing a white wedding dress flashed up, Santiago was beside her in a tuxedo. A person off camera spoke. "I now pronounce you…husband and wife."

Santiago kissed Tahlia's cheek then picked up her left hand, flashing the huge rocks on her finger for the camera. "We are finally married. I'm so happy, my dear, aren't you?"

The image changed to Tahlia and Santiago being intimate, naked in each other's arms. "Oh, Tahlia, I knew our wedding night would be amazing," he said.

It changed again to Tahlia sitting in a chair reading a book, then her eating a sumptuous meal at the dining table.

Finally, Tahlia swimming in the ocean, walking up to the beach, her summer dress surrounding her bulging belly. The footage cut to Santiago rubbing his hand over her stomach as she sat in the chair beside him on the beach. "Oh, my dear, our son grows inside of you, getting bigger and stronger every day. How far are you now, over five months. I can't wait to hold him in my arms and bathe him. Hand down my name. I'm so proud."

The image faded to black then Santiago himself came on. "Hello, Diega, Vegas. Yes, Vegas I know you're there, because I know you're out of your coma and getting stronger all the time. And Diega, how lonely and sad you've been without Tahlia." He smirked. "Now, onto more important things. As you can see, yes, Tahlia is alive, so no, that wasn't her in the cave. And yes, we did marry just as I said we would, after all, we did conceive our son. I couldn't let Tahlia be an unwed mother. She's healthy now, having pneumonia after I took her away, but she and the baby are doing fine. We're *all* doing fine. And *I* am going to be a Daddy. So, I'll let you go, and maybe, I'll send you a DVD when our son is born."

The image faded to black, and the DVD stopped. Diega and Vegas stood there in silence staring at the screen, both lost in their thoughts until Vegas smashed his fist through the monitor. Diega wasn't surprised, he'd wanted to do that himself.

"Where are they?" Vegas demanded, turning to Diega. *"Where, are, they?"*

"I don't know," Diega stormed back. "But my men are raiding every island they come across, even ones that aren't on maps, so they *will* find her."

"We *need* to find her," Vegas said vehemently.

"I know." Diega's voice was harsh. He didn't need Vegas telling him something he already knew.

"How long has she been gone now?" Vegas asked, his tone softer.

"Five months, one week," Diega answered, standing at the window.

"So," Vegas said, walking over to stand beside him. "He got her pregnant after all." His eyes stared stonily at the view.

Diega bowed his head in anger and disgust at his Tahlia being pregnant to a man he hated with every fibre of his being. *Oh, my God, she's pregnant. He got her pregnant. Damn that bastard for raping her. I will kill him! Just over five months, she looks a little bigger, but that could just be weight gain. But what if she is bigger? That means she's more pregnant and that could mean…* "I'll kill him for that," he said softly.

"Get in line," Vegas replied.

*****

He stared at the image on the screen. It repulsed him, seeing that vile animal with his Tahlia. But then she is a filthy vile whore, and the two of them deserve each other.

No, he thought viciously, *I can't let her go yet. I won't let her go, not when she could be carrying* MY *baby. I know it's my baby, and no other man will have her or raise my son.* MY SON. *He is my son, and I will teach her to never screw around on me again.* NEVER AGAIN! *After all, look at the position she's in now.*

He glanced at himself in the mirror hanging on the wall. A fine, masculine man stared back, controlling him with his gaze.

"You did this," the man in the mirror hissed. "You did this and now look, he has her somewhere, and you don't. You don't even know what he's planning, don't even know what he's up to. He has her. And he won't let her go."

"That's all right," he said, straightening his tie. "I know where she is and what she's been up to. I'll take care of him so he will not be a problem."

With one last glance at Tahlia, he walked out the door.

*****

For the next two months, Diega and Vegas did one of two things. Argue over their mutual problem, which Vegas hated and defiantly disagreed with, or try to track down Tahlia. They would have explosive arguments over Diega finding out about his past, and Vegas would throw every ounce of anger at him. Telling him how much he hated him, how much he wished Diega was dead, and how dare he take his Tahlia away from him.

They were in the middle of a knock down drag out fight when Mark Dalton came running into Diega's office. "We've found them!"

Diega and Vegas stopped fighting, both of them still holding each other by the collar and panting for breath. "What!" they said in unison as they both looked at him, not believing what they'd heard.

"We've found them," Mark repeated, rolling out a map on Diega's desk. "Here," he said, pointing to nothing on the map. Diega and Vegas crowded around the desk.

"There's nothin' there, where you pointin' to?" Vegas gasped.

"The island's not on the map, but the yacht has scoured the ocean, and we've used the latest technology to scan each island. Many small islands aren't on the map because they're so small or uninhabitable. But we've found one that is. The yacht stopped out of range and used the satellite to scan and photograph. There's a huge mansion and a runway for a small plane. We've also got photos of people on the beach. It can only be

Santiago and Miss Tahlia."

"How long will it take for us to get there?" Diega asked.

"It's the Indian ocean, the other side of the world. We could take the plane to the west coast of Australia, then either fly straight to the island or take the yacht."

Diega thought for a few moments as he paced his office.

"Well?" Vegas demanded his hands on his hips.

"We'll take the plane to Australia, so make sure the fleet is in position to attack. Then we'll fly in and land. It has to be a precise attack, he can't know we're coming until we're on land. We'll raid the island, find Tahlia, and bring her home," Diega said.

"I'll call the fleet to prepare. It will take a day or so for them to converge in formation," Mark said, rolling up the map.

"Are the boats armed?" Diega asked.

"Yes, sir."

"The crew armed and ready?"

"Sir. Fifty men on each ship, four ships in total."

"Good. Get ready as quickly as you can. Vegas and I will leave in," he looked at his watch, "two hours. We'll land in Australia and wait for the fleet."

"Sir." Mark ran out the door.

"I can' believe we found her," Vegas said, looking around in amazement. "I can' believe we found her."

"Halfway around the world," Diega said distractedly, "he took her halfway around the world just to get her away from me."

Vegas moved uneasily at the comment. "Do we have a plan?" he asked.

"Besides going in with an army of men and guns?" Diega asked, glancing at Vegas. "Have you ever flown?"

Vegas shook his head. "Besides your chopper, nope, never."

"Not nervous are you?"

"Won' know till I get on the plane now, will I."

"All right, go pack a bag, we'll head for the airport soon."

Vegas walked out, leaving Diega to stand at the window, lost in his own thoughts. He was packing his bag when the realisation truly sunk in. His Tahlia was pregnant to Santiago. *That bastard! I will kill him for touchin' her.* He remembered the photos and the DVD of Santiago naked on top of Tahlia. *God that was so long ago,* he thought. *So much has happened since the bomb, her death, my coma.*

Tahlia was alive, and all he had to think about was rescuing her and getting her to love him again. And he would do it. *I will go down there with Diega an' fly to her rescue, bringin' her home to Las Vegas. Or maybe we'll go somewhere else. But the baby? Could I be a father to another man's baby?* He loved his Tahlia greatly, but the question disturbed him because he just didn't know the answer.

*****

Meeting downstairs, Vegas settled into Diega's BMW. He didn't want to spend time with him, but had to if he was going to get Tahlia back. As Diega sped away from the hotel toward the private airport he owned, neither of them spoke.

"Did you consider my proposition?" Diega asked finally.

"I wan' nothin' from you," Vegas said, staring stonily out the passenger window with his arms crossed.

"Vegas."

"Nothin'!"

Within minutes they arrived at the airport and drove to the hangar where Diega's plane was located. They alighted and grabbed their bags. "Michael, take my car back to the hotel," Diega said to one of his bodyguards.

Ascending the stairs, Diega and Vegas entered the plane. While Diega spoke to the pilots, Vegas moved to the back. He picked a seat, sat down, and buckled himself in, wanting to be as far away from Diega as possible.

"We'll be leaving in a few minutes," Diega told him, settling into his own seat at the front of the plane and clicking his belt.

Thank God, he ain' near me, Vegas thought with a sigh.

Ten minutes later they were winging their way to Perth, Western Australia.

Vegas threw off his belt, leaned back in his seat, and put the footrest up. "Nice," he drawled, a big grin on his face. "We gettin' any food an' drink on this flight?" he demanded.

Diega motioned to someone, and a stewardess appeared at Vegas' side.

"We have chicken, steak, or fish, all with vegetables. Which one would you like?"

"The chicken, an' bring me a beer."

Diega busied himself with some papers, which he

spread over the small table set out in front of him.

Vegas watched, wondering about his parents. *They're dead, nuff said,* he thought. *I guess I should be thankful to him. He saved my life, givin' me a transfusion an' all.*

He'd never been in a coma before and didn't want to be in one again. It was hell, a prison that he didn't want to be trapped in, paralysed, unable to move. Only feeling pain in his shoulder and his head. He rubbed his shoulder.

It was a few months now, but it still ached, and he couldn't lift his arm too high above his head. *Damn Diega for shootin' me in the same shoulder. It could have healed quicker.* He glanced at Diega then turned to watch the sunset through the window as night-time fell.

The stewardess pulled the curtains over the windows, and brought Diega and Vegas their meals, and afterwards, their blankets. Vegas settled in, putting the seat full out to form a bed. Wrapping the blanket around himself, he lay back waiting for sleep to come. *God this is great,* he thought. *Hot stewardess, comfy bed, good food. There's nothin' else I need. Nothin' else I wan'. Nothin' 'cept Tahlia.*

Diega glanced at his watch. 1:00 a.m. *Is that U.S. time...? I don't know, who cares.* He sighed and leaned back in his seat. Deciding to call it a night, he put his papers away and glanced over at Vegas. *Vegas,* he thought. *What do I do with you?*

He rested his hand on his chin and gazed at the man asleep at the other end of the plane. *He has his mother's eyes and his father's brow. God, his parents,* Diega thought. I knew them so well. *And Vegas never had. Never would.*

He stood and walked over to his travel companion, looking down at him. *What do we do?* he asked himself, watching Vegas sleep peacefully. *What do we do?*

Hours later, they landed in Perth, Western Australia, in the early evening, and drove to their hotel which was close by. The security team was already there. "What do we have?" Diega asked as they walked in.

"There's been no movement to or from the island. So, we take that to mean he has no idea that we know. The fleet is in place, and we can make our attack in the next day or two," Mark replied.

"How far is the island?" Diega asked.

"One thousand miles from the coast. It will take a while to get there."

"Have we planned it, so the fleet arrives when we do?"

"Yes, sir."

"Good. We should leave tonight, so we can raid at dawn, maybe even during the night. Can we do that?"

"If you don't mind flying at night, but you won't be able to see the runway. We should go in at dawn?"

"Right, you're right." Diega ran his hand through his hair. "Were you able to get any images from inside the house? Find where Tahlia is?"

"No, sir. The place is well secured, can't get any images at all."

"All right." Diega sighed and paced the room, thinking things through.

Vegas was sitting in a chair and had so far watched

silently. "Well?" he asked.

After a few moments, Diega finally turned to Vegas and his chief. "We go in tonight and raid at dawn. Make sure the doctors are ready to tend to Tahlia. I want her out of there the minute she's found. Get her on the plane and wait for us. Have another doctor on standby in case we need one. How big is Santiago's place?"

"Three storeys high, expansive. There would be a lot of rooms, many underground tunnels and bunkers possibly leading to the other side of the island, even to the runway that's set back from the house."

"All right. I want a team on floors one, two, and three, and another team will search for any underground escape routes. Have four more teams come at the island from each direction and move in. One guards the runway, one guards the house, the rest take down his men because Santiago is mine."

"Sir. I'll go ready the plans."

"This is gonna be big," Vegas said, watching Diega. "I wan' my turn with Santiago."

"Why?" Diega asked, and sat down opposite Vegas at the table.

"I have my reasons," was all he said.

The time came for them to go and they drove back to the airport. Boarding the plane, Diega sat beside his pilot in the cockpit, Vegas sat behind him.

"This is going to take a while," Diega said to him, "get comfortable."

It was very late, maybe even morning, and Vegas couldn't, wouldn't sleep. Thoughts tormented his mind. His past, his parents, real and adopted, Diega, Tahlia,

Santiago. *Oh, God, what am I gonna do when I come face to face with Santiago? An' Tahlia? Will she wanna see me?* He didn't know, so he shut down his mind as the plane took off.

*****

Tahlia was tossing and turning in her bed having bizarre dreams. She was in her third trimester, and her stomach protruded as she rolled onto her side. Waking with a jolt, she sat bolt upright.

Something was wrong.

Something was happening.

Something was outside.

Rushing to the French doors, she flung them open and stepped out onto the balcony. In the distance, she could just make out the faint sound of a plane. And it was getting closer. The sky was becoming light, and she could just make out a dark shape on the water.

She was scared. Something serious was going down, and she didn't know what to do. "Okay, get a grip. You need to…need to…get dressed an' prepare yourself." Running inside, she quickly washed and dressed, winding clothes around her body hoping it would protect the baby, strapping them with the masking tape that she'd stolen and hidden in her closet. Pulling on her boots and a sweater, she pulled her hair into a ponytail and sat on the end of the bed. Waiting.

*****

Diega and his pilot flew toward the island. They could see it on the horizon and were getting closer by the second. It was still dark out, but the sky was losing the darkness quickly, and Diega could see his fleet on all four sides of the island. He knew they were prepared, and his men would already be on the island waiting for his arrival.

"That the island?" Vegas asked, grabbing Diega's seat and leaning forward.

"That's the island," Diega answered. "We'll be landing shortly, buckle up."

Vegas strapped himself in, ready. Ready for raiding the island. Ready for killing Santiago. Ready for seeing his Tahlia again. *The first thin' I'll say is sorry,* he thought. *Sorry for hurtin' her an' tryin' to rape her. Sorry for cheatin' on her an' bein' a bastard.* He wanted her back, and he couldn't wait.

Diega had his own thoughts. *We're almost there sweetheart, hang on just a little bit longer. We're almost there. I'll rescue you and bring you home where you belong. And I promise I will love the baby just as much as I love you. The baby's a part of you and so it is a part of me.*

*****

He's coming, he's coming. Oh, my God, he can't be coming. How dare he come here and try to take her away from me. How dare he, he can't do that. I won't let him.

He dressed quickly and strapped a gun to his waist.

Looking out over the water, he saw a dark shape. Damn, a boat. And is that plane I hear. Well, it looks like Diega has come prepared for an unfortunate event that will ultimately end in defeat. His defeat.

"There's only one thing you need to know, gentlemen. I will kill you. I will kill all of you."

*****

Santiago was being shaken awake.

"Sir, sir, wake up, we're being raided," one of his henchmen yelled.

"What do you mean, we're being raided?" he demanded groggily, getting out of bed and throwing his robe on.

"There's a plane coming and ships out at sea all around us, we're being raided."

Santiago ran for his balcony and saw the dark shape in the water. "Are you sure they're boats?" He heard the plane. "Get the men ready, secure the house, get someone to Tahlia's room. Now!"

He dressed quickly and loaded two guns, putting them into their holsters and strapping them to his ankle and waist. Running next door to Tahlia's room, he saw she was already dressed. "You've prepared yourself I see. Come with me." He grabbed her arm and led her out of her room.

"Where are we going?" she demanded, trying to pull her arm away. "What's going on? Tell me."

"We're being attacked. I need to get you to safety," Santiago said, tightening his grip.

"What do you mean, we're being attacked," she cried. "Oh, my God, are they going to kill us, what's happening?"

Santiago stopped at a painting on the wall and pulled a light sconce down. The wall moved, and a panel slid up to reveal a lift, making Tahlia gasp in surprise. They went down four levels, and when the doors opened, she saw tunnels in three different directions. Santiago moved her down the one on the right, turning corner after corner.

"Where are we going?" she asked again. She tripped over some loose rock, and his fingers dug into her arm to pulled her along.

"Right here, my dear," he said.

They stopped in front of a metal door bolted into the hard rock of the tunnel. He opened the door, clicked a switch, and escorted her into a brightened room. There was a bed against the wall in front of her with blankets and pillows. But that was it. No windows, no chair, no nothing. Just the bed and the overhead light bulb.

"You'll be safe here. Don't worry, I'll be back for you." He shut and locked the door, leaving her alone.

"Diega, God I hope it's you," she whispered.

*****

Diega landed the plane expertly, and saw his teams had subdued Santiago's men as they attempted to fight back, so they had no interference as they taxied to a stop. Leaving the plane, Diega and Vegas met up with the leader of team five.

"We've secured and scanned the area, the house is

this way," he said, leading them toward the house.

A huge explosion rocked through the island, and diving for cover, they hit the ground as it shook. After getting clearance, they ran for the house with guns drawn.

Four teams merged on the house.

Team one went to floor one, team two went to floor two, team three went to floor three, and team four went to check for any basements and underground areas. Diega and Vegas waited for word, hearing shouting and gunfire on the other floors.

Then silence…

Three teams came running.

"Floors are empty, sir, except for a few of his henchmen who we killed."

"So, where are they?" Diega murmured, gazing around at the luxurious surroundings.

The leader of team four found them. "Sir, we found a hidden lift that goes down into a mass of underground tunnels."

"All right, let's go," Diega said, and they made their way to the lift. "Teams one and two go out and help the other teams, team three, ten of you stay here, the rest, come down as fast as you can." They rode down to meet up with team four. "What have you done?" Diega asked when they emerged into the rocky underground cavern.

"We've sent ten men left, ten ahead, and ten to the right, they're reporting back. The place is a maze. Multiple tunnels leading from the main ones, some dead ends, some merging with others. It's going to take a while to search the whole area."

The rest of team three arrived, and Diega gave orders. "All right, fifteen more men down the left, fifteen ahead, and fifteen right. Ten of you stay here. Be ready. And shoot to kill." He turned to Vegas. "Which way will you go?" he asked, handing him a gun.

"I'll go straight," Vegas said, checking the cartridge.

"I'll go right. Everyone, go."

They spread out with each team moving quickly down their tunnel. Diega had his own gun drawn, ready to shoot Santiago. Coming to a cross section, he debated which way to go. "Teams of five, go." He stood a moment and closed his eyes, willing Tahlia to lead him. He sensed it. Straight.

He moved on swiftly until he and the team arrived at more tunnels. This time they forked out in three prongs. "Oh, my God, which way now?" The other teams joined them.

"Nothing, sir."

"All right, go." He closed his eyes again. "God, Tahlia, where are you, please tell me, where you are." He waited a moment. "Where, are, you?" he breathed. "Tell me where you are."

"Diega."

His eyes flew open. "Tahlia," he shouted, "Tahlia."

"Diega." It sounded as if it was coming from the left tunnel.

He ran.

*****

Where are they? Where is Tahlia? Damn him for hiding her from me so I can't find her. He pulled his gun, prepared for shooting if he had to. Damn those bastards. Damn all three of them. How dare they come here and take her from me, especially being so big now, she must be due soon. With MY SON. That's right, MY SON. Not his. Not theirs. MINE.

He ran down a tunnel trying to keep out of their way. Not that it mattered, he knew the tunnels like the back of his hand. He knew where he was going.

What's that? He quickly pulled back into a crevice so he wouldn't be seen. A group of men in uniforms ran past him, holding rifles close to their chests. Ah, Diega. He saw him run past, shouting Tahlia's name. The sound of the men faded, and he stepped back into the tunnel undetected.

So, I wonder where the others are? I must be careful. I don't want to be caught, I don't want them to know I'm here. They can't know I've been here until I get Tahlia out.

And I will get her out.

*****

Vegas was having a similar problem. Tunnels shooting in different directions making him unsure of which way to go. The teams were far ahead of him, and he was on his own. Hearing a sound behind him, he turned, but not quickly enough, being struck over the back of the head with a sickly thud.

After a few moments of blackness and dizziness, he

became vaguely aware that he was being dragged along a tunnel and into a room. He was thrown into a chair as the door slammed shut and was bolted behind him. Shaking his head to clear the fog, he strained his eyes in the darkness.

A bright white light flashed on overhead.

"Hello, Vegas."

Vegas shot out of his chair and blinked rapidly.

Four henchmen stepped forward, hands on guns ready to shoot.

"It seems we have a little unfinished business."

"I have no business with you," Vegas said, swaying on his feet and reaching for his gun.

"Looking for this?" Santiago asked, holding the gun in his line of vision. "You won't need it."

He walked toward Vegas making him back up against the wall. "We *do* have unfinished business. Business concerning a person you were supposed to kill."

"Doesn' matter anymore, does it?" Vegas spat.

"No, actually, it doesn't. It's funny," Santiago said, walking around, "how the things *you* fail at improves the lives of others. Maybe I should thank you for not going through with it. I mean…had you have done it, we wouldn't be here now. Thank you, Vegas."

Vegas eyed him suspiciously. "What are you up to?"

"Why would I be up to anything. I'm just thanking you for not doing your job."

"What do you want?"

"I want Tahlia to know the truth," Santiago said, his eyes glistening with absolute evil.

*****

Diega was running, running, running, zigzagging along tunnel after tunnel. He didn't know how long he'd been going, or where his security teams were, and yes he was lost. He stopped and bent over, gasping for breath. As he straightened, his eyes widened in surprise. Right there in front of him was a door in the wall.

"Tahlia, can you hear me?" He pounded on the door and tried to open it, but was unable to as a padlock was attached to the bolt. He shot it off, slid the bolt back, and pushed the door open. There in front of him…

"Diega?"

"Tahlia."

They ran for each other.

Tahlia collapsed against Diega and he caged her in his arms, both of them sobbing uncontrollably

"Oh, my Tahlia, my sweet, sweet Tahlia." He kissed her deeply, tasting her like he hadn't in so long. "I've missed you so much." He planted kisses over her face.

"I've missed you so much too," she mumbled, kissing him back hungrily.

"Oh, how touching."

They broke apart and Diega spun around, aiming his gun straight at the person who'd spoken.

"Santiago," he spat, readying himself to shoot as Tahlia clung to his shirt, his arm protectively out in front of her and the baby within.

"You don't want to shoot me, Diega," Santiago said smugly as he walked into the room.

"Why not?" He was so ready to shoot.

"Because there's something you need to know. Especially Tahlia." He stood to face them.

"And what would that be?" Diega asked.

Tahlia was crying, desperately clinging to Diega as she stood behind him.

"The truth about the death of Wayne Brady," Santiago said, spreading his hands.

That caught both Diega and Tahlia's attention.

"What about Wayne?" she demanded through her tears. "I didn't kill him."

"I know you didn't, my dear. But don't you want to know who did?"

"You know who killed Wayne Brady?" Diega asked. "How?"

"Well, you know how you had your PIs look into Wayne's past? How he worked for a guy, who worked for a mobster." He laughed.

"I know you're the mobster the guy was working for," Diega said, "so essentially, Wayne worked for you."

"That's true," Santiago replied, "but did you find out who my right-hand man was? The man Wayne answered to?"

"No, I didn't," Diega replied slowly.

Tahlia was definitely intrigued by the conversation going on. She would finally learn who had tried to kill her.

"Pity," Santiago said. "It would have saved you all the trouble you've gone to. Would you like to meet him? Tahlia, do you want to meet the man who killed your boyfriend, the man who tried to kill you?"

"Yes," she whispered, more scared now that she was

going to meet her would be killer. The man that had stalked her. The man that had chased her. The man that had tried to kill her.

Santiago turned slightly to his left. "You can come in now."

The man stumbled into the room with his hands tied in front of him, and one of Santiago's henchmen holding a gun to his back.

Diega and Tahlia were both stunned to the core. As she gazed into the man's eyes, her whole world crumbled as deep pools of blue stared back.

"No. No. No, no, no, no, no," she screamed.

Even Diega wavered, his arm dropping slightly as the air rushed out of him.

Tahlia was clinging to him, sobbing. "No, no, how could you?" She shook her head, totally unbelieving.

*****

He heard her scream. Oh, my God, Tahlia, what are they doing to you? He ran in the direction the scream had come from, trying to be quiet. He didn't want them to know he was there, but he had to get Tahlia out somehow. He saw a faint light that became brighter and brighter as he ran toward it, finally coming to a door in the wall. He stopped a few feet from the door, and slowly stepped up to peer inside of the room. He almost gasped.

There was HIS Tahlia with the men he hated so much. The men that had ruined her. The men that had taken her from him and violated her against her will.

Taking and tasting her, every inch of her sweet suckable flesh. The men that had come inside of her over and over again as she screamed in pain at the torture. The torture he too had inflicted upon her as she lay under his muscular, manly body as HE came inside of her and kept on coming. He remembered the taste of her. The feel of her. Her body imprinted in his memory as it was on his body.

They were the men he hated with a passion.

They were the men he would kill with a vengeance.

*****

Santiago was watching the scene in amusement, relishing the pain in their eyes. He looked at the man who was staring at Tahlia.

"How could you?" she whispered. "How could you?" She broke down, holding onto Diega tightly and barely able to stand.

"I'm sorry, baby," he whispered back. "I'm so sorry."

"Sorry," she screamed. "*You're sorry?* You were gonna kill me, you killed Wayne. Then you were gonna kill me…how could you?" she ended in a whisper.

"Baby." Vegas took a step toward her, reaching out his bound hands as best he could. "Once I met you I didn' wanna kill you."

"Oh, well, that's just perfect isn't it," she spat. "I slept with you. I slept with you that first night, an' so many nights after, an' you had been, *was,* my boyfriend's killer."

"Baby, listen, please," Vegas was begging now.

"Yeah, I worked for Santiago, an' yeah he told me to kill Wayne 'cause he was rippin' us off. Wayne invited me there that night to pay me, he said he had a gift for me. But when I got there, he didn' have my money, an' he lied to me an'—"

"So you killed him?" Tahlia screamed.

Vegas looked at her. "That was my job, baby."

"Your job. Oh, my God." The revelation hit her. "He was going to give me to you. He said I was your gift… but you tried to kill me instead."

"I…I…" He shrugged and shook his head sadly. "I'm sorry."

"Were you the one following me?" she asked.

His eyes were mournful. "Yeah, baby. When I didn' kill you, I followed you, keepin' an' eye on you. New York, Miami. I was the one who banged on your trailer to scare you, an' I followed you again. Problem was, you stopped on the side of the road an' I ended up ahead of you. I pulled into the gas station where we met." He shrugged again. "You know the rest."

"Did you really kill the attendant?" she asked.

He looked down at his hands. "Yeah, baby, I did."

"Oh, my God, an' I just let you in. Into my car, into my life, into my body. Oh, my God." She wiped at her tears and was sick to her stomach.

"I love you, baby," Vegas said, taking a step toward her. "When I met you, I knew I couldn' kill you. I just couldn'. You made me feel things I never felt with a woman, an' I fell in love with you, baby. I fell in love for the first time *ever.* With *you.*"

"Oh, God, I'm gonna be sick," she said, grabbing

Diega's arm.

Diega was sick as well, not believing what he'd heard. He and Santiago had been silent while watching the interaction, now, Santiago snorted.

"He just wanted to control you, that's why he didn't kill you after you met. That's all he does with women, control them. That's why you were always worried the police were after you, why he told you about hearing it on the radio, and you should get rid of the car. Why he never told you about his illegal activities with his pal Manny, and why he certainly didn't want you with any other man."

Tahlia shook her head at Vegas, disbelieving what she was hearing, disgusted and betrayed as he stood there gazing back at her forlornly.

Santiago glanced at his watch. "Well, I hate to break up this little party but—"

An explosion ripped through the ground and chunks of dirt fell from the ceiling.

*****

The earth shook under his feet, and he fell against the wall, desperately grabbing at any jutting rocks to hold himself up. Damn it, I didn't know there were more explosives around the place. I would've gotten Tahlia out sooner. He glanced into the room and saw Tahlia standing, seemingly okay. At least no rocks fell on her, he thought, relieved. Now, how do I get her out of there…?

*****

"You okay?" Diega turned to Tahlia.

"Yeah," she said, looking up at the unstable roof.

"Ah, yes," Santiago said, straightening himself, "I forgot all about the explosives I planted. Where was I? Oh, right, we need to be off, so Tahlia isn't here when the other bombs go off. After all, I need to keep my wife safe and sound and protect our baby. I'm going to be a father," he chortled proudly.

"No, you're not," Tahlia spat. "You stupid bastard, the baby's not even yours. I found out I was pregnant the day you had your goons grab me."

Three sets of deep blue eyes stared back at her.

"What!" Santiago cried.

"The baby's not yours. I was already pregnant," she yelled, staring at all of them.

The news stunned all three men.

"Why the hell did you keep it from me?" Santiago screamed.

"So you wouldn't hurt me or the baby, you idiot," Tahlia screamed back. "If you knew it wasn't yours, you probly would've killed me just to get back at all of us."

"Well, if it's not my baby…" Santiago's voice trailed off as he tried to figure it out.

Tahlia's gaze flitted back and forth between Diega and Vegas, the two men she loved more than anything in the world. Biting her lip, she cried in misery, and hot tears rolled.

Diega was somewhat surprised. She'd looked more pregnant than Santiago had said she was, but the problem now, was he the father or Vegas?

Vegas stood in shock. Tahlia was pregnant…to him? *I'm the father,* he thought, *but she slept with Diega too, only for two weeks, but the timin's right. Oh, my God! I'm gonna be a father.*

"I'm not going to be a father?" Santiago seemed confused, but then the confusion cleared. "Well, I'm not going to be a father, but I *will* be a grandfather. Vegas, my son," he said, slapping Vegas on the back. "You're going to be a father. You make me so proud."

"What?" Tahlia, Vegas and Diega stared at Santiago.

"Oh, that's right, you all don't know that either." He motioned to his henchman. "Cut him loose." He watched as Vegas was freed from his ties. "Do you remember I used to come around to your house sometimes when you were young? And when your father killed your mother, and you ran away from your foster home, I found you on the streets and took you under my wings?"

Vegas stared at him strangely and rubbed his wrists. "Yeah."

"I did that because…I'm your father."

"What?" all three of them said again.

"That's right." Santiago clamped his hands on Vegas' shoulders. "Vegas, I am your biological father."

Chapter 31

Vegas and Diega looked at each other. Considering the information they knew, it was impossible.

"What makes you think you're his father?" Diega asked, wanting to know.

"Because I had a DNA test done," Santiago said, looking from Diega to Vegas. "When I found out about the doctor selling babies, I tracked you down to your adoptive parents. That's why I befriended them, so I could watch over you. That's why when you ran away, I took you under my wing. And you don't have to worry about your adopted father, I killed him for what he did to you and your mother."

"You did a DNA test?" Vegas asked, exchanging another look with Diega.

"Yes. I took a lock of your hair, and a lock of your mother's, and had the test done. You are her son. *Our* son. Mine and Rosalee's son."

"Rosalee?" Tahlia said, looking curiously at Diega.

"Yes," Santiago said, glancing at her. "Rosalee Montiamo."

Tahlia's brows shot up in shock. "Oh, my God, Diega." She gazed at her lover.

He seemed like a mix of surprise and knowing.

"That's right," Santiago continued, "Rosalee Montiamo and I were having an affair for years on and off." He looked at Vegas again. "You are *our* son. *My* blood. My DNA runs through you."

"No, it doesn't!" Diega said, once again levelling his gun at Santiago's head. "*You are not* his father."

Santiago turned to Diega. "Yes, I am, Diega. In fact, I'm your father too."

"What!" Diega was astounded, laughing at the thought of Santiago being his father. "You have *got* to be kidding me." He laughed again. "You are *nothing* but a liar. My mother never had an affair with you, and you are *not* our father."

"But I am," Santiago stormed, upset at Diega's insolence. "I ran the test, Vegas is Rosalee's son, your brother."

Diega stared him down. "You stupid bastard, I already know Vegas is my brother. I've known since he was in a coma. But you are *not* our father, you only ran the test to confirm he was Rosalee's son, *not* yours." Diega readied his gun. "*I did* run full tests. *And you, are not, our father.* The blood of Ricardo Montiamo runs through both our veins. *He* is *our* father. *Not* you."

Santiago was astounded.

Another explosion rocked them, and steadying themselves, they faced off again.

"I'm not your father?" Santiago asked, unbelieving. "But Rosalee and I were seeing each other both times she became pregnant, and then I heard she'd lost the baby." He turned to Vegas and his face crinkled. "My son."

"I'm not your son," Vegas said in a low voice. "You

may have been some sick version of a role model, but you were never my father."

"No! No! I *am* your father," Santiago bellowed as he shook. "No, this can't be happening. First my baby, then my sons. No, no."

*****

Well, well, well, he thought, that's very interesting. And so hilarious that their lives are falling apart before my very eyes. He wanted to laugh out loud but restrained himself as he glanced back into the room. It doesn't help me get Tahlia out of there, though. What the hell am I going to do damn it?

Between his three enemies and the henchmen, he didn't know if he'd be able to take them all out without Tahlia being hurt, or he himself being shot.

He heard footsteps running down the tunnel, coming closer and closer. Damn it, Diega's men.

Quickly looking around, he noticed a large opening in the wall. It must have happened in the explosions, he thought, and slipping over to it, he disappeared from existence.

*****

Two of Diega's teams pounced on the room, aiming their guns at Santiago and shooting his henchmen dead when they tried to shoot back.

"Sir, explosions are going off, the house is falling apart. Do you want us to take him?"

"No. We're done here," Diega told his team, facing off against his arch nemesis who gazed back at him with a steely look of determination in his eyes.

"Santiago, my enemy. You may have thought you won this game. Taking Tahlia away from me, believing you were our father. But you didn't, and you aren't. And so this is the end of the line for you."

Santiago stood straight and proud, ready to defy everyone around him.

Diega levelled the gun and pulled the trigger, blowing a bullet through Santiago's forehead.

Smack bang. Dead centre.

Santiago took a step backward, still straight and proud, his eyes boring into Diega's. Then, with the supreme finesse he possessed while alive, his lifeless body fell to the ground as another explosion ripped through the tunnels and into the room.

*****

What was that? He panicked, oh, God, another explosion. He saw rubble falling in the tunnel outside of his hiding place. I have to get out of here and get Tahlia. I have to get out of here before the place collapses.

The ceiling started to cave in as he struggled to leave the hole in the wall.

"No, no, no, Tahlia, no," he screamed, the whole tunnel collapsing in front of him before he could get out.

Rocks and dirt came falling down, burying him in the wall and knocking him to the ground, covering him in debris.

One last thought crossed his mind before leaving.
Tahlia.

*****

"Arggghhh," Tahlia screamed, doubling over in pain. "Oh, my God, the baby, ahh."

Diega and Vegas reached for her.

"Oh, my God, the baby's coming, the baby's coming." She screamed in pain and clutched her stomach, feeling the baby pushing from the inside, wanting to get out.

"Not yet!" Diega commanded. "Get the doctor down here and have the plane ready to go," he told his team. "Get on the bed," he said, turning to Tahlia.

"What?" She groaned.

"Get on the bed. It looks like the baby's coming and he's coming now." Diega helped her pull down her jeans, yanking them off as she sat on the side of the bed. Her water had broken all over them and it looked gross.

She ripped off the extra clothes she had wound around herself and turned on the bed, so she was in position.

Diega knelt between her spread legs. "We're going to have to do this ourselves," he said, staring at her determinedly. "Can you do it?"

She nodded, screaming as another contraction gripped her stomach.

Diega turned to Vegas who was rooted to the spot. "Get on the bed behind her, support her. We're bringing a baby into the world."

Vegas hesitated a moment before moving into action. He sat on the bed behind Tahlia, his legs bent either side of her. She lifted her legs up and over, so they were on the outside of his, helping to keep them apart.

He grabbed her hands. "Squeeze, baby, you can do this," he murmured in her ear.

Tahlia looked over her right shoulder at him. Hating him. Loving him. Both at the same time. "Aaaahhh," she screamed, her head thrusting back into his shoulder.

"I see the baby's head, he's coming," Diega cried excitedly.

"He's barely over seven months, I think he's too young."

"You think?" Diega asked, looking up at her.

"I don't know how pregnant I am, except it might be around the time we – aaaahhh."

"Push, Tahlia, push," Diega commanded, and she pushed with all her might.

"Aaaahhh," she screamed, pushing back against Vegas as the baby slid out of her. She was gripping his hands so tightly they were white, the pain was that intense.

"We need something to wrap him in," Diega said, as the premature baby cried his first cry. He looked around. "Grab a pillowcase from the pillow," he told Vegas, who reached back. Diega wrapped the baby in it, putting him in Tahlia's arms. "It's a boy," Diega said. "You have a son."

He was tiny and beautiful, and Tahlia fell madly in love instantly.

Vegas was leaning over her right shoulder, stroking the baby's head. "Oh, my God. Oh, my God. I have a son."

Tahlia gazed at him, knowing he was right.

There was a look of full and total elation on his face as he looked down at his brand-new baby boy. "I have a son," he said again.

"And I have a nephew," Diega said.

Tahlia turned to look mournfully at him. There was sadness in his eyes, knowing he wasn't the father.

The doctor rushed in with two nurses. "You've had the baby, let me check him."

Tahlia handed over her son.

"Who wants to cut the umbilical cord?" the doctor asked.

They looked at Vegas.

"Can I?" he asked tentatively.

The doctor handed him the scissors and he cut the baby's cord. "Oh, my God," Vegas said, "oh, my God."

Tahlia collapsed against him, completely exhausted.

The doctor examined the baby, then handed him to the nurses who cleaned and wrapped him while the doctor checked over Tahlia.

Vegas stood and took his son into his arms as the nurses helped clean her up as well.

He held him gently, not wanting to drop him or break him, taking one tiny hand between two of his fingers. "Hello, little one. I'm your Daddy. That's right, I'm your Daddy."

Tahlia struggled to stand as she gazed at the man holding her son.

Vegas turned to her. "Do you have a name?" he asked softly.

"I thought of calling him Christian."

"Christian," he smiled, "I like that. Hello, baby Christian." He kissed his tiny son on his tiny forehead. "My son, Christian Casnova."

"Montiamo," Diega choked as he corrected him. He'd been watching the scene with difficulty and it was tearing him apart.

Vegas looked at him.

"You are a Montiamo. It's only right that your son has the name," Diega said softly, gazing at the tiny bundle in his brother's arms.

"I can't believe you two are brothers," Tahlia said, her eyes going from one to the other.

"Join the club, baby," Vegas drawled and stepped toward her, seriousness taking over the situation. "Tahlia, I'm so sorry, baby, I'm so sorry. I fell out with Santiago 'cause I didn' kill you. Then I met you an' fell in love with you, an' I couldn' kill you. I couldn'. I love you, baby, an' I am so sorry, for everythin' I did."

Tahlia wiped her tears away. "I hate you for what you did to me," she looked at her son, "but I love you, too." She reached out and touched her baby's head. "You gave me my son."

"It's time to get out of here," Diega said, as Vegas handed Christian to his mother.

Another bomb exploded.

"Aaaahhh," Tahlia screamed, shielding the baby as she fell onto the bed.

"Help her," Diega yelled to his team as parts of the ceiling caved in and Christian screamed.

"Arghhh," Vegas cried. A large clump of rock had landed on his leg as he lay on the ground where he'd fallen.

"Get her out of here, protect them at all cost," Diega yelled at his men.

The team swarmed around Tahlia and the baby and shuttled them out of the room as the doctor checked Vegas and his leg.

"It might be broken, you'll need to help him," he told Diega.

"All right, go, get out," Diega said to the doctor and reached for Vegas. "Give me your right arm," he commanded, grabbing his right hand.

Pulling him to his feet, and sliding his left arm around his waist, Diega wrapped Vegas' right arm around his neck to support his weight.

They ignored Santiago as they stepped over his lifeless body and out of the cell into the tunnel, turning left. His team had left large glow sticks along the ground at intervals so they could find their way out. They moved quickly as another explosion rippled through the ground and up through their bodies.

"Arghhh," Vegas grimaced.

"You okay?" Diega asked.

"Yeah, just hurts." Vegas glanced at Diega "I saw the look on your face. You hate that the baby's mine."

Diega glanced at his brother. "If that's the way it is, then so be it. At least the baby's not Santiago's."

"Amen to that," Vegas agreed.

Moving down another tunnel, Vegas spoke again. "You hate me. You must hate me bein' the father?"

Diega stopped walking, and letting go, turned to face Vegas. "I don't hate you. I hate what you did to Tahlia.

You hurt her badly, and that is unforgivable. And now, we find out that you were the one who was trying to kill her. *You* were Santiago's right-hand man." Diega couldn't put his words together. "What were you… thinking…doing? What the hell was wrong with you?"

"My life sucked growin' up an' he was there to take me in. You may not like how my life turned out, but I had no choice. I didn' ask to be stolen an' adopted. I didn' ask for rotten parents. I didn' ask for my father to kill my mother an' try an' kill me. I didn' ask for any of it. I didn' have the life you did. I didn' have two lovin' parents." Vegas wiped the steady fall of tears from his face.

Diega was also crying. "Our mother died when I was fifteen, you would have been ten. She was killed because she was shuffling through papers on the passenger seat. Articles about the doctor who sold babies, the doctor who said you were dead, and *maybe*, if he hadn't stolen you and you were still with us, then *maybe* Mom wouldn't have been distracted by papers and wouldn't have driven through a stop sign and been hit by a truck, then *maybe* Dad wouldn't have fallen apart because he lost the love of his life, and I wouldn't still be mourning her death."

He tried to catch his breath. "Life sucks sometimes, Vegas, and I'm sorry your life sucked, but it wasn't my fault. It wasn't our mother's or father's or Tahlia's. It was the doctor's. Our parents are gone, but I'm still here. I don't hate you. I hate what you've done. You're my brother, I've finally found you, and I can't hate you."

"Sir." A team was coming back for them just as an

explosion blew them apart.

*****

Tahlia was boarding Diega's plane when the explosion blasted the mansion in every direction and made the runway shake.

"No! No. Where are they? Where are they?" she screamed. "Where are they?" She tried to run down the stairs to go back to the house, but was restrained. Feeling a sting in her arm, she turned.

"It's a sedative, you need rest," the doctor said.

All she saw was black.

*****

Diega's team helped him out from under the rubble. "Help Vegas," he cried, waving them away as he swayed to his feet.

"I don't think we can, sir."

Diega turned in the direction Vegas had been standing. There was a pile of dirt and rocks. "Vegas? Vegas?" Diega stumbled over the rocks, calling his name. "Help me get him out," he yelled to his team. "We have to get him out."

Pushing and pulling rocks and rubble, they uncovered his face then his body. "Vegas, Vegas." Diega slapped him to wake him up. He groaned. "Vegas, wake up, wake up."

He opened his eyes slowly, choking on the blood he spat up.

"Get the doctor, where's the doctor?"

"I'm here." The doctor did a quick examination, then gravely looked at Diega. "He would have extensive internal injuries, a lot of rock fell on him. He has broken ribs, so his lungs are punctured. He won't survive you getting him out."

Diega lifted Vegas into his arms. "We're going to get you out of here. I won't leave you here."

"No…no," Vegas said, his voice low and croaky. "I won' last." He coughed and more blood came up. "Look, I've done a lot of thinkin' these last few months. I don' like you bein' my brother 'cause I hated you, but, I never had a brother, an' it's been kinda nice to argue an' fight with you." He coughed again, his face screwing up in pain.

"Take it easy, you'll be okay," Diega said, holding him tight.

"Tell Tahlia, I really do love her. She's the only woman I ever loved. She changed me…for a while, an' I hurt her, an' I hate myself for that. Tell my son about me, make sure he knows who his old man is…was. The good parts anyway." He coughed again, choking up more blood. "I know that you'll look after them, 'cause you love her too. You're probly better for her than I am. You can give her everythin' she wants, raise the baby better than I can. I wan' you to take care of them."

"You know I will," Diega said, wiping his brother's face and kissing his forehead. "You're my brother…I love you." He sobbed.

"Yeah…I, um, mmm, you're not so bad yourself," Vegas drawled. "There's some letters in my room.

One's for Tahlia. Make sure she gets it."

"I will," Diega promised.

"Tell her, I love her…an'…our…bay…be," Vegas murmured, his eyes closing.

"I will."

Diega watched in complete agony as his newfound brother slipped away.

*****

Tahlia slowly opened her eyes. They burned, making her blink a few times. Moving her head, she saw she was lying in a bed in a white room with the sun shining through the window.

"Tahlia."

She moved her head in the direction of the voice, and her heart sang when she saw Diega sitting beside her bed. "Hey," she said quietly.

"Hello," Diega replied, smiling softly.

She breathed in, looking around. "Where are we?"

"You're in a private hospital in Las Vegas."

"How'd we get here?"

"We flew to Australia, then back here."

"When was that?"

"Two days ago."

"Two days! Oh, my God." She tried to sit up, but her body protested. "Uhhh…ahh, God that hurts," she said as Diega stood to help her lay back. "Where's the baby?"

"It's okay," Diega said, sitting back down. "He's in the nursery. He's doing fine, gaining strength, and growing every day."

She sighed and gazed at Diega. "That's good. I suppose Vegas is there watching him? Unable to tear himself away."

Diega looked away, unable to meet her eyes.

She felt the panic grow. "What's wrong?"

He looked at his hands as they lay on the bed. Opening his mouth, he tried to speak.

"What's wrong?" she repeated, trying to keep her fears under control.

"Vegas…he…didn't make it," he choked, tears rolling down his face.

"What do you mean, he didn't make it?" She was freaking out now. "Diega?"

"One of the explosions caused a partial cave-in. Vegas…was buried underneath. He suffered internal injuries." He wiped his face. "He…he…died."

Her head moved mechanically from side to side. "No…nooo." Her world fell apart. "Nooo." She pulled the covers up to her face as tears poured forth, her body racked with spasms.

After a few moments, Diega stood and pulled Tahlia into his arms. "I'm so sorry," he whispered into her hair, holding her close. "I'm so sorry."

They held each other tightly, crying together.

"Where is he?" she asked, pulling back.

"Down in the morgue."

"I want to be alone for a while. I need to be alone."

"Okay," he said, stroking her hair. "I need to do some things, you sleep, okay." He left Tahlia to rest. He had something important to do.

Thirty minutes later, he stood in another hospital

room. "Thank you, doctor, when will the results be in?" he asked, shaking the doctor's hand.

"I'll get them to speed it through, about this time tomorrow."

"Thank you, I'll see you then."

Diega walked back to Tahlia's room and found her gone. She wasn't in the bathroom, so he ran to the nurses' station. "Where's Tahlia?"

"She asked for directions to the morgue."

Diega thanked her and took the lift down to the basement.

*****

Tahlia stopped at the door labelled Morgue. She didn't know if she wanted to do it, but she also knew she had to. Pushing the door open, she saw a sheet covered body on one of the tables.

"Oh, God," she whispered, standing still with shock. Gathering her emotions, she walked into the room and noticed the assistant. "Is…this…Vegas?" she asked.

"Yes, ma'am. Would you like a moment?"

"Yes. Thank you."

The assistant left her with the body.

Vegas' body.

She grabbed the corner of the sheet and slowly pulled it back to reveal his head and shoulders.

He looked cold.

Cold and blue.

"Oh, God," she sobbed, her hands covering her mouth. She squeezed her eyes tightly shut, not wanting to believe, wishing it weren't real.

She opened them. He was still lying there. Lying on a slab in a morgue covered by a thin white sheet.

"Oh, God, Vegas." Her left hand went to his forehead and stroked his hair. Resting it on his head, she put her right hand over his heart.

A heart that no longer beat.

Tahlia allowed her tears to flow, letting out months of anguish and pain. "I love you," she gasped. "I still love you…so much."

She broke down, putting her head on his chest and willing him to come back. Come back to her. Come back to their son. Come back to life. "Come back," she cried, sobbing for several minutes, not wanting to let go. Not wanting to believe it was real. Not wanting to believe that he was dead.

DEAD.

She was still crying when Diega quietly stepped into the room. He paused a moment, watching the woman he loved grieve over the man that was her lover. His brother.

Moving to stand behind her, he gently grasped her arms and pulled her back against him. Wrapping his own arms around her, they clung to each other.

"It hurts so much," she sobbed, gripping the arms around her.

"I know, sweetheart. I know," Diega whispered through his pain.

They cried their tears and gazed down at the man who'd affected both their lives so much. Finally, Diega pulled the sheet back over his brother. Wrapping his arms around Tahlia, he led her back to her room, feeling every ounce of her pain.

*****

The next day, Diega entered the doctor's office. "Are they ready?" he asked.

"They are," the doctor replied and handed him a piece of paper.

Diega read what was written on it and smiled grimly. "Thank you, doctor." He left the office and put the paper in his pocket. He needed to talk to Tahlia.

Walking into her room, he found her gone again just as a nurse rushed in. "Where's Tahlia?" he asked.

The nurse looked scared, making Diega uneasy.

"Where's Tahlia?" he demanded.

"We don't know, sir." She backed hesitantly into the wall behind her.

"*What do you mean, you don't know?*" Diega asked, his anger rising.

"She's gone, sir." She picked at her cardigan hem.

"Gone! How could she be gone?" he yelled.

She jumped. "We don't know. Either last night or early this morning. She went to the nursery. The baby's gone too. I just found out."

"The baby's gone?" Diega shouted. "How could they be gone? How the hell could she leave with a baby?"

"We don't know, sir. She wasn't under lock and key. No one noticed." She shrugged a nonchalant shoulder.

"No one noticing isn't good enough," he yelled. "The baby was premature, and Tahlia was under stress.

This isn't good enough. I want the hospital searched top to bottom. She *has* to be here somewhere."

The hospital administrator came running in. "Mr Montiamo, we've gone through the surveillance tapes. The young lady left early this morning. Apparently, no one noticed."

"Apparently," Diega thundered, storming out of the hospital.

That damn feeling of dread resurfacing…

Again.

*****

Tahlia stopped the car on the side of the highway. She'd acquired it that morning after withdrawing her money from her account. Fortunately, her singing job had paid well, and she'd managed to save most of it. Buying a nondescript sedan and baby seat, she bought some clothes for her and Christian and made sure she was stocked up on food. She packed the car to excess with everything they would need, as she didn't know how long they were going to be on the road. Or where they would stop, and they were about to head out of the city.

She sat there, looking in the rear-view mirror at Las Vegas, now a fair distance behind her. It had been over a year since she'd arrived with Vegas, the man who'd changed her life. Changed her life so much he'd given her a baby. She gazed at her son in his car seat. He was sleeping peacefully, completely healthy and happy, thank God. His tiny hands clasped the other, and he gurgled softly.

"I'm gonna miss your Daddy so much," she whispered to him, tears pouring down her cheeks. For a few minutes, she sobbed quietly, remembering her year in a new town. Her year with a new life. Her year with two new men. She loved Diega, but Vegas had been the one to change her, and with him gone and her with his baby, she just couldn't stay.

Wiping her face and blowing her nose, she took a few deep breaths to calm herself, and taking one last look in the rear-view, she accelerated back onto the highway.

"Goodbye, Vegas."

Chapter 32

Tahlia stepped out onto the porch of the small two bedroom farmhouse with her son in her arms. The weather was warm, as summer had arrived, and she sat down on the bench seat to enjoy the day. She'd been there for a month, having driven east for two weeks, then found somewhere to live. The town was appropriate to settle in, and the house was nice and small, working well within her budget.

She was listening to her baby gurgle when she saw dirt and dust being kicked up on the road at the edge of the property. Worried, she stood, ready to run inside and barricade them both in. Instead of continuing past on the road, the car turned into her driveway heading for the house.

She stepped toward the door, but stopped mid-stride as she noticed who was behind the wheel. Oh, my God! She couldn't move.

The car rolled to a stop in front of the house and a man emerged from the driver's side. He walked slowly up the porch stairs, removed his sunglasses, and gazed lovingly at her. "Hello."

"Hey." She melted as Diega enveloped her and the baby into his warm, loving embrace. Holding her tightly, he kissed her, with the passion he hadn't felt in so long.

"I finally found you…*again*," he said, smiling softly and glancing at the little boy cradled in his mother's arms. "Hello, Christian." He stroked the baby's head and leaned down to plant a kiss on it, getting a gurgling cry in return. How he had missed them both so much, going absolutely insane at them disappearing again. Doing everything within his power, he had finally tracked them down to a small town several states away. Tahlia wasn't using her credit card, so she had been hard to trace. But he'd done it. Flying to the closest city in his private plane, and driving to the town where she and Christian now lived.

Hidden away from the outside world. Away from the pain and anguish she would have been enduring after losing her lover. The man that was the father of her child. Her heart would have been breaking, and he'd wanted to help put it back together, piece by piece, with all the love he had for her.

He had been enduring it too. Grieving for the brother he'd only just found, and all the years they'd missed. Never knowing each other, only ever fighting for Tahlia, and then trying to find her. He had never bothered talking to Vegas, not taking the time, only knowing what he'd been up to in his previous life. And now he regretted it deeply. Wishing he had known him longer, told him sooner about them being brothers so that maybe, things could have changed.

"How did you find us?" she asked.

He smiled at her endearingly. "Tahlia."

"All right, stupid question," she said, softly grinning. "Why are you here?"

"To take you both home."

"I can't go home," she whispered, her face falling as she looked away.

"Of course you can."

"No, I can't."

"Why not?"

"'Cause."

"'Cause why?"

"'Cause the baby's not yours," she said mournfully, glancing up at him with tears welling in her eyes. "He's not yours." She turned and put Christian in his bassinette then sat down on the bench seat, wiping the falling tears from her face.

"Tahlia," Diega said, sitting beside her. "There's something you need to know."

"Please, just, leave an' forget about me an' the baby, an' just go home an' live your life. Get married an' have kids of your own, forget about ever meeting me." Pain tore at her heart, ripping it to shreds. She so desperately wanted him with a fierceness she'd never known. But she couldn't be with him knowing he would never be happy raising a child that was not his own.

"Stop talking nonsense and just listen a minute." He sighed. "When you were in the hospital I had a test run."

"What sort of test?" she asked.

"A DNA test."

Confusion fell over her, and her brow descended. "Why would you...oh." It hit her. "You mean you an' the baby?"

"Yes."

She glanced away, unable to meet Diega's gaze. "I'm sorry," she said.

"Why?" Confusion now besieged him.

"I'm sorry you had to find out for real that he's not yours."

Diega's laughter was soft, low and sexy.

"What's so funny?" she asked, wiping away more tears and looking at him.

"You," he said, returning her look.

"Me?" She frowned.

"Yes. You."

"Why?" She had no idea what he was talking about.

"Because you're still assuming you know the paternity of your baby."

"What do you mean?" Now she was really confused.

"I had the test done to see if Vegas or I, am Christian's father." A sly smile crossed his lips, and he watched her face. "It seems that our time at my retreat was…*very* fruitful."

She shook her head, brow furrowed. "Wait…what do you…" The light dawned, and her eyes widened. "You," she whispered, blinking away her tears.

"Me," Diega replied, a grin spreading across his face. He stood and picked the baby up from his bassinette then sat back down beside her.

"You," she whispered again, still unbelieving.

"Me. I am the baby's father." He gazed down at the smiling baby boy cradled so lovingly in his arms.

"You're his father? Are you sure?" She felt relief and

happiness raining down on her.

"Yes, I'm sure," Diega said, smiling at the woman he loved.

She leaned her head on his shoulder, tears of joy rolling down her face as all of her emotions started to overflow.

"Let me take you and our son home," he said softly, gazing deeply into her eyes. Hoping that every emotion he was feeling was being picked up by Tahlia.

She looked at him. "Our son."

Diega's grin grew bigger. "*Our* son." He looked down at the baby. "Hello, Christian, I'm your father. I'm going to take you and Mommy home."

*****

Tahlia laid the rose on the grave.

The grave of Vegas Montiamo.

Diega had buried half of his ashes with their mother and father, placing a plaque with his name, birth, and death dates on the grave. She touched the plaque and murmured a few loving words, then moved to stand beside Diega who was holding baby Christian. They had come back to Las Vegas and were standing at his family's graves in the cemetery.

"God, I hate this," she said.

"I know. So do I. Just when I found my brother… he's taken from me." He handed Christian to her, watching as she held him. The huge ruby and diamond heart-shaped engagement ring he'd bought was on her finger, fitting snuggly next to her wedding ring. They had married the week they arrived home. It was a small affair. So small only five people attended. He and Tahlia, the celebrant, Kate and Mandy, who was overjoyed that Tahlia was alive and back safe and sound. Oh, and baby Christian, make that six.

He had her marriage to Santiago annulled, but since he was dead, it didn't really matter. Ironically, she inherited Santiago's fortune upon his death, and not wanting any reminder of him, had donated it all to charity. And she had forgiven Diega for spying on her in her suite, thankful that he'd been watching when Vegas was about to attack her, and warned him if he ever did it again he'd be punished and she would leave.

He gazed down at them both. His wife. His beautiful Tahlia, his wife. And his baby son. Christian Vegas Montiamo, named for his uncle.

Pride overwhelmed him.

"I don't know if I want to stay here," she said.

"What do you mean?" he asked softly.

She gazed up at him. "I don't know if I want to live here in Las Vegas anymore. Everything started off great when I first got here an' you hired me. I became a star thanks to you, but then things got really ugly, an' I don't know if I want to be here anymore. Too many bad memories I just don't want to think about."

"Okay," Diega said, brushing a strand of her hair aside. "Maybe we can go on our honeymoon. Travel for a year or two, live abroad, or somewhere else here in the states for a while. Where would you like to go?"

"Maybe Australia. I was born there, an' didn't see any of it the last time we were there." She grinned wryly.

"Maybe we could just spend a few months there and travel all over, see the different cities. Then go to Hawaii for a while. Maybe?" she asked hopefully with a sweet smile on her lips.

Diega grinned at her cheekiness. "All right, my love, Australia and Hawaii it is. I'll call the airport to have them ready the plane, and Kate so she can get our belongings together."

"Instead of taking a lot of clothes in cases an' stuff," Tahlia interrupted, a sly smile crossing her lips, "can we just buy everything we need as we go?"

Diega's eyes narrowed. "You just want a whole new wardrobe, don't you?"

"Or," she replied, "it would make it easier for you to keep me naked." A mischievous expression spread across her face.

Diega laughed softly at his wife's remark. *His wife. Tahlia was his wife.* Finally. "You just might be right," he said, kissing her lips gently before becoming serious. "There's just one last thing we need to do. Then we'll go."

They walked away from the grave.

Father, mother, baby.

A little family, bound in love.

An hour later, Tahlia stepped out of the lift.

"Are you ready?" Diega asked.

She looked at him and shrugged. "No! I don't think I ever will be."

"Sweetheart. I know this is hard, but we have to do it."

She sighed dejectedly. "I know. Okay, let's go."

They sat on the Harley.

The Harley belonged to Vegas.

The Harley belonged to them.

When they had arrived back in Las Vegas, Diega found the letters Vegas had told him about. One was for Tahlia, expressing great sorrow at the way he'd treated her. The other was his will. He didn't own much, but what he did have he wanted Tahlia and the baby to have.

They rode out into the desert with Tahlia holding onto a small urn. Vegas had wanted to be cremated if he died. A part of his ashes buried with his real parents, a part scattered across the desert of the place he was born in and named after.

Vegas.

Diega stopped. "Are you ready?" he yelled over his shoulder.

"No," she yelled back and sighed. "But let's do it anyway. For him."

With a nod, he gunned the bike, and roaring across the desert, Tahlia gently kissed the urn before unscrewing the lid.

The urn that held the man she loved.

Holding it above her head, she shook Vegas into the wind.

To blow wild and free.

About the Author

L.J. has been writing since 2006, when her first of many novels, ***The Road To Vegas,*** was born. In 2016 she created the ***Porn Star Brothers*** series about three sizzlingly hot Australian born Greek Island raised brothers who became the hottest porn stars in '70s America.

L.J. lives in Australia, loves '80s music, disaster movies, and collecting Jackie Collins books as Jackie is her inspiration and mentor.

*L.J. **Diva*** is the adult pen name for author Tiara King. You can find more about Tiara on her website; follow her on social media, or visit her publishing house, Royal Star Publishing.

Socials

tiaraking.com.au/ljdiva

royalstarpublishing.com.au

Sign up for *Tiara's* Newsletter…

Make sure you're always in the know and never miss free exclusives, the latest news, book updates, and so much more with newsletters from…

tiaraking.com.au

Have you read these?

The Porn Star Brothers Series

Porn Star Brothers
Forever
Love Never Dies
Stefan: The New Generation
DeLuca
Spiros & Jenny
And Always

The Illicit Things Series

Her
Him
Madam X

A Novel Investigation Series

Designs in Crime
A Killer Plot
Murder on the Set
A Novel Investigation (omnibus)

Or these?

NOVELS

Burning Desires
Anything for You
Falling for London
The Road to Vegas
Hollywood Dreams
The Billionaire's Dirty Little Secret

SHORT STORIES

The Body
The Perfect Plot
The Star of Your Own Crime Scene

www.ingramcontent.com/pod-product-compliance
Lightning Source LLC
Chambersburg PA
CBHW030656190726

48286CB00001B/50